Son
of
Perdition

The Ahab's Legacy Series

by Louise Gouge

Ahab's Bride

Hannah Rose

Son of Perdition

Son of Perdition

Book Three of Ahab's Legacy

Louise M. Gouge

RiverOak®

Good News in Fiction

COOK COMMUNICATIONS MINISTRIES
Colorado Springs, Colorado • Paris, Ontario
KINGSWAY COMMUNICATIONS LTD
Eastbourne, England

RiverOak® is an imprint of
Cook Communications Ministries, Colorado Springs, CO 80918
Cook Communications, Paris, Ontario
Kingsway Communications, Eastbourne, England

SON OF PERDITION

This story is a work of fiction. While some characters and events are taken from the pages of history, the main characters and events are the product of the author's imagination.

Cover Design: Marks & Whetstone
Sunrise/Monet 1873 © Planet Art

First Printing, 2006
Printed in the United States of America

1 2 3 4 5 6 7 8 9 10 Printing/Year 11 10 09 08 07 06

Published in association with the literary agency of Les Stobbe, 300 Doubleday Road, Tryon, NC 28782

Unless otherwise noted, Scripture quotations are taken from the King James Version of the Bible. (Public Domain.) Italics in Scripture quotations are added by the author for emphasis. Scripture quotations marked (NIV) taken from the HOLY BIBLE, NEW INTERNATIONAL VERSION®. Copyright © 1973, 1978, 1984 International Bible Society. Used by permission of Zondervan. All rights reserved.

Library of Congress Cataloging-in-Publication Data

Gouge, Louise M. (Louise Myra), 1944-
  Son of perdition / Louise M. Gouge.
     p. cm. -- (Ahab's legacy ; no. 3)
  ISBN 1-58919-041-6
  1. Ship captains' spouses--Fiction. 2. Ahab, Captain (Fictitious character)--Fiction. 3. Nantucket Island (Mass.)--Fiction. 4. Mothers and sons--Fiction. 5. Whalers' spouses--Fiction. 6. Widows--Fiction. I. Title.
  PS3557.O839S66 2005
  813'.6--dc22

                                        2005016659

Acknowledgments

I am indebted to the following people for their invaluable
assistance in the development of *Son of Perdition:*

* Gloria Ganno, researcher extraordinaire, for her
  advice on historical details of nineteenth-century
  Boston
* Mark L. Hayes, historian, Naval Historical Center,
  Washington, D.C., for his advice on the Civil War
* Jean Russo, Ph.D., Historic Annapolis Foundation,
  for her advice on historical details of the city of
  Annapolis
* Charles M. Todorich, author of *The Spirited Years: A
  History of the Antebellum Naval Academy*, for his advice
  on historical details of the United States Naval
  Academy

Numerous scenes in my novel were inspired by and based
on real historic events as recounted in Charles Todorich's *The
Spirited Years* and Admiral George Dewey's *An Autobiography of
George Dewey*. Every effort was made to give due respect
and honor to the real life faculty and students of the United
States Naval Academy and to the Civil War heroes borrowed for
my fictional tale. And of course I am deeply indebted to
Herman Melville for his great American novel *Moby Dick*, upon
which my Ahab's Legacy series is based.

For my book, some direct quotations were taken from *An
Autobiography of George Dewey* and *Moby Dick*, both of which are
in the public domain. Quotations from *The Spirited Years* were
used by permission of the author. All these quotations remain
unmarked so as not to interrupt the flow of my fiction tale.

Loving thanks go out to my son Timothy—a truly spiritual man who has honored God since childhood—for permitting me to use his name for my not-so-perfect protagonist.

As always, this book is dedicated to my dear husband, David, who is my inspiration and loving support.

Louise M. Gouge

Prologue

Hannah closed the book, laid her head back against her chair, and let her tears flow. So the stories she heard over the years were true. The man called Ishmael was not just telling a tall tale in this account, nor did he bear a grudge despite his own torment. She had met him when he came to Nantucket, rescued by the whale ship *Rachel* all those years ago. The islanders had gathered at the Congregational church to hear him tell of the *Pequod*'s last days, and his story seemed credible. But of Ahab's final moments he had not spoken, perhaps because he was in a church, or perhaps because he wished to spare her and her son the agony she now felt.

She had long known it must be true. But just as she tried to deny herself all claims to happiness after becoming a widow, she tried to deny the monstrous evil her husband committed on his last, fatal voyage.

Now, in the privacy of her bedroom, her tears poured forth in racking sobs. Had she done all she could to save him? Was it her fault he could not be kept from his fateful course? And if her love and devotion could not save him, why couldn't their darling son's sweet charms or his very existence give Ahab cause to abandon his vengeful quest?

A strong, gentle hand touched her shoulder. "Hannah, I told you this book could not bring you peace. Come, my dear. I cannot bear to see your grief renewed this way."

Her gentle second husband pulled her up into his strong arms where she sobbed until no more tears came. At last he lifted her face and brushed her cheek with a hand roughened by years at sea, and she gazed up into gray eyes filled with compassion. Only he knew, only he understood her suffering. And only he could give her comfort.

"Oh, David, how can I bear it? How can I live with this awful truth? Ahab, poor Ahab. He's truly lost. Now I know beyond all doubt he is in perdition, separated from God forever."

She laid her head against David's great, broad chest and felt his deep sigh. He had respected Ahab and had protected her and her son long before marrying her. Despite his strong Christian principles, David supported her deception when she changed her last name to avoid public censure for Ahab's deeds. But did it pain him to see her grieve her lost love?

"Forgive me." Hannah wiped her tears with his handkerchief. "I love you so much. Please don't think …"

He touched her lips with his finger. "Shh. I understand. We have both suffered great loss. Remember when I returned from my last whaling voyage? Instead of being greeted by my dear Eliza and little Lizzie, I found they had been dead for nearly six years. It was almost more than I could bear."

"Yes, I know, and I don't dismiss your grief. But think of the difference. When I sat beside their deathbeds, I saw only peace and faith in God reflected in their eyes. I saw their souls depart into eternal happiness. One day you'll be reunited. But Ahab—" She held up the book recounting his demise. "Ahab died cursing God, spewing out hatred, and rejecting to his last breath the grace our Lord extended toward him even in the final moments of his life. And for days before that, poor, good Mr. Starbuck did all he could to urge him to salvation."

"As did you, dear one. You bear no fault for Ahab's decision. You must relinquish this guilt. No one can bear such a burden. I do not expect you to forget him, but God, in his great mercy, has granted us a new life together. Think of your son and pray that he will make a wiser choice than his father."

She lifted the volume. "I do think of Timothy, and I know he must never see this book."

David considered her words for a moment. "Mmm. Not now, of course. But when he's older, he is certain to encounter someone who has read or heard the story. Perhaps it would be best to prepare him."

A short, mirthless laugh escaped her. "But surely by then, some new tragedy will have enthralled the seafaring world, and he can reflect on his father's sins in solitude."

"We must pray that will be so. But listen, Deborah is stirring." He walked over to the elegant wooden cradle where their infant daughter slept, and his face glowed. "How beautiful she is, and so sweet tempered. So like her mother." He turned to Hannah, gave her a tender smile, and reached out his arms. "Put away your sorrow, my dear one, and rejoice in this new life God has given us."

Hannah came to snuggle in his embrace. "I never should have read the book." She shuddered involuntarily. "Or at least not so soon after Deborah's birth. Mattie tells me many other women she has helped with birthing feel sadness for several weeks, even months, no matter how happy they are to have their baby."

David bent down and placed a kiss behind her ear. "What shall I say to cheer you?"

His deep murmur sent a pleasant shiver down her spine, and she leaned against him. He was right. She must choose to be thankful for all God had done for them and within them.

"You always know just what to say ... and do." She lifted her face to receive his gentle kiss. As more pleasant feelings began to flood her, she permitted herself a last wistful thought about Ahab's fatal choices. She would never forget him, but now she could honestly admit to herself that the dear one who now held her in his arms was by far the better man to raise her son. And, oh, how she did love this David Lazarus.

The sudden noise of pounding fists reverberated through their bedroom door.

"Mother, may we come in?" Timothy's muted voice accompanied the sound.

"Movver, me come in?" his little brother's voice echoed.

Tiny Deborah stirred once more and began to whimper.

David chuckled, and Hannah's laughter dispelled the last of her dismal mood.

"Shall we never have any privacy?" He released her, strode across the room to admit the boys, and stopped to tuck her book into a bureau drawer before opening the door.

"Probably not." She gave him a merry smile.

Ten-year-old Timothy jogged in and dumped two-year-old Matthew from his back onto their parents' bed. Matthew squealed and bounced up to leap off. Timothy and David both lunged to catch him before he hit the floor, but David, laughing heartily, caught him and tossed him nearly to the ceiling. The towheaded toddler squealed once more and begged to be tossed again.

Hannah gasped at the near-accident, and then laughed too, for she was learning to cope with the frights her sons gave her. Deborah chimed into the chaos with a cry signaling that dinner must no longer be delayed. In response, a familiar ache in Hannah's full breasts reminded her that she needed her daughter as much as the six-week-old infant needed her.

"Take your high jinks outside, please. Deborah is hungry."

"No, Mother, let us stay." Dark-haired Timothy gave her a winsome smile. "We won't look."

Matthew clambered onto the arm of Hannah's chair as she opened the front of her morning dress and prepared to nurse. "Deebee," he cooed.

"Come, boys, let's leave your mother and sister in peace." David started to gather the two, but Matthew resisted with a little whine.

Timothy appealed to Hannah with his dark eyes. "I want to hear more about our trip."

Moved as always by her eldest son's pleas, Hannah bent her head in acquiescence while David tilted his in mock consternation.

"So much for discipline."

Timothy lifted his chin, and his upper lip arched in a triumphant smirk that made her heart twist. How like his father he was. He plopped down onto the window seat and folded up his legs. "Are we really going this time? I mean, will we really get on a ship and sail to England? No changing our minds *this time?*"

"Lord willing, we will." David sat on Hannah's delicate fainting couch, his large frame looking out of place.

Another, darker Ahab look darted across Timothy's face, and Hannah winced. Deborah whimpered at her breast, and Hannah took a deep, calming breath so the baby would not be disturbed. How could she forget all that Ahab had done when his son wore his face and had his black hair and deep, dark eyes? When that son often seemed to resent his stepfather's trust in God?

"Why can't we just get on a ship and go?" Timothy's expression lost its glower, but he still appeared cross.

"But, my darling, aren't you being foolish?" said Hannah. "If we, you and I, had gone to Europe several years ago when we first planned, we would not have Prince Albert's great new exhibition to see in London. Nor would we have your little brother and sister to take with us." She glanced at David and then back at her oldest child. "Nor would we have …"

Timothy leapt from his perch and ran to throw his arms around David. "I'm sorry, Laz. I'm glad you are going with us." He giggled boyishly. "No. I'm glad you are taking us. Mother would probably get us lost in the Sahara Desert or something."

Hannah permitted his teasing without protest, but one of his words stung. How she wished Timothy would address David as Papa or Father. But when they had married three years before, she and David gave him permission to choose the name he liked the most. With memories of his own father lingering, he chose Laz. Yet she harbored a hope that one day he would change his mind.

As for the trip abroad, his impatience was directly her fault. All his life, in fact, all *her* life, she had longed to travel abroad and never stopped talking about it. Not until she married David and observed the depths of his faith could she join him in praying "Not my will, but thine be done" in matters both large and small. Small matters such as asking for a sunny day for a picnic. Large matters such as a trip to Europe or even more important, the regular voyages of his ship, the *Hannah Rose*.

David. Her mighty Viking. If only Timothy could understand how bold, how courageous this man was, he would not be so slow to adopt his faith or to accept him as father. For years, David had sailed to Norfolk, Virginia, to import cotton to Massachusetts mills where it was spun into fabric for sale around the globe. But another cargo reflected David's true courage. With each cotton shipment came another, far more precious cargo: men, women, and children delivered to freedom from slavery in the South.

Hannah could see Timothy suspected something. But just as he had kept the secret of his father's name, he kept quiet about the covert activities in their home and the townhouse adjoining it. He rarely even hinted to her that anything might be out of the ordinary, as though by instinct he knew it was a matter of life and death.

But one day, in the not-so-distant future, her bright young son would learn the whole truth. As soon as their little family returned from their trip abroad, David would take Timothy on his first voyage to Norfolk as his cabin boy. He would learn the true purpose for the trips and be subjected to the same discipline as any other sailor. Then there would be no thought of how David might be related to him, for favoritism had no place at sea.

With much fear but a persistent, growing faith, Hannah would loosen her maternal grasp on her eldest child, trusting David and God to bring him to manhood.

Chapter One

ஐ

Spring 1857

Timothy Jacobs stood on the topgallant crosstrees high above the deck of the *Hannah Rose*, his heart pounding with excitement as he breathed in the salty Atlantic air. The sixteen-year-old loved his turn in the "crow's nest" and often lingered after his watch was over, dreaming of the day he would have his own command. Today, however, he remained aloft for another reason. For the first time in eleven years, he would set foot on Nantucket, the island of his birth, and he wanted to be the first on the ship to see the small, windblown bit of land.

The ship could stay berthed in the whaling port for only a few hours, for it must hasten home to Boston to deliver its fragile cargo to safety. But Laz had said the time had come for Timothy to visit his birthplace, if only for a short while.

Impatience surged through him, and then a twinge of guilt. Good manners required him to visit his relatives before doing anything else, but he saw them often enough during their annual visits to Boston. Fortunately, they lived in the house where Timothy had been born. He could complete his family duty while he toured the house, seeking memories of the father whom Timothy had last seen when he was only three years old.

"What news?" shouted Laz from the deck far below.

"Nothing yet, Captain." Timothy gave him a quick salute.

At sea, his stepfather received the respect due a superior officer.

On land, Timothy honored him as a good friend. Even with three children of his own, Laz never showed favoritism. Laz and Mother even depended on Timothy to be like a third parent to his younger half siblings, and he loved the little tadpoles every bit as much as if they shared the same father. Timothy never resented Mother's love for her second husband, for Laz had deeply respected her first one, Captain Ahab, Timothy's father.

Often, as Timothy grew up, Laz told him the story of how Captain Ahab once saved his life. When he had been a young whaling captain with his first command, Laz had unknowingly shipped with a mutinous crew. When their two ships gammed in the South Pacific, Ahab had seen what the green Lazarus had not and promptly hired away the treacherous first mate. After Ahab's ship, the *Pequod*, sailed off, a young Christian boy revealed the plans for the thwarted mutiny, and Laz had forever felt gratitude and respect for Ahab's kindness and wisdom.

Laz seemed to understand Timothy's need to know of his father's good deeds. All of his life, in the seafaring community where they lived, he had heard whispers of the "infamous" Ahab and his lost ship. Even if no such hints existed, the fact that Mother changed their last name from Ahab to Jacobs bespoke some sort of disgrace. But Timothy remembered a strong, dark giant who had taught him how to tie sailors' knots, playfully scowled at him at the supper table, and carried him about Nantucket on his shoulders.

And so it was with excitement—and a measure of trepidation— that Timothy stared across the Atlantic waters, searching for the island he had viewed only from afar in the five years he had sailed the Norfolk route with Laz.

Timothy sent an appreciative glance down to his stepfather, who now stood at the ship's helm, his eyes on the vast ocean before him. No other captain would take a side trip like this just to fulfill a third mate's lifelong wish.

This was the best time to do it, Laz had said as they sailed out of Norfolk. None of the five rescued slaves hidden in the hold of the *Hannah Rose* was a child or infant who might cry out as the ship docked in Nantucket Harbor, thereby alerting authorities of the ship's illegal cargo. Quaker Nantucket had never permitted slavery on its shores, but these days many off-islanders lived there, some of whom might agree with the nation's fugitive slave laws, which Congress recently had made stronger. Such scoundrels could and would expose the ship's clandestine activity and perhaps arrest the entire crew. As captain, Laz would pay the highest price, perhaps being imprisoned for many years.

Therefore, they could stay only a short time in Nantucket, and Timothy planned to make the most of it. Gazing once again across the waters, he felt his heart jolt with excitement.

"Land ho!"

Jemima Starbuck stood in the windswept Nantucket graveyard and brushed the dried dirt from the tall black pillar, shaking her head in sorrow over the chinks gouged from it. Why did Isaiah keep doing this? What satisfaction did her older brother receive from battering this marble memorial to the man whom he blamed for killing their father? Now that Mother was gone, Isaiah blamed Captain Ahab for her death too, for Mary Starbuck had never stopped grieving the death of her lifelong love, who had been first mate on the *Pequod*'s final voyage.

Isaiah was not the only person who continued to show contempt for the dead captain. Island lore kept alive the story of how Ahab had never followed rules or customs, how he had pursued a certain white whale, seeking revenge against it for biting off his leg, and how he refused the pleas of Jemima's gentle father to return to the business of harvesting oil from the thousands of other, more placid whales that surrounded them in the vast Pacific waters. Finally, the worst of all in Nantucket's way of thinking, how he failed to assist the captain of the *Rachel* in searching for his young son, lost to the white whale Ahab had stirred to fury. Then just a few years ago, the only survivor of that great whale's deadly wrath against the *Pequod* had written a book recounting the tragic events some had thought to be only rumors. Now everyone knew them to be true.

Jemima could not bring herself to read the book by the one who called himself Ishmael. Isaiah had read it last year, sharing with her the parts that described their father's brave last days. But, while she loved hearing of Papa's courage, the story only renewed the rage Isaiah had felt since childhood. In frustration, he often came to the Nantucket graveyard where the captain's widow had long ago erected a memorial. There, he cursed the captain and battered his monument, as though by striking the shiny stone and slathering it with mud, he himself could punish the guilty man. Why must he be so foolish?

Was it not enough that Ishmael recounted Ahab's awful end? That the mad captain died cursing God? That he was eternally lost? But then, until Isaiah became a Christian, he would never be able to comprehend the importance of forgiving—or his own need to be forgiven. Every day, she prayed for her beloved brother, pleading with her merciful heavenly Father to bring Isaiah to salvation.

A strong breeze blew Jemima's long blond hair across her face, and she wished for her bonnet to hold it back. Mother would be shocked at how often her daughter neglected to cover her head upon leaving home. That neglect really must stop or people might think her mother failed to raise her daughter properly.

Reminded of her dear one, Jemima glanced across the road toward the Quaker graveyard where Mother lay buried in an unmarked grave. Although Jemima accepted many Quaker views, she did not embrace them all. Because the Society of Friends regarded grave markers or adornments as prideful, she could not place bright, fragrant bouquets of flowers on the grave as they did on gravestones over here. She and her mother had shared a love of flowers, and Jemima's sorrow might have eased if she could put some there. But, denied that comfort, she contented herself with cleaning away the evidence of her brother's futile rage toward a long-lost sinner. Through this simple task, she found healing for her own grieving heart.

Most of the dirt was gone now, except for traces caked into the carving. Her fingers covered with a worn linen handkerchief, Jemima traced the letters, reading each word softly to herself:

This Monument Erected in Memory of
Captain Ahab
of Nantucket, Aged 58 Years,
Who Perished with His Ship, the *Pequod*,
In the South Pacific Ocean
November 27, 1845.
All Hands Lost Save One.
Committed to Merciful God
By His Loving Wife and Son.

Despite all that he had done, his family had loved this man. Jemima's eyes grew misty as she considered their loss.

"What are you doing?"

A stern, masculine voice jolted Jemima from her reverie. She turned and looked up into the stormy black eyes of a tall young man.

"Oh! Oh, you startled me." She brushed away her tears with the back of her hand.

His angry expression dissolved, replaced by one of surprise.

"Forgive me." He bent forward with a well-executed bow, and when he straightened, the storm had disappeared. "I didn't mean to frighten you."

For a moment, Jemima could not breathe. Then fire seemed to rise up from her heart to the top of her head, burning her face on the way. Who was this handsome youth? She could recognize every person who lived on Nantucket Island, and she had never laid eyes on him. But what were these strange feelings racing through her? Not fear. No, not at all. The only word she could think of was awe, for he was the finest-looking young man she had ever seen.

They stood silently for a moment, gazing at each other. Then he glanced behind her and cleared his throat.

"Did you know him?" He nodded toward the monument.

She giggled, and her face flamed again. "I was just a baby when he died."

He winced, shook his head slightly, and gave her a sad smile. "Of course. Foolish question."

"Oh, no. Not foolish at all. Many people say I look older than I am."

He chuckled. "I've always had that problem as well. Too tall."

"Oh, I would not say *too* tall." No, not too tall at all. What fine figure of a man—nearing perfection!

He smiled his appreciation of her remark and then turned his gaze once more to the monument.

She glanced at it too and then back at him. "Did you?"

"Did I … oh, did I know him?"

"Yes." She gave him an encouraging smile.

He stared at her for a moment, and she could see he was considering his answer.

"What were you doing before?" He jerked his head toward the stone. "I mean, when I walked up, you were doing something to it. What were you doing?"

Jemima pursed her lips for a moment. She would not reveal her brother's actions.

"Dirt had collected in the letters. I was trying to clean it out."

Her words seemed to move him. He turned away, cleared his throat, and rubbed the back of his neck before turning back.

"Thank you," he whispered.

She breathed out a sob. Was this Captain Ahab's son, listed here on the monument, of whom her mother sometimes had spoken?

"Timothy?"

He gave her a brief nod, and his dark brow furrowed. "But who are you?"

"Jemima!" At that moment, Isaiah raced into the graveyard where they stood. He threw his arm protectively around her and glared up at the much taller youth. "What do you want with my sister, you son of a madman?"

Timothy stepped back, his tanned face suddenly pale. "Isaiah?"

"Isaiah," cried Jemima. "What a cruel thing for you to say. Oh, Timothy, I'm so sorry—"

"No!" shouted Isaiah, moving away from her toward Timothy. "Never apologize to this sort. Never apologize for me. As for you, you son of Ahab, what makes you think you can show your face on this island? Do you think people here don't remember what your father did?"

Timothy's face grew stormy once again, and his stance showed him ready for whatever came.

"Oh, Isaiah," said Jemima, "Timothy was your very first friend in this world. Mother told me. How can you blame him for what his father did? It wasn't his fault."

"The sins of the fathers shall be visited on their children unto the third and fourth generation," Isaiah growled. "And just in case God forgets to do his job, I plan to see it gets done."

She gasped, looking at Timothy to see his reaction to her brother's blasphemous words. To her sorrow, she saw only an arrogant sneer on his handsome, elegant face. But what could she expect in response to her brother's attack?

"I did not come here to cause trouble." Timothy leveled an unflinching glare at Isaiah, and his hands clenched at his sides. "I suggest you leave quietly, and I will forget we ever met."

"You think you're going to drop anchor here and give orders?" Isaiah took a step toward Timothy.

"Isaiah." Jemima grasped his arm. "Please take me home."

He stared at her as if she were a stranger and then gave her a curt nod. "Come, Jemima. The smell of this place sickens me." He pulled her down the path toward the graveyard entrance.

Jemima glanced over her shoulder, and her heart ached to see the handsome young man kneeling on the ground and sobbing like a small child against his father's memorial.

Once Isaiah and Jemima entered their tiny, two-room home, Isaiah slammed the door as hard as he dared. If he slammed it too hard, as he had after Mother died, the hinges might break and they would have the expense of replacing them again. He and Jemima could not afford another new set of hinges or even to pay the black-smith to repair broken ones. Like their poverty, sometimes the walls of this dark shack seemed like a prison.

While Jemima retreated to her room, probably to read her Bible and pray for him, Isaiah flung himself down on the fragile wooden chair in front of his desk, the only thing he owned that had once belonged to his father. Somehow, when Mother had sold their large house on Orange Street ten years before, she managed to keep the simple but elegant oak secretary. The tall desk was their sole memorial of their father, other than a few books in the bookcase that sat atop it.

Mother had lived in poverty all but a few years of her life, and now he felt powerless to prevent Jemima's suffering the same fate. They had been charity cases, unable to hold up their heads among the proud people of Nantucket. Even when he had gone to sea as a cabin boy, his payment had been too low to provide much support. And though he had performed admirably as a whaler—far beyond his years, Captain Chase had said—Mother had suffered too much in his absence, fearing to lose him as she had Father.

But Isaiah's most compelling reason he could not return to the sea was the waning whale oil trade in Nantucket. These days, few ships from the island sailed around the Horn to the Pacific whaling grounds, and many more capable men than he were quick to seize all the available berths on those ships. He stayed home, therefore, and became a man-of-all-work for women whose husbands lived more at sea than on land; but at sixteen, he lacked enough experience to do all the necessary jobs, so few people hired him.

With Mother gone, he could return to whaling or perhaps sign aboard a merchant vessel, but then who would take care of Jemima? She was not quite fourteen, and he would not permit her to go into service as a live-in maid for their wealthier Starbuck relatives. He felt sufficiently shamed that his pretty, kindhearted sister had performed day work for several old, retired captains, two of whom had aggressively proposed marriage to her, frightening the child out of her wits. That was when Isaiah had put his foot down. She could be a clerk in Mrs. Lyons' dry goods store over on Petticoat Row, where good Mr. Lyons could keep a protective eye on her, but she would no longer clean any home other than her own.

That Ahab fellow—what audacity he had to come back to Nantucket. Obviously he had never been in want of anything. Fine clothes and shiny black boots so new they barely had a dent or scuff. His mother probably never sewed for other people late into the night just to put food on the table. Probably went from one rich husband to another, never missing a meal. Probably threw away her dresses if they got a little tear and ordered a new pair of shoes twice a year, maybe even more often.

Then young Ahab stands there by that marble abomination and

grieves his father's death. Did he not comprehend that to grieve him was to condone his murders?

Forgive, Mother had always said. *Forgive*, echoed Jemima. But even if he could forgive what Captain Ahab did to Father and to Isaiah himself, how could he forgive the hardship and pain he had caused in the lives of his kindhearted mother and sister?

A vague memory flitted into his thoughts—a merry, dark-haired playfellow wrestling and giggling with him as little boys do. With the memory, a tender, nostalgic twinge arced over his heart, unable to gain entry. For Isaiah Starbuck had hardened his soul to the gentle spirit of his sister and her God.

How would he provide for Jemima? What choices did he have? Continue his feeble efforts as a man-of-all-work or seek something else? His father's distant cousin, Matthew Starbuck, had mentioned the availability of an appointment to the United States Naval Academy at Annapolis, Maryland. Such appointments were hard to come by, and despite his excellent marks in school, Isaiah doubted that, with all the worthy candidates in Massachusetts, he could be chosen. Such luck never came his way. But even if it did, he could not accept, for he would never desert Jemima.

Chapter Two

ℰℐ

"Tell me what happened." David Lazarus lounged back in his captain's chair, gazing across the desk at Timothy. Although they were at sea, his words were not a command, only an invitation to confide in him, as Timothy had done since childhood.

Seated in the captain's small cabin of the *Hannah Rose*, Timothy stared down at his hands and then peered out the porthole. The ship now sailed home to Boston with First Mate Seamus Callahan at the helm. In a few short hours, all personal matters must be set aside so they could deliver their hidden cargo to safety and, of course, unload the cotton shipment. Then he and Laz would go home, and Mother would easily discern, as she always could, that her firstborn was troubled. Best to unburden himself now and tell Laz everything that had happened at the graveyard. Best to clear his mind and his heart so he could perform his duty to those who depended on him.

"There was a girl …" Timothy paused, recalling her lovely face, her thick blond curls blowing in the breeze, and her dark, kind eyes. Jemima Starbuck. Somehow, he imagined he had loved her since she was born.

Laz leaned forward, a look of puzzlement, and perhaps amusement, on his face. "A girl? You're this upset about a girl?" He offered a half-smile of encouragement.

Timothy nodded and then shook his head. "Yes. I mean, no. She didn't upset me. She was just there. She was wiping dirt off of my father's memorial. Reverently, almost like she knew him, cared for him. She never told me why. Her brother came up and …" Timothy bit his lip and frowned so hard his forehead ached. "… he said my father was a murderer ... a madman."

His eyes burned, but he gritted back the threatening, childish tears. "Laz, you must tell me the truth about my father. Why do people hate him? Why did Mother change our name? You and Mother have always told me my father was not evil, but even Aunt Abigail and Cousin Daniel won't explain to me what he did. What makes people hate him so much?"

Leaning back once more, Laz brushed his hand across his bewhiskered chin but kept a placid gaze on Timothy. At last, he said, "How can I call him evil when he saved my life and—"

"You always say that!" Timothy shouted and jumped forward in his chair, then remembered himself and cringed back. "Sorry, sir."

Laz's expression never changed. For a moment, he continued to watch Timothy, as if carefully choosing his words. "When we arrive home, tell your mother we at last had time to visit Nantucket. Then ask her to let you read the book about your father. It was written several years ago by a man who survived your father's last voyage. I think it will explain to you why some people feel differently about Captain Ahab than we do."

Released from the pilot boat that guided her into Boston Harbor, the *Hannah Rose* glided into her berth at Commercial Wharf. The ship's eighteen sailors sprang into action under the direction of the officers, Captain Lazarus, First Mate Seamus Callahan, Second Mate Paddy Callahan, and Third Mate Timothy Jacobs. The captain shipped a crew of various skin hues: deeply tanned English Americans, sunburned Irish, sun-browned Portuguese, and free blacks whose skin tones ranged from bronze to obsidian, all with a common purpose. All staunch abolitionists. All committed to risking their lives to free slaves from bondage despite the laws of the land.

While the sailors dropped anchor, threw out ropes, and readied the cargo, dockworkers seized the lines. They helped set the gangplank in place and prepared to board and unload bales of cotton. In the beehive of activity, no one seemed to pay particular notice as three dark-skinned sailors carried various bundles from the hold. No gaze followed as, one by one, the three descended the gangplank, set down their burdens, spoke with a waiting man, and then drifted away into the crowded dock and disappeared. No gaze, that is, but one—that of David Lazarus, who stood on the quarterdeck and took in every detail without turn of head or movement of muscle.

Timothy never failed to be amazed at the way Laz could know everything that happened on his ship and on the surrounding docks yet never seem to peer around or change the calm expression on his face. Even the time a few years back when the Port Authority, alerted by some unknown source, sent officers to check the *Hannah Rose* for runaway slaves, Laz never lost his head. He appeared to be mildly annoyed by the officers but fully cooperated with their search, even showing them around the ship, where, of course, no evidence of illegal traffic could be found.

When Timothy questioned him later, admitting his own heart had nearly burst with fear, Laz confessed to feeling some alarm at the thought of being imprisoned, but only because such a separation would distress the family. Timothy stood in awe of Laz's calm courage and tried to emulate him in every way so he too could become a worthy leader of men, perhaps a merchant captain like Laz or, even better, a naval officer.

But no matter how courageous, good, or clever his stepfather was, today the specter of his real father haunted Timothy. He despaired of grieving his mother, but he must know the truth about Captain Ahab. And so he worked in a fury to unload the cotton, as though only by his efforts would the task be properly completed.

Arriving home was always an event, despite the shortness of the voyages. After less than two weeks' separation, the three younger members of the household swarmed over their father and elder brother like ants, and Mother added to the melee with her enthusiastic embraces and demands to know every detail of the trip. Just as Timothy thought, the moment he and Laz stepped into the foyer of their Louisburg Square home, her eyes widened and her mouth formed a thin line as she gazed up at him.

How he hated to hurt her, his beautiful, kindhearted, and gracious mother. But she had shielded him for too long. He must know the truth. Giving her a quick hug, he pulled back and offered the best smile he could muster, but could see she was not fooled. And so, amidst the noise made by his siblings, he resorted to playfully chucking her under the chin and turning his shoulder to hers to measure how much he had grown in the past two weeks, one of their favorite rituals.

Had it only been last year he had grown taller than she—the tallest lady in Boston, he was certain. Even the Queen of England had remarked on her height. The monarch encountered the family at the London Exhibition of 1851 when they had at last made their tour of Europe. Across the exhibition floor, the queen had spied Mother and Laz, who was far taller than most men, and insisted on meeting these giant Americans. The encounter had amused Laz, amazed Mother, and awed Timothy, who at ten years of age had been taller than the diminutive monarch. At the end of their ten-month tour, all their friends at home enjoyed hearing about that event the most.

"Timbee, Timbee, up, up." Two-year-old Grace flung her arms around his knees to demand attention, almost knocking him down.

He blew out a sigh of feigned exasperation. "Very well, little mite. Come up here." He lifted the squirming, giggling redhead, and she grabbed him around the neck and shouted in his ear.

"Bwing me? Bwing me?"

Timothy winced, overplaying the discomfort her shrill voice gave him, but also trying to make a point to his parents. He had never been permitted to behave as Gracie did, and to be fair, neither had Matthew or Deborah. He supposed his parents indulged her because both Mother and baby almost died at her birth. And, because of that, he spoiled her a little bit too. He dug in his pocket and brought forth a stick of licorice. Prize in hand, candy in mouth, Grace wiggled to get down.

Laz was having his own share of action. Eight-year-old Matthew eagerly reported his improved performance at computation, and six-year-old Deborah wanted to show off her new frock. But in the midst of all the commotion, Timothy saw the strain on Mother's face.

"Matthew, take your sisters and find Mademoiselle Trudeau," Mother said. "I'm sure your father and brother would like to bathe after being so long at sea."

All three begged to stay until Laz cleared his throat and gave them one of his looks. Not so stern as he might give a recalcitrant crewmember, but severe enough that even Gracie knew he meant business. Deborah grasped her little sister's hand, and Matthew led them up the narrow front staircase on his assigned quest.

Timothy started to follow, but Mother touched his arm. "Tell me about your voyage." She gazed up at him, her clear green eyes radiating love, concern, and questions.

He shrugged and glanced toward the stairs. "You were right. I do want to bathe. We can talk later."

She looked at Laz, who nodded his agreement. "We'll feel better after we wash."

"Did you have a big shipment?" she persisted.

Laz nodded again. "Five extra bales. Three were picked up near the docks and two will be delivered to Mr. Hayden's house after dark."

Mother smiled her pleasure. "Well, then, we'll finish talking when you two take your sea smell out of my front hallway and bathe it away." She drew her hand across Timothy's cheek. "Hmm, look at all those dark whiskers. I do believe you'll need to start shaving."

He bent to kiss her before continuing up the stairs. "Mother, I've been shaving for at least a month. I'm a man now, don't you know?"

"I know." She whispered the words with a catch in her voice, and Timothy felt a lump in his own throat. He would rather die than hurt her.

Soon stirring up lather in his shaving cup, he studied his face in the washstand mirror, admiring the fine black whiskers scattered about on his cheeks, chin, and above his upper lip. Of course, there were not so many as Mother implied, but perhaps that was her way of telling him she was ready to accept him as a grown-up. That she knew he was ready to hear an adult version of the story about his father, one beyond all the happy reminiscences she often shared with him.

Using the brush Laz had given him, Timothy daubed the thick lather on his face, getting a large amount on one ear and accidentally brushing a glob across his nose. Shaving was tricky business, and he was glad Matthew was not watching or the little scamp would fall on the floor laughing.

Timothy took his freshly stropped razor and began scraping whiskers from his neck. Between swipes of the blade, he considered his features. Mother always said if he wondered what his father had looked like, he should just study his own face in the mirror.

Papa had been tall and strong and a very successful whaling captain. According to Mother, his crews respected him, as did the entire whaling community. Laz always agreed. Timothy was glad Papa had saved Laz's life all those years ago. No boy ever had a finer stepfather, one who understood and accepted Timothy's need to know about his real father.

His face now smooth and whisker-free, he patted on a soothing ambergris balm and then ran a comb through his thick black hair.

Try as he might, he could not envision the swath of white that had blazed through his father's dark mane or the savage scar that a lightning bolt had slashed down his face to his chest. Mother always said the scar made Papa appear even more dashing and handsome and that, other than the scar, Timothy looked just like him. But then, didn't all mothers think their sons handsome? Still, from the way some of the young ladies at church behaved around him, he surmised that he possessed at least passing good features.

He himself thought the face tolerable, but he was most proud of his tall, sturdy frame. Years of sailing, whether in the family's sailboat or on a voyage to Norfolk, had built a strong back and limbs. He did not shy away from any heavy work, despite the family wealth that could have turned him into an indolent, self-indulgent dandy like his childhood friend Charles.

Timothy finished his ablutions and began to dress. But first, he studied his reflection in his wardrobe mirror, turning this way and that, admiring the breadth of his strapping chest and the length of his muscular legs. Before stepping into his trousers, he reached down and rubbed his right knee, another of his rituals. What had it been like for Papa to lose his leg? How had he borne the pain of the injury or the indignity of stumbling around on an ivory pole after being such a powerful and self-reliant man?

Sometimes Timothy thought he could remember playing with the crudely carved whalebone limb while sitting on Papa's lap. Other times, he decided that, because Mother often told him the story, he was claiming the memory as his own. Papa's tragic injury always made Timothy shudder. What horror for him to have suffered that way.

Chasing off the dismal thoughts, he drew up his trousers, then turned to the mirror again, bending his arms and flexing his muscles to increase their already impressive size. Not so grand as Laz's, but he would catch up soon. As he donned a clean white shirt, affixed his white cravat, and pulled on a fresh jacket, he was pleased with the young man who gazed back at him through the mirror.

Did Jemima think him handsome? The thought surprised him and made his heart ache a little. Even if she did find him as appealing as he found her, what difference did it make? He probably would never see her again, at least if Isaiah had his way. And it was not even Timothy's fault but his father's. Was he like his father in more than appearance? If Papa had done something wicked, was he somehow destined to do something wicked as well?

Gazing once more into his wardrobe mirror, he studied his eyes. No, he could see no wickedness there. No glint of avarice, cruelty, or decadence, such as he had seen in the eyes of slave catchers or malicious mariners by the waterfront. More than that, he felt certain his pure-hearted mother could never have loved a man who was wicked.

No matter what anyone said, he would still love his father, still be proud of him. Maybe he did not need to read the book Laz spoke of. After all, as well read as Timothy was, he had never heard of it, despite living in Boston, where every thinking person belonged to a literary circle. Maybe the book would give no insights at all into his father's deeds that so shocked everyone. Maybe no one other than Laz and the Nantucket whaling community even knew of its existence. And, after all, Nantucket was truly a very tiny island, especially in the eyes of one who had traveled the world, as Timothy had. Even the house where he had been born and his father's monument were much smaller than he remembered. Small island. Small people. What did it matter if a few of those islanders thought ill of Captain Ahab?

Even if the book contained true accusations and Timothy's father was indeed deemed by some people to be evil, what difference did it make? Long ago, almost before he could consciously decide it, Timothy had chosen to be good, like Uncle Jeremiah and

Laz. He always helped Mother, even when he would rather be with friends. He worked at Grace Seamen's Mission, doing everyday chores to help Uncle Jeremiah keep costs low. On every voyage to Norfolk, Timothy renewed his vow to help people who could not help themselves, whether they were down-on-their-luck mariners or escaped slaves.

Bathed, shaved, and dressed in his clean black suit, Timothy squared his shoulders before the wardrobe mirror. No, he decided, he did not need to read the book. Despite what Isaiah had said—and Timothy felt certain the other youth had misused the Scriptures—his father's sins would not be visited on him. For he had every intention of being a good man, the very best, in fact, no matter what anyone else said. No one, not even God, would ever find fault in him.

As he descended the front stairs, he could hear an unfamiliar woman's voice coming from the front parlor. He expelled a soft sigh of relief. If Mother had a visitor, he could easily avoid the subject of Nantucket and the book about Papa. Standing outside the parlor door, he waited for a break in the conversation before entering. He did not intend to eavesdrop, but the woman spoke so loudly, he could not help but hear her affected Southern dialect.

"Oh, it was so romantic, Mrs. Jacobs, I mean, Mrs. Lazarus. Forgive me. I just can't seem to get it through my silly little head that you have remarried. Aren't you fortunate, at your age? Anyway, there he was, my dear Captain Longwood, just about to sail away to the Mexican War way back in forty-seven, June eighth, it was, and he comes to my dear daddy's house very late at night and proposes to me. Why, dear Mama and Daddy hardly knew what to think, this son of a wealthy plantation owner so in love with their little Amanda that he insisted on marriage that very night. Can you imagine?"

"My dear, don't you think ...?" A man attempted to interrupt her.

"Not at all, my darling Duncan. We all know that Mrs. Jacobs—I mean, Mrs. Lazarus—thought very highly of you, just as we all did, you being a war hero and everything. Why, she just has to be interested in how we decided to marry, aren't you, Mrs. Ja— Lazarus? And here we've been married almost ten years, with three fine sons growing up back down there on our plantation outside of Richmond."

The woman took a quick breath, but resumed her story before anyone else could speak. "Whitney was born just nine months after we were wed." She stopped to giggle. "His dear daddy was still at war. Can you imagine how happy Duncan was to come home and find a beautiful baby boy just waiting for him? Looks just like his daddy, Whitney does. And let me tell you, my dear, that certainly set Mr. and Mrs. Longwood's minds at ease. At last they had an heir, Duncan's older brother's wife being barren and all. But not I, oh, no, not I. Three sons, and all as healthy as can be."

Timothy felt his face burn. What a dreadful woman, to say such things to his mother in her own home. But a vague memory shot through his mind, memory of a Captain Longwood, who called on Mother and him several times when they lived in the townhouse next door. Was that the man who just now had tried without success to silence his boorish wife?

"Timothy?" Laz appeared at his shoulder and spoke in a quiet voice. "Shouldn't we go in?" His expression gently chided, and Timothy gave him a sheepish grin.

As the two entered the room, relief flooded Mother's face. "David, Timothy, see who has come to call. You remember Captain Longwood? And this is his wife, Amanda. Her parents are Mr. and Mrs. Burns of the mercantile Burns."

The dark-haired naval captain stood and took a step toward Laz and Timothy, his hand extended. "Captain Lazarus, how good to see you."

Laz shook his hand warmly—or perhaps just with good manners.

Timothy could not tell which, for in awkward social situations, his stepfather's face wore a pleasantly bland expression. This situation felt very awkward to Timothy.

"Welcome, Captain Longwood, Mrs. Longwood." Laz stepped near the divan where the plump, brown-haired woman sat. He bent to kiss her offered hand and then glanced toward Timothy. "You recall our son, Timothy?"

"Timothy." Captain Longwood was already shaking his hand with unmistakable enthusiasm. "What a fine young man you have grown up to be ... and so tall." Longwood's rich Southern accent and handsome naval uniform completed the youth's memory of him. The only difference was that he found himself looking down at the now-graying captain who had towered over him all those years ago.

"Sir, how good to see you again. It's been a long time."

Mrs. Longwood bounced up off the divan and came forward, her hand extended for a kiss. "Why, my goodness, what a fine young man." She repeated her husband's sentiments while Timothy performed the proper honors. "So tall and handsome. I'll wager all the young ladies just simply swoon—"

"Amanda!" Captain Longwood shot a brief, angry glare at her before regaining a pleasant, if somewhat strained smile. "My dear, we do not have much time, and I do have an important purpose in coming here."

"Why, of course, my *dear*." Mrs. Longwood's nostrils flared, and her smile seemed more forced than her husband's. "*Do* go on."

"Mrs. Lazarus." Longwood bowed to Mother and then to Laz. "Captain, I hope you know that I have always held you both in high esteem. Dear lady, I have not forgotten a promise made to you long ago concerning this excellent son of yours." He clapped Timothy on the shoulder. "I have in my power to recommend to my friend, Congressman Hopkins from right here in Massachusetts, a worthy young man to be appointed as an officer candidate to our United

States Naval Academy at Annapolis. I would like your permission to confer that honor on your son."

Timothy felt his jaw drop, and the air involuntarily fled from his lungs. Annapolis! He had heard of it from sailors at the mission and long ago decided no other college would do for him. However, wealth could not purchase acceptance at the academy, for it must come by congressional appointment. This generous offer from Captain Longwood could fulfill his fondest wishes, his dearest dreams. He stared at his mother and then at Laz, pleading with his eyes for them to say yes. They appeared to be as stunned as he.

"Well, what do you say?" Longwood chuckled, seeming to understand their silence.

"Oh," Mother breathed out, her tone filled with dismay. "Oh, I don't know. Harvard is right nearby, and I had hoped ..."

"What an honor." Laz's face beamed with surprise and appreciation, but he quickly turned to Mother. "Hannah, dear, this is a truly splendid honor."

"Oh, Mother, do say yes," said Timothy. "You must say yes." How could he bear it if she would not permit him to accept?

"Yes, Mother, you must say yes," Longwood echoed with a grin.

She looked from Laz to Timothy to Longwood and back to Laz, her eyes suddenly brimming with tears. "How can I refuse? This world is designed to steal children from their mothers, is it not?" She tried to laugh, but it sounded more like a sob.

"You are the best mother there ever was." Timothy hurried to cross the few steps separating them and pulled her into his arms. Stepping back, he shrugged an apology to the others, none of whom seemed to mind his emotional display.

"And you will be the best naval officer there ever was." Mother reached up to caress his newly shaved cheek, and her intense stare held many meanings. "I cannot wait to see you in your uniform."

"Ah, yes." Mrs. Longwood gazed at her husband's attire up and down and then cast a knowing look at Mother. "We do like men in uniform, don't we?"

Mother blinked and cocked her head, as she did when shocked, but gave no response.

"Thank you, my dear." Captain Longwood gave his wife a polite nod and then sauntered over to Timothy and his mother. "This autumn, I will be leaving active duty to take a teaching post at the academy, so I shall keep an eye on our boy here."

Her eyes still damp, Mother smiled her gratitude. "Knowing that will make his absence much easier to bear."

"Now that does not mean I will extend any favoritism toward you, my boy." The captain gave Timothy a warning look.

"No, sir. I would not expect it." Timothy jerked his head toward Laz with a rueful look and a short laugh. "On shipboard, he never has either."

The captain threw his head back and laughed. "Good man, your stepfather. He's raised you well." Then he turned to Mother with a look Timothy could not discern. "A very good man, your husband."

"Yes, he is." Mother's face turned rosy pink.

The three of them glanced across the room where Mrs. Longwood clung to Laz's arm and attempted to charm him with fluttering lashes and coy smiles. The captain coughed softly, and Mother did not indicate anything was amiss. Timothy had to bite back a grin at the smooth manner with which Laz disengaged himself from the unpleasant woman, offering her lemonade that the housekeeper had brought.

"The formal offer will come by post, but I wanted to come in person with the news," said Captain Longwood.

"You will always have our gratitude," said Mother.

The captain gazed at her for a moment, an undecipherable expression on his face. He lifted Mother's hand to kiss it and whispered, "An atonement, dearest lady."

She gasped softly, and her eyebrows arched. But then she gave him a tender smile and almost imperceptible nod.

Timothy shifted and cleared his throat. "Captain, what must I do to prepare?"

The captain laughed. "All in good time, my boy. All the information you need will arrive by post. But I admire your enthusiasm."

Timothy offered an exaggerated salute and a broad grin. "Thank you, sir."

Annapolis—a dream come true. Surely God was smiling on Timothy's righteous life. So much for Isaiah Starbuck's bitter prophecy against him.

Chapter Three

⍋

Jemima watched the Brant Point lighthouse recede from view across the choppy waters of the Atlantic as she stood at the rail of the *Moss* sailing toward New Bedford. Although she was saying good-bye to Nantucket, an island she had never once left since birth, no tears filled her eyes. All tears had been shed in the privacy of her tiny room in the shack she had shared with her mother and brother for over ten years. Useless weeping might cause sorrow for Isaiah, who had almost turned down a heaven-sent opportunity to attend the Naval Academy so he could stay in Nantucket and provide for her. But God intervened, making clear his will for her brother, though Isaiah could not yet acknowledge divine providence.

Despite twinges of sorrow over leaving the only home she had ever known, she felt an unexpected happiness as she embarked on this great adventure. Isaiah's future was now secure, but what doors would God open for her? She had heard Boston, her ultimate destination, was a much larger city than Nantucket, with many fine churches, historical sites, and libraries with even more books than her beloved Athenaeum. On her half-day off from work, she would be able to indulge in her favorite pastime, reading classical literature and history, and perhaps someday she could become a schoolteacher. The thought made her heart leap with joy. *Thank you, Father, for this wonderful gift.*

A sudden gust of warm July wind blew her bonnet back from her face and set loose several strands of hair. She tried to tuck them into place, but the stiff breeze made the task impossible. Oh, how she wished to remove the cumbersome bonnet and let every curl blow free. But many off-islanders were aboard the schooner, and if she uncovered her head, they would surely be scandalized and think ill of all Nantucket ladies. However, after losing the struggle with the stray locks, she loosened the ties a bit to let the wind sneak under the hat and dry her perspiration-dampened hair.

As the afternoon sun continued to beat down, Jemima grew drowsy. She had stayed up late last night talking with Aunt Charity Coffin. The dear old saint had always been kind to Jemima's little family, making sure they never starved, though she possessed very little herself.

Aunt Charity could have much more if she didn't give it all away. Just like Mother, she kept only enough of her meager income to survive and gave the rest to those she deemed less fortunate. Although she had suffered many losses, she remained generous, loving, and strong, never giving in to bitterness or despair. She lived with her son Josiah but often visited her daughter in Boston.

Wherever she was, Aunt Charity always seemed to find some needy soul whom she could help. And somehow, that kindhearted busybody had learned of Isaiah's opportunity to go to the Naval Academy and his concerns about leaving Jemima alone in Nantucket. She had written to her daughter, whose husband once ministered in a Nantucket church, and obtained a chambermaid position for Jemima at the pastor's Boston mission. She would live in the servants' quarters in the attic of their home. Isaiah readily agreed to the arrangement, for Mother had often spoken kindly of the Reverend Jeremiah Harris and his Nantucket wife, the former Kerenhappuch Coffin.

And so, just one week after her fourteenth birthday, Jemima and Isaiah boarded the schooner *Moss* and left Nantucket, not knowing if they would ever see the island of their birth again. What would the future hold? As if to respond to her unspoken prayer, the boat hit a swell, which forced her to grip the rail to keep her footing. For a moment she felt alarmed. Was this God's answer? Would her life become a troubled sea? A moment of doubt, of near despair, made her want to cry out to the schooner captain, "Wait! Take me back."

But she knew beyond all doubt that God willed for Isaiah to attend the academy, and she would not ruin his future, no matter how rough the seas of her own life became. Willing away her last sad thoughts, she determined to reassure Isaiah that he had made the right decision for their future.

"Are you all right?" Isaiah joined her, his feet steady on the rolling deck. At that moment, a hard wave struck the schooner, and he held her fast against the rail to keep them both upright.

Jemima laughed, suddenly giddy. "Oh, yes, I am more than all right. And see, I told you I would not get sick."

He smiled down at her. "Aunt Charity's ginger jub?"

"Yes, I drank some awhile ago. But I was determined, too."

"That's my girl."

The unrestrained joy on his face made her heart leap with happiness. She needed nothing more to know that leaving Nantucket was the right thing to do. Since he learned of his appointment, he had even stood taller, making the most of his five feet nine inches and broad, muscular shoulders. She tried to imagine what he would look like in his military uniform. Sometimes his expression could be very severe, which she supposed would make him a good officer. Like her, he had thick blond hair and dark eyes, but would the strong, sturdy Nantucket features that she found so endearing cause others to avoid him as unapproachable? She prayed that her reserved brother would show his new classmates what a likable fellow he could be when he tried.

Isaiah could not hide his excitement. After he settled Jemima at Reverend Harris's house, he would be off to Annapolis, there to find day labor until classes began in the fall. Jemima would be safe with the minister. Of that Isaiah was certain. Otherwise he would not have permitted her to accept such a menial position. But, although her work would be difficult, she was a hardy if slender girl and could manage any household duty.

The two of them must have inherited their father's good health, for Mother had always been frail. Even in his dim memories of childhood, she seemed fragile. How he wished he could have taken Mother to Boston too, for the city boasted the finest physicians in the land. They might have been able to help her. His thoughts began to depress him, and an old, haunting question came to mind: *Why had his good, gentle mother suffered so much?*

"This is a great adventure." Jemima broke into his reverie.

"Yes." He gazed at her pretty face, already womanly despite her tender age. Her eyes radiated love, and on impulse he hugged her. "Thank you again for making this sacrifice."

Her arms around him, she patted his back. "I have told you it is no sacrifice, but you are most welcomed anyway, brother dear. Just promise you will do well in school. That is all that matters."

"I will send you money when I can. The navy pays us, you know."

She laughed. "But I will be making my own money. Reverend Harris has offered a very generous salary, a place to sleep, and meals as well. You'll come see me after your first two years, and I will be fat as a goose."

Isaiah released a sigh that rivaled the wind whipping around them. "I hope so, sister dear."

"Just you wait and see." Jemima laughed again, and as her laughter wafted across the waters of the Atlantic Ocean, so did Isaiah's last bit of gloom. Finally they could be—would be happy—both of them. He laughed with her, and as he did, he made up his mind. He would work very hard at his studies, become the best officer in the United States Navy and, for the rest of his life, do everything in his power to give his beautiful, beloved, unselfish sister all the happiness in the world.

The railway train from New Bedford to Boston was crowded, noisy, and dirty. The smoke from the steam engine blew into the cars, causing Jemima to cough from time to time. Unlike windswept Nantucket, where only the docks reeked of whaling, the mainland harbored many unidentifiable foul smells and many loud people. But for Jemima, the sights more than made up for the bit of unpleasantness. Used to the flatness of her island home, she delighted in seeing the hills and mountains of the rest of Massachusetts. Riding in the bumpy railway car was a treat, despite the boisterousness of some of her fellow passengers. With Isaiah sitting beside her, she felt no fear in this new experience, only wonder and excitement.

When the train chugged and huffed into the station near Boston's North End, the brother and sister disembarked and joined the throng of other passengers rushing to various destinations within the city. Many hurried to claim luggage or to engage train station workers to carry trunks or secure waiting carriages for hire.

Jemima and Isaiah needed no assistance, for each carried only a small, tattered valise containing all their worldly possessions. The shack where they had lived belonged to one of their wealthy relatives. Their father's old desk had been sold to Josiah Coffin to pay for passage on the boat and train. Other than a few often-mended clothes, they brought only one item from their past: Mother's old Bible. Although Jemima had offered it to Isaiah, certain she would have access to another Bible at her employer's home, he said he would have little time for such reading.

Nor did the two travelers hire a carriage, for they were used to walking and the mission was not far from the railway station. As they traversed the busy streets, Jemima paused frequently, stunned by sights such as fancy carriages pulled by matching horses or awed by the strange languages and dialects of the diverse races around her. Although Nantucket was visited by whalers of many nations, she had never frequented the rough docks and thus had known few foreigners. Isaiah did not seem to mind her pauses, for he too stopped from time to time to look around the bustling city.

After asking directions once or twice along the way, they arrived at Grace Seamen's Mission in Boston's North Square, not far from the docks. The five-story clapboard building wore a new coat of yellow paint, with white trim around windows and entrance. Six handsome gables stuck out from the top floor, and the double front doors appeared welcoming. Next door stood a pretty little white chapel, and beyond it, the three-story clapboard home of Reverend Harris and his family. Dark green shutters graced the elegant yellow house, and Jemima saw lacy white curtains through the front windows.

"We should go to the back door, don't you think?" asked Jemima. "I mean, with my being a chambermaid …"

"No." Isaiah bristled at her remark. "Our instructions were to go to the house, but they did not say the back door. Chambermaid or not, you are as good as anyone else. I will not have you acting as if you are lower than these people, and I will not have them treating you as if you were. You are here to accept an honest job, one that they need you to do. You hold your head up, Jemima Starbuck, and do not let anyone make you lower it."

She did lower her head, but only to hide her smile. Isaiah was anxious for her, and it endeared him to her all the more.

"Well?" He lifted her chin, and his glare demanded an answer.

Jemima giggled. "Brother dear, if you arrive at Reverend Harris's door with your shoulders hunched up like that, he will think you have come for a fight."

She could see he was trying not to smile but was losing the battle. He let go of her with a mild snort, relaxed his posture, and turned toward the house.

"All right, then. Let's go." He took her hand, and they climbed the front stairs of Jemima's new home.

Isaiah rang the doorbell, and then stepped back and stood in front of Jemima. She was right, of course. Now that they had arrived, he felt anxious about leaving her here with strangers, even though Mrs. Harris was from Nantucket. Jemima seemed satisfied to work for a minister, but Isaiah found no such comfort. Once they made their decision to leave the island, he had vacillated between great happiness for his own future and dismal fear for hers. Now that they were here, fear was winning.

The door swung open, and a short, matronly woman in a prim black dress gazed at them, eyebrows arched. "Yes?"

"I'm Starbuck, and this is my sister. She's to work for the minister …"

"Isaiah, Jemima," cried another, younger matron descending the front staircase. "Do come in, children. How wonderful to see you at last."

The blond lady of medium height barely allowed them to step into the foyer before she pulled them both into her arms and then stepped back and studied them both up and down.

"Mother has written me all about you," she said to Jemima, "and you're everything she described. As for you …" She gazed at Isaiah, her dark eyes bright with genuine pleasure. "I knew you when you were a tiny baby, and look how you have grown into such a fine young man. I am Kerry Harris, of course, and this is Mrs. Maples, our housekeeper."

"How do, ma'am?" Isaiah bowed toward each woman, though his cheeks burned with embarrassment over being hugged. The people of Nantucket generally were not so effusive in their actions, but he had to admit that he felt encouraged by Mrs. Harris's warm welcome. Perhaps his fears for Jemima were unnecessary.

Jemima curtsied. "Mrs. Harris. Mrs. Maples."

"Now, tell me, did you have a good trip? No, wait. Let's go into the front parlor and have some refreshments. Mrs. Maples, please bring us a pitcher of lemonade."

"Yes, Mrs. Harris." The gray-haired older woman turned and walked down the center hallway.

"Now, let's gam." As Mrs. Harris directed them into the front parlor, her grasp on Isaiah's arm felt much like Mother's, both gentle and firm at the same time.

Once seated, Isaiah forced himself not to stare at the beautiful furnishings of the spacious, bright room. Although his own wealthy relatives possessed fine homes with elegant decorations, he was surprised to see a minister's home so lavishly outfitted with brocade divans, upholstered chairs, and shiny mahogany tables holding floral arrangements, leather-bound books, and pretty glass figurines.

"You'll be wanting to know how your mother is," Jemima said to Mrs. Harris.

"How thoughtful of you, dear." Mrs. Harris leaned forward expectantly. "I never can tell from Mother's letters, for she will only write of the needs of others, never her own."

"Oh, yes. She is so good and kind. Aunt Charity still amazes us all. As frail as she appears, she never seems to get sick. She must be seventy-five years old, but you would think she's just a girl. And she …"

A commotion in the hallway stopped Jemima. Then three blond young ladies of stair-step heights rushed into the parlor, all giggling.

"Mother, we've finished the sewing. May we take it over to Miss Clara?"

The eldest—or so she appeared to Isaiah—addressed her mother, but the other two crowded close behind, and one clung to the other's arm. Jemima jumped up from her chair, but Isaiah stood more slowly, and his cheeks burned. He did not mind rising when ladies entered the room, but he knew Jemima had just acknowledged her servant position when she stood for these spoiled young misses in their fancy ribbon-and-lace dresses.

"Ah, how wonderful, my darlings," Mrs. Harris said. "Yes, you may take them to Mrs. Callahan. But first, you must meet new friends, Isaiah and Jemima Starbuck." She turned to her guests. "Isaiah, Jemima, these are my daughters, Lacy, Molly, and Daisy."

The two younger girls giggled and curtsied, but Lacy hurried to Jemima and embraced her. "I'm so pleased to meet you at last. I've heard of you all my life, and now it's so wonderful to meet you."

"Thank you." Jemima's eyes glowed with shy pleasure.

"And Isaiah." Lacy turned and approached him, her hand held out to shake his. But she stopped and blinked, and, if he was not mistaken, she began to blush. "How nice to meet you."

She seemed to lose her breath, and he wondered what was wrong with the way he looked. Perhaps his dusty, wrinkled clothes offended her, or perhaps he still carried the smell of the sea, or worse, hard work. For his part, he felt a little breathless, too. Although she had the usual blond, dark-eyed looks of all Nantucket beauties, her pert little nose and winsome dimples would make her stand out from even the prettiest girls back home.

He cleared his throat and bowed. "Miss Harris." He touched her hand, not quite having the courage to shake it.

The two other girls had greeted Jemima with friendly embraces and now walked toward Isaiah, the younger guiding the older. When they drew near, he worked to subdue his shock. The middle sister was blind, yet her face beamed with the same kind smile Lacy and Daisy wore.

"We're so pleased to have you here." Molly reached out almost in the right direction.

With great care, he took her slender, pale hand in both of his. "Miss Molly, I'm pleased to meet you, too." He turned then to greet Daisy, glancing back at Lacy for only an instant, but long enough to see her warm smile, a smile he felt clear down to his toes.

"Well, now," said Mrs. Harris, "you girls must run along. It's getting late, and I'm certain Mrs. Callahan will want to inspect your work before it grows too dark."

Taking their leave, the two younger sisters hurried from the room to obey, but Lacy seemed reluctant to follow them.

"Are you taking sewing lessons, Miss Harris?" Isaiah's face heated up again. Why had he blurted out such a foolish question just to spend another moment in her presence?

Lacy gave him a sweet, dimpled smile. "Why, no, we've sewn all our lives. We have just completed some shirts for the mission clothing shop. Mariners often have no one to sew for them, and we make shirts they can buy for a very small price. The proceeds benefit the mission so Father can help more needy seamen."

"Oh." No other words would come. What a mistake he had made to judge Lacy so quickly. This lovely young lady was not spoiled at all.

"Lacy," said Mrs. Harris, "I think you need some help to carry the shirts. Isaiah, would you mind? Then Lacy can introduce you to Reverend Harris. He has made plans for you to stay in the mission tonight."

"Yes, ma'am. I would be proud to help." Isaiah turned to Jemima. "With your leave?"

Jemima patted his arm. "Yes, you go on. I'm sure Mrs. Harris has some work for me to do."

"Nonsense, my dear. There will be work aplenty for all of us tomorrow and every day after that. Tonight, you and Isaiah must join our family and tell us all about Nantucket."

Awed by her unexpected kindness, Isaiah traded a look with Jemima, whose eyes sparkled. He knew what she was thinking. She believed her God had blessed them by bringing them to this place. Maybe she was right.

Chapter Four

ઈઝ

Jemima knelt down, swished a large rag in her wooden bucket, wrung it hard, and began to swab the floor of the water closet. The varnished wooden floors of these small rooms were easy to clean, as was most of Grace Seamen's Mission Inn. After the first few days, she still enjoyed her new job. The time would surely come soon when she would grow homesick for her island, and she already missed Isaiah. But for now, she felt content, despite her chapped hands and sore knees.

She found this work easier than her labors back home, for though some people in Nantucket had well water piped into their homes, Jemima and Isaiah had to carry it in buckets from the city well. Here at the mission, she could scrub the rooms on each of the three guest floors and then just dump the dirty water down the commode in the water closet at the end of the hallways. No need to carry buckets up and down the stairs, sloshing water all the way.

The guest rooms required daily dusting, sweeping, and lamp polishing. Most of the men smoked pipes or cigars, so she could never completely get rid of the smell. How glad she was that Isaiah never took up such a habit. She hoped he would not be influenced to do so at the academy. But then, he was not easily influenced.

After a seaman left on a voyage, the vacated room must be thoroughly cleaned, sheets changed, and blankets beaten on the clotheslines out back. Some of the mariners were less than fastidious, and Jemima said many thankful prayers that she did not have to launder the bedding, which sometimes crawled with vermin.

Cleaning thirty guest rooms—as well as the library, parlors, and galley on the first floor, not to mention helping with kitchen chores—kept her and Jewel busy all the long day, six and a half days a week.

Jewel Macy tried to work hard, but sometimes she forgot what to do. Older than Jemima by at least five years, she seemed younger in many ways. Jemima was learning to guide her to stay with a task until it was completed lest the two of them be forced to work far into the evening to finish all their duties. Still, Jemima could not be annoyed with her new friend, for she worked as best she could.

Jemima could not guess what ailed Jewel. As young as she was, her thin, fine hair was a dull, brownish gray and her skin ashen. Her bent, bony frame seemed to cry out for nourishment, but her abdomen bulged oddly. Still, the young woman had a pleasant temperament, and her faith in God was sweetly childlike. Although she could recite a few simple Bible verses, she could not read. When Jemima tried to teach her other verses, she could not seem to recall them just moments later. At least she knew the most important verse, John 3:16, and understood that it meant one day she would go to heaven and be with God.

At the end of each day, Jewel hurried to join her sister much as a small child would rush to meet her mother after a separation. Jemima could only surmise that Jewel was one of God's special children placed on earth to teach others how to be compassionate.

Jewel's sister, Clara Callahan, managed the mission clothing shop next door. Jemima learned at their first meeting that the young women's father, like her own, had been a Nantucket whaler who had died at sea. Jemima hoped they would have a chance to talk more about it one day.

The mission thrived under the leadership of Reverend Harris, the kindest man Jemima had ever met. Who else would hire someone like Jewel? Or big, bearish Mr. Jonathan Lazarus, who could hardly hear? Or Clara's chatty husband, Paddy Callahan, who seemed to think everyone should listen to his long-winded sea stories? Or Jemima herself, an orphan who needed a job? Under Reverend Harris's gentle guidance, they all worked to make the mission a place where seamen could find rest from their labors, refuge from waterfront criminals, and restoration for their souls.

"Jemima, what shall I do with this?" Jewel stood outside the water closet with an armload of sheets.

Jemima looked up from her nearly completed scrubbing. "Just put them down the laundry chute."

Jewel bobbed her head, but still stood watching Jemima.

"It's right there, dear." Jemima poked her head into the hallway and pointed toward a small door halfway up the wall. "Just open it and stuff them in."

"But what if I fall down the hole?"

Jemima stared up at her and sighed. They had this discussion several times a day.

"You won't fall. Let me help you."

She stood slowly, for her legs ached from kneeling on the hard floor. But as she rose, her hemline caught under her foot, and she fell back down. Her knee struck the floor, and one arm landed in the bucket of filthy water, which overturned and thoroughly drenched the side of her skirt clear through to her skin.

"Oh, dear, what a mess!"

"Poor Jemima." Jewel dropped the bedding and reached down to help her up.

"Ouch." Although her knee stung from the fall, the worst damage was to her skirt and underskirt. "Goodness. Clumsy me. Now I must go change, for we'll be serving dinner soon. Go put those sheets down the chute while I clean up this mess."

Jewel managed her assignment, and Jemima soon had much of the water sopped up and flushed down the commode. They went down the back stairs to the kitchen, where the mission supervisor's wife was preparing the noon meal.

"Mrs. Lazarus, I'm afraid I've made a mess of myself. I'll run over to the parsonage to change and be right back."

Maria Lazarus looked up from kneading bread dough and studied Jemima with a frown. "You best hurry. I need help right quick. Elana is too much with child to help serving dinner." The short, plump woman tilted her head to Jewel. "You, Jewel, come butter my bread pans, girl."

"Yes, ma'am." Jewel hastened to obey.

Jemima ran out the back door and down the porch steps. As she crossed the narrow backyard to the alley, she chided herself again for her clumsiness. Mrs. Lazarus was not a hard taskmistress, but she had many responsibilities and depended on her girls to complete their jobs on schedule.

A warm summer breeze blew against Jemima, and her wet skirts clung to her legs, making it difficult to run. She gathered the offending garments up to her knees and raced to the parsonage, praying no one watched her scandalous action. At the back door, she slowed her pace, not wanting to make a clamor as she entered.

Like Maria Lazarus, the Harrises' cook was preparing dinner in the kitchen. Gray-haired Mrs. Cook glanced up from chopping carrots and smiled at Jemima.

"My, my, that was fast. Betty went over to fetch you not thirty seconds ago, and here you are."

Jemima stopped, her heart pounding from her run. "You sent for me?"

"Mrs. Harris did. Betty's to finish your work at the mission today. Mrs. H. has a guest who wants to meet you. They're in the front parlor."

"Oh, my. And I'm such a mess. Who would want to meet me?"

Mrs. Cook chuckled. "You won't find out by wringing your hands and pacing back and forth. Run upstairs, child, and change your skirt. I'll tell Mrs. Harris you'll be down in a minute."

"Yes, of course." Jemima blew out an anxious breath and then ran up the back stairs to the small attic room she shared with Betty, the Harris's housemaid. After changing clothes, she checked her appearance in the tiny mirror above the washstand. The pitcher held just enough water for her to wash away the smudges on her face, and she quickly donned a clean mobcap. Never one to linger over her toilette, she smoothed her fresh apron and returned to the kitchen.

"It's all right, missy," Mrs. Cook said. "You can go right to the parlor. Just knock afore you go in."

"Thank you."

Her heart racing with anxious anticipation and a good measure of reluctance, Jemima tiptoed down the hallway. She did not know anyone in Boston, other than the Harris and Lazarus families. Isaiah had been gone only three days, but she already hoped to receive a letter. Had something happened to him?

At the parlor entrance, she knocked and then slid the mahogany door halfway down its track into the wall pocket.

"You wanted to see me, Mrs. Harris?"

"Yes, Jemima. Come in, dear child." Mrs. Harris beckoned from her chair.

The guest, a tall, striking lady dressed in an elegant green summer dress, stood and took a step toward her.

"Jemima," she whispered, tears sparkling in her beautiful green eyes. Before the girl could move or respond, the woman strode across the room and pulled her into her arms. "Oh, Jemima, dear child, you are the very image of your mother."

Jemima trembled with sudden emotion, and her eyes stung. Who was this person? How did she know Mother?

Regaining her composure, the woman stood back but still held Jemima's hands. "You must forgive me, please. I was just so startled to see your resemblance to my dear friend, Mary Starbuck. But then, you took after her as a baby." She laughed softly. "I'm Mrs. Lazarus, and I …" She bit her lip.

"Go on, Hannah," said Mrs. Harris. "Tell her."

"I used to live in Nantucket. Shall we sit down?" She pulled Jemima to the divan.

Mrs. Lazarus glanced at Mrs. Harris, an odd look on her face, as if she felt self-conscious, and Mrs. Harris seemed annoyed with her friend. Jemima watched the two women with a mixture of trepidation and curiosity. Was this elegant lady related to the couple of the same name who managed the mission? She searched her memory but could not recall her mother ever mentioning a friend named Hannah Lazarus.

"Did you know that my mother died last winter?" Jemima hoped it was not too forward of her to speak.

"Yes." Again tears filled Mrs. Lazarus's eyes. "I was grieved to receive the news. We … we did not manage to keep in touch after I left Nantucket."

Jemima gave her a polite nod. The lady clearly felt the loss. But why would a society lady keep in touch with a poor whaling widow on a distant island? Jemima peered at Mrs. Harris and then looked back at Mrs. Lazarus, waiting to learn why she had been summoned.

"Are you well, Jemima?"

"Yes, ma'am. My brother and I inherited our father's sturdy constitution. We never seem to get sick."

"Ah, and how is Isaiah? Have you heard from him yet?"

"No, ma'am. He'll probably write once he gets settled in. Do you know that he's gone down to Annapolis, Maryland, to attend the Naval Academy?"

"Yes, I know. Kerry … Mrs. Harris told me. How wonderful for him to have such a grand opportunity. You must be pleased."

Jemima bobbed her head. "Oh, yes, ma'am. Isaiah is very smart, and he knows the sea. I expect he'll do very well there."

Mrs. Lazarus blinked at Mrs. Harris and then took a deep breath, as if trying to gain courage, which increased Jemima's curiosity all the more.

"My son also will be attending the academy."

"How grand, Mrs. Lazarus. Perhaps he and Isaiah will become friends." Surely there would be no class distinctions among the midshipmen. At least Jemima hoped not, for Isaiah did not take such arrogance lightly. But then, after both boys—men, she corrected herself—became officers, they would be equals in every way.

"Dear child," said Mrs. Lazarus, "they once were the best of friends."

Jemima frowned. "I don't understand."

"Isaiah was my son's first playmate."

"Ma'am?"

Mrs. Lazarus stared down at her hands, then gazed back at Jemima with sorrow-filled eyes. "My first husband was Captain Ahab."

Jemima gasped, and her eyes stung again. She scooted back from the woman, but then realized how her gesture might be misconstrued.

"I'm sorry. I am so sorry. It's just … it's a shock to meet you here." She drew in a quick breath to regain her composure. "You're Timothy's mother."

The woman bent toward Jemima with a frown. "Yes, but how do you know my son?"

"Did he not tell you?"

Mrs. Lazarus gave her head a little shake. "No."

"He came to Nantucket last spring."

"Yes. I knew that. He wished to visit the memorial we erected to his father and the others who died aboard the *Pequod*."

"Did he not tell you of meeting my brother and me there?"

A look of comprehension lit Mrs. Lazarus's face. "Ah. I wondered why he spoke so little of it. May I assume that all did not go well at that meeting?"

Jemima glanced away, gathering her thoughts. The truth was always best, no matter what the consequences. She looked back at the lady. "No, ma'am. My brother was not pleased to see him."

Mrs. Lazarus shrugged her understanding. "And you, Jemima? Do you resent us as well?"

Jemima's face burned. She had no idea why she had reacted with such feeling a moment ago. "No, ma'am. You lost your husband, and Timothy lost his father, just as we lost our father. None of us is at fault." She hesitated for a moment. "Mrs. Lazarus, my mother sometimes spoke of you and your son, of course with your former name. Why did you never write to her?"

"Ah, dear child, I did. She never answered." Mrs. Lazarus gazed at her evenly. "But even before I left the island, shortly after the news of the ship's sinking arrived in Nantucket, she drew away from me. I don't think she meant to blame me for the accident, for many whaling ships have gone down over the years. I think she simply felt the need to retreat into the embrace of her closest circle, of which I could not be a part." Her eyes exuded sadness. "I so much wanted to help her ... and you children as well ..."

Jemima sat up straight. "Help us? But why? We are not related." She regretted her words immediately. Why had such wicked pride filled her heart? While Mrs. Lazarus did not seem offended, she did appear to be hurt. "Forgive me. I don't mean to speak rudely. But the Starbuck family has helped us through the years. In fact, our distant cousin arranged for Isaiah's appointment to the Naval Academy."

"I understand why you ask. But, you see, my father owned whaling ships. He always considered it his responsibility to care for the families of his crews, especially when one of the men died. I felt I should do no less than he in ministering to those who might be destitute when the family provider perished."

"You're very generous, Mrs. Lazarus. But the late Captains Peleg and Bildad owned the *Pequod*. Why would you feel an owner's responsibility?" She did not add that the two old captains had been notorious for their parsimony and never helped them at all. But since Captain Bildad had been Mrs. Harris's uncle, Jemima must not speak ill of him.

"My husband was also part owner of the ship," said Mrs. Lazarus.

"Ah. I see. I did not know that." Jemima felt another twinge of remorse for her silly pride. "I wish my mother had responded to your letters, but only because it is sad to think of her losing a friend."

Mrs. Lazarus questioned Mrs. Harris with her eyes, and Mrs. Harris gave her a slight nod.

"I could not help you before, Jemima, but I would like to do something for you now."

"You would?" Oh, what a silly thing to say.

"Yes. Mrs. Harris tells me you want to become a teacher or a governess. I would like to arrange for your schooling."

Jemima's heart seemed to twist oddly. She had begun to feel so much confidence in earning her own way. She even planned to send money to Isaiah. Isaiah! He would never permit her to receive assistance from Captain Ahab's widow. Could she accept and not tell him? No, of course not. She could not bear lies or deceit. But how could she refuse this opportunity for her own future? Surely it was a gift from God. Surely this was the very thing she had prayed for.

Mrs. Lazarus gave her a gentle smile. "You are very quiet, Jemima, but your eyes reveal your struggle. You may consider my offer for as long as you like. There's no hurry."

Jemima laughed, and the rush of air bursting from her lungs seemed to dispel all her misgivings. "Oh, ma'am, I will not keep you waiting. I accept your offer. Please forgive me for my hesitation. It's just the shock of meeting you ..."

"We won't speak another word about it." Mrs. Lazarus hesitated, her brow furrowed. "There is one thing."

"Yes, ma'am?"

"You see, we suffered some difficulty after ... after the accident. Timothy was very small then, and to protect him, I took another last name, one from my relatives in Indiana. Of course, I am remarried and have a new name. But my son's last name is now Jacobs. I hope you understand the need never to refer to our past."

Jemima studied her benefactress, whose demeanor reflected only kindness. She had not asked Jemima to lie, merely not to reveal painful things. Did not the proverb say, "A talebearer revealeth secrets: but he that is of a faithful spirit concealeth the matter"?

"Oh, yes, of course." Keeping Timothy's secret was the least she could do to demonstrate her gratitude to this kind, kind lady—the very instrument of God to answer Jemima's prayers.

Chapter Five

ॐ

Timothy ran forward, scooped up the ball, and hurled it to his friend. "Catch it, Ezra. Hurry, lad! He's almost home. He's almost home."

The dark-skinned youth leapt up to snatch the ball, flung himself at the runner, and tagged his leg just in time. With Ezra's game-winning move, his fellow players cheered, while the opposing side offered good-natured, if grumbling, congratulations.

Timothy ran to Ezra and clapped a hand on the shorter boy's shoulder. "Good play, lad. We make a great team."

"Yes, sir, we do at that."

As the two boys left the small, vacant lot, Timothy frowned. "Don't do that."

Ezra glanced up at him. "Do what?"

"Call me 'sir.'"

Ezra shrugged. "Best do it when we're around other people. We're tempting trouble enough when you come over here to my neighborhood. If anybody thinks I don't have proper respect for you, it could get bad."

Timothy glanced back at the disbanding group of a dozen black youths with only two or three unkempt white street scamps sprinkled among them. Then he looked at people passing by on the street, some of whom stared at the boys. "Aw, who cares? I never let anyone tell me what to say or whom to be friends with."

Ezra's dark brow furrowed, and he shrugged. "No, you don't. But I have to."

Timothy stopped for a moment and then resumed his walk. It was true. Ezra must be careful, even here in Boston. Although he had always been free, someone still might try to steal him off the streets and sell him into slavery down south. Timothy's stomach turned at the idea. It annoyed him almost to distraction that Ezra always walked a half step behind as though he were Timothy's servant.

"Say," he said, "this Massachusetts game sure is getting popular. I've heard that groups in some cities have put together baseball leagues, and people can watch them play."

"Wouldn't that be grand?" Ezra spoke softly, but his tone conveyed excitement. "I'd love to play in a league."

Timothy chuckled. "If they do it here in Boston, you and I could play on one of the teams. We're awful good together." He glanced over his shoulder to see Ezra shaking his head.

"Yes, I can see them letting *me* play."

Timothy frowned. "Well, they should."

When they neared Phillips Street, where Ezra lived, he paused, but Timothy beckoned him along.

"Why not come for dinner? Your aunt will be glad to see you."

Ezra furrowed his brow as if weighing the decision. "I'd sure like to see her, but I'm working with my pop this afternoon. He just gave me this morning off 'cause you came by and he knows you're leaving town soon. I don't think he had any idea we'd be out playing ball where folks could see us." He hung his head for a moment, then looked up at Timothy. "We can't do this again. It could get bad for both of us."

Timothy watched him, anger rising like a fire in his chest. "Why? We're friends. Why can't we walk and play together any time we want?" He leaned back against a lamppost, jammed his hands in his trouser pockets, and glared at a passing wagon driver who was watching them.

Ezra stood with his shoulders stooped and his head bobbing

respectfully. "Hmm" was his only response.

"Why?" Timothy repeated.

Ezra shrugged. "One name."

"Huh?"

"Dred Scott."

Huffing out a great sigh of exasperation, Timothy shook his head. "Laz says that was a dark day for our country. He says it's making a lot of people change their minds about Negroes and slavery."

Ezra shifted uncomfortably. "Yes. It's pretty hard to hear that a hard-working man has no rights in this country just because ..." He stopped and glanced around, shrugging off the rest of his thought.

"Just because of his skin color," Timothy finished for him. "Listen, I'm not worried about myself, but I don't want to cause you any trouble." He gave Ezra a half-smile. "Promise you'll come see your Aunt Patience before I leave."

Ezra gazed back with affection. "I promise."

Timothy started to offer his hand to Ezra to shake, but the other youth ducked his head again and took a step back to fend off the friendly gesture. Timothy shrugged. "Farewell then, my friend."

"And you, my friend."

With a wave of his hand, Timothy turned toward home, jogging the three blocks to dispel his frustration. Running always cleared his mind, and his long legs covered the distance quickly; his thoughts moved even faster.

What would it take to change this country and people's minds about the worth of a man? What did a man have to do to prove himself worthy of respect?

The high regard of others had come as a birthright to Timothy, due simply to his family's wealth. But he always made certain he deserved that unearned esteem. During his few years in public school, he spoke his own mind and refused to go along with boys who got into mischief. That attitude had led to a few fights when other lads called him a coward. But then, he always won, which earned him plenty of respect from his peers.

Ezra John's life had been very different. He first came to Timothy's house at seven years old to serve as an apprentice to old John, Mother's man-of-all-jobs. The nephew of Patience, the family cook, and just a year younger than Timothy, Ezra proved clever and diligent. When he finished his work, he and Timothy sometimes played for an hour or so in the backyard, where twelve-foot-high privacy fences with locked gates prevented prying eyes from noticing a black boy and a white boy tossing a ball or wrestling happily on the ground. Every evening Ezra returned to his own neighborhood just a few blocks away, a place Timothy had not been permitted to visit, though he had not understood why.

When Mother married Laz and she and Timothy moved into Laz's adjoining Louisburg Square townhouse, Timothy thought Ezra's family should move into the newly vacated house. Then Mother and Laz explained to Timothy that his friend's family would never be permitted to live in Louisburg Square, for most white people held strong prejudices toward different races. Even some people of European descent were considered inferior, such as the Irish and the Portuguese, who now flooded the Boston area seeking better lives just as English settlers once had done.

But no segment of the population was as vilified as the Negroes, whose ancestors had no choice of whether to immigrate to America. Kidnapped from their homes and families in Africa and sold into cruel slavery, the Negro races suffered the greatest injustice of all in this so-called land of freedom. Though some lived freely after purchasing their freedom or fleeing their bonds, the majority of the Negro inhabitants of America were treated as possessions.

And then, only last March the United States Supreme Court decided that Dred Scott, a slave who had sued for his freedom, was not a man but a piece of property. Further, the nation's highest court ruled that not even free Negroes possessed the rights of citizenship. No wonder Ezra toed the mark. Although he was never a slave, someone could still kidnap the strong, able young man and take him south, where no one would acknowledge his rights or stand up for him.

The Court's decision was not accepted placidly by all Americans. Even calm, controlled Laz raged at the contradiction between the rights granted to whites and forbidden to Negroes, and he vowed to intensify his efforts to free as many people as possible from their bondage in the South.

Timothy felt great pride in his stepfather and mother for their courage in helping those who sought freedom. On more occasions than he could count since they had become a family, a frightened individual had been smuggled into their home in a trunk or in disguise. If guests came or, as had happened twice, a slave catcher demanded to search the premises, as the law permitted, the refugee slipped through one of the secret doors between the two townhouses and eluded detection.

At eleven, Timothy discovered the hidden basement door. Instead of scolding, Laz put him in charge of keeping Matthew away from it. The trust of his stepfather was far more valuable to Timothy than the fun that showing off the escape route to friends would have been.

He rounded the corner of Pinckney Street and entered Louisburg Square, slowing his pace to take in the view. Soon he would leave town, and although he would return one day, he sensed it would never seem the same, and nostalgia gripped him.

In the center of the square, surrounded by a black wrought-iron fence, lay a narrow, grassy mall wherein stood two marble statues, one of Columbus and the other of Aristides the Just. When Timothy and Mother first moved into the neighborhood no statues had stood there, and he had played tag, hoops, or mumble-peg with other boys within the fence. Some time later, the adults decided to forbid children the park's pleasures, and not without justification. One errant boy broke a finger from the Columbus statue, and legend claimed he tossed it in the river down the hill. Though he could not prove it, Timothy felt certain the guilty party was his old friend Charles Atwood. Even now, Charles avoided all discussion of the event.

Today, elm trees flourished in the mall and flower beds bloomed in abundance, sending fresh floral fragrances throughout the neighborhood. But in his mind's eye, Timothy saw himself running there with two other lads—good friends and then cousins when Mother married their uncle, David. Estevam Lazarus—now called Stef, all grown up and a missionary out west after three years at Andover Seminary—had pulled Timothy out of several scrapes when they were small. Stef's brother Paolo, a year younger than Timothy and an eternal optimist, had cheered his brother and friend on in all their endeavors even as his own health declined. The dark-haired boy, more like his diminutive mother than his tall, robust father, succumbed to yellow fever during the 1852 epidemic. Although five years had passed, Timothy found himself choking back bitter sorrow at the thought of gentle Pal.

Or perhaps that memory only renewed the foolish melancholy he felt these days. After all, he was about to embark on the greatest adventure of his life. At the Naval Academy he could prove himself a man and a worthy leader of other men, like his father and Laz. He had no doubt he would meet that challenge with distinction. Still, when he thought of leaving Mother, Laz, and his three pesky little tadpoles, he could not keep the lump from his throat. He would be gone for two whole years before his first furlough.

Reaching his house in the center of the block, he gazed up at the four-story, red brick edifice. Home. No matter where he went or how long he was gone, coming home would always stir his spirit. With a deep breath to chase away his lingering sadness, he bounded up the five front steps in two strides.

The family sat at dinner, so he hastened to wash, change his shirt, and don a suit jacket before joining them. As usual, the atmosphere in the dining room was lively, with every member, even the youngest, participating in the conversation. Although most families sent their younger offspring to the kitchen for meals, Laz and Mother believed having them at the dinner table taught the children many valuable lessons.

Of course, no one ever mentioned the household's covert activities, for Deborah and Gracie were still too young to comprehend such things. But each child understood the sacred duty of keeping secrets. Each one expressed ideas and opinions freely. And each one's comments, no matter how childish, were given consideration. That way, Mother, Laz, or Mademoiselle Trudeau could help them learn to reason for themselves or, if needed, teach them proper behavior.

"Did you see Ezra?" Mother asked as she passed a serving bowl to Timothy.

"Yes, ma'am. We played the Massachusetts game, and our team won." Timothy served himself a helping of summer squash, then passed the bowl to Matthew. "I won't be able to do that again, at least not for some time." He glanced at Laz, who returned an understanding look.

"Will you play ball with me again before you leave?" Matthew gazed up at Timothy, admiration glowing in his eyes.

"And me," Deborah said.

"Me, me," Gracie added.

"But, *ma petites*," said Mademoiselle Trudeau, "young ladies do not play this game. It is not done."

Gracie puckered up to cry, but Laz cleared his throat, and she sniffed back her protest. Deborah sighed with disappointment at her governess' pronouncement.

"Tell you what, little mites," Timothy said. "I will take you all to Tremont House for an ice cream this afternoon. Then we will go to the Common and catch tadpoles in the pond."

Mademoiselle wrinkled her nose, but everyone else laughed.

Timothy turned to Mother. "May I take them?"

"Yes, you may. Just don't let Gracie fall into the water this time."

While the three younger children chirped their happiness over the coming adventure, Mother gazed at Timothy with a sober expression.

"I went over to the mission this morning. Kerry and Jeremiah send their regards."

"Umm," Timothy mumbled around a mouthful of potatoes. "Regards back."

She frowned her disapproval of his poor manners. "I also saw a friend of yours."

"A friend? Is Stef back early?"

"No. It was Jemima Starbuck."

Timothy gulped down his bite and began to cough. When he had recovered with the help of a sip of water, he stared at Mother, his heart pounding wildly, absurdly. "Jemima? Why was she at the mission?"

"She began working there this week. Aunt Charity arranged it and—"

"But why didn't you tell me sooner? When did you find out?"

"I learned of it only this morning."

"But what's she doing? What kind of work?" Apprehension surged through Timothy, destroying his appetite. The mission had only one kind of work for young women. To think of lovely Jemima cleaning up after dirty, smelly seamen was too much to bear.

"Never mind. Just tell me why you failed to mention meeting her when you visited Nantucket." Mother stared hard at him, and he returned a frown.

"It was … I didn't …" There was no appropriate answer to Mother's question. To say he forgot Jemima would be a lie, for he would never forget any detail of meeting the prettiest girl he had ever seen, no matter how brief their encounter.

"My dear," said Laz, "Timothy has had enough on his mind

preparing for the Naval Academy. I'm sure he meant to tell you. And, after all, we've made another trip to Norfolk since then. The lad's been busy."

Mother shot him a look of annoyance. "Well, you certainly could have mentioned it to me," she murmured, then turned back to Timothy. "Jemima is living with Uncle Jeremiah and Aunt Kerry and working at the mission inn for now. In the fall, she will begin taking classes at Boston Normal School in preparation for becoming a teacher."

"A teacher?" Timothy sat back in his chair. He could barely put his thoughts together. Jemima. Here in Boston. And he had not even known it. "I must go see her right away." He started to rise but recalled his manners. "May I be excused?"

"Are we going for ice cream?" Deborah gazed at him, her round, green eyes radiating trust.

Timothy glanced at Mother, then at Laz, then at Matthew and Gracie, all of whom stared at him with varying degrees of concern. Flopping back in his chair, he sighed. He never broke a promise, no matter what it cost him.

"Yes, ladybug. We will go for ice cream."

"But, *mon chéri*," said Mademoiselle, "the young ladies must take their naps, no? And Master Matthew must work on his multiplication tables, as he does every day after dinner. And so, you must visit Miss Starbuck, then return and take the children for their escapade. I shall have them ready to go by four o'clock."

"Oh, what a wonderful plan," said Mother.

"I agree," Laz added. "And you may take the phaeton."

"Thank you, Mademoiselle, Mother, Laz." Timothy looked around the table, beaming his appreciation.

But halfway to the mission, he realized he had no idea why his parents were encouraging him to visit Jemima. Nor did he know what to say when he got there.

Chapter Six

ॐ

Timothy tugged the reins, guiding Babe to a stop near the curb in front of the Harris residence. Ordinarily, he would have jumped from the buggy, secured the horse, and bounded up the stairs without a thought, for this had been a second home for him for many years. But today he viewed the house with deep concern. Today he noticed the North End's unpleasant smells of sewage and horses and the roughness of the residents and wished Uncle Jeremiah would take Laz's advice to move his family to a better neighborhood.

While the mission location could not be matched for convenience to the seaport docks—where many worthy seamen needed a clean, reputable place to lay over between voyages—it was hardly the place to raise three respectable young ladies and their fragile little brother. Nor was it an appropriate place for the lovely Miss Jemima Starbuck to reside. The notion that any passing, degenerate, scurvy old letch might set eyes on her made Timothy's stomach turn.

Or perhaps something else caused this queasy feeling. From the moment he met her in the Nantucket graveyard, he never considered another girl worth a second glance. And now, learning from Mother that Isaiah was not with her, Timothy would not rest until he discovered if she had similar feelings toward him. Their meeting had been so brief, so fraught with other emotions. Was it too much to hope that she might care for him in some small way?

His hands shook as he tied Babe's reins to the curbside post. What if she did not wish to see him? Mother's news that Isaiah would be his classmate at the academy was bad enough, but what if Isaiah had influenced Jemima's feelings about him because of his father? Drawing in and blowing out a deep breath, Timothy stared up at the yellow three-story house, squared his shoulders, and strode up the stairs to ring the doorbell. Soon a short, round, bustling figure appeared and opened the door.

"Why, Master Timothy, come right in." Mrs. Maples greeted him with a warm smile. "You don't usually ring. Did you forget your key? Why so formal today?"

Stepping inside, Timothy doffed his black cap and shrugged. "Um, I was wondering if Miss Starbuck is receiving visitors."

Mrs. Maples stared at him with a blank expression for just an instant before recovering herself. "*Miss* Starbuck? Receiving visitors? Why, I'll inquire, Master Timothy. Won't you have a seat in the front parlor?"

She bustled up the front staircase muttering to herself, but Timothy could not make out what the funny old dear said.

He hung his cap on the hall tree and wandered into the parlor— a familiar, homey room where he had often played as a child. Now it suddenly seemed alien to him. Where should he sit? On the divan? A chair? Which chair? By the window or by the hearth? No. Never mind sitting, for he would rise as soon as she entered. What would she think of him? What should he say? No coherent thought would answer those questions.

In a few moments, Mrs. Maples returned, perplexity written across her face. "Master Timothy, Jemima, eh, Miss Starbuck will be down shortly. Won't you be seated? I'll bring some lemonade as soon as she arrives."

"Thank you." Timothy sat down on the edge of a settee near the center of the large room. "Oh, Mrs. Maples?"

She stopped in the doorway. "Sir?"

"It's awful quiet around here today. Where is everyone?"

The housekeeper bobbed her head in agreement with his observa-
tion. "Reverend's at the mission. Miss Kerry and the young missies
are out taking tea with Mrs. Munroe. And of course, wee Master
Samuel is taking his afternoon nap."

"Ah, how is he?" Timothy felt a twinge of guilt for not visiting
more often.

"Oh, he has his ups and downs. But his spirits are good, as ever
they are. There never was a sweeter, more compliant boy. So
accepting of his pain."

Timothy nodded, and Mrs. Maples left him alone with his
musings.

Despite a racking cough the physicians could not cure, six-year-
old Sammy was a good little lad who made everyone smile even
though they sensed he would not be with them for long. The child
told everyone who would listen how pleased he was to be named for
the biblical prophet Samuel, and he proclaimed 1 Samuel 3:10 as his
favorite Bible verse: "Speak, Lord, for thy servant heareth." Indeed,
the sweet child seemed to hear heavenly messages, for he brought
joy to everyone who met him. Timothy wondered why God allowed
such suffering, especially in this loving family who had served him
all their lives.

"Mr. Jacobs?" Jemima stood in the parlor doorway, her blond hair
tucked into a mobcap and a starched apron over her plain white
blouse and brown skirt. Despite her servant's clothing, her flawless
face radiated with character and grace, and her dark eyes exuded
the same peace he had noticed in the graveyard. "You wished to see
me, sir?"

Timothy sat stunned for a moment, then quickly rose. "Yes. Yes, I
wish to see you." A lump filled his throat, and he coughed
awkwardly. "Yes, please come in. Sit down."

A soft smile on her lips, Jemima complied with his request and, as
she drew near, a blush appeared on her cheeks, enhancing her

already flawless beauty. Was this a good sign? Or was she distressed to see him?

She sat in a chair across from the dainty settee, which he now realized was too small for his large frame. So he chose the chair next to hers. In an instant he understood his error, for she drew back, her smile fading. He stood immediately and walked to the cold hearth, biting his lip and toying with a pewter letter opener he found on the mahogany mantel. He had no idea what to say.

"Sir, is there something …?"

"Miss Starbuck, I'm an idiot …"

They both spoke at once, and then stopped, chuckling with embarrassment. But then their gazes met, and their laughter dissolved into pleasant gaiety, as though they had known each other forever. At least it seemed so to Timothy.

"Sir?" She looked at him expectantly.

He crossed the room, sat back down on the settee, and hoped it would not collapse. But at least by his sitting here, she would not misunderstand his intentions. He stared down at his hands, chewed his lip, and took a deep breath for courage.

"Miss Starbuck, our first meeting—in the graveyard, I mean, not when we were small children, for you probably don't remember that—it was under unusual and not the best circumstances."

He ventured a look at her. She was nodding, and her eyes were bright with acceptance. His courage grew.

"I would like to begin again."

Her brightness faded, and bewilderment replaced acceptance. "Sir?"

Timothy blew out a sigh of frustration. "Don't call me 'sir.' All the wrong people call me 'sir.' I don't feel like a 'sir.'"

"Yes, sir. Oh, I mean … forgive me." Jemima's face grew rosy pink again.

"Oh, no, I don't mean … I'm not angry." Timothy slapped his

forehead and threw himself against the settee back, which groaned its displeasure. He sat up quickly, then stood, ran his hands through his hair, and stumbled back toward the hearth, where he leaned his elbows on the mantel and rested his chin on his hands. "I can't say anything right," he mumbled.

Jemima appeared beside him, and for the first time he took in how comfortable, how very pleasant her medium height felt next to his much taller stature. A wave of protectiveness surged through him.

"Mr. Jacobs, shall we do as you suggested and begin again?"

He chuckled. "Yes. Thank you. That would be grand. And, to begin again, please call me Timothy."

Her blush returned, and she stepped back. "Oh, no, sir, I could not."

"But why not?" He turned to face her.

She looked down at the floor. "Sir, I am a servant in this place. I will not take liberties when addressing my employer's friends."

"But are *we* not friends, Jemima?" His voice squeaked with heart-felt pathos, and his face grew warm. Had Isaiah destroyed any chance he might have with her?

She stared up at him, her eyes round with childlike confusion. And perhaps a small measure of expectation. His plummeting heart swung back up into his throat as he waited for her response.

"I … I don't know if that's proper." The expression of puzzlement on her face was so endearing, he almost laughed as she continued. "I mean, with your mother being my benefactress …"

"My mother your … what?" He quickly regretted his vehement tone, for she took another step back and blinked, perhaps afraid. "Forgive me. I don't know what you're talking about."

"Why, Mrs. Lazarus was here just this morning offering to pay for my education so I can become a schoolteacher. She's even offered to find an appropriate school and make all the arrangements."

Timothy slumped against the mantel. "Oh." Mother had

mentioned Jemima's school plans, but not her own part in them. No wonder Jemima was reticent. She must think he wished to use Mother's generosity to some unseemly advantage. "Well, I must say my mother never stops surprising me. I didn't know. In fact, I didn't know you were in Boston until Mother informed me at dinner today. Had I known, I would've come to see you much sooner. And not because of what she's doing, but because ... because, after meeting you, I wanted to see you again."

A smile once more graced Jemima's face, and happiness shone in her eyes. She took a quick, deep breath and gazed up at him. "From the moment we met in the graveyard, I've wished to be your friend, but doubted it would be possible. Perhaps God has granted me that which I didn't possess faith enough to ask of him."

Timothy swayed with dizziness and expelled a long sigh of relief. "Oh, I cannot think God would deny us such ..." He wished to say "happiness," but feared it would be misconstrued. "... such friendship." He stepped toward her and reached out to capture her hand. "Let's sit and talk."

Jemima did not pull her hand away but permitted him to lead her to the long divan, where he sat her at one end and took his place at the other. There they sipped Mrs. Maples' lemonade and shared childhood stories until the mantel clock chimed the half-hour at three-thirty.

"Oh, bother," said Timothy. "I must go. I've promised my little brother and sisters I would take them for ice cream." He paused, struck with a new plan. "Won't you come with us, Jemima? It would be grand to have you. Have you seen the Public Gardens? Or the Common? Or the capitol? Do say you'll come, for I'd love for you to meet my family, I mean, the rest of my family."

She considered for a moment. "Oh, Timothy, I'd love it, too. But I must help Mrs. Lazarus with supper at the mission. I've been given this half day off only because of Mrs. Harris's generosity. She felt I should recover from the shock and excitement of your mother's offer." Jemima giggled. "I told her, respectfully, of course, that she must know we Nantucket girls are sturdier souls than to faint away when life takes a turn, whether up or down. After all, she's a Nantucket girl herself. Still, she insisted I take some time for myself."

Timothy gazed at her, his heart swelling with happiness despite her refusal. What a sensible, responsible, beautiful girl. Just listening to her talk, no matter what she said, was like hearing music. But doubt darted across his mind. What if she was only being polite by visiting with him like this? What if she longed for him to leave, despite their pleasant chat?

"Another time, then?"

She ducked her chin and smiled, a blush returning to her fair cheeks. "Oh, yes. Most certainly, another time."

As she raised her lovely dark eyes to gaze at him again, doubt fled before the onslaught of raging ecstasy in his heart.

Isaiah squirmed around on the lumpy straw mattress, trying to find a comfortable position. His old bed back in Nantucket had been easier to sleep on than this fleabag in Mrs. Doone's basement. It didn't help that his back, arms, and legs ached from his first few days on a fishing boat that sailed daily from the Annapolis docks. Although he could perform his share of duties, the job took muscles too long unused. Several years had passed since his whaling voyage, and no other work had put this strain on him.

Then there was this uneasiness over living in a strange woman's basement. Isaiah didn't mind that her narrow East Street home was humble and ill furnished or that this six- by eight-foot cubicle could hardly be called a room. Who was he to demand luxurious accommodations? By the time he'd found this place, he'd spent two days searching for work and two nights sleeping on the streets and was grateful to have a roof over his head at last. But Widow Doone and her daughter Meg had latched onto him as if he were a gift from above. Meg, who appeared a couple of years older than he, found many reasons to be in the same room, often coming so close he felt uncomfortable. She was moderately clean and not unpleasant to look at. But her uncultured dialect betrayed a lack of education, and her familiarity after only two days was disconcerting.

On the other hand, Mrs. Doone's slave Bebe kept Isaiah's room clean, and Mrs. Doone knew how to make a tough cut of beef into a chewable and hearty stew, which made remaining here tolerable—even beneficial. He would need his strength to keep working until classes began in October.

The job had been difficult to find too. Here in Maryland, slaves did much of the manual labor. An inexperienced young outsider must look long and hard for work and must be willing to perform menial tasks side by side with the Negroes hired out by their masters to the dock managers.

Isaiah had no objections to either, although he was bothered by the conditions of his fellow workers. While he was free to come and go at will, the slaves must return to their masters each day, and at the end of the week turn over their earnings to those who held them in bondage. This disparity and, in fact, the whole idea of slavery sickened him, as it did every Nantucketer. Although Mrs. Doone seemed to treat Bebe well enough, Meg's behavior toward the thin old woman was less than kind.

Yet he had learned that poverty held people like him in bondage almost as strongly as any physical chains. Although his employer might not beat him—as slave owners often beat their chattels—he had the power to destroy Isaiah's reputation and prevent him from getting another job.

Isaiah coped with this cruel condition by reminding himself his employment was temporary. In two months, he would move out of this shabby place and into student quarters at the academy, just a few blocks away on the Severn River. He would start earning his navy pay, not a large amount but more than his current salary. Then he would prove himself a man worthy of respect, a prospect no slave could ever hope to attain.

A scratching sound near the door interrupted his musings. A rat, he was certain, for one had crawled across him last night. He picked up his shoe from beside his cot, preparing to hurl it into the darkness.

"Mr. Starbuck?" Meg's muffled, whispered voice sounded through the flimsy door of his tiny, blackened room. "Isaiah?"

He could hear her rattling the latch. Surely she would not enter. He slowly lowered his shoe to the floor and scrunched down under his light blanket. If he pretended to be asleep, she would go away. Wouldn't she?

The door hinges creaked, and his eyes popped open. Just as quickly, he shut them, but not before taking in a sight that sent strange, unwanted feelings surging through him. Lit by a dim light from behind, her womanly form was silhouetted in the doorway, lightly shrouded in a gauzy white nightgown. He stifled a groan.

"Isaiah?" She knelt by his cot and gave him a gentle shake.

There was no escape.

"Mmm." He pretended to be half awakened. "Go away, Jemima. It's too early to get up."

She giggled. "I'm not your sister, Isaiah."

He bolted upright, pulling his blanket up to cover his bare chest. "Miss Doone!"

"Shh. Let's not wake Mother."

"Miss Doone, you should *not* be here. You should ..."

Again, she giggled. "Your back hurts from all that hard work you been doin'. I brought some liniment to rub on it."

"What ...?"

"I said 'Shh.' Now lie back down and turn over, and I'll make it feel all better."

A vision of Lacy Harris darted across Isaiah's mind. Sweet, pure Lacy. Her kindness and unfeigned interest in him had caused him to think … what? Despite the Harris family's warm welcome, Isaiah could not permit himself to hope Lacy's feelings might go beyond Christian charity. After all, his sister was their chambermaid.

"Are you gonna turn over, or do I have to …"

"No." Isaiah gulped. "I'll turn over."

Humming a soft, soothing tune, Meg worked the odiferous liniment into his aching shoulders. As long as he was able, Isaiah resisted the nearly overwhelming sensation of relief that flowed through him as his pain subsided. But at last he surrendered to Meg's artful ministrations.

Chapter Seven

A dull light filtered through the dirty basement window, announcing that the summer's early dawn had arrived. Breakfast smells wafted through the door, and Isaiah stirred, looking forward to another of Mrs. Doone's hearty meals. According to his habit, he lay for a moment anticipating the coming day—or maybe bracing himself for the pain it would bring. Then he noticed his back and shoulders no longer ached. *Then* he remembered. Meg!

Last night was an unexpected new experience. But Meg knew exactly what she was doing. He still could not figure out whether he was wise to let her do it. He only knew he felt so superb afterward that he fell asleep easily.

A movement beside him woke him fully. He turned his head to discover himself not alone.

"Miss Doone! What are you doing here?"

She drew in a deep, sleepy breath and yawned. "Hmmm. Is it morning already?" Her eyes popped open, and she rolled off the cot, gasping out a profanity as she hit the dirt floor. "Isaiah! Mr. Starbuck. Oh, my mama's going to kill me." Her gaze darted about the room as if she were looking for an escape. Her voice fell to a whisper. "Oh, me, oh, my, I never meant to fall asleep." Glancing down at her thin nightgown, she tugged on the bed's one blanket to cover herself.

Although only clothed in undergarments himself, Isaiah relinquished it gladly. "You'd better go. Now. Please." He aped her quiet tone, adding considerably more urgency.

Meg nodded. "Yeah, I better. But what if Mama sees me? She'll kill me." Again, she glanced frantically around the room, as if some help could be found in the tiny, dimly lit space. Her glance rested on him once more. "Or she'll kill you."

"Me? Why me?" He drew back against the wall, horrid images filling his mind.

"Oh, there was this other fella here last month. A smooth-tongued type. He was ..." She stopped, stared down, and shook her head. "Never mind. Mama just don't want me hanging around the boarders. Said the next fella that casts sheep's eyes at me is gonna end up married." She offered him a crooked, embarrassed smile.

Isaiah's hair seemed to stand on end, stinging like tiny needles all over his body. Even if he cared for this person, midshipmen could not be married. He would lose his appointment at the academy. His whole future would be lost. Lacy would be lost long before he could earn a respectable station in life from which to court her.

He stared beyond Meg to the half-open door. "Can't you go out the back way and up the outside stairs? Don't those stairs lead to the second-floor hallway?"

She gave him a saucy grin. "So you noticed. You been planning to come up that way?"

He blew out an exasperated sigh. "No. Not at all. Now you need to get out of here before your mother hears us."

"Aw, she's half deaf."

"Miss Doone, please leave."

Meg stared back down at her hands, and he could not tell whether it was from truly hurt feelings or just pretension.

"Awright, I'll go." She pouted. "And we'll just hope Mama don't see me."

Isaiah was tempted to pray to Jemima's God that the older woman was indeed partly deaf and perhaps a little blind too, so she would not catch her errant daughter escaping this scandalous situation. But he shook off the thought, deciding action was far more practical than prayer.

"You wait until I get dressed. I'll go up for breakfast and distract your mother so you can get out of here."

"Sounds good to me." Letting the blanket slip off her shoulders, she leaned against the cot and stared at him.

"Quit looking at me," he hissed. He found his trousers and quickly pulled them on, ignoring his need for the chamber pot.

She smiled. "I saw you plenty last night, even in the dark."

Isaiah froze. "You did not. And don't think you can say anything … well, anything wicked happened here."

Meg seemed stunned. "No. I never would do that." She turned away, but not before he saw tears—real, honest tears—start to slide down her cheek. "But I hoped …"

"Well, don't hope. It's not going to happen."

The misery on her face sent a guilty twinge through his middle. "Look, Miss Doone, don't think so little of yourself. You're a …" He started to say she was pretty but feared that might be misunderstood. "You're a decent girl. I know you are."

"I suppose. But after that other fella …"

"See here, I don't know what happened with him, and I don't want to. But the next time you come too close to me, I'll be setting sail and telling your mother why."

She stared up at him, her eyes round with fear and a small measure of pathos. "I won't. I promise I won't. Just don't leave."

He finished buttoning his shirt, tucked it into his trousers, and pulled on his well-worn shoes. "I'll go aloft now. Then you can scud up the back stairs."

"Scud?" She wrinkled her brow in confusion so honest and charming, he almost laughed.

"That's how Nantucketers say 'hurry up and go.'"

An embarrassed smirk scampered across her face. "Will you tell me about Nantucket and whaling sometime?"

He grabbed his cap and jacket, glancing over his shoulder as he went out the door. "Maybe. If you mind your manners." He did not like the sound of her giggle following him up the stairs.

Later, as he tramped through the streets toward the docks, he pondered his situation. Should he find another place to live or could he trust Meg to behave? In fact, could he trust himself to behave? Last night he had felt sorely tempted to return the favor … and more, as Meg massaged his back. But something had restrained him, an even stronger feeling he could not define. Maybe he had some subconscious fear of being trapped into marriage, which was not the way he wanted to enter that part of manhood. Not when he had good advice for another way to manage those temptations.

When he had sailed around the Horn with Captain Chase, the ship had lain over on a South Pacific island where villagers offered the whalers generous hospitality. At eleven years of age, Isaiah had been too young to participate in all the activities, but he had known plenty well what went on inside the grass huts and behind the bushes. Seeing how troubled he was by the giggling island girls who kept pestering him, the captain had offered some suggestions.

"These island folks think a bit differently than folks back home. When you're old enough, these girls can teach you all you want to know. But if you're back home when you decide to, eh, become a man, here's what you do. Don't hook up with a girl who's got a mother, or worse, a father, or you'll end up married to someone you don't care a fig for. Instead, find a girl who's glad to be with you for a couple of coins. Just make sure she's clean."

What he had meant by clean, Isaiah was not certain, but he would be sure to find out before he "became a man." For now, he just wanted to stay out of trouble and make some money before entering the academy in October. Tonight, he would be certain to prop a board or a broom handle against the door of his room so Meg could not enter again. And he would work very hard every day to be certain he was too tired to give in to any temptation himself. At least until he had those couple of coins in his pocket.

Despite having to stop and help Jewel several times, Jemima flew through her morning chores at the mission. Her mind raced from one future possibility to another, making every physical task seem easier.

Shaking out the small rug in one of the guest rooms, she laid it across the ladder-back chair, waved the floating dust particles away from her itching nose, and swept up the rest from the wooden floor. The summer day was dry and hot, and dust clung to everything. Perhaps she should mop this room and use a damp cloth to clean the windowsills, chair, and tabletop. Usually, she disliked going back to redo a chore, but today it did not bother her at all, for she felt far too happy to mind any inconvenience.

Yesterday had brought so many lovely surprises. What she had always counted distant dreams were about to become reality. Not only would she be able to attend school and study all the subjects she loved, but one day she would be able to teach little children as she had been taught by the good women of Nantucket.

What would she have done without those ladies? By island tradition, they had made it their mission to be certain every Nantucket child was educated—even the poorest—as she and Isaiah had been. An important part of the education was learning that, while people might have different stations and different occupations in life, they all had the same worth in the eyes of God.

How Jemima wished Isaiah could believe that. He struggled so much and felt so much shame for their poverty, as if it were somehow his fault. But such an idea was foolish. Nantucket men, whether wealthy or poor, had a reputation of being hard workers, and her brother never shirked any duty he was given, no matter how difficult.

Dear Isaiah. Last night, despite her own happiness, she had felt a deep, strong stirring of concern for her beloved brother. Her inner agitation kept her awake far into the night, as she prayed alternately for him and for herself. She offered praise and thanks for her own unexpected blessing through Mrs. Hannah Lazarus. She pleaded anxiously for Isaiah to be protected from harm and temptation, though she could not imagine her self-controlled brother getting into any trouble. Perhaps her vague concerns for him had to do with his forthcoming shock of discovering Timothy was to be his classmate.

If only Isaiah did not have this unreasonable hatred for Timothy. What a lovely thing it would be if they could once again become friends.

The room now dusted and wiped down, Jemima moved to the water closet at the end of the hall. She dumped her bucket, refilled it from the faucet, added lye soap from the crock in the storage closet, knelt down, and began to scrub.

Wringing out her washrag, she laughed softly, sharing a joke with her Lord. "While I'm down here on my knees, I might as well pray," she whispered. This was her favorite pastime while doing house-work—a secret she had learned from her mother as the best way to avoid boredom over the repetition of her labor. It also kept her thoughts close to those she loved.

Now, Lord, you know where Isaiah is and what he's doing. Please protect him from harm. And if you don't mind, please let me hear from him soon. Help me not to worry if I don't, but to trust you. And, Lord, please help him not to hate Timothy or blame him for Papa's death, for after all, one day he and Timothy will be brothers.

With a gasp, Jemima paused in her chore and sat back on her heels. What on earth had she just prayed? A giddy, happy feeling swept through her and, try as she might, she could not think of one sensible, sobering thought with which to suppress it. At this moment, with all her heart, she believed that one day, despite the disparity in their situations, she would marry Timothy. Was God truly speaking to her, or was this merely her own dearest wish?

Only time would tell.

Chapter Eight

&

"A man should never let his appetites control him, no matter how strong they seem." Laz kept his gaze on his fishing line, which draped over the side of the skiff and hung deep in the waters of Boston Bay, but he bent his head in Timothy's direction.

"Aye, sir." Watching his own line, Timothy waited, certain his stepfather would continue, and also certain that eating too much food was not the appetite under discussion. Both of them had lean, strong bodies from working hard and refusing extra helpings of Patience's excellent cooking. Long ago, the dear old cook had given up encouraging them to eat more, for neither liked to feel overstuffed.

"Look lively." Laz spoke in a hushed tone, but nodded toward Timothy's line.

The spun cotton strand jerked beneath the water's surface with an irregular rhythm. Timothy bided his time, then yanked back his hard line to set the hook and jumped up to land his catch.

"Easy," said Laz, laughing. "Don't swamp us. Bring him in. Bring him in."

The small skiff's gunwale listed close to the bay's surface, but Laz quickly jumped to the port side to balance the boat and keep it from taking on water.

"Look at him. Look at him!" With a laugh, Timothy hauled in the thrashing fish, a fat, silver-striped bass. "Must be ten pounds, easy." He unhooked the thirty-inch fish, held on tight as it continued to fight, and stuffed it into a canvas bag in the bottom of the boat.

Laz clapped him on the shoulder. "Good job. You played him just right."

"Wow! Some fish. Can't wait to show it to Mother." Timothy returned to his seat to rebait his hook with a strip of shad.

"Ah, well, she never gets too excited about fish, you know." Laz laughed, clearly delighted with Timothy's success. "Now Matthew— that's another thing altogether. He'll be green with envy that you caught the big one today."

"He sure will, the little scamp. He was so proud of that big dogfish last time. Too bad he had to catch a poison fish. He just couldn't understand why we didn't want to take it home for Patience to cook for dinner." He laughed at the memory. "Say, why didn't we bring him? He wasn't too happy being left with the girls."

Laz pulled up his line to check his bait. "He'll get plenty more turns in due time. This was our trip today, the last one for who knows how long."

Timothy gave him a crooked grin. "Thank you, Laz. But I never mind the little guy tagging along. I was a lot younger when you started bringing me out here."

"No, you never do seem to mind. You're a fine big brother. Matthew and the girls will miss you when you leave."

Timothy grunted to disguise the sudden lump in his throat. "Me, too." He glanced sidelong at Laz. "So, what about appetites?"

The older man chuckled lightly. "Women."

Timothy took a turn at chuckling, but with considerably less light-ness. "We had this talk a few years ago, Laz. I know all about that sort of thing."

Now Laz pursed his lips, obviously trying not to laugh outright. Timothy felt his face burn. He hunched his shoulders forward and concentrated on the fishing line. After a few moments of silence, he glanced again at Laz.

"All right, then. What about women?"

"You've read in the Bible about the strange woman."

"Yes, sir." Timothy was tempted to roll his eyes in annoyance, but respect for his stepfather tempered his attitude. If Laz brought him all the way out here on the bay to have a talk with him about women, however unnecessary Timothy considered the discussion, so be it. He would listen.

But, true to his nature, Laz did not preach. "Well, then, tell me what the Scriptures say."

"Um, which Scriptures?"

"Let's say Proverbs. What does Proverbs say about the strange woman?"

Still working his line, Timothy blew out a deep breath. "Says flee from her. Says go not nigh the door to her house, 'cause it's a trap. Says she'll steal your money." He wrinkled his brow, recalling and listing other verses. "Her end is bitter. Her feet go down to death. Only a fool has anything to do with her." He stifled a mischievous grin. "And she might make you very, very sick."

"Hmm. Sounds like you have the right idea." Laz concentrated on his fishing line as well, but Timothy noticed his half-grin.

After a few moments of silence, Timothy shifted uncomfortably in his seat. Although he felt certain that he knew how to handle the matter, Laz seemed concerned.

"Question," he said.

"Yes?"

"All those seven or so years you were out on that last whaling voyage?"

"Yes."

Timothy stared at him. "You never, um, looked at another woman?"

Laz gazed placidly back. "Never."

"How'd you manage?"

"Prayed, read my Bible and some books I'd brought along. Mostly, though, thought of my Eliza. And I thought of how I wanted young men to treat my little Lizzie when she grew up."

"Mm." Timothy considered his little sisters and Jemima and understood just what Laz meant.

"It was a matter of honor, son. Honor toward God. Honor toward my wife, to whom I had promised to be faithful. Honor toward myself. A little pleasure for a short time might lead to a lifetime of regret."

Timothy continued to watch the man who had never told him a lie. "Were you ever tempted, really tempted?"

Laz threw back his head and laughed out loud. "Why, to be sure, my boy. To be sure. A man can get mighty lonely on a long voyage, and some of those islands in the South Pacific are known for their, eh, hospitality."

"Hmm." Timothy had heard all this before, some of it from sources not as respectable as his stepfather. "And so—"

"And so we found other places to replenish our food and water."

Timothy grinned. "How'd the men take it?"

"Some took it better than others. But I had shipped a Christian crew, and they knew what they were in for before they sailed."

"Mm." Timothy watched his bobber duck under the surface again and sat ready if the fish took the line.

Distant sounds wafted across the water: tugboat horns, working men calling to one another on the docks, train whistles. Seagulls and pelicans circled overhead, begging a share of the catch, or dove into the bay to grab their own. The two men in the boat sat silent for some time.

"You'll do fine, son."

Timothy nodded his appreciation for Laz's remark. Not every fishing trip they had taken over the years included instruction about how to live wisely. But when they did, he could hardly complain, for Laz was a man of few words and the best stepfather a boy ever had. Still, Timothy could not help but wonder what his own father would tell him about this matter of women. Not a question he could ask Mother, of course, so he would never know. More important, would

Papa have had the same confidence in Timothy's character that Laz expressed? Another mystery he would never solve.

A stiff wind came up, and without a word but with a shared instinct, the two men packed in their gear and their catch and began the trip back toward the shore. Not far into their endeavor, Laz paused his rowing, and Timothy followed suit.

"The most important things a man can give the lady he loves are honest character, a pure body, and a spirit submitted to the Almighty."

Laz appeared to be considering if anything else should be said, but finally gave his head a sharp nod and resumed his rowing.

Timothy huffed out a long, quiet breath, expressing both his efforts against the increasingly stronger waves and his relief that the conversation had ended. As his departure for the academy grew nearer, some undefined list of happenings seemed to be completing itself. Sometimes, he almost felt like a person who knew he was going to die and was putting his affairs in order. And, in a way, Timothy was dying, at least to his old life and the last remnants of his childhood. Despite those occasional twinges of emotion regarding his family, he approached the milestone without the least bit of trepidation.

One thing he would do before he left: make sure Jemima knew he cared for her. And if she returned his feelings, he might even pledge his affection to her. Did Jemima like Shakespeare? Perhaps he could use a Shakespearean sonnet to express himself. But maybe he should not make a pledge, for she might think him too forward. Maybe he should just give her a book of poetry and mark passages that expressed his feelings.

What should he do?

Not a question he would ask Laz.

Jemima fidgeted in her chair in the Harrises' front parlor and rose every few moments to look out the window. Each time she left her chair, Lacy giggled.

"Do sit still, Jemima," said Lacy. "He said three o'clock, and it's only two forty-five. Timothy is always punctual but never early."

"Oh, my, I know I'm being silly, but—" She stopped, unable to think of a way to explain her own uncharacteristic nervousness.

"I understand." Lacy gave her a sweet, knowing smile. "There *is* one young man whose presence makes me all aflutter."

Jemima smiled back, certain she knew who that young man was. From the moment they had met until Isaiah had left for Maryland a few days later, he and Lacy had cast shy glances at each other every time they were in the same room. Despite her brother's shabby clothes and worn shoes, fashionable Lacy seemed enchanted by his youthful manliness. Even Reverend Harris did not seem to mind the subtle, innocent flirtation between his oldest daughter and his chambermaid's brother. Perhaps it was a result of Mrs. Harris's influence, for she was a girl from Nantucket, where many an impoverished boy had worked hard and become a respectable leader of men. The Harrises could see Isaiah's trustworthiness and potential. They admired his good character and expected great things of him.

Her brother had never taken an interest in any girl, and his sweetly befuddled manner in Lacy's presence brought joy to Jemima's heart. And, she decided, since Reverend Harris would never consent to a union between the two until Isaiah believed in the Lord Jesus Christ, her brother would gain salvation *and* a wife.

"I said—" Lacy tapped Jemima's hand. "Tell me again what Timothy said to you after church on Sunday."

Jemima jumped and then laughed. How foolish her musings could be sometimes. Yet imagine how pleasant it would be to have this dear, unselfish girl for a sister. Even now, Jemima wore one of Lacy's pretty blue frocks so she could look nice for her outing. Although a little short, it fit nicely and made her feel more elegant than she ever had in her life.

"He was very charming. He said he had asked your father if he could call to take me out for ice cream at the Tremont House. He said he would bring along Matthew for a chaperone if your father thought he should."

"That's just like our Timothy." Lacy giggled in girlish conspiracy. "He's always been the perfect gentleman, even when Molly, Daisy, and I have pestered him to distraction. He has never said a cross word to any of us."

Jemima studied her new friend's expression. If Lacy thought so much of Timothy, how could she have failed to fall in love with him?

As if sensing the question, Lacy tilted her head in mock annoyance. "Of course, he does tease us endlessly, as well, just like a big brother. And, like a brother, he's often taken us out for ice cream. I think that's why Father did not insist on a chaperone for you today. Timothy is family, and so are you."

The ring of the doorbell interrupted their cozy chat, and Mrs. Maples soon announced Timothy's arrival.

Black dome-crowned hat in hand, Timothy stood in the parlor doorway wearing a smart black suit, starched white shirt, and shiny black half-boots. "Good afternoon." His deep voice squeaked a little, and Jemima could see that, despite his perfect manners, he was as nervous as she.

"Good afternoon, Timothy. Do come in." Lacy spoke as both girls rose and walked to greet him. "Just give me a moment and I'll fetch my bonnet."

"*Your* bonnet?" Timothy's voice ascended even higher.

"Why, yes." Lacy appeared earnest. "Didn't you know I'm going with you as a chaperone?"

He laughed out loud, and his demeanor became relaxed. "What do you think, Jemima? Should we let her go with us?"

"Why, I—" Jemima's face grew warm. As much as she liked Lacy's company—

"Don't be silly." Lacy laughed. "Why, la, I don't care a whit for ice cream."

"Not much," Timothy quipped. "Well, then, that's settled. Shall we go, Jemima?"

"Oh, yes." Jemima blinked in momentary confusion and then laughed. She must get used to these teasing ways. She grabbed her bonnet from the divan, checked her reflection in the hall tree mirror, and tucked her unruly curls beneath the headpiece. "This will be a grand adventure. I've never been to a real hotel."

Timothy started to speak, then stopped, apparently reconsidering his words. At last, he said, "It will be a grand adventure, won't it?"

As Timothy drove the phaeton through the busy, crowded streets, he pointed out Paul Revere's house right near the mission, the far off Bunker Hill monument, the spire of the Old North Church, and other historic sites. Watching Jemima's wide-eyed interest and delight, he felt his heart warm immeasurably. He was glad he had not teased her about never being in a hotel, for that might have wounded her feelings. She did not seem overly sensitive, but he must be careful. He would rather die than hurt her.

In his left jacket pocket, wrapped in brown paper, lay a small book of poetry. He had decided Shakespeare's sonnets were the best choice, since Mother often told him she and Papa had read those poems together. Was this the time to ask Jemima if she liked the Bard? Then, if she said no, he could take her to Brattle Bookstore and find another poet's work. But would that be proper? He had not thought to ask Mother.

He knew only one thing without doubt. He must make certain this lovely young lady understood exactly how he felt. Despite their young years, it was not too soon to pledge their love. Mother once told him that, among Nantucket folk, many girls as young as fourteen secured such a pledge before their beaux set sail to hunt whales, and then married after a two-, three-, or five-year voyage. Most mainlanders did not begin courting until at least seventeen, usually older. But even Mother and Laz approved of Timothy's interest in Jemima, trusting him to know his own mind and heart.

His own heart told him more than once that his fondness for her had begun long ago. When he and Isaiah had minded the pretty, smiling baby while their mothers chatted, Jemima often reached up, patted his cheek or grabbed his nose and giggled. The simple gestures had filled his heart with happiness, though he could not say why. After he and Mother moved to Boston, he had named his beloved, ill-fated yellow kitten for the blond toddler left behind in Nantucket.

Now, as if a dream had come true, she sat beside him, a toddler no longer, but a beautiful young lady. They drove through the streets of Boston, chatting about the city's great history or remarking over the diversity of its burgeoning population. He could see she would be an excellent teacher, for she made many astute observations about both scenery and people. Still, he hoped that, by the time her schooling was complete, they would marry, and she would have no need to work.

They entered the Tremont House and walked up the graceful staircase to the second floor restaurant. Jemima's eyes grew wide with obvious wonder as she gazed around at the beautiful draperies, marble sculptures, and courteous, uniformed staff. Through her eyes, he saw anew what a lovely hotel this was.

Settled at last in the sunny, spacious dining room, they ordered ice cream from a nervous, newly trained waiter who could neither take his eyes off of Jemima nor get their simple order straight. When he brought two slices of lemon pie, the headwaiter scolded him tersely until Jemima insisted it had always been her fondest wish to taste lemon pie in this very hotel. The waiters bowed their gratitude to the lady, the older man insisted they have both pie and ice cream, and the younger one seemed so smitten with her that Timothy, using one of Laz's tactics, cleared his throat in an authoritative manner and sent the boy scooting away to fetch the correct order.

"My, that was much ado about nothing," Jemima said with a little laugh.

Before Timothy could comment that the hotel's waiters usually had more thorough training, he grasped the importance of her words to his purpose, and his heart leapt.

"Why, Miss Starbuck," he teased. "Do you like Shakespeare?"

"Why, yes, Mr. Jacobs," she responded in kind. "I love Shakespeare. In fact, I enjoy *Much Ado about Nothing* more than all the others because of the witty repartee between Beatrice and Benedick, although some of the meanings elude me. And, of course, I like the play because the romance of Hero and Claudio ends happily. I find it much more appealing than the tale of poor Romeo and Juliet, which is often held up as the epitome of love stories."

He watched while the young waiter set their order in place, then waved him away. "Then you prefer the comedies?"

"Yes, indeed." Jemima picked up her spoon, dug into the ice treat, and took a bite. "Mmm. Delicious. As I was saying, the comedies are so uplifting. Do we not have enough grief in this world? Why go about entertaining ourselves with imagined unhappiness?"

"What a sensible opinion." Timothy gazed at her, struck by such wisdom in one so young, and was rewarded with a sweet smile. Encouraged, he cleared his throat again, this time with a small twinge of nervousness. "If you like romantic writings, do you number the Bard's sonnets among your favorite poems?"

Jemima now placed a bite of pie between her lips and glanced away as if thinking how to answer him. While she chewed, Timothy did not move. Was she pausing to finish her bite, or did she really have to consider her response?

"Hmm," she said at last. "I would say his sonnets are certainly some of the most beautiful poetry ever written. While I would not wish to disparage Byron, Keats, or the more recent and extremely gifted Brownings, I am of the opinion that William Shakespeare is the master of them all."

Timothy exhaled an explosion of relief, and then felt his face grow hot with embarrassment. He had not realized he was holding his breath. "Well, then, will you accept—" He reached down and struggled to bring the book out of its snug hiding place in his pocket. With a quick, frustrated yank, which was accompanied by the sound of ripping threads, he produced the brown package. He rolled his eyes and shook his head, but Jemima laughed merrily.

"That will require mending."

"Here." He thrust the gift across the table. "It's for you."

Her laughter receded into a pleased smile. "Oh, my. Oh, Timothy." Hesitating only a moment, she reached out to take it. She slipped off the twine tied around the paper and took out the tan leather volume.

"How very pretty." She held it up and sniffed. "I love the smell of new leather." She opened the book and read the inscription.

"'August 15, 1857. To Jemima, from your friend Timothy.'" She gazed across the table, her cheeks aglow with a lovely blush. "Oh, Timothy, it's so sweet of you to give me this token of our friendship. And how grand to have the very first book in my own personal library. I will need many books for teaching, you know. You *are* a friend. A very good, dear friend."

Timothy felt the strain of his smile, the one his sister Deborah called his crooked, silly grin. Jemima did not understand what he was trying to say at all. He should have underlined some of the passages that could reveal his feelings. But what could he do now? How could he talk so easily with her for hours about history, poetry, and people on the streets, yet when he wanted to tell her what was in his heart, his brain refused to supply the words? The best he could come up with was, "I'm glad you like it."

Jemima fanned the unslit pages for a moment. "I can hardly wait to cut them and read every word on every page." She closed the book, set it on the table, and, after hesitating a bit, stared at him intently.

"Timothy, there is something very important I must ask you."

His heart leapt once more. Was she one of those Nantucket girls who took the initiative in romance? If so, he would not reproach her. "Yes. Anything." *Just say you love me, and I will tell you all my heart.*

To his surprise, she bowed her head for a moment, almost as if in prayer, before gazing at him with a sober expression. "I believe very strongly that I am responsible to my Lord for the souls of all my friends."

"Souls?" There went his voice, squeaking again like an adolescent's.

Her eyes twinkled, and she pursed her lips. But then she grew sober once more. "What I mean to say is that it is important to be certain all my friends know my Lord Jesus Christ."

Timothy slumped back in his chair. She had completely missed his point, and probably had no idea what his gift was supposed to represent—his very heart!

"How could I not know all about the Lord? With Jeremiah Harris as my pastor and David Lazarus as my stepfather, do you think I could grow up without knowing all that?"

Disappointment seemed to dart across her face, but she nodded and smiled again. "Knowing is very important, but it's only the first step. Do you recall the passage in the gospel of John, chapter three? Our Lord's conversation with Nicodemus?"

"Of course. That's one of Uncle Jeremiah's favorites. He never preaches a sermon without 'Ye must be born again' fitting in somewhere." He spoke almost flippantly and hoped she would laugh ... or at least smile. But her sober expression never wavered.

"But have you?"

"Huh?" Not the most gentlemanly sound to make.

"Have you been born again?"

Her gaze bored into him with an intensity that stirred an unbidden resentment in his chest. He would not be pushed—even by Jemima—to say words everyone else seemed to think were important. He knew how to please God, and he worked at it every day. But to say that might destroy his chances with her. He toyed with his spoon and cleared his throat yet again.

"Some people don't express their thoughts about religion as well as others, but don't worry about me. I have always paid attention to Uncle Jeremiah's preaching, and I have always done what he … and the Scriptures, say is important to do."

Jemima tilted her head and frowned, as if uncertain of his meaning, but he would say no more. Her concern did not surprise him, for he had seen her deep faith the moment they met in Nantucket. The same peaceful spirit he saw in his Mother and Aunt Kerry was evident in her eyes. But, with those same eyes, she must be able to see his goodness and have faith in him, or all was lost. Just as despair began to slither into his heart, she smiled brightly.

"Ah, I see. I understand. Many people have difficulty expressing their faith. The Society of Friends, in which my Mother was raised, teaches that each soul must find its Inner Light to God. Why, the silence in our—their—worship meetings is not from lack of deep spiritual stirring, but rather from each person's quiet communion with the Lord."

Relief filled him at her understanding. How he wished to reach across the table and take her hand, but such a public display would be improper. And so, he merely smiled, trying to express his appreciation of her words with a tender gaze. He must have succeeded, for she beamed at him and blushed happily.

In the seven weeks before he left for Annapolis, they spent numerous idyllic afternoons strolling through the Public Gardens or visiting fashionable tearooms on Beacon Hill. Sometimes the Harris sisters accompanied them, trailing behind as they sauntered through the gardens, but usually they went alone. They spoke of their upcoming educational adventures, discussed the arts and literature, and shyly read a few of the more benign sonnets from the book he had given her.

They even discussed Isaiah, but only for a short while, pledging to each other to pray often for Jemima's disagreeable brother. Timothy planned to do more than pray. Somehow, no matter what it took, he would win Isaiah over, for he could not bear to see Jemima grieved by her brother's disapproval.

When at last the eve of his departure arrived, he visited her once more at the Harrises' house, where the family bid him good-bye and then left the young couple in the front parlor.

This is it. I have to tell her how I feel. She must know that I care. If I don't, she might meet someone else. His heart felt near to bursting. Why could he not open his mouth?

She turned her lovely face up to him, her eyes exuding melancholy encouragement and her lips graced by a sweet, sad smile. "You wished to ask me something?"

Timothy swallowed hard. "Yes," he whispered. "I wonder if you would mind if ... if I write to you."

Chapter Nine

&

*J*E-mi-ma, je-MI-ma, je-mi-MA, je-mi-ma, JE-mi-ma, je-MI-ma, je-mi-MA.

The rhythm of the train's iron wheels beat in time with Timothy's heart as he stared out the window, barely aware of the autumn-painted landscape or the pungent, sooty odor of the steam engine's smoke.

She had looked so sweet, so beautiful when he left her in Aunt Kerry's front parlor the day before. Tiny tears sparkled like diamonds in her dark eyes, but her smile radiated bright encouragement to warm his soul.

"We will both be so busy with our studies," she had said. "We'll not have a moment to think of anything else."

"Yes," he had agreed. But the expression in her eyes belied her words, and he knew he would think of nothing else but Jemima every day, no matter how demanding his studies became.

"Mama. *Mama!*" A child's shrill tones pierced through Timothy's hazy daydreams and almost his eardrums. He glanced over his shoulder at the passengers in the seat behind him, half expecting to see his youngest sister. Instead, a dark-haired girl about Gracie's age glared back and stuck her tongue out at him. The bedraggled mother dozed beside her, so Timothy stuck his tongue out at the imp, who giggled and hid her face in her mother's shoulder.

From across the aisle came a snicker, and Timothy turned to see a young man about his own age grinning at his childish behavior.

"You have younger brothers and sisters," the sandy-haired youth said.

Timothy laughed. "Yes. You?"

"No. I'm the youngest of eight. I do the pestering in my family."
He stuck his hand across the aisle. "Jackson Hartley."

Timothy scooted nearer to shake it. "Timothy Jacobs."

"Going far?" Hartley asked.

"Maryland. Annapolis."

Hartley's face lit up with delight. "The Naval Academy?"

Timothy nodded. "Yes. You, too?"

"Yes. By gum, I just had a feeling I'd meet a shipmate along the
way."

"Shipmate? I think it's 'midshipman.'" Timothy hoped he did not
sound arrogant.

"I dunno. Maybe so. I've heard that at West Point they're called
plebes their first year and then cadets after that. But we'll find out
soon enough, won't we?" Hartley clapped his hands on his knees and
gave a happy chortle. "Yes, sir, I knew the Lord would send a friend
right away. My ma prayed for it, and she generally gets what she
prays for."

Timothy grinned, liking the lad right away for his guileless talk.
"I'm from Boston. Where're you from?"

"Middlebury, Vermont. I'm a dyed-in-the-wool inlander. This'll
be my first time to see the ocean, much less sail on it. Not sure I'll
do that well, but who's gonna turn down an appointment from
Congress giving a body a free education? Not me, I'll tell you that.
I'm the first one in my family to go to school. We're farmers,
don'tcha know. But I always craved book learning, so the family let
me have my head." Hartley paused, then guffawed and slapped his
knee. "Let me have my head. Book learning. Good joke, don'tcha
think?"

Timothy laughed again at his jolly new friend. "Yes. Very funny."

"How 'bout you? Why the Naval Academy?"

"Always wanted to, I guess. I've sailed with my stepfather since I was ten. He's a cotton importer and sails down to Norfolk all the time."

"You lucky dog." Hartley shook his head and gave Timothy a mock-envious look. "Say, I've never tackled anything I couldn't whip, but I'll be looking to you to teach me the ropes."

"You can count on it, Hartley."

"Call me Jack, short for Jackson. And I'll call you Jake, short for Jacobs. Jack and Jake. Folks'll think we're twins."

Yet again, Timothy laughed. No one would ever think they were twins, for even seated he could see Hartley was a much shorter man, perhaps no more than five foot seven. Hartley's round face seemed almost babyish, while Timothy's face was long and lean. Hartley's sandy hair and deep blue eyes were in stark contrast to Timothy's dark features. But clearly, the fellow would be a grand companion. Rather than Jack, Timothy might call him Hart, for he seemed to have such a good, merry heart.

Timothy wondered if his own mother, like Hartley's, had prayed he would soon find a new friend. Undoubtedly she had, for she, too, seemed to "get what she prays for." Mother prayed for everything, even Deborah's lost doll or Matthew's request for bugle lessons, though her money could buy anything her children asked for.

"Did your mother bawl when you left?" Hartley asked.

"Some. My little sisters fussed quite a bit, though."

"Land sakes, my three sisters made a racket." Hartley chuckled and waved his hand in dismissal, but a glint of tenderness shone in his eyes. "Women. Always bawlin'."

Timothy's heart dipped as he recalled the tears of one particular young lady. "Yes. That's something, isn't it?"

The train rumbled, chugged, jerked, and skidded to a stop at a small railway station, its wheels squealing their complaint on the tracks. The conductor called the town's name, and numerous people in Timothy's car gathered their things and began to disembark. The little girl behind him swatted his head as her mother lifted her from the seat, but the woman did not notice as she struggled down the aisle with child and baggage. The girl, however, peeked over the mother's shoulder and stared wide-eyed at him.

"I think she likes you," Hartley said with a smirk.

Timothy rubbed his head and grinned ruefully. Her slap had not hurt, only surprised him. "Yes, I noticed." *Someone should smack the little brat.*

As the car began to fill with new passengers, Hartley moved his much-mended valise across the aisle and took the seat beside Timothy. Soon the train lurched forward and began to accelerate down the tracks.

Hartley's light-hearted chatter provided a pleasant diversion from Timothy's former solitary doldrums. In all things, this new companion appeared innocent and honest, having spent his entire life on a farm and in the small Vermont village nearby. Timothy knew he would have to protect the boy, even after he learned Hartley was almost a year older than he, for more sophisticated fellows would be sure to torment him as a rustic. Even now, Hartley's knees bounced and his hands spun about in nervous gestures to emphasize his various observations about life or the passing scenery. Obviously, Timothy's new friend was frightened.

He himself felt less than bold in this new adventure, but he was careful to mask his anxiety. Years of watching Laz go calmly about his dangerous concealment of escaped slaves had taught Timothy the value of a tranquil exterior, no matter how much emotion might riot within him. He learned long ago that a lift of the chin, a narrowed gaze, and a deep, quiet breath steadied him, gave him time to sort things out, and fooled anyone who might think they had him in a corner.

The ploy had worked in public school when other lads tried to start fights and on shipboard when boredom caused the crew to turn mischievous. Observing his facade of serenity in any situation, men proclaimed him a born leader, for nothing seemed to disconcert him. He felt a surge of excitement at the prospect of likewise impressing his superiors at the academy, both upperclassmen and faculty. Only Mother, Laz, and Uncle Jeremiah could read what lay beneath, and his true thoughts and feelings were safe with them.

Soon he would be at the head of his class at the academy. But for now, it was pleasant enough to see his own calm demeanor had extended to Hartley, who now dozed tranquilly beside him as the train swept them along toward their grand new adventure.

"Jemima, are you certain you won't reconsider?" Mrs. Lazarus set her teacup on the coffee table in the front parlor of the Harris home. "Your daily walk to Boston Normal School will be so much shorter if you live with us rather than here in the North End."

Jemima started to answer, but was silenced by the chorus of protests from the Harris children.

"Aunt Hannah, you cannot take her from us," Daisy cried.

"She's like a sister," Molly added.

"My twin sister," Lacy put in, squeezing Jemima's hand.

"And she knows lots of games." Samuel shuffled across the room to Mrs. Lazarus's chair, leaned into her open arms, and gazed plaintively at her.

"But, my darling." Mrs. Lazarus pulled the sickly boy onto her lap. "Think of how exhausted she'll be walking all that distance each day. She'll have no energy for games or even for her studies."

"Oh, Mrs. Lazarus," said Jemima, "you know us Nantucketers. We traipse from one end of the island to the other and don't think a thing of it." She glanced around the room at the two opposing forces: Mrs. Harris with her four children versus Mrs. Lazarus flanked by Matthew and Deborah. "Still, you're so generous to give me this opportunity. Will it put you out to have me here instead of with you? I mean, was there some work I should assist with at your house?" Jemima's face began to burn. Her words had not come out as she intended. Mrs. Lazarus expected no service for providing Jemima's education.

But Mrs. Lazarus did not seem to mind. "Only to fill the empty place at our dinner table, my dear."

She gave Jemima a fond look that spoke of the one who owned a large part of both their hearts. Gazing at Mrs. Lazarus's beautiful countenance, Jemima saw traces of Timothy, despite their claims that he more closely resembled his father.

Jemima's blush now felt like a warm glow. Never had she experienced such love as from these two families. The destitute orphan had become a valued child so beloved that Reverend and Mrs. Harris even spoke of adopting her, an offer she was still considering.

But perhaps she had known this feeling, after all. Long ago, Mother had sat beside her, Bible in hand, and read of God's love, a love that could not be fully understood until a person realized that salvation through Jesus Christ was free to all who would simply believe in him. And from the moment of accepting that great, free gift, she, who had not known a father's love, never again felt like an orphan.

"I would like very much to visit you often, if that's all right." Jemima glanced around the room, her eyes resting on Mrs. Harris before she gazed back at her benefactress. "But I am certain this is where the Lord wants me to live."

Mrs. Lazarus sighed, but she also smiled. "Very well. I understand." She hugged Samuel again and patted his cheek. "There, my little man, you have another older sister, though you already have plenty to spoil you. Or shall I take you home with me to give Matthew a new brother while his own is away?"

Samuel giggled and squirmed from her embrace. He trudged over to the divan, plopped down beside Jemima, and turned to her an adoring gaze. "She's not my sister, Aunt Hannah. I'm going to marry her."

All the girls laughed softly at his remark. Matthew rolled his eyes and made a disagreeable sound that brought a reproving glance from his mother. Mrs. Harris blinked back tears. Reading Mrs. Harris's thoughts, Jemima placed her arm around the frail boy.

"Why, I would be honored, sir." Jemima spoke playfully, but even if her heart were not already claimed, this gallant little knight would probably not live long enough to marry her or anyone else.

"Then it's decided." Lacy leaned against Jemima's other side. "We shan't lose you after all."

The Harris children cheered, Deborah and Matthew sighed their disappointment, and Mrs. Lazarus accepted the decision with good grace. "No, Lacy, I concede to you the victory. But I hasten to add, Jemima, that we will claim your company for dinner every Sunday after church. And of course we must see to your wardrobe, for you will need new clothes for the coming school year."

"Will you come back and visit?" Meg stood just outside the door of Isaiah's tiny room, wringing her hands and wiping tears off her cheeks. "At least maybe come for Sunday dinner?"

Isaiah bent over his valise and arranged his folded, freshly ironed extra shirt. "Maybe." He tried not to sound brusque. "They might not permit us to leave the academy, at least not at first."

"Don't seem fair to me." Meg's tone was both teasing and tearful. "A man's gotta have some fun in the middle of all that schooling."

Isaiah stood straight and stared hard at her. "I have appreciated your mother's hospitality, and yours, Miss Doone. You both have extended courtesies beyond what a boarder might expect, such as ironing my shirts and packing my dinner for work each day. That's why I insisted on painting the front porch last month and why I hauled in all that coal to fill the bin so you won't have to. I expect you have enough in there now to keep the furnace going for a month or more. I believe we can call our accounts even. Would you not agree?"

Meg nodded mutely and hung her head. Her wilted expression moved him, but he could not permit her to see his concern, for it would only promote false hopes. In two months of living here, after that one near-disastrous night, he studiously avoided any action that might encourage her. Yet she still clung to hope, or perhaps desperation. But he was leaving, and some other boarder would move in, perhaps someone who would take a special liking to her. And she would do herself a favor in hunting a husband if she would just learn to hold back a bit. No mistake about it, the girl sold herself too short.

"Marse Starbuck, Miz Doone sent this cranberry bread down for you to take along to school." Bebe bustled down the last basement step and over to Isaiah's room.

He accepted the wrapped package, placed it in his bag, and smiled at the slender, dark-skinned old woman. "Thank you, Miss Bebe. But haven't I told you not to call me 'Marse'? Isaiah will do fine."

She threw back her head and cackled. "Law, listen to you. You be a good man, Mr. Starbuck, and you be a fine officer one day. Kin I hep you with that packin'?"

"We don't need you," Meg hissed. "Now git up them stairs and start cleaning, you lazy ol'—"

"Miss Doone, if you don't mind." Isaiah lifted his valise and started out the door, making sure not to brush against Meg.

He took the stairs two at a time, with Meg and Bebe scrambling after him. In the kitchen, Mrs. Doone stood at the stove stirring a pot of stew, and its aroma, along with that of baking bread, made his mouth water.

"Mr. Starbuck, I do wish you'd change your mind and stay for dinner. They won't feed you this well over at the academy, I'll swear."

"Thank you, ma'am. I do appreciate it. But I'm sure they'll take care of us. Now let me say a proper good-bye."

He reached out to her. She wiped a hand on her apron, then thrust it toward him. A blush spread across her pale, sunken cheeks as he bent to place a kiss on her fingers.

"Gracious, what a gentleman. We're going to miss you, boy. I know they let you out of school from time to time, for I've seen those cadets around town looking so handsome in their uniforms, and you'll look mighty fine in yours, being such a good-looking fellow already. Do promise to come back for a visit. A young man needs a place to call home, you being an orphan and all."

"Thank you, ma'am." He gave her a small, noncommittal smile.

She took a deep breath and leaned toward him. "And a young man needs a sweetheart, too. Someone to give him a reason to stay on the straight and narrow. Now my Meg's a good girl. You can't find better."

Isaiah barely kept from grimacing. Mrs. Doone's hints had not stopped since he moved in, but she had never been this audacious.

"Ma'am, you and Miss Doone and Bebe have been very hospitable. I will not forget your kindness."

Like her daughter's, the woman's expression fell. "Well, you think about it. We're not going any place."

Isaiah did not know how long the three women stood on the front porch waving good-bye, for he studiously resisted turning back to look. However, he did think about Mrs. Doone's last words to him. She was right. He needed a girl. But he already had one over on Jarbo Alley, one he could visit whenever he had a few extra coins, yet who would never claim any permanent attachment. In fact, the second time he went to see her she didn't even recall his name. In subsequent visits, he didn't correct her when she called him Elijah, for he suspected her real name was not Merry.

A warm feeling spread through his belly as he recalled all she had taught him. He gave his head a little shake. This hunger for her company must be curbed, for he doubted midshipmen were permitted to leave the grounds very often, at least to begin with.

The impressive red brick archway at the Naval Academy entrance came into sight, and all fleshly appetites evaporated, replaced by a mighty surge of joy. Here was his dream about to be fulfilled. He would forget the outside world and devote himself to his studies. Because he would earn superior grades, he would be at the top of his class, and because of his cleverness, the officers would clearly comprehend that he was a born leader. Promotion would come swiftly. Even before he donned a uniform, he could feel the officer's epaulets on his shoulders.

Head lifted with pride, Isaiah Starbuck marched toward the arched gateway, the portal to his future ... and success.

Chapter Ten

§

For a moment, Isaiah thought someone had slammed a fist into his stomach. He could not breathe, his knees nearly buckled, and a haze seemed to form over his eyes. Drawing in a deep, desperate breath, he blinked hard to clear his vision, but it did no good. The loathsome specter, the insufferable person, still stood in the center of the academy yard, surrounded by other men who were laughing at some clever remark the tall youth had made. Ahab, the embodiment of everything Isaiah hated, already admired, already the leader.

To his horror, Ahab spied him, and from the scoundrel's self-satisfied and thoroughly unsurprised expression of recognition, he clearly had expected Isaiah to be here. But how did he know? *Whom* did he know?

In an instant, Ahab's appearance changed, the condescension becoming a facade of friendly welcome.

"Starbuck! Over here." Ahab beckoned with a broad gesture. "Come meet some of our classmates."

A violent, unbidden shudder quaked through Isaiah's body, and he felt near to retching. The man was acting as if they were friends, even to the point of reaching out to offer a handshake. The other youths in the small group had also turned friendly, expectant faces toward the newcomer.

With no hesitation, Isaiah spat hard on the ground and turned away, consigning the lot of them to the ranks of his own personal enemies, a place formerly inhabited only by men named Ahab—

father and son. Behind him he could hear the astonishment, even outrage, in the voices of the others. But Ahab's voice was calm.

"Never mind, lads. He's from Nantucket. The island sits a way off shore, so maybe the isolation affected his manners."

The insult was not to be borne. Isaiah whipped around, flung down his valise, raced toward the group, and hurled himself at the taller youth, slamming him to the ground and knocking the wind from both of them. Barely taking time to regain his breath, Isaiah began to slug his adversary. For an instant, Ahab merely shielded himself, but then with both hands he stuck a solid blow to Isaiah's chest that sent him flying. As Isaiah landed on his back with a painful thump, Ahab rolled over on top of him and pressed his shoulders into the grass.

"Are you mad, Starbuck? What do you think you're doing?"

Before Isaiah could answer or strike another blow, other men grabbed both Ahab and him and pulled them to their feet, holding them apart.

"What's the meaning of this?" A tall, uniformed midshipman stood facing them, his hands on his hips. "You plebes trying to get kicked out on your first day?"

"No, sir," Ahab said. "Just a misunderstanding."

His words stunned Isaiah. Ahab could have blamed him for the fight. Why hadn't he?

The upperclassman glared at Isaiah. "Well? What do you have to say?"

He shook his head. "Nothing."

"Nothing? Nothing what?"

"Huh?" Isaiah stared at the youth, whose severe expression seemed to foreshadow doom. What a fool he had been to attack Ahab that way. Had he just destroyed his own future?

"You answer 'sir,' plebe. Do you understand me?"

"Yes, sir."

"That's 'aye, sir,' boy."

Isaiah cringed at his foolish error. Every child on Nantucket Island knew how to answer an officer, whether whaler or sailor.

"Aye, sir."

The midshipman glanced around at the assembled crowd. "This is no way to begin your officer training. I will make it abundantly clear to all of you plebes that this kind of behavior will not be tolerated." He stared again at Ahab and Isaiah. "You and you, follow me. I'm taking you to the superintendent's office. He's our new commanding officer, posted here just last month, and he'll probably decide to make an example of you two." He scanned the group. "And the rest of you men had better understand we're here to learn how to fight on the same side—for our country, in the spirit of corps—not to fight each other."

In a short time, Timothy and Isaiah stood stiffly before the super-intendent, both staring straight ahead, for Midshipman George Dewey, the upperclassman who had intervened in the fight, had briefed them on how to stand at attention.

A portly, balding man with a ruff of thick white hair half-circling his head, Captain George S. Blake was a dignified presence, even seated behind his broad oak desk. He quietly observed the two young men for a moment. Standing behind him, Captain Duncan Longwood also studied them.

Timothy took long, slow, deep breaths, not moving his chest, to hide and control his emotions. A surge of contempt rolled through him as he realized Starbuck was still panting. Did the man have no self-control?

"Very well," said Captain Blake. "What's this all about? What do you two men have to say for yourselves? Mr. Jacobs, you first."

"Sir, I have no quarrel with my shipmate here." Timothy ventured a glance at the officer and saw to his satisfaction the surprise registered in his expression.

The superintendent nodded his head curtly. "Indeed? You, Mr. Starbuck, what do you have to say for yourself?"

In the corner of his eye, Timothy saw Isaiah's chin go up defensively.

"Sir, I am concerned about the reputation of the Naval Academy and the officers our school turns out—"

"Save the bilgewater, Starbuck," the commander broke in. "Why were you fighting this man?"

Isaiah's loud gulp sounded throughout the room. "Sir, he is not who he says he is. His real name is not Jacobs. It's Ahab. Should a man be here who misrepresents himself by using a false name?"

Timothy's gaze darted to Captain Longwood, who stood watching the proceedings with concern. Still Timothy forced himself to stay calm.

Blake continued to stare at Isaiah for a moment, then turned to Timothy. "We can settle this part of the problem very quickly. Mr. Jacobs, does this man speak the truth?"

"My name is Timothy Jacob, sir." Not a lie. Jacob *was* his real middle name. He was careful to slur the *s*, but not too much. "I will swear it on the Holy Bible, if you like."

The superintendent studied his face, and despite his best efforts at staying calm, Timothy could feel heat rising up his neck.

"Sir, if you will permit me?" Captain Longwood moved to Blake's side.

"Yes, of course, Longwood."

"I have known Mr. Jacobs since he was a small child. I know his family in Boston. He is here on my recommendation, and I will vouch for him."

Timothy's knees almost buckled from the mixture of relief and shame that flooded him. Longwood had not lied. He said what he thought to be true. Yet Timothy could not ignore his feelings of guilt. It was one thing to tell lies in order to protect escaping slaves. It was another thing entirely to lie for self-protection or to cause someone else to misrepresent the truth. But Timothy would not relent.

Longwood leveled a stare at Isaiah, assessing him, challenging him. "I'll warrant it's just a case of mistaken identity."

Captain Blake nodded, apparently satisfied with Longwood's reasoning. Now he too stared at Isaiah. "Mr. Starbuck, becoming an officer in the United States Navy requires discipline, self-control, moral rectitude, and great care in decision-making. If you do not possess or aspire to obtain those qualities, perhaps you should reconsider being here at the Naval Academy."

"Sir, may I have permission to speak?" Timothy burst out. How could he ever face Jemima if Isaiah were expelled? Even now, he could sense Isaiah trembling beside him, but whether from anger or fear, he did not know.

"Yes, Mr. Jacobs?" The superintendent turned his attention to Timothy.

"Sir, I … well, I …" How could he tell another lie? What could he possibly say?

"Go on."

"Mr. Starbuck *is* from Nantucket, sir." He inclined his head toward Captain Blake and spoke as if it were a sufficient explanation, as if the superintendent should know what he meant.

An uncertain frown darted across the man's face. Timothy could see that behind him, Longwood was stifling a smile, which quickly disappeared when the superintendent turned to him.

"Longwood, what do you think?"

The captain lifted his chin and regarded the two. "Sir, I think once these men are squared away with registration and quarters, they will need some extra duties to release their youthful energies. If you turn them over to me, I will see that they have neither the time nor strength to engage in fighting each other."

"Very good. I place them in your charge." Blake turned back to the miscreants. "First thing in the morning, you will report to Captain Longwood."

"Aye, sir," Timothy and Isaiah chorused.

"Dismissed."

"Aye, sir," they repeated again and turned to leave.

As Isaiah hurried out the door, Blake called, "Jacobs."

Timothy turned. "Aye, sir?"

A wily look stole over the superintendent's face. "Nantucket, eh?"

Timothy blinked, and then grinned broadly, at last losing his composure. The superintendent had not been fooled at all. "Aye, sir." He did his best to sound entirely innocent of any attempt at subterfuge.

"Get out of here, boy, before I discipline you for insubordination."

"Aye, sir." Timothy hurried from the office, leaning for a moment against the wall just outside the door. Inside, he could hear the superintendent and Captain Longwood chortling, and he breathed a great sigh of relief.

He strode up the hall, down the stairs, and out onto the front walkway. Like the balmy heat of the early October sunshine, a warm feeling spread through him. He had protected Isaiah, despite the other's hatred for him, which meant his enemy now owed him. But most of all, Timothy had protected Jemima from the shame of having a brother who had been tossed out of the Naval Academy. Although she would never know what he had done, his feeling of satisfaction was so intense that he knew he wanted to spend his life protecting her.

"You think you're smart, don't you?" Isaiah sprang from behind a large oak tree beside the walkway and faced Timothy, his fists balled up at his sides.

Timothy stopped, heaved a sigh of exasperation, and stuck his hands in his pockets, effecting one of Laz's poses when he wanted to defuse a bad situation.

"Great Zeus, Starbuck, haven't you caused enough trouble? Why can't you let it go? I don't owe you anything and you don't owe me, even though I saved your hide in there."

He could see the rage in Isaiah's eyes, and once again felt stunned.

"I will get the better of you one day," Isaiah muttered. "I will prove you are your father's son, and then no hoodwinked old superintendent will help you out." He whipped around and strode away, leaving Timothy to shake his head in confusion over such senseless, unbounded hatred.

Jemima stared at the two letters lying on the bed she shared with Lacy, unable to decide in what order to read them. Sisterly duty contended she should begin with Isaiah's, for it was the first he had written in the two months since he had gone to Annapolis. But her heart yearned even more to hear what Timothy would say. He had left Boston only a week ago, and here was his letter already. Her dear brother could take a lesson in thoughtfulness from Timothy, but she would never tell him that.

"Why not let me read Isaiah's letter, and you can read Timothy's?" Lacy sat on the edge of the bed, her eyes twinkling.

Jemima laughed. "Shame on my brother for not writing sooner, and to both of us. I wonder what he's been doing all this time."

"Only one way to find out." Lacy snatched up the ivory envelope, danced across the room toward her desk, and pulled open the drawer.

"Very well. Go ahead and open it." Jemima giggled at her friend's playfulness, still not certain how to respond. Daisy, or even blind Molly, would have hooted in protest and chased Lacy if she took something from them, though all in fun. Jemima's heart welled up with happiness at being included in such loving, teasing ways. She and Isaiah used to tease each other too, but after Mother's death, he had become too sober, too sad, something Mother never would have wanted. In the months before they left Nantucket, he seemed to wear a perpetual frown.

Lacy walked back across the room and thrust the letter and a pewter opener at Jemima. "Here. Open this one first." Her tone was light, but her eyes revealed the depth of her interest.

With a wistful glance toward Timothy's letter, Jemima took the missive and carefully slit open the envelope. Pulling out the single page, she felt her heart sink as much as Lacy's expression did. Her brother. A man of few words.

The girls plopped down on the bed facing each other, and Jemima read aloud the neat, small script:

> *Dear Sister:*
>
> *Annapolis is a fair city with narrow streets, clapboard houses, and several grand, pre-Revolutionary brick manses. If you came here, you might think you were back home in Nantucket. Because the streets have no cobblestones, they are often muddy.*
>
> *When I first arrived, I found a clean boarding house where they served good food. I worked as a fisherman for a few weeks and then found a job working the ferry across the Severn River. My arms grew strong pulling the ropes.*
>
> *You no longer have to worry that I will feel alone here at the Naval Academy. I have a new friend. His name is Francis Bartholomew, and we share a room. My classes are not hard, for my memory is better than most, and my daily recitations are always perfect. You will be proud of me.*
>
> *Our rooms have gaslights and gas heat. I shall not be cold this winter, as you feared.*
>
> *I would like a letter from you.*
>
> *Your loving brother,*
> *Isaiah*

Jemima turned the letter over.

P. S. Please give Reverend and Mrs. Harris my regards and gratitude for giving you a job at the mission. But hold your head up, for I will not always permit you to be a chambermaid.

P. P. S. If you see Lacy, please tell her hello for me, if she remembers me. Molly and Daisy, too.

"Oh," cried Lacy. "If I remember him. Oh, that man!" She crossed her arms and put on an artificial pout, but then she laughed. "Your dear brother may be a man of few words, but he is well-spoken in what he does say."

"Yes, very well-spoken." Jemima folded the letter and placed it back in its envelope. The moment she had read Lacy's name aloud from Isaiah's letter, her friend had beamed with happiness. "I'm so pleased to hear his recitations are going perfectly. I wish I could say the same for mine."

"But, my dear, you are a full two years younger than your classmates. You will catch them soon."

"Hmm. I hope so." Jemima slit open her second letter.

Lacy sighed. "Well, I'm certain Timothy is doing well, for he always does. I'll leave you to read his letter in peace." She hopped off the bed and bent to kiss Jemima's cheek. "Thank you for sharing your brother's letter with me. When are you going to tell him about your schooling?"

"Right away, now that he is living at the academy." She watched Lacy cross the room toward the door. "Shall I give him a message from you?"

Lacy spun around. "From me? Goodness, what would I have to say to a young man in naval officer training?" She turned back toward the door, and then turned yet again to face Jemima. "On the other hand, I might think of something. When you've finished your letter to him, let me know. Perhaps I shall have a postscript to add." She cocked her head in a saucy pose. "Yes, perhaps a postscript is exactly what Midshipman Starbuck needs."

Chapter Eleven

&

Jemima drummed her fingers on the desk and gazed out the window, wishing for a more peaceful view to inspire her letter writing. Even though her Nantucket home had been humble, at least it sat beside a windswept green meadow where sheep grazed, birds sang, and flowers bloomed beyond the fence. She did not wish to be ungrateful for her new home with the Harris family, but this noisy, smelly North End neighborhood was not conducive to study or to deciding what to say to Timothy.

His four-page letter was much more descriptive than Isaiah's, and his tone more cheerful, even when he told of seeing Isaiah their first day at the academy. "My friends and I invited him to join us, but he declined, seeming to prefer solitude over our fellowship. Never fear, however, for I shall continue to offer the olive branch, and one day he will come about."

Jemima whispered a prayer that Isaiah would indeed have a change of heart. Neither his penchant for solitude nor his misplaced bitterness did him any good and might even damage his chances for becoming an officer.

Timothy went on to describe the academy, which stood on the banks of the Severn River at the site of an old army fort. Its numerous buildings included a recitation hall, hospital, dormitories, faculty residences, a chapel, and a parade ground. Timothy told of his square, spartan room, its plain iron cot, one bureau and chair per student, a shared table, washstand, and Jackson Hartley, the fine young man with whom he would share them.

*Our uniforms are made by tailors on Maryland Avenue in
the city of Annapolis, but we purchase them from the
academy storekeeper along with our other requirements. The
uniforms are quite handsome, being made of dark blue wool
and sporting gold anchors on the collar and shiny brass
buttons down the front. Our caps have a broad, gold braid
band and an anchor insignia. They are flattened and cocked
to one side with a jaunty flair. I wish you could see me all
decked out.*

Timothy also reminisced about their strolls in the Public Gardens
and their chats about Shakespeare while they enjoyed ice cream at
Tremont House. Although he would much prefer to be in her
company now, he added, his memories would carry him until they
met again, which could be sooner than the expected two years' separation. He wondered if she would like to be his guest at the annual
ball in January. With her permission, he would write his parents and
ask them to bring her to the academy then, for the affair was a grand
gala, and he thought she would enjoy it immensely. Her presence
would ensure his own enjoyment of the event.

Jemima's heart beat faster as she read about the ball. What would
she wear for such an occasion? Was it truly possible that Captain and
Mrs. Lazarus would escort her all the way to Annapolis for such a friv-
olous purpose? Could she secure permission from the headmistress at
her school to miss classes? What would Reverend and Mrs. Harris
have to say about dancing? Why, she did not even know how to dance
and did not own an appropriate dress, shoes, gloves, or—

Jemima laughed. Here she was all in a dither, as she often had been
since meeting Timothy. But that would not solve her dilemma.

"Lord, if you will for me to attend this ball, please work out all the
details," she whispered. She dipped her quill pen into the ink foun-
tain and began to write:

Dear Timothy,

   I was so pleased to receive your letter and to know your
studies are going well. I am struggling to catch up with my
classmates, who all seem to know so much more than I. But
I forge on, and every day it becomes a little easier.

She wrote of having Sunday dinner with his family, of shopping trips with his mother, of helping Lacy and her sisters sew for the mission store, and how much she missed their trips to the hotel for ice cream, though soon it would be too cold for such icy treats. The words seemed to flow onto the first page and another sheet as well, almost as though she were talking with him. By the time she reached the end, her last words came without any reservation:

Thank you for your kind invitation to the ball. You have my
permission to write to your parents about conveying me to
Annapolis in January.

Of course, her attendance at the gala would reveal to Isaiah her friendship with Timothy. But strangely, the thought did not disturb her. As much as she loved her brother, she would neither keep her feelings a secret from him nor permit his anger to control her future.

"Say, Starbuck, how do you do it?" Francis Bartholomew clapped Isaiah on the shoulder and slumped down into his own chair in their dormitory room. "Every day, every class, your recitations are flawless."

Isaiah shrugged, trying not to grin like a fool. "Aw, it's nothing you couldn't do, Frank."

"Ha!" Frank gave his head a shake. "I'm forty-two in our class, and you're number one … you and that Jacobs fellow." He twirled a pencil on the table they shared for a desk and stacked and unstacked his books. "Say, what shakes there, friend? Why do you let that fellow get to you?"

Isaiah snorted. "He doesn't get to me."

"Hey, this is your roommate here, bud. You can tell me and, word of honor, it won't get past me."

Isaiah hunched his shoulders over, rested his chin on his fists, and blew out a long breath. Maybe Frank would understand. His life had been hard too. Although not an orphan, he was one of fourteen children, and his parents barely eked out a living on a farm in Ohio. Like Isaiah's, his academy appointment had been granted through the influence of a wealthy relative.

"So tell me." Frank gave Isaiah's arm a little shove with his fist, and then leaned back and balanced his chair on its rear legs.

Maybe it would feel good, Isaiah decided, to say it out loud to someone who, unlike Jemima, would not preach at him.

"His father murdered my father."

"What?" Frank bolted forward, and the front legs of his chair hit the floor with a thud. "Murdered?"

Isaiah nodded once.

"Thunderation, that is bad." Frank brushed a hand across his chin. "But that's not Jacobs' fault. I mean, we can't control what our fathers do."

Isaiah shook his head. "Don't you know the Bible, lad? Every evil thing his father ever did, including murdering my father, shall be visited on the son to the third and fourth generation. The father's dead. He got off easy. But, you just watch, this *Jacobs* fellow will follow in his footsteps. Then he'll get what they both deserve."

Frank scratched his head. "Well," he drawled, "I'm not sure I agree with you about that, but I do think the man is pretty arrogant. I mean, from the first day, he marched in here like he owned the place." He chuckled. "He and that Beauchamp fellow keep showing off how they can talk French already, and him acting like he had the divine right of kings or something."

Isaiah laughed, and the laughter felt good clear down to his belly.

Frank did understand. "Yep. Exactly so. The divine right of kings." *And wouldn't I like to knock off his crown?*

"In fact, there's a passel of these fellows who think they own the place. Rich kids, every last one of them."

"Yep." Isaiah lifted his chin. "But we can give them a run for their money."

"How's that?"

"We can work hard, harder than they do 'cause they're used to things being handed to them. And we can beat the tar out of them with our grades."

"Maybe you can, but I'm way down the list, and I see no hope of raising my rank."

Isaiah lifted one of their textbooks. "You wanted to know how I do it, how I have perfect recitations every day?" He shook the book at Frank. "Stick with me, and I'll turn you into a scholar. I have some tricks up my sleeve for learning things fast, and I'll teach them to you."

His brow wrinkled, Frank picked up another book and fanned its pages. "I don't know, Isaiah. I'd like to have a few good times while I'm young. Your nose is always in the books. You never go anywhere or have any fun."

Isaiah shrugged. "I wouldn't say 'never.' I have my share of fun from time to time. It's just that I plan to do something important with my life, and if that means burning the midnight oil, then so be it."

Frank stared out the window as if deep in thought. Then he turned to Isaiah. "I promised my folks I'd do my best here at the academy and make them proud. If Providence put me in a room with a smart man like you, then I guess I'd be a fool not to make the most of it." His expression lightened until a big grin split his long face. "Yessir, I think I'll throw in with you, Starbuck. We'll give those rich 'kings' a real run for their money."

Isaiah stuck out his hand. "Deal?"

"Deal." Frank gripped his hand and shook it firmly.

Warm satisfaction filled Isaiah's breast. Bartholomew was a good man, and the first real friend he had ever made on his own. With a medium build, reddish brown hair, steady eyes, and, most important, impeccable character, this was a fellow he would not mind introducing to his sister. He would have to be clever about it, though, so Jemima would not resent his brotherly machinations. Maybe he could invite her to the naval ball in January. He had not thought of attending, but if he saved his pay, he could buy her a train ticket and take her himself. He would make certain Frank attended and met her, and leave the rest to them.

Then another idea wedged its way into his mind. Reverend and Mrs. Harris had been good to both Jemima and him, and he could see they respected him for his appointment to the academy. Why not write to them and ask if both Lacy and Jemima could attend the ball? That way, Jemima could meet this fine fellow Bartholomew, and Isaiah could find out if he had any chance for a future with Miss Lacy Harris.

The plan sounded good, but he would sleep on it. If nothing came to mind to counter the idea, he would rise before first light and write to the minister.

Timothy raced up the stairs, taking three at a time, with several of his classmates trailing behind him. No one ever could catch him, and he was the only one to reach the second floor a third time without breathing hard.

This daily, after-class routine provided all the exercise these cadets had. Timothy wondered how the academy faculty expected their students to become seaworthy sailors when they offered no formal sports or athletic activities. As soon as he gained some rank, he would suggest to the superintendent that he add some sort of physical education to the curriculum. For now, he himself would lead his small crew of seven through this daily ritual to shake off the lethargy that built up while sitting through morning classes. These few would be stronger than the rest, whose only exercise came through marching and artillery drill.

Reaching the second floor, Timothy plopped down on the landing and leaned back against the newel post, grinning at his friends who dragged themselves up the last few steps. It pleased him to see Hartley arrive right behind him. As short as his friend was, he was strong and sturdy from a lifetime of laboring on his family's farm.

"Good work, men." Timothy gazed around the group. "Next week, we'll do this six times instead of just three."

Wheezing laughter met his comment, and he laughed too.

"If I run up any more stairs," Jean-André Beauchamp puffed out, "I'll collapse for the rest of the day."

"Yup, me too, Jake." Ernie Wilson lay draped on the staircase like a limp rag doll, staring at Timothy with a plea for mercy in his eyes.

"Land sakes, Beauchamp." Timothy mimicked his friend's Southern drawl. "Are all you New Orleans dandies so weak-limbed?"

Beauchamp shook his finger at him in protest. "I do believe I should challenge you to a duel for that insult, Mr. Jacobs—" He paused for a deep breath. "But I'm a bit winded right now."

Timothy chuckled. "I'll accept that challenge. Let's see, if I'm not mistaken, I choose the weapon, is that right? Well, I'd say some of those breakfast biscuits at ten paces. What do you think?"

The group gave up a mixture of groans and laughter.

"Mercy, how I miss my Aunt Sukey's biscuits," moaned Beauchamp. "The best in all New Orleans—no, in all Louisiana. I should write my father and insist he send Sukey to cook for the academy. These Northern Negroes don't know how to."

This brought a protest from Wilson, who reminded Beauchamp that his home state of Maryland was most certainly not a Northern state, and furthermore, he would pit his family's cook against any, and he would prove it by ordering some biscuits sent down from his home in Baltimore. "Even one or two days old, they'd be better than the hardtack they feed us here."

While the rest of the group laughed, Timothy's stomach turned, his cheerful mood broken. How stupid of him to mention food, for that was sure to start a bragging competition. He would be pleased to boast of Patience's cooking, but refused to mention her name in the same context as these others. Unlike the free, well-paid woman who had cooked for the Lazarus family for years, Beauchamp's and Wilson's cooks, drivers, and housekeepers all were slaves. Beauchamp even brought along his own personal steward, Cordell, who of course was a slave.

In his many academy expectations, Timothy never imagined some cadets might be Southern men to whom owning slaves was as natural as breathing. When these conversations arose, so did his turmoil. How could he be friends with people whose most deeply held philosophies were so opposite of his? Yet, in all other ways, he was forced to admit that they were decent, honest, courageous Christian gentlemen, beside whom he would be proud to fight in the service of their country.

"Say, Jake, why the long face?" Hart nudged Timothy, his eyes conveying empathy. The two of them once talked long into the night about the slavery issue. Near his remote farm in Vermont, Hart had seen few Negroes and known no abolitionists. But he found no fault with either his Southern friends or Timothy. Hart was a peacemaker, able to look at both sides of an issue with impartiality.

"Nothing. Just all this talk about food makes me hungry." He jumped up and started down the stairs, skipping many along the way. "Last one to mess is a chowderhead."

Thundering footsteps followed him down to the first floor and out the door, where the small group immediately stopped, fell into formation, and at Timothy's command, marched down Stribling Row toward the mess hall.

With each beat of his cadence, Timothy tried to think of ways to persuade Beau and Wils that slavery was unchristian … more than that, downright evil. Like it or not, he must do it. But when and how?

Chapter Twelve

&

Jemima forced herself to walk at her usual pace, although she wanted to skip all the way home. Today she had performed her recitations without serious error and at last grasped the difficult mathematical concept of dividing fractions, which had tormented her for weeks. Now she no longer doubted her aptitude for becoming a teacher. But she subdued her giddiness, not wanting to appear childish when she met Reverend Harris at their customary spot, from which he escorted her every day through the worst part of the North End.

The brisk November breeze moved her along swiftly. And a good thing, too, for she had stayed after her last class to gam with her favorite teacher. Darkness had fallen, and the only light shone from dim gas street lamps along the way. No time to peek into store windows and admire the latest fashions. She clutched her books and pulled her shawl up to meet the back of her bonnet. Despite the garment's heavy woolen fabric, a sudden chill swept down her neck, and not just because of the wind. Turning the corner of North Street, she searched in vain for Reverend Harris.

Where was he? Had something happened at the mission? Should she risk walking the rest of the way alone? Even in his company, even in daylight, her heart always beat faster when walking on this street. After dark it grew worse as local taverns spilled their boisterous patrons into the streets, and boldly dressed women strutted about, some smoking cigars like the men they accompanied. If she could scud unnoticed through this obstacle course, how happy she would be, but more than once men had approached and offered to buy her a drink. She had given no answer but kept her eyes straight ahead, recited a Bible verse, and continued walking. As winter approached and darkness came earlier, she appreciated Reverend Harris's insistence on meeting her each day. He had not missed the appointment until now.

Why, oh, why had she stayed late at school? Nothing short of foolish pride had caused her to bask in her favorite teacher's praise for so long. Now, as she wended her way through the crowds, their rowdiness alarmed her. *Goodness, Lord, don't these people feel the cold wind? Do the alcoholic spirits they drink keep them warm?*

Ahead, a man and a woman stood in the center of the sidewalk leering at her. She shuddered and tried to avoid them, but they side-stepped to block her.

"Say, dearie, I see you here every day. What a pretty thing you are." The thin, pockmarked woman reached out a bony finger to touch Jemima's cheek, but Jemima jumped back with a gasp and again tried to walk around them.

"Would you like a job ... a good job?" The unkempt man stood in her way, his breath reeking of alcohol. "Then you could hire a buggy to take you around town."

Jemima refused to look at him, but stared at the woman. "The Lord is my shepherd. I shall not want. He maketh me to lie down in green pastures ..."

The coarse woman threw her head back and cackled. "I've got a better place for you to lie down, sweets. Come along, and I'll show you." Her tone commanding, she reached for Jemima's arm as the man grabbed the other. Jemima's books and shawl fell to the ground.

"No! Let me go! Someone help me."

As the two dragged her toward a nearby alley, Jemima looked around desperately for help, horrified that no one seemed to notice her dilemma. If these two pulled her into the darkness, all would be lost.

"Yea, though I walk through the valley of the shadow of death, I shall fear no evil …" Jemima gasped out the words. "… for thou art with me!"

"Quiet," the woman hissed. "Nobody's going to kill you."

"Shut your face," the man growled.

"Stop!" a third voice commanded. "Let her go."

Released suddenly, Jemima fell back and landed on the ground, while the man raised his arms as if to ward off a blow. The woman backed against the alley wall, her hands also lifted.

"Easy, Reverend. It was a mistake. We thought she was one of our girls who owed us money and—"

"Don't bother lying, Mrs. Baker. I saw everything." The newcomer lowered his elegant, carved cane and turned to Jemima, his tone now gentle. "May I assist you, Miss Starbuck?"

The two miscreants disappeared into the shadows, and Jemima stared up at her tall, young rescuer, whose dark, handsome features were visible even in the dim light. After a brief hesitation, she accepted his proffered hand and was pulled to her feet.

"Seamus, Paddy, over here," he called over his shoulder, then scooped up her shawl, gave it a shake, and handed it to her. "Are you injured?"

His kind expression should have encouraged her, but perhaps he was merely masquerading as a hero. Perhaps all these people worked together. How did he know her name? Whom did he just call?

"Um, I must find my books." Still trembling, she flung her shawl around her shoulders and began to search the ground nearby. But he found the books first, as tightly strapped together as when she left school.

"A bit dusty, but no harm done." He brushed away the dirt, handed them to her, lifted his tall beaver hat, and bowed. "Please permit me to introduce myself."

"Oh, my, I'm certain that is not appropriate." She sidled past him and started away, then turned back, her face burning. "Please forgive my poor manners. Thank you so much for saving me from those dreadful people. If you ever attend services at Grace Seamen's Mission, I would be pleased to be properly introduced."

"You can be certain I will attend services there. The mission is my home."

"Your home?"

He nodded, his dark eyes twinkling. "Lived there all my life, except the first five years."

"Miss Starbuck, you're safe, thanks be to God." Seamus Callahan and his brother Paddy jogged up, relief written across their weathered faces. "You gave us a scare, missy. What's the meaning of not showing up to meet the Reverend when you're supposed to? The womenfolk and wee Sammy are beside themselves with worry, and the Reverend called out the militia. There are a hundred and fifty men out searching for you from here to outer Mongolia." Seamus paused only long enough for a quick breath. "I see you met our other reverend."

"I'm so sorry, Mr. Callahan. How very thoughtless of me." Then Seamus's last words sank in. "Oh, you must be Estevam Lazarus."

The younger man bowed again. "At your service, Miss Starbuck."

"My boy, we best be getting her back so Reverend can recall the armada." Paddy glanced at their surroundings, his eyes filled with concern.

The minister followed his glance. "You're right." He offered his arm to Jemima. "May we escort you?"

"Thank you, Reverend Lazarus." She relinquished her books back into his care and took his arm.

"You must call me Stef, as all my friends do." His gentle smile dispelled the last of her fright.

"I will, Stef, but alas I have no byname, so you must call me Jemima."

Delivered safely back home by her three rescuers and surrounded by the family in the front parlor, Jemima was still apologizing as she bid them good night. "Perhaps I should move into Mrs. Lazarus's home after all."

"We would all be distressed if you left." Reverend Harris's countenance was lined with concern.

"You have become a daughter to us." Mrs. Harris's kind gaze reminded Jemima of her own mother.

"And our sister," said Lacy, with her sisters and brother voicing their agreement.

Tears stung Jemima's eyes. "How could I leave you? Surely God brought me here to replace the parents I lost. But he has provided for my schooling too, and I am certain it is his will that I become a teacher."

Reverend Harris gave his wife a questioning look and again she nodded. "Perhaps it is time, Jeremiah. As much as I love our home and being close to the mission, this neighborhood is filled with too much evil. God expects us to use our heads in times like these."

The Harris children sat up in expectation.

"We're going to move." Daisy clapped her hands. "I just knew it."

"You did not," Sammy said.

"Did, too."

"Now, Sammy." Mrs. Harris set her hand on his. "You know Daisy is our best guesser. And she's right."

"Is this my fault?" Jemima searched the parents' faces.

They both smiled their reassurance.

"No, my child." Reverend Harris took his wife's hand. "As my dear Kerry says, God expects us to use our heads. For years Captain and Mrs. Lazarus, and others as well, have expressed their concern over our living here in Sodom and Gomorrah. It's simply time for us to pay heed to those concerns."

Timothy squirmed about in his bed, trying to find comfort for his six-foot-three-inch frame in the six-foot-long cot. But more than the bed's inadequacy, he struggled to cope with the persistent impulses that accompanied his nightly dreams of Jemima. Shamed by such visions of one so pure, he longed to discuss again with Laz exactly how he had managed to endure all those years at sea. Of course, he had been married to his loved one and felt committed to vows he considered sacred. While Timothy hoped likewise to pledge himself to Jemima one day, that happy occasion was at least four years hence. Did she care enough for him to wait until he graduated, or would someone else win her heart? For his part, how could he endure these powerful urges for that long without seeking some relief?

Several of his classmates had no such dilemma. Beauchamp did not go into detail about his experience, but he did confide that he often pined for the company of a certain quadroon girl on his father's plantation. Timothy wondered if that slave girl longed for her young master as well. Although he himself had, well, *admired* a certain shapely serving girl who worked for his parents, he never considered using his position to advantage. Not only was such behavior unseemly, but Laz would never tolerate it. Some of Timothy's fellow students apparently had a different paternal example.

Against Timothy's advice, sometimes Beauchamp joined a few upperclassmen in going over the wall to find female companionship. Upon return, with the discretion of a true gentleman, he refused to discuss his activities, but he always looked like the cat that got the cream. Timothy deduced that, once a man started down that road, it would be difficult to backtrack. Best to wait until marriage. But, oh, how hard the wait.

He consoled himself as best he could, reciting those Proverbs about the strange woman and wishing desperately for a cold dip in Severn River.

Isaiah stood at attention in front of Commander Blake's desk, trembling with fear, if only inside his chest. Beside the superintendent's desk stood Mrs. Doone and Meg, whose appearance had changed considerably since he last saw her two months before. Now she looked as if she were concealing a small pillow beneath her skirt front, but from the dismal, teary expression on her face—and her mother's, it was obvious that no pillow caused her round appearance.

"Mr. Starbuck." Blake's grave expression sent a new chill coursing through Isaiah's chest. "Mrs. Doone is the widow of a sea captain who, though not in the United States Navy, was a man of worthy reputation. This genteel lady is from a decent family and has raised her daughter in kind. Mrs. Doone tells me you were a boarder in her home from mid-August until October and that you spent considerable time with Miss Doone. Do her memories agree with yours?"

"Aye, sir." Isaiah tried to sound detached. "I was a boarder at Mrs. Doone's house."

"And did you spend time with Miss Doone?"

Isaiah kept his eyes on Blake. "Sir, I painted their front porch, cleaned the attic, and carried in coal. Sometimes Miss Doone was present while I worked at their house, but I also worked on the Severn ferry twelve to fourteen hours a day, six or seven days a week, sir." Isaiah fervently hoped the superintendent would comprehend how tired he had been from all that hard labor.

Blake, however, merely stared at him. "I will not waste time on this." He stood, and his formidable presence sent another chill through Isaiah. "Starbuck, a gentleman takes responsibility for his actions. If you are the cause of this young woman's, eh, condition, you must own up to it and do your duty by her." He leaned forward, both hands on his desk, and glared into Isaiah's eyes. "Boy, do not lie to me. Are you responsible for Miss Doone's condition?"

Isaiah returned his stare. "No, sir, I am not."

"Oh!" Meg wailed and threw herself into her mother's arms. "How could you be so cruel?"

"Commander Blake." Mrs. Doone's thin body quaked, and her sunken eyes exuded misery. "Even though this young man denies it, you must force him to admit the truth." She dabbed at her eyes with a handkerchief and looked at Isaiah with reproach, but also a measure of gentleness. "I understand he doesn't want to lose his place here at the academy. Lord knows, a young man has to have an occupation in order to support a family. But look at my girl here. She can't go through this shame without the child's father. Do something. I beg you."

Isaiah's face burned, and he swallowed hard. *God, help me*. The silent prayer came without conscious thought.

"Well, Starbuck." Blake stood tall again and glared at him.

"Sir, I am not responsible for this." Try though he might, Isaiah could not keep the tremor from his voice.

Meg howled again, and Mrs. Doone began to weep as well.

Blake shot a glance at the women and once more looked at Isaiah. "Mr. Starbuck, did you, eh, share a bed with this young woman?"

Isaiah opened his mouth, but no words would form.

"Starbuck, answer me." Blake's face grew red. "Did you sleep with this girl?"

Isaiah's jaw worked, but still no sound would come. Shared a bed with her? Yes. Slept with her? Yes, *slept!* But no one would believe they only slept. And it would do no good to lie. Blake had a reputation of seeing through any deception the cadets attempted. A wave of dizziness swept over Isaiah. All was lost. His future as a naval officer. Lacy. Everything.

"Answer me, Mr. Starbuck. On your honor, did you know this young woman in the biblical sense?"

At the superintendent's reworded question, Isaiah almost fell forward with relief. He would not have to try useless subterfuge, after all. "No, sir, I did not. I will swear it on the Bible, sir. I did not."

Blake heaved a great sigh. He studied Isaiah, who continued to return a frank stare, his chin held high. Then the superintendent looked back at the women.

"Mrs. Doone, I am at a loss here. Starbuck is one of our best students and, I believe, a young man of honor. Yet I can see you also feel you have spoken the truth. Take your daughter home, and I promise you I will get to the bottom of this. If indeed Mr. Starbuck is the father of your daughter's child, I will personally see to it that he does the honorable thing."

With a tearful thank-you, Mrs. Doone herded Meg toward the door, where both turned reproachful eyes on Isaiah. "I'm counting on you, Commander Blake. Everything, *everything* depends on you."

As the door shut behind them, Blake once again pinioned Isaiah with a stare. "I do not know what defense you can manage for yourself, Starbuck." He thought for a moment. "Perhaps after a night of drinking, you did not recall all your actions with the young lady."

"Sir, I do not drink. And I have an excellent memory."

Blake considered his words. "That you do. Your daily recitations prove it." He ran his hand through his white hair. "I will help you as best I can, but I spoke the truth when I said I believe Mrs. Doone."

"Aye, sir." Isaiah nodded. "Mrs. Doone is a truthful woman. But I am not responsible for Miss Doone's condition."

Blake jerked to his full height and frowned. "Do you realize what you are saying, man?" Again, Isaiah nodded. "Aye, sir, I do."

"And you realize that if we do not learn any facts to the contrary, we must accept Mrs. Doone's account and find some way to make restitution?"

Isaiah winced. "I ... I guess so, sir." No, he would never marry Meg, no matter what anyone said. He would leave Annapolis and go somewhere, anywhere, to escape that fate.

"Very well. We will see what can be done. Dismissed."

Outside in the icy December wind, Isaiah shuddered, but not from the cold. How would he ever exonerate himself from this charge? He would have to prove that Meg was lying, but how? Whether or not the superintendent ultimately chose to believe him, his honor was at stake. A gentleman never ruined a lady's reputation, even if it damaged his own. But then, Meg was not a lady, despite her mother's claims. How blind the old woman was.

And what a fool he had been not to find another boarding house after Meg fell asleep beside him that night. Instinct warned, but appetite for Mrs. Doone's good cooking had won out. He would never again make such a weak, foolish choice.

Across the academy yard, Ahab and his cronies dashed about, warming themselves with a game of bandy, carefree for an hour before going to their studies. Isaiah's stomach lurched. Today he had faltered in a history recitation, but Ahab—*Jacobs*, he corrected himself—had spouted details of the English Reformation with ease. Everyone knew his rich family had taken a tour of Europe. Ahab never let them forget it.

"When we were in England," he had bragged, "the queen herself recommended that we visit Hampton Court, where Henry the Eighth lived with several of his wives. Not all at once, you understand. He managed to dispose of them with some regularity." The classroom had erupted in laughter. Even the professor, Captain Longwood, had chuckled, permitting Ahab to continue an informal recitation no other student could get away with. "Of course, we have Henry to thank for the Reformation in England, although his original purpose was to annul his marriage to his first wife and marry Anne Boleyn, who ..."

All his weasely little sycophants had listened with mouths agape, but Isaiah had nudged Bartholomew and they traded their secret signal of disgust and boredom, as they always did when Ahab talked.

Ahab. Everywhere Isaiah turned, his adversary prospered. If he were ever accused of fathering a by-blow, he could simply pay the girl off and be done with her. No one would ever know it happened. Like Henry VIII, he would not be forced to deal with an unwanted female.

Striding toward his dormitory with his jacket hunched up around his neck, Isaiah shoved his adversary from his thoughts and set his mind on how to solve the problem with Meg. There had to be a solution. There just had to be.

Chapter Thirteen

ଆ

*H*e got a girl in trouble?" Timothy's hair seemed to stand on end as he stared at Beauchamp. "Where in blazes did you hear that?"

Hands behind his head, Beauchamp lounged back on Timothy's cot, his pretty-boy lips puckered into a triumphant smirk. "My boy Cordell talks with all the other stewards, and they know everything about everybody here at the academy, and in town, too. The girl's mother had old Starbuck dragged into Blake's office to confront him with it, and now he's got to marry her."

Timothy felt bile rising in his throat. What a fool Starbuck was. This was just another example of his lack of self-control. Maybe it would be best if he left the academy, but Timothy could take no pleasure in the thought.

"If she's that kind of girl, maybe Starbuck's not the guilty man."

Beauchamp grunted in disgust. "Oh, he denies it, all right. Didn't even have the honor to take responsibility."

"Say, Jake." Hart leaned his elbows on the table in the center of their room. "You look mighty glum about this. I'd think you'd be glad to be rid of the fellow. He's had it in for you since day one, but you keep defending him."

"Ha!" Beauchamp grinned and tilted his head knowingly. "I'll wager Starbuck has a sister. A pretty sister. Right, Jake?"

Heat crept up Timothy's neck. "Where'd you get that crazy idea, Beau?"

Beauchamp snickered. "It's always a lady. And your red face proves I'm right."

Timothy blew out a sigh and slumped down into his chair. "Aw, you're just a featherhead. Besides, no matter what, we gotta do something. Maybe he isn't responsible. Maybe he's being put on the spot because the real culprit left town."

Hart and Beau traded looks and shook their heads.

"Don't know why you care," Hart said.

"A lady." Beau spoke in an artificial whisper. "I will bet you fifty bucks."

"Forget about that," Timothy said. "I mean to help him. Somehow."

Beau sat up on the bed. "Say, I can send Cordell to scout around town. He's a clever boy. If there's something to know, he can find it out."

Timothy frowned. So far he had managed to avoid any discussion of Cordell's presence at the academy. Would it be condoning slavery to accept Beau's offer? But no other solution came to mind. "Sure. Good idea. But don't say anything to anybody else. Let's just keep this amongst the three of us. Agreed?"

He put out his fist and Hart clamped his hand on it, while Beau jumped up from the cot to join the three-handed ritual to cement their pledge.

"Agreed," they chorused.

"I'll do it right away." Beau walked toward the door, then turned back. "You're a good man, Jake. Can't say I'd do this for a man who's out to get me."

"Same here," Hart put in.

Timothy shrugged in an off-handed manner, but their admiration sent a wave of satisfaction through him. He was a good leader to his little band of fellow students, and in time to come he would make a good officer, a great one. Of that he was certain.

Two days later, Beau reported back to Hart and Timothy's room. "Cordell found out the girl's name: Meg Doone. He made friends with Bebe, Mrs. Doone's girl. I told you he's clever. Put on he was a free black and asked for work at the back door. Bebe took a liking to him because he looks like her son. She fed him and let the cat out of the bag plenty."

Beau chomped down on an apple and sat back in a chair, a pleased expression on his cherubic face.

"Spill it, man." Timothy wanted to grab his friend and shake the information out of him. But at the same time, he wondered how the young black man had felt pretending to be free. If Cordell ever indicated a desire to make freedom a reality, Timothy knew he must help him, no matter what it did to his friendship with Beau. But that was not a problem Timothy could solve now, so he would deal with the one he could solve. "What news?"

"Well, this girl, Meg, tried to get Starbuck into her grip, but another fella lived there before him, a dandy of some kind. He's the scoundrel."

"How does Bebe know for sure?"

A shadow passed over Beau's face, and he cleared his throat. "You know, Jake, there're some things a gentleman never discusses, so I hope you won't think less of me for mentioning certain delicate matters."

Timothy gave him a questioning stare. What could be more private than their pact to save Isaiah?

"I mean," Beau continued, "that is to say … well, Bebe washes the laundry."

Still mystified, Timothy scratched his head. "And so …?"

Hart snorted, and Timothy glared at him.

"Sorry." Hart sniggered. "I have older sisters."

"Ah. I see." Timothy grimaced at his own stupidity. "Does that mean she's not … eh … *enceinte?*" He chose a word he had found in his French textbook, one Mademoiselle had never taught him, but his face grew warm as he said it.

"Oh, no, she's in trouble, all right. But Bebe knows who's truly to blame."

Timothy tilted his head and frowned, still not understanding all the implications of Beau's statement but unwilling to let his friends see his *naïveté*. "Well, then, that solves the problem. We get Bebe to tell Old Blake, and Starbuck is out of hot water."

Beau shook his head. "It's not that easy. No one takes the word of a chattel against his master, or in this case, her mistress. No, we have to be clever about it."

As his friends wrinkled their brows in obvious concentration on how to rescue Isaiah, Timothy dealt with another troublesome thought. Back home, if Patience said something, people believed it as truth, at least in the Lazarus household. Why would Bebe's testimony not be sufficient? How difficult he found it to act as though he accepted these untenable conditions. But if he revealed his abolitionist views, it might come around to betray Laz's work of rescuing slaves. For now, and only for now, he must ignore the fire in his heart when these things came up. *For now*, he must concentrate on how to rescue Starbuck.

"I have it." Beau slapped the table. "I'll simply send Cordell back out to find the man, and if he's still around, we'll corner him and make him own up."

"You mean the three of us?" Hart frowned. "I'm not sure I want to get into that kind of scrape for a fella I don't even like. I can't afford the demerits if we got caught."

"I don't blame you, Hart. It's not your battle," Timothy said. "I'll take care of it."

"Not without me," Beau said.

Timothy regarded his Southern friend. Six feet tall and slender but energetic, he had proved his mettle several times over in games, fencing, and fisticuffs. Despite his bush of curly golden hair, boyish blue eyes, and cherubic face, he would do well in a fight if it came to that.

"The game is on, then. Send out your man."

Isaiah had his things in order, what few there were. Frank would buy his uniforms, and another student would buy his books. The money would be enough to help him get out of town. Maybe he would go out West. With the decline in whaling, many Nantucketers had gone to California in '49, and some had stayed even after they failed to find gold. He might find a Starbuck cousin, a Chase, or a Folger who would give him a job. He would walk up to Baltimore and ship out on the first merchant vessel heading around the Horn.

Now that Jemima had found a benefactor, she would not need him or his paltry ability to care for her. The lady who paid her living expenses while she attended school, this Mrs. Lazarus, sounded kind-hearted, and from Jemima's letters he knew Reverend and Mrs. Harris treated his sister as well as they treated their own daughters. To think he and Jemima had left Nantucket for his benefit. How had he failed to realize that his luck would never change? But as long as Jemima had a good home and good friends, he was free to make his own way in the world.

Commander Blake had sent orders for Isaiah to report to his office during the afternoon study hour. As strict as the superintendent was about students using that time to learn their lessons, he must have made his decision about Meg, and so Isaiah's heart had sunk upon receiving the note. His academy days were over.

He marched from the dormitory without his coat, accepting the bitter wind blustering in from the waterfront as typical of his harsh life. No real opportunities had blown his way, not until his appointment to the academy. And then a vile blizzard named Meg had stormed in and swept away the only good thing ever to happen to him.

He reached the administration building, squared his shoulders, climbed the stairs, and entered. Despite the injustice of his dismissal, he would take this interview like a man. But he would never marry that girl.

Standing at attention in front of Blake's desk for the third time in less than two months, Isaiah stared straight ahead. This time his heart did not clamor to get out of his chest, and his dinner did not threaten to come up. Other than his cold cheeks, which stung from the heat of the gas furnace, every part of him felt dead.

After seeing to some other business, Commander Blake shut his office door and walked around his desk to face Isaiah. To the younger man's shock, Blake beamed with obvious pleasure. How could the man be so sadistic?

"Starbuck." The superintendent picked up his pipe and filled it with fresh, fragrant cherry tobacco, then lit it and puffed before continuing. "I won't waste your time or mine. You're in the clear, lad."

"Sir?" Isaiah's voice squeaked like a girl's.

Blake guffawed. "That's right, my boy. As a gentleman, I cannot discuss the details, but you have been completely exonerated. No one will ever lay this charge against you again."

The room seemed to move, and suddenly Isaiah found himself seated in a chair with a small glass of whiskey being waved under his nose. He moved back, hoping Blake would not be offended by his refusal to drink the spirits.

"That's enough." The superintendent spoke to the steward who held the glass. Where the man had come from, Isaiah had no idea.

Blake regarded him with a tender, almost paternal smile. "I'm very pleased for you, Starbuck. You have potential, and I will do everything in my power to see you succeed here at the academy. My wife is also very fond of all our fine young men, and she has granted me permission to invite you to our home. Would you do us the honor of coming for dinner after services this Sunday?"

Isaiah swallowed the lump in his throat and commanded the burning in his eyes to disappear. "Aye, sir. I would be honored."

"All right, then, lad. You're dismissed."

With great effort, Isaiah did not hop down the stairs of the administration building, did not skip along the pavement to his dormitory, and did not cast off his hat and fling it into the air. Clouds might cover the sky, but an exhilarating sun shone in his heart. Even the icy wind could not chill him now. Beyond all hope—indeed he had not dared to hope—he had been delivered.

Far across the yard he saw Ahab, and Isaiah smirked. Ahab and that foppish Beauchamp had sneaked over the wall a few nights ago and come back with their pretty faces banged up, earning thirty demerits each. Unlike those two fools who were always inciting each other to trouble, Isaiah kept to himself, kept his nose clean. Never mind that the other cadets put him in Coventry, shunning him because he studied hard and never broke the rules. One day, he would be their superior officer, and then they would see what was what. For now, they could shun him all they wanted. By the power of some mystical hand, he'd been cleared. He was free. And he would never go near another female—except Mrs. Blake, of course—as long as he remained at the academy.

Chapter Fourteen

&

Jemima and Lacy traded yet another look, both trying not to giggle with excitement. Ever since they had boarded the first train in Boston, they struggled to appear grown-up, or at least a little older than their fourteen and a half years. After all, they were on their way to the Naval Academy ball, invited by the young men who owned their hearts. Dressed in their new wardrobes—Jemima's provided by Mrs. Hannah Lazarus—they had agreed to help each other appear as mature as possible, befitting this grand adventure. Reverend Harris had come along to chaperone them, but his presence had helped only a little, for he loved to tease them and each gentle jab brought forth more childish giggles from the girls.

After they made numerous transfers from one railroad line to another, the Annapolis and Elkridge train now rushed them along the last twenty-one miles of their journey. With each passing mile through the winter-clad forests of Maryland, Jemima wondered how she and her dear friend would manage not to embarrass their escorts.

As it was, Isaiah's upcoming shock at learning she came not to see him but Timothy would be difficult enough to deal with. More than once in writing to him, she almost had given it away, then tore up her letter and started anew. Telling him in person would be much better, she was certain.

After many prayers, she revealed the whole situation to Lacy, despite her fears that Lacy would think less of Isaiah. But although her friend was sad to hear of it, she instead promised to pray for the man she cared about and for the other one who was as dear to her as a brother. Then she insisted Jemima must tell Reverend and Mrs. Harris, for their prayers, and perhaps their intervention, would surely bring about a solution.

In midafternoon, the train burst from the bleak forest and soon chugged into the Annapolis station. After the little party disembarked, Reverend Harris found a porter to carry their luggage and a carriage to take them to their lodging.

Reverend Harris had written his old seminary friend, Reverend Frederick Easton, to ask if he, with his daughter and ward, might visit for a week in January. By return post, Reverend and Mrs. Easton expressed their delight at the prospect of hosting the little party, especially since they were coming to attend the Naval Academy ball. The Eastons explained that they frequently entertained the midshipmen in their home and were diligent to encourage the young men when studies and loneliness threatened to overwhelm them.

This last bit of news heartened Jemima, for she often wondered if Isaiah had anyone to lift his spirits. Although he had written much about his roommate and also told her of an invitation to Commander Blake's home for Sunday dinner, he never mentioned being lonely. But then, he wouldn't. Only when she was with him could Jemima cajole him into sharing his deepest thoughts and feelings.

"Your carriage awaits, miladies." Reverend Harris swept off his brown stovepipe hat and bowed grandly to the girls. "May I assist you, Miss Starbuck?"

He reached out to Jemima and helped her climb into the covered buggy, a large, older model, four-passenger brougham with padded seats and unfurled isinglass shades to keep out the wind. Drawn by a single horse, the conveyance soon sped the group through the streets of the small city.

Jemima shivered with delight over her adventure as Lacy pulled her into a loving embrace.

"There, don't be worried. Timothy will be so pleased to see you. I know you've fretted over these two inches you've grown since October, but he's so tall, he won't even notice."

Jemima giggled, and then tried to modulate her voice into a more ladylike laugh. "Oh, I'm not worried about that any longer. Your mother says God designed each of us according to his purpose, and we must trust in that. Being five feet six inches has the advantage of making me seem as mature as my schoolmates. Still, I confess I have prayed not to grow any taller."

She turned to Reverend Harris—*Uncle Jeremiah*, she reminded herself—who sat across from the girls. "I greatly enjoyed my lessons with the dance master. Thank you for arranging for me to go with Lacy. Now I won't put Timothy entirely to shame at the ball."

Uncle Jeremiah smiled and gave her a little bow. "You would never shame him, my child. Nevertheless, it was my pleasure to arrange the lessons."

"I needed the practice as well," Lacy said. "It's been some time since I've danced at a social."

"Oh, indeed, years and years. One can hardly believe the old dear can still walk, much less dance." Uncle Jeremiah leveled his teasing gaze on his daughter, and both girls laughed.

As often happened, Jemima had difficulty turning away from the minister's handsome, paternal face. Despite a sprinkling of gray in his short, brownish-blond hair and a few wrinkles around his bright blue eyes, he glowed with youthful vitality. But she found most compelling the way he viewed people, as if he could see deep into their souls. What a wonderful gift for a minister to possess, especially one who never condemned, but only encouraged people to find peace with God and to rest in his loving arms.

His sermons were not thundering diatribes reverberating off the walls of Grace Seamen's Chapel and warning of eternal damnation for disobedient sinners. Rather his gentle words reverberated within the hearts of his listeners, persuading them to the righteousness found in Christ. During Jemima's five months in Boston, she had seen countless rough seamen and even women of the street come weeping to the altar when they realized that salvation was a free gift, not something they must earn. Uncle Jeremiah truly understood the meaning of God's grace.

For her part, just being with the pastor soothed her, for he filled the empty spot that had always been in her heart, the spot left by her father's death. Until she came to live with the Harrises, she had not realized how very much a girl needs a father.

"Ah, here we are."

Uncle Jeremiah reached for the carriage door, swung it open, and hopped out with the eagerness of a youth. He helped Lacy and Jemima disembark and gave instructions to the driver concerning their luggage.

The Eastons gave their guests a warm welcome. About the same age as Uncle Jeremiah, Reverend Easton was a short man with dark gray hair and evidence of a hearty appetite beneath his well-made suit. Mrs. Easton stood as tall as her husband and almost as round, but she appeared much younger. No gray touched her light brown hair, and her round face had not one wrinkle. Mrs. Easton informed her guests that her two children would be brought downstairs directly as soon as their nurse dressed them after their naps.

"Why, Miss Starbuck," Mrs. Easton said while leading everyone into the large front parlor, "you could be mistaken for a Harris with that lovely blond hair and those dark eyes."

"Thank you, ma'am." Jemima took a seat next to Lacy on a blue brocade divan. "Mrs. Harris's people and mine are distant relations, our forebears having settled Nantucket Island in the sixteen-hundreds."

"Ah, I see." The lady bobbed her head, and her abundant corkscrew curls bounced. "Miss Harris, I do believe you two will be the prettiest young ladies at the ball. Do you think you can contain your excitement for two days until Saturday?"

"Oh, I do hope so, ma'am. It truly is thrilling to be here." Lacy's eyes sparkled.

"And Reverend Harris," Mrs. Easton said, "how grand of you to bring these lovely girls for the ball. Our young midshipmen need all the encouragement they can get, for they are our country's future defenders, and their course of study is difficult. Yet not every father would permit his daughter and ward to attend such an affair."

Uncle Jeremiah chuckled. "I certainly would not have sent them by themselves, nor could we have undertaken the adventure without your generous hospitality."

"Believe me, dear sir, we are so pleased to have you."

"Well, Reverend Harris." Reverend Easton clapped Uncle Jeremiah on the shoulder. "You and I have some twenty or so years to catch up on. Shall we adjourn to the back parlor for a smoke while Mrs. Easton advises these charming young ladies concerning their upcoming event?"

"Hurry up, Frank." Isaiah grabbed his roommate's hat from the hat stand and pulled him along toward the door, even though Frank was still buttoning his jacket. "What's the matter with you? We're going to be late."

"No skin off my nose. It's your girl we're going to see." Frank took his cap from Isaiah and adjusted it on his head while they descended the dormitory stairs.

"Yes, well, uh, that's just it." Isaiah avoided his friend's gaze. "You see, my sister is there, too. I couldn't exactly invite Miss Harris and not invite my own sister, now could I?"

"Awright," Frank drawled. "And that means …?"

"Well, uh, she won't have an escort for tonight and you don't have a guest, so I thought …"

Frank expelled a long, steamy breath into the cold morning air. "So that's your game. You sneak. Why didn't you tell me?"

"You aren't mad, are you?" Isaiah resisted the urge to grab Frank's arm again and drag him toward the front gate of the academy.

"Naw, I'm not mad, but my girl back home might be."

"Your girl?" Isaiah's heart seemed to plummet into his stomach. "You have a girl? How come you never said so?" So much for his plans to find Jemima a husband he approved of.

"And how come you never said your sister was coming?"

Isaiah shook his head. "I'm sorry, pal. I don't want to get you in trouble with your girl. She's not here in town, is she?"

Frank lowered his chin and stared at Isaiah as if he were a fool. "If she was in town, I'd be taking her to the ball, now, wouldn't I?"

They walked in silence for a few moments, and Isaiah thought of several ways to solve the dilemma. At last he clapped Frank on the shoulder.

"Tell you what, just write your girl and tell her the whole thing. Say I put you on the spot. She can't be mad if you tell her the only honorable thing to do was play along. Why do you think our professors talk to us all the time about fine manners and such? Once we're officers, we'll be in the company of ladies wherever we go. If you marry her, she'll have to get used to it."

Frank shrugged. "I guess so."

Again they walked in silence, and Isaiah's thoughts turned to Lacy. When they saw each other, would she still think well of him? He had never thought much of his looks, and girls had never paid much attention to him. But Lacy had seemed pleased enough with his appearance to smile at him often during his short stay in Boston. He was a little taller now—almost five feet eleven inches—and had better posture, a quality quickly acquired here at the academy with so much standing at attention. Even in class no slouching was permitted. If his leaner, more mature face no longer appealed to

Lacy, at least his military bearing would impress her.

Jemima had insisted he write to Lacy, and once he had started, it turned out to be much easier than expected. And Lacy's responses had been cheerful, gracious, and everything he had remembered her to be. He still read them over and over again.

They found Reverend Easton's fine house with no difficulty. A servant showed them into a large front parlor even more ornate than Commander Blake's. While waiting for their hostess and her guests, Isaiah had to remind himself not to gawk at the lavish, elegant furnishings of this grand house, even grander than the Harrises' home. How could a minister afford to own such fine things? He sighed, his heart once again sinking. He did not belong in this place. He did not deserve the affections of a well-born girl. He should just stand up and leave before Lacy entered the room.

"Cheer up, pal," Frank whispered. "I'll help you out. I won't let on to your sister that you've botched it."

Giving his friend a rueful smile, Isaiah nodded his appreciation. Thank goodness Frank had no idea what he truly was thinking.

"Stop fussing with your hair, Lacy. You'll ruin it." Jemima took the brush from her friend and set it on the bedroom dressing table. "You look beautiful. Perfectly beautiful. My poor brother will keel over in his boots when he sees you."

Lacy giggled and Jemima joined in with her. Once again they checked each other up, down, and around to be certain every detail appeared flawless. Lacy's green muslin morning gown and Jemima's own blue one had been made from the same fashion plate, and even their lace and sashes had been cut the same. Mrs. Lazarus had given each girl a tiny vial of perfume, with directions to use the contents sparingly. Both girls agreed that wearing the lovely rose-petal fragrance made them feel very grown-up.

A tap sounded on the door, and Mrs. Easton's Negro servant woman peered into the room. "Miz Lacy, Miz Jemima, your gentlemen callers has arrived."

The girls traded looks, clasped hands, and giggled once again. Then suddenly Lacy straightened, lifted her chin, and transformed herself from a schoolgirl into an elegant lady. Jemima had seen her do it before when, as the oldest child in a large family, she needed to take charge of her younger siblings. This remarkable feat set an example that Jemima now sought to emulate. With one last glance in the mirror, the two girls walked arm-in-arm from their guest bedroom.

As they reached the top of the stairs, Jemima paused. Had the servant said "callers"? Had Timothy come too? Had Isaiah made friends with him at last? *Oh, please, Lord, let it be so.*

"Coming?" Lacy tugged on Jemima's arm.

"Oh, yes."

At the parlor door, they both composed themselves again, and then entered.

"Ah, here they are." Mrs. Easton said.

Jemima did not realize she was holding her breath until she saw Isaiah and an unfamiliar young man, both of whom jumped up to attention. Then an explosive cry escaped her.

"Isaiah!" She rushed to her brother and fell into his arms, crying for joy. "Oh, you look so handsome! How tall you are! How strong! Oh, how can I stand any more of these long separations?" Her heart felt near to bursting. Oh, how she loved him.

"There, now, Sis, don't do this." Despite his words, he pressed her head into his shoulder and kissed her temple. "Shh." He bent near her ear and whispered, "You smell mighty good."

Jemima pulled back, brushed the tears from her cheeks and glanced around, her face growing warm. "Please forgive me."

"Never mind, dahlin'." Mrs. Easton came over and patted her on the back. "We understand. Why, I still miss my dear brothers down in South Carolina. Family is always family."

Isaiah cleared his throat and stepped away from Jemima. "Sis, may I present my friend and roommate, the man I've written you about, Francis Bartholomew. Frank, this is my sister, Miss Jemima Starbuck."

"I reckon she better be." Frank chuckled and reached out to Jemima. "How do, Miss Starbuck." He bent to kiss her hand, a little clumsily, but charming, nonetheless.

"I'm fine, Mr. Bartholomew, and so pleased to meet you." But why had Isaiah brought this friend?

Another party in the room cleared her throat, and Jemima gasped. "Oh, I've completely forgotten my manners. Here's Miss Harris." She stepped back and beckoned to her friend.

"Mr. Starbuck, how nice to see you." Lacy glided across the room and lifted her hand to Isaiah. "Thank you for inviting me to the ball."

Although Lacy appeared the epitome of poise, her eyes twinkled with delight as she gazed at Isaiah. Jemima's heart swelled with happiness to see her brother's enraptured expression as he lifted Lacy's hand to his lips. They were meant to be together, of that Jemima was certain.

"Now, you young people just sit right here and visit all you want." Mrs. Easton glanced around the group and smiled. "I'll have Serena bring tea. The reverends are over at the church, but they'll be home for dinner in an hour, and you young gentlemen must stay and have a bite with us. Right now, I'm going upstairs to check on my little babies before their morning naps."

An awkward silence fell over the room for several moments until Lacy turned to Isaiah's friend to ask where he came from. Hearing he hailed from Ohio, the girls both plied him with questions about his home state.

"It was the first state beyond the Alleghany Mountains to be admitted to the Union." Pride in his home shone in Mr. Bartholomew's face, and he seemed comfortable with himself.

Jemima liked him. What a good friend for Isaiah to have, though there was another she wished could be included in her brother's too-small circle. Fortunately, or to her way of thinking, unfortunately, Timothy would not be visiting her until this afternoon. By that time, Uncle Jeremiah planned to take Isaiah aside for a serious discussion. With the minister's gift of persuasion, he would no doubt resolve all of Isaiah's difficulties by the time Timothy arrived.

Timothy brushed his thick black hair and applied a small amount of fragrant macassar oil to make it smooth and shiny like Captain Longwood's. The captain always looked flawless, from his neatly trimmed hair to his spotless uniform to his shiny black half-boots. Timothy tried to emulate him in every aspect of his own appearance. To dress thus for military inspection was a duty, but to dress for the lady he loved was a delight. And for Jemima's first view of him in his uniform, every detail must be flawless. He stood back from his small mirror, checked one last time, and gave himself a nod of satisfaction. She would be proud of him.

Outside in the sunny, cold day, he walked briskly toward the home of Reverend Easton. He was a little disappointed that Uncle Jeremiah rather than his parents had brought Jemima to Annapolis. Yet, hastened by the exhilaration in his heart over seeing her again, he covered the half-mile in only a few minutes and soon stood in the foyer of the old mansion, delivering his hat and outer jacket to the Negro servant. The old woman then showed him to a back parlor.

"Miz Easton will be right in, sir." The woman curtsied and then left the room.

As they had passed the closed front parlor door, Timothy heard voices and hoped he was not intruding. Uncle Jeremiah had told him to come in the afternoon, but in his excitement over the prospect of seeing friends from home, he felt certain they would forgive his early arrival. Had he made a mistake in coming before the appointed time?

"Why, you must be Mr. Jacobs." A plump and pleasant lady entered the room and extended her hand in greeting. "I'm Mrs. Easton. You're early, dear boy."

"I hope you'll forgive me, ma'am." Timothy kissed her hand in greeting. "I found it too difficult to wait."

"I understand completely. Now you just be seated, and I'll see to everything. As it turns out, Reverend Harris and my husband are over at the church at present, but they will be home any moment now."

She left the room, but he could not think of sitting down to wait. He ambled about, first looking out the back window at the wintry scene of barren bushes and a frozen pond, which looked just perfect for skating. Did Jemima know how to skate? If not, he would teach her.

Next he checked his appearance in a tiny mirror on the wall to be certain his cap had not put a dent in his hair, and was relieved to see no such damage. Then he turned to a side table to peruse a book of photographs, which included scenes he recognized from England. His mind quickly filled with pleasant memories. One day he must take Jemima to Europe, perhaps on their wedding trip. The thought made his heart leap.

"Timothy!"

There she stood, more beautiful than he remembered. For a moment, time seemed to stand still. Then he crossed the room in three long strides, pulled her into his arms, and kissed her full on the lips. For one blissful instant, he was lost in euphoria until reality slammed through the parlor door.

"Get your filthy hands off my sister!"

Timothy stepped back, both appalled and pleased at what he had done. Jemima looked dazed, but a tiny, happy smile flitted across her face before she turned to her brother in astonishment.

Isaiah, holding his fists up ready to fight, shoved his way between the two of them and stood facing Timothy.

"What do you mean manhandling my sister that way? Jemima, go to your room. I'll handle this."

"Oh, Isaiah!" cried Jemima.

"Mr. Starbuck, please recall your manners." Mrs. Easton's voice resounded with authority as she stepped between the two youths.

Isaiah lowered his fists and shook his head, as though trying to control his temper. "Mrs. Easton, begging your pardon, ma'am, but this scoundrel just kissed my sister, and he doesn't even know her. I have a right and a responsibility to call him out."

The room filled with a growing audience, including a tall Negro manservant who looked able enough to stop any ill-advised behavior in his mistress's house.

Lacy took Isaiah's arm. "Mr. Starbuck, please escort me back to the front parlor."

He stared at her, his face blazing with color. "I'm sorry, Miss Harris, but I will not leave my sister in the company of this—" he glared at his adversary "—this *person*."

"What's going on here?" Reverend Easton's voice thundered down the hallway, and soon he and Uncle Jeremiah joined the throng.

"Timothy, good to see you, lad." Uncle Jeremiah wended his way through the crowd and clapped a hand on Timothy's shoulder. "Isaiah, good to see you, too, my boy." He stepped over to him and shook his hand, then glanced back at Timothy.

"We were delighted to accept the invitations you two young men so kindly sent to my daughter and Miss Starbuck. The young ladies are looking forward to this evening's ball with happy anticipation, and I'm sure you gentlemen must be as well."

He leveled a look on Isaiah that Timothy knew well, and it was all he could do to keep from smirking. In those few words and glances, Jeremiah had informed Isaiah of how things stood. Now it would be

LOUISE M. GOUGE

up to Isaiah to decide whether to be on the inside or out. For his good friend Lacy's sake, he almost hoped the fool would storm out the door and out of their lives forever. But then what would Jemima do? Even now, her sweet face was flushed with pink and lined with anguish that Timothy longed to soothe away.

Isaiah's face, however, was drained of color as he stared at Jeremiah. Trembling slightly, he gave the minister a brief nod. "Yes, sir. I'm honored to escort Miss Harris to the ball. Thank you for bringing her and my sister."

His words sounded like a stiff classroom recitation, but everyone in the room seemed to breathe a sigh of relief.

Chapter Fifteen

ஜ

"They all conspired against me." Isaiah lay on his cot and stared at the ceiling of his room, trying not to throw up the fine dinner he had forced down at the Easton house. "Lacy. Reverend Harris. My own sister."

Frank snickered wryly. "I wouldn't say Miss Harris conspired against you unless it was to get you to the altar 'bout an hour after you graduate from this place."

Isaiah shot an angry glare at him, wanting to slug him, not because his words were a lie but because they were a wonderful truth undoubtedly now destroyed. Oh, yes, for that one blissful hour when he, Lacy, Frank, and Jemima had gammed in the Eastons' front parlor, he imagined spending his life with the lovely young lady who seemed to care for him more than just a little. But vile reality crashed into his dream in the form of Ahab, with all his superior attitude and hidden, filthy lust for Jemima.

He could forgive Lacy, for he learned this day she grew up with Ahab and always considered him a brother. He could forgive Reverend Harris, for a minister was required to be good to everyone. But he would never forgive Jemima for her secret friendship with Ahab. She never should have encouraged him. She should have respected Isaiah's feelings. In fact, she should feel the same way. Ahab's father had murdered their father. How could she think of caring for such a man? Couldn't she see what a proud, arrogant fellow he was, the type to woo and win a girl, then discard her?

"Aw, cool down, Starbuck." Frank spun a pencil on the table, a habit Isaiah had never minded before but which now bothered him almost to distraction. "This Jacobs fellow isn't so bad once you get to know him. He was a real gentleman at dinner, acting like we're all friends, complimenting your recitations and such. You oughta let it go, lad. There's no profit in making him your enemy. You'll lose out in the end. For my part, from now on I'm gonna give him a friendly nod next time I see him."

Isaiah rolled over to face the wall. "*Et tu, Brute?*"

"How's that?"

"Nothing."

So now he was truly alone. Even gaining Reverend Harris's approval to court Lacy seemed out of reach.

Or was it?

Isaiah bolted up on his cot, staring at his roommate. "Frank, I'm an idiot."

Frank smiled broadly. "You're gonna make peace with Jacobs?"

"Great malarkey, no. Never. He's his father's son through and through."

Frank shook his head, but Isaiah ignored the gesture. "No, but I just realized something. All through dinner, Reverend Harris never once acted as if he disliked me."

"No, he didn't." Frank nodded. "Not at all. Just the opposite."

"Right. So that means I still have a chance with Lacy."

"Any fool could see that."

"You think so?"

Frank laughed. "Are you blind? Her father went to the trouble of bringing her all the way down here from Boston, and she was making cow eyes at you all through dinner."

Isaiah slumped back against the wall and smiled. "Yes. Yes, she was." He glanced across the room at his new uniform hanging on the closet door. When he had ordered it from the academy store-keeper, he had wondered if it was a foolish expense to have a second one. But now he would be able to hold his head up with any midshipmen. Once in uniform, all the men appeared the same. None rich. None poor.

Tonight he would be the most charming fourth-class cadet at the ball. Lacy would be proud of him. Reverend Harris would be impressed.

After the ball, no one would ever again be privy to his hatred for Ahab. But one day, he would see his arrogant adversary fall.

"I'm sorry I kissed you."

Timothy stood beside Jemima in the academy mess hall, which had been cleared of tables for the ball. Across the room, a marine band played a waltz, and Mrs. Blake and other faculty wives mingled with the crowd, encouraging shy young people to join the few couples whirling about the dance floor with varying degrees of skill.

Jemima's delicate pink gown cast a glow on her fair cheeks, and she smelled like a summer rose. She gazed up at him, her eyes exuding such innocence that he felt true remorse for his impulsive kiss in the Eastons' parlor. How could he have been so ill mannered, so disrespectful of her?

"Please forgive me."

She gave him a sweet, playful smile. "I don't think you're sorry at all." Then her expression grew grave. "Oh, perhaps you *are* sorry."

"No, that's not what I meant." He glanced around them, but the other guests were busy with their own affairs. "It was very ... um, pleasant. It's just that ..."

How could he explain that the kiss had set his blood on fire when she didn't even seem to know how things were between men and women? He recalled a Bible verse Laz once pointed out: "Stir not up, nor awake my love, till he please." Jemima was a true innocent, and he must not stir up womanly senses in her, but rather protect her, even from himself, even if it hurt her feelings.

"I think we should not kiss again until we are betrothed."

"Oh." Instead of appearing hurt, she beamed. "Yes, I see. Very well, then. Until we are betrothed."

At that moment, his own words struck him with their full import. At last he had told her how he felt, what his full intentions were, and her broad, artless smile revealed her acceptance. He reached out to take her hand.

"Miss Starbuck, may I have this dance?"

"Mr. Jacobs, I would be delighted."

Timothy's matter-of-fact remark about their betrothal made Jemima's heart feel much lighter than her feet. Despite her dance lessons, she must work hard to keep her eyes on Timothy's face instead of the floor. He seemed to understand her nervousness and lack of skill, for he carefully guided her around the dance area, winking and grinning when she stepped on his toes. He even caught her when she stumbled, and dipped gracefully to make it look like a deliberate movement. After just a few musical numbers, her steps became more certain, and they began to move as one.

"Ready for more lemonade?" He tilted his head in the direction of the refreshment table, where Lacy and Isaiah stood, and his eyes asked another question.

She gripped his hand and blew out a short breath. "Ready."

As they neared the table and the other couple noticed them, Jemima could tell Isaiah was struggling not to show his anger. Earlier this evening she had observed her brother and her friend, and they truly were having a good time. Lacy seemed determined to be the center of Isaiah's attention, and until now she had succeeded.

"Isaiah!" Jemima released Timothy's hand and grabbed her brother's arm. "I noticed you and Lacy dancing a while ago. Where on earth did you learn to dance so well? I've been stepping all over Timothy's feet, but he assures me I haven't broken his toes."

Isaiah bent near her ear and mumbled, "What a shame." Then he stood straight and affected a cheerful pose. "Mrs. Blake made certain we all learned the social graces. It seems one cannot be a successful naval officer without learning to dance, use the right fork, and discuss poetry with the ladies, though what those things have to do with sailing a ship or defending our country, I cannot imagine."

Jemima, Lacy, and Timothy laughed, and if Jemima did not know her brother so well, she might believe the sincerity of his pleasant demeanor.

"Ah, well," said Timothy, "table etiquette is a necessary bore, but dancing with a lovely lady reminds us of why we are defending our country."

He gazed fondly at Jemima, and she felt Isaiah bristle.

"But, Isaiah, I never dreamed you were so smooth on your feet. You must dance with me." She took his hand to pull him away, but he resisted.

"One moment, Jemima. Miss Harris, may I have your leave to dance with my sister? I'm sure this *gentleman* will attend you."

Lacy gave him a bright smile. "Of course, Mr. Starbuck." She stepped over to Timothy and took his arm, and once again Isaiah stiffened.

"Come, Brother, before this set is over." Jemima tugged him along to the dance floor.

As he pulled her into dance position and began to lead her about the room, his face became a smiling mask. "You're doing very well, Sis. Just try to relax."

"I might say the same to you."

He snorted. "Of course. Relax, when my own sister keeps secrets from me."

"It was not—" She stopped. With him so cross, how could she tell him the rest? Still, she must do it. "You know it always works better for us to talk in person."

"Your letters are very informative about *unimportant* things."

"Now you're just being unkind. I write you about my schooling, which is just as important as yours." She tripped a little, and he caught her.

"Yes, it is, and I don't intend to be unkind. But you must know how you've hurt me by taking up with the son of our father's murderer."

She let him twirl her through several steps before answering. "Father's death was not Timothy's fault. And besides, sometimes our hearts make choices for us. You, for instance, were smitten with a certain young lady from the moment you met her, and she feels the same way."

Isaiah glanced across the room where Timothy and Lacy sat talking. "She's wonderful, isn't she?" He turned back to Jemima. "Say, don't change the subject. I don't want you to accept his attentions any longer, but I suppose you're a true Nantucket girl. You'll do it your way, no matter what I say." His eyes conveyed disappointment, and Jemima sighed.

"I must tell you everything."

Now Isaiah tripped, but quickly regained his steps. "What now?" Horror darted across his face, and his grip on her waist tightened. "What have you done?"

"Why, nothing. What would I have done?"

He blew out a little sigh and relaxed, apparently relieved. "Nothing. Go on."

Jemima took a breath for courage, and then blurted out, "Timothy's mother is my benefactress."

Isaiah stopped moving, and she thought he would fall forward. People danced about them, and another cadet nudged him to get out of the way. Like a wooden puppet, he moved again, stiffly, clutching her hand and waist, making all the right steps, but seeming not to see.

"Isaiah, did you hear me? Captain Ahab's widow feels responsible for us. She tried to help Mother, but Mother told her the Starbucks would care for us." Tears stung her eyes. "Do you hear me, Brother? Do you know what I'm saying?"

He stared at her, his eyes appearing glazed. "Of course, Jemima. You're telling me that if I want to keep my sister's friendship and earn the affection of another young lady, I must bow down and kiss the feet of my sworn enemy."

Chapter Sixteen

ॐ

March 1858

Timothy trudged through patches of frozen snow on the Annapolis streets, a gloomy chill clutching his heart like winter's icy hold on the land. A block ahead he saw Hartley, Wilson, and Beauchamp headed toward the academy, warming themselves by punching and shoving each other in good humor. But he did not try to catch them, for he had much to consider.

What would today mean to his future? What had Captain Longwood expected of him? Even the invitation to Sunday dinner had made him uncomfortable. As much as all the midshipmen liked their history professor, none relished dining in his home, where his silly wife flirted with them and his three bratty little sons battered their uncomfortable guests without parental reproof. Many found excuses for not accepting the invitations.

Today, however, after attending church services in the academy chapel, while Hart, Wils, and Beau accepted the hospitality of a family with marriageable daughters, Timothy was invited to the Longwoods' home. Of course he could not refuse, for he felt ever grateful to the captain for his appointment and friendship. When he arrived at the handsome brick mansion on Prince George Street, he discovered Mrs. Longwood and her sons had departed for their Richmond plantation. In their place, the captain introduced his new housekeeper, Señora Cervantes, who acted as hostess, and her lovely daughter, Consuela, who joined them at table.

Meeting the widowed Anna Cervantes had shocked Timothy, for she could be his aunt, so closely did she resemble Hannah Lazarus. Elegantly tall, with classical features, porcelain complexion, and deep auburn hair, the once-wealthy Spanish lady had been impoverished by the 1847 war in Mexico. Longwood had rescued her and her daughter from some sort of dreadful fate at the end of that conflict, and their gratitude was evident in their devotion to him. This recent employment of the two women in Longwood's home encouraged Timothy. Perhaps the captain was reconsidering his way of life and would one day free his slaves and pay them for their labors.

His discomfort resulted from Longwood's idea that Consuela should become his language tutor. Although Mademoiselle Trudeau had taught him to read, speak, and write French, he needed help with Spanish. But how could the captain suggest he spend time with the lovely girl with the soulful eyes, when Timothy had told him his heart was claimed? And how could Timothy graciously refuse, for refuse he must?

Just two months ago, Uncle Jeremiah had brought Jemima and Lacy down from Boston for the academy ball. During those few short days, he and his sweetheart had reaffirmed their mutual devotion. No woman but Jemima, not even beautiful Consuela, could move his heart. Still, in her warm, charming presence, he needed to remind himself of Laz's admonitions about keeping his mind faithful. Despite his need for tutoring, he must avoid being alone with Consuela, for he would neither play with her affections nor place his own heart in temptation's way. He blew out a great sigh of frustration. How could he refuse Longwood without causing offense?

"Jake," Beau called from up the block. "Come join us. We're planning a snowball fight."

Shaking off his mood, Timothy laughed. Beau had seen little snow growing up in Louisiana but took to winter fun with infectious enthusiasm. "Coming." He sprinted to join his friends. Of the seven or eight close friends from their first academy term, only the four of them remained, for almost a fourth of the plebe class had dropped out. But even though his little group often argued late into the night over slavery, states' rights, and other complex issues, Timothy loved these friends like brothers. Maybe they could advise him about his dilemma.

After an hour of energetic frolicking on the parade grounds, Timothy and his friends lounged about Beau and Wils' dormitory room, careless of their sweaty, disheveled appearance. Tomorrow would be soon enough to return to military discipline.

"So, Jake." Wils' eyebrows wiggled, a signal his impish humor was about to surface "How was the delightful Mrs. Longwood today?"

"Now, Wils," Beau chided, "a gentleman never speaks ill of a lady." But his face revealed his struggle not to snicker.

"What makes you think I was speaking ill ..."

"She wasn't there." Timothy broke in, determined not to discuss his benefactor's wife. "She and the boys are down in Richmond. But Longwood's hired a housekeeper. She and her daughter both work for him." He started to say something to his two Southern friends about paid employees as opposed to slaves, but that would only reopen an old argument rather than solve his problem. "Señora Cervantes and Consuela are from Spain, but Longwood saved their lives in the Mexican War. Colonel Cervantes was killed and the Mexican government seized their fortune, so he found them a place to live in Florida until recently. Now they're working for the Longwoods and—"

Beau stared at him, a strange look in his bright blue eyes. "Uh, Jake—"

"Yes?"

Beau cast a beseeching glance at Wils, who in turn glanced at Hart. Hart surveyed the group with a quizzical look. "What is it, Beau?"

Beau cleared his throat, scratched his head, and studied his muddied boots for a moment. "Um, I don't want to suggest anything

… no, maybe I do want to suggest it. Maybe you shouldn't go see Old Longwood until the Missus is back in town."

Wils drew in a breath, seeming to understand. "Ah, good idea, Beau."

"What are you talking about?" Timothy and Hart chorused almost in unison.

Beau screwed his face up as if preparing to take castor oil. "It doesn't exactly sound to me like the lady is keeping house … exactly … if you know what I mean."

Unbidden rage lifted Timothy from his chair, and he leveled a hard stare at his friend. "I thought a *gentleman* didn't speak ill of a lady, Beau, especially one he doesn't even know." But even as he ground out the words, truth smacked him full in the face. The last thing Longwood had said to him today was, "We all understand a young man can be lonely away from home." Had he meant for Consuela to provide more than tutoring?

"Now, Jake," Beau said, lifting both hands in a calming gesture. "Forget I said anything." His boyish face wore a paternal expression. "But just think about it."

Timothy's hackled posture slumped, and humiliation flamed in his face. But this revelation—for he had not the slightest doubt Beau's conjecture was correct—solved his problem. He most definitely would not return to Longwood's house, no matter what he owed the captain. But how would he excuse himself?

April 1858

"Sit still." Jemima laughed at Stef's fumbling attempt to hold the loop of wool over his hands while she rolled it into a ball. "You said you've done this before, but you keep causing tangles."

Seated across from her in the parlor of the Harrises' new home on Chambers Street in the West End, Stef gave her an innocent grin. "Never said I did it *well*."

She laughed again. "Some help you are. You would be more help to Uncle Jeremiah over at the mission."

"Ah, but since he has moved his charming family to this neighborhood, we have no lovely young ladies to keep company with over there." Stef's smile seemed more serious now, and his brown-eyed gaze more intense.

Jemima softened her own smile and studied her lopsided ball of dark blue yarn. In the past few months—no, longer than that—since the night last fall when Stef rescued her from those horrid people on North Street, his attentions had increased. Several times, she had ignored certain of his remarks, and she regularly read Timothy's letters to him. But Reverend Estevam Lazarus seemed to disregard her attempts to deflect his courting.

Even worse was the effect of his visits on thirteen-year-old Molly, for Stef treated her like a child and was far too solicitous of her blindness. Yet Molly's devotion to Stef equaled Jemima's feelings for Timothy. If Stef would only notice what a capable young lady Molly was becoming, perhaps he would turn his attentions to her or at least wait for her to reach courting age.

"You're very quiet. Have I said something wrong?"

She wound the last few feet of yarn onto the ball before answering. "Not at all. It's just that …" She must be forthright with him. "Perhaps I have misinterpreted your visits. If so, please forgive me. You know I love Timothy, and while we are not yet betrothed, we do have an understanding."

Stef took the ball of yarn and tossed it from one hand to the other, his sober expression contradicting his playful action.

"An understanding. Yes." He squeezed the yarn as if trying to make it round. At last he leveled a somber gaze into her eyes. "I love Timothy too. He, my little brother, and I used to be inseparable. When Pal died, I felt as if a huge chunk had been cut out of me. Timothy and I grieved together many times. Still, I know when God calls me home to heaven, Pal will be there waiting for me."

Jemima reached out to pat his hand, and he relaxed his grip on the yarn.

"If I could be sure Timothy is a Christian too, I would deny my own heart …" Stef set the ball of yarn on the table beside him. "Forgive me. As much as I care for you, I must remember what is most important—my cousin's salvation."

Jemima drew back. "But why do you say that? Timothy and I have discussed this, and he assures me that all is well. Some people don't express their religious convictions as easily as others."

Stef's gaze became pastoral. "He expresses himself quite admirably on matters that interest him."

Jemima grabbed the yarn from the table and stuffed it into the large cloth bag beside her. "There. Three pounds of wool rolled and ready to be knitted into a fine, warm sweater for his midshipman cruise. Captain Lazarus tells me it can get very cold out on the ocean even in the summer." She stood and would have walked away, but Stef caught her hand.

"What if you're wrong?" His dark eyes radiated concern and brotherly affection. "At least pray about it."

She loosed her hand from his grasp. "As the apostle Paul said, 'God forbid that I should sin against the Lord in ceasing to pray' for him."

Stef pursed his lips, and his eyes twinkled. "Um, that's the prophet Samuel you're quoting. Old Testament."

"Oh." Jemima's face grew warm, but she giggled, then quickly sobered. "Dearest Stef, I do 'pray without ceasing' for Timothy. Now *that* is the apostle Paul. First Thessalonians. New Testament." She tried to give him a playful smirk, but only tears would come. "You pray too."

"Sweet Jemima, I have done so since childhood."

June 1858

Isaiah placed his new wool sweater in his duffel bag, making sure not to snag it on the metal end of his rolled-up razor strop. The dark blue garment was flawless, but even with stitches all askew, he would treasure it, for Lacy had made it with her own hands. He took it out again, held it to his face, and breathed in the earthy smell of sheep, a nostalgic scent reminding him of Nantucket's annual sheep-shearing celebration. But the sweater also bore the fragrance of Lacy's perfume, and he could imagine her delicate hands lovingly looping each stitch from needle to needle ... all for him.

A wavy pattern surged across the sweater front like breakers on the beach, and Isaiah's heart stirred with excitement. Soon he would be back out on the ocean, feeling for the first time since his youthful whaling voyage the freedom of the endless seas. But more than anything, he would finally show his classmates what being in the navy was all about. For, of the forty-two newly promoted third-class students, only he and Ahab had ever hoisted a sail or climbed rigging.

But memories of Lacy vied with his excitement about the cruise. At the ball, she had looked even more beautiful than he recalled. He could not imagine why she cared enough to make the winter railroad trip from Boston, but clearly she did care. And why had Reverend Harris put himself out to bring Jemima and Lacy so far just for one social event? Perhaps good fortune had smiled on Isaiah at last.

He had endured a few unsettling moments alone with the pastor, whose intense gaze seemed to bore deep into his soul. But somehow he had passed the interview, responding in a satisfactory manner to questions about his spiritual condition. Or so it seemed. Thank his lucky stars for Mother's Bible reading to Jemima and him all through their childhood. He did not resent the reverend's grilling at all. One day when he had a daughter of his own, he would put her suitors through their paces with an even sterner hand.

On her visit, lovely Lacy had been all the more endearing because of her pretty confusion over the language of the academy. She who had always understood his quaint Nantucket sayings could not seem to grasp the way each class was referenced.

"But, Isaiah …" She had sat beside him, blond curls bobbing and dark eyes round and blinking. "… why are you called a fourth-class midshipman when you're only in your first year of school? And why are the boys … I mean, the *men* who are in their last year called first-class midshipmen when they've been here almost four years?"

He struggled to answer without chuckling at her sweet ignorance. "It's about rank. The lower the rank, the higher the number."

She still appeared confused, so he added, "Just think about it like this. It's better to be first class than fourth class in anything. Being first class means we will have arrived at the top. As for what we're called, our actual designation now is acting midshipmen, but when we graduate, we will be promoted to passed midshipmen."

"Oh."

Was he mistaken, or had a wily look darted across her pretty face? Was she joshing with him? But she gave him an innocent smile and suggested they join the other guests dancing to a Strauss waltz.

The memory of Lacy in his arms made Isaiah ache inside and out. How could he wait another year before seeing her again? But wait he must, and so he forced his mind to the task at hand: packing for the summer cruise.

As in years before, newly promoted first- and third-class midshipmen would sail on a practice cruise to Europe to learn seamanship, navigation, and gunnery. The academy's old but seaworthy training vessel was a 117-foot, sixteen-gun, three-masted sloop christened the *Preble*. The midshipmen had been warned to pack lightly, for their below-deck lockers would hold uniforms, toilet articles, and little else. One thing was certain. Isaiah would find room for his new blue sweater.

He glanced about to make sure he had left everything in order. His new roommate, Will Sampson, had already gone to the ship. Isaiah felt a pang of loneliness, missing Frank Bartholomew, who had dropped out shortly after the ball. Now he was truly alone here at the academy. Sampson, who gave Isaiah and Ahab some serious competition for first place in their class, already had a group of friends, some of whom disliked Isaiah because he had reported their disreputable behavior. Let them all put him in Coventry. Let them shun him as they did Alfred Mahan, a good, upright man in the first class. Isaiah would not break the rules or let others get by with doing it either.

The duffel bag tightly packed, he tied it closed, slung it over his shoulder, and headed out the door. In the hallway stood Ahab holding up a dark blue woolen sweater with a wavy pattern across its front.

"My girl knitted it for me." He spoke to several friends gathered around. "Pretty smart looking, don't you think?"

Isaiah returned to his room and slumped down in a chair, dropping his duffel bag to the floor. It didn't mean anything. Nothing at all. Jemima lived with Lacy. They did everything together. Naturally they would economize by dyeing their wool the same color. But why choose the same stitching pattern? It couldn't be Lacy's fault, for he had convinced her that he bore no ill feelings against the man she called Timothy Jacobs.

But Jemima knew better and had knitted Ahab a matching sweater anyway.

Chapter Seventeen

&

*I*saiah grabbed his dinner plate from the table and held it high, letting crockery bowls and pewter mugs slide past him and crash to the galley deck. While servants vainly strove to keep order, the first-class midshipmen downed their meal as the *Preble* plunged from wave crest to trough and back up again. Across the galley, Ahab kept his seat and laughed like a baboon at every plummet. Of the third class, only Isaiah and Ahab stayed at table and not just kept their stomachs but continued to eat their molasses-covered fat pork and hardtack. The rest of their class either hung over the side on the upper deck or clutched a chamber pot in their quarters.

With mess seat, locker, hammock, and watch station assigned to each of the ninety-seven midshipmen on board, Isaiah never had to rub shoulders with his adversary. His newfound good luck had placed them in different divisions for every part of the cruise. What did he care that none of his classmates paid attention to his ability to scale the ropes like a monkey and cling to the rigging no matter how rough the sea? He had earned the respect of Commander Craven, and Alfred Mahan, first captain among the first-class men, had given him more than a few nods of affirmation for his performances. Mahan's father, Colonel Dennis Hart Mahan, held a prominent, influential position on the West Point faculty up in New York, so Alfred's approval carried the weight of real military experience.

The *Preble* was scheduled to visit Plymouth, England; Brest, France; and Madeira, Spain, plus a few smaller ports. Once they reached Madeira, maybe Mahan would condescend to let him tag along for some sightseeing. They would be in port only for a short while, and Isaiah planned to purchase a Spanish mantilla for Lacy. With no experience in such matters, he hoped Mahan would at least suggest a reputable merchant.

For now he amused himself by watching the misery of those who shunned him. To those who mattered—and to himself—he had proved he had inherited his father's Nantucket seamanship, which no whaler or sailor of any other port could surpass.

Along with other three-man teams, Timothy, Hart, and Beau clambered up the ratlines to practice furling sail. On the deck below, first-class midshipmen scrutinized each team's performance. With longer legs and a lifetime of experience, Timothy reached the stirrups before his friends, but soon all three stood on the footrope below the spar and gathered the heavy, coarse sail into place.

"Keep fast that tricing-line!" cried Midshipman Mahan from below.

"Look lively," Timothy prodded. "We have to beat Wilson's team."

With a stiff wind stirring up enough spray to make the exercise a wet adventure, the three youths slung gaskets around the furled canvas, tied them securely, and each raised a hand in triumph. Then, just as Hart reached for a line to begin his descent, the *Preble* heeled sharply to starboard. His feet slipped off the footrope and he flailed about, grasping the rigging with only one hand. Timothy and Beau leapt to his aid and clutched his forearms while his feet dangled wildly.

"Help!" Hart stared at the deck far below, his eyes wide with terror.

"Don't look down," Timothy ordered. "Look at me, Hart. Look at me." He gripped his friend with both hands and wove his own legs securely in the rigging.

"God, help us, please!" cried Beau. "Mercy, Lord, mercy."

On the deck, a first-class midshipman shouted orders, and several men scrambled up to assist. Before they reached their endangered shipmate, Timothy bent forward, grasped him around the waist, and hauled the smaller man into the ropes. Hart trembled violently, but he seized the wet lines in a death grip while Timothy and Beau slung their arms around him.

"I'll never make it." Hart stared wild-eyed at Timothy. "I might as well drop out now."

"I do declare, boy." Beau's almost-jovial tone belied the fear on his face. "If you're planning to drop out, don't do it this way."

Timothy and Hart both tried to laugh, but their relief erupted in choking sobs. "You'll be all right. Hush, now." Timothy jerked his head in the direction of one ascending first classman. "Don't let him see your fear."

"What's going on up here?" Mahan shouted. "Don't you men know better than to fool around? You could be killed with this kind of foolishness."

"Sir, begging your pardon, sir ..." Hart still clutched the lines to his chest. "I fell and these men saved my life."

Mahan's military mask slipped for only an instant, and Timothy saw real concern in his eyes. "I know what happened. Now get below, all of you." He swung out in the ropes while the three under-classmen descended. As they worked their way past him, he clasped their shoulders and murmured, "Good work, Jacobs, Beauchamp."

Below deck in their quarters, Hart lay in his hammock, arms crossed over his face. "I can't go back up there. I can't. I'm not a coward. I've faced mountain lions and rattlesnakes back home and climbed trees as high as that mast. But I can't hang on to slippery lines when a ship is pitching around like that. I just can't."

Timothy and Beau exchanged a look.

"Why, I do declare ..." Timothy parroted Beau's Southern drawl. "Never thought I'd hear Jackson Hartley say 'I can't.'"

Hart scowled at him. "Well, hear it now."

But after dark that night and many days following, Hart did climb the ratlines, with Timothy and Beau beside him, refusing to let him quit.

The *Preble* made the Atlantic crossing in a few short weeks, but food rations grew scarce. Never before in his life had Timothy been hungry, nor had he ever eaten weevily rice, wormy cheese, or rancid butter. Now he ate them to survive. At night he dreamed of Patience's mouth-watering chicken and dumplings or her spicy apple pie, only to awaken to a breakfast of salt horse or pork and beans. Prior to the cruise, he had tried to prepare himself to suffer what every midshipman would suffer, whether sleeping in stifling quarters, where hammocks hung just one foot apart, or eating rancid food. Never did he imagine how hungry they all would be.

Commander Craven, who had perfected the organization and training routines of the summer cruises, gave his usual orders to keep to sea as long as possible without entering port. While this was good practice in endurance for the midshipmen, the edict also prevented the ship's cooks from acquiring fresh supplies along the way. This year, coming alongside a small fleet of French fishing boats on the Banks, Craven permitted the purchase of some six hundred pounds of cod and halibut, all of which was devoured before the *Preble* reached Brest. The men arrived with empty stomachs and little money to remedy the situation. Like his classmates who planned to sell personal equipment and even articles of clothing, Timothy decided to relinquish his sextant to buy fresh fruit and bread once they docked. He felt tempted to sell his sweater, but how could he hurt Jemima by trading her gift just to quiet his aching stomach?

Many times he wished he had brought extra money aboard to buy food secretly from the ship's cooks, for he would have shared with those who needed it most. Other times, he and his friends grumbled that the navy would do well to feed its midshipmen better if those in charge expected said sailors to be of any use to the country. At last, hungry near to starving, he nonetheless embraced this enforced stoicism, determined not to be defeated by mere appetite.

Isaiah watched across the deck where Ahab and his friends languidly performed their duties. He laughed to himself at the plight of the hungry rich boys. What did they know of suffering? Which of their mothers had died of illness a few good meals might have cured? Yet for him, hunger had been a cruel friend that taught him endurance and fueled his ambitions for a better life. The gnawing in his belly infused him with a strength Ahab would never know. After his experience at the Doone house, he would never again sell his good judgment for a mess of potage.

Soon enough for him, and only him, the *Preble* made port at Brest, where he tucked his carefully saved money into his inside jacket pocket and set out to see the fair French city. Locating a street market, he perused the rows of vendors and then indulged himself with a fresh orange, a day-old loaf of bread, and a small block of cheese. Across the street, he noticed several of his shipmates as they bought long loaves of bread, hollowed them out, and stuffed bottles of wine inside to smuggle aboard the ship. He snorted his contempt. Those fools thought no one would report them, but they were wrong. If the captain wondered about their drunkenness, Isaiah would be glad to tell him how it came about. For his own beverage, he found that this town's public water, while it could not match Nantucket's spring water, tasted far better than the brackish residue at the bottom of the shipboard tanks.

The market also boasted stalls of fabric, lace, perfumes, glass figurines, and countless other items, with vendors eager to bargain. Isaiah wandered from one to the other, trying to imagine what Lacy might like. Never in his life had he dreamed he could buy such gifts for his loved one. On his long-ago whaling voyage, Captain Chase had bought many things for Mrs. Chase back home in Nantucket. Isaiah had only managed to carve a few scrimshaw items for Mother and Jemima. Yet now he longed to spoil Lacy with fine, rich presents, if only he could decide which to buy. At last, he surrendered to his indecision and determined to purchase the lace mantilla later in Madeira.

With all hands back on board, a little better nourished though not sated, the replenished *Preble* departed from Brest. Just windward of a dangerous point on the French coast, the ship hit heavy seas and a violent headwind that carried away part of the bowsprit rigging. With much struggle, the youthful crew held their stations and did not flinch, but hastily rigged substitutes for the two lost chain bobstays. As they sailed beyond the danger, Craven called the entire crew on deck for a prayer of thanks. "Had our bowsprit gave in, we never could have cut clear, my lads. We would have been lost. Consider that and bend your knee to thank God for his providence and mercy."

Hat in hand, Isaiah bowed on the deck with the rest of the crew, grateful for whatever power had saved the ship. But during this storm, he had not fully kept his stomach, and a fever kept creeping up from his bowels to his skull and back down again. Over the next hours and days, as the ship sailed southwestward toward Spain, he watched his shipmates to see if anyone else appeared ill. Other than the few who still had not mastered their *mal de mer*, none did. He kept to his duties, however, for no one would ever accuse him of slacking.

At the port of Madeira, he wandered ashore despite a blazing fever, but only as far as the open-air market on the docks. There he found a pretty black lace mantilla for Lacy. With no energy to bargain, he paid the first price the old woman vendor named. She seemed disappointed when he refused to haggle. Back on the ship, he spent the rest of the liberty time in his hammock, wishing his head would go ahead and explode, for then it would cease to pound.

The ship under way once again, Isaiah threw himself into his duties, riding fever waves like the ship rode the undulating seas. Off duty, he kept to his hammock and many times bemoaned his solitary life among so many people. Was there not one good-hearted man to notice his flushed complexion, his pouring sweat in the face of cold winds, his vomiting, diarrhea, and violent chills? Perhaps they all assumed he had at last succumbed to seasickness.

Fevered dreams of Lacy drifted through his mind, and he often did not know whether he was awake or asleep. He felt certain he sat at table and ate during his assigned times, but had no strength to prove it. Days and nights ran together in a hazy, unending fog.

The *Preble* sailed past the Azores and took a north by northwest heading. After their stormy adventures, the midshipmen cheered the calmer winds that blew them over milder waves than on their first crossing. At midway home, during the 4:00 p.m. abandon-ship drill, Isaiah heard someone order him to hoist sails. His mouth dry and his limbs aching, he nonetheless began to scramble up the rigging. Some fifty or sixty feet up, he heard shouts below and glanced down to see fiery-eyed devils beckoning him to Hades. Isaiah gasped and turned his face upward, only to see another devil leer at him from the rigging. He reached out to grasp the ropes, but none met his fingers. A great dark bird flew past his head, hissing, "Fly, Starbuck, fly."

With one last lunge for the ropes, he did fly, plunging to the deck in surrender to his tormenters. And the world turned black.

Timothy stood outside the captain's cabin, trembling and heart-sick. He had failed Jemima. If Isaiah died, how could she ever forgive him? Somehow he must convince Craven to sail to Boston, where the country's best physicians could heal Isaiah's injuries, whatever they might be.

Timothy had not seen the fall, but Wils reported that instead of taking his post for abandon-ship drill, Starbuck had climbed the ropes. By the time anyone noticed, he was about fifteen feet up and refused commands to come down. Then he lost hold and fell. Rumor had it Starbuck was still unconscious, so they would have to wait to learn what he was doing up there.

With a hesitant knock on the captain's cabin door, Timothy took a deep breath to steady himself.

"Enter."

Timothy ducked his head under the low door frame and moved to stand, hat under arm, before the captain's desk. "Sir, I'm distressed about my shipmate Starbuck's accident. I would like to offer a … um … a proposition to help out, if I may, sir."

Craven's eyes widened. "Why would you do that, Jacobs? This man is not your friend."

Timothy felt his own eyes widen, but he should not be surprised. Like Laz, this captain missed nothing that happened on his ship. "Well, sir, my girl is his sister and …" He paused, his face flaming at Craven's expression of disbelief. "… Miss Starbuck lives with my pastor's family in Boston, sir. She's Starbuck's only living relative."

"Hmm. I see. All right, then, what do you propose?"

Timothy cleared his throat, stalling. He had not thought this through. "Sir, I would like to offer to pay for whatever it costs for the *Preble* to sail up to Boston, where Miss Starbuck and Reverend Harris can make sure Starbuck sees the best physicians."

Craven's skeptical expression deepened. "Are you wasting my time, boy?"

Timothy shook his head vigorously. "No, sir. My family has money. They'll back my offer, I promise you."

"Why do you think they would take on such an expense?"

"Because, sir, that's the way they are." No need to boast of Mother and Laz's philanthropy.

Craven's gaze bored into Timothy, but Timothy did not flinch. Now that the words were out, he knew the plan was good.

Still studying him, Craven sat back in his chair. "I see no reason the *Preble* can't sail to Boston. One more practice at entering a busy harbor will do the lads some good." He sat forward. "Keep your money, Jacobs. Dismissed." He took up his pen and bent over the log before him.

"Sir?"

"What is it, boy?"

"Well, sir, as you noticed, Starbuck doesn't exactly ... uh ... like me. I'd just as soon he never knew I spoke to you."

Craven snorted. "Did you speak to me, Jacobs? Can't a captain come up with an idea to help a worthy midshipman injured in the line of duty? Now get out of here." The light in his eyes contradicted his gruff tone.

"Thank you, sir."

Timothy ducked back out of the cabin, his heart lightened. Craven's acceptance of his idea made him want to lift up a hearty cheer, but then his shipmates would want to know why. He could not risk Starbuck or anyone knowing what he had done.

In the dark passage, he turned toward the stairs. To his surprise, he bumped into Hart, whose face mirrored surprise and ... guilt?

"What are you doing?"

"Nothing. Polishing lamps." Hart brushed his sleeve over an unlit lantern hanging nearby and gave him a crooked grin.

"Hartley?"

"All right, then, I was listening."

Shoving him toward the stairs, Timothy blew out a long sigh. "Why don't you keep your nose where it belongs?"

Hart shrugged. "Dunno. Guess I'm still trying to figure out why you look out for that man. You're real decent, Jake, real decent."

"That's fine. Thank you. Now just keep your mouth shut. Swear it."

Hart shrugged again. "Who am I gonna tell? Starbuck?"

Timothy eyed him. "Have you heard how he's doing?"

"Sampson said he hasn't waked up yet. Say, it's a good thing Flusser's father is a doctor. Flusser told the first-class men not to lift Starbuck right after he hit the deck. Dr. Ross said he was right 'cause it could worsen the injuries. He had them put Starbuck on a plank and carried him down to sick bay. Said he has a bad fever, so maybe he was sick before. Maybe that's why he was acting crazy."

Timothy's heart dropped. He had promised Jemima he would keep an eye on Isaiah, but had he failed to notice an illness? If the man would only meet him halfway, this awful accident might never have happened. Timothy could not do it all himself. But that thought failed to cheer him. If Isaiah died, not only might Jemima never forgive him, he would never forgive himself.

Chapter Eighteen

ℰℐ

"Typhoid!"

The word spread quickly throughout the ship, and every man, including Timothy, searched his memory for any possible contacts with Starbuck. The ship's surgeon, Dr. Ross, ordered a scrub down of the midshipman quarters, told the cooks to clean everything in the kitchen with boiling water, and advised every man on board to report a fever or any other symptoms immediately. As the days wore on, no one else became ill, although Timothy felt heartsick to think that Isaiah's isolation, no matter how much he deserved it, had protected the rest of them.

One good piece of news circulated among the crew. Starbuck suffered no life-threatening injuries. Although bruises covered his body and he probably had several broken ribs and perhaps a mild concussion, his neck and back appeared sound, and no limbs had broken in the fall. Nevertheless, Dr. Ross told Captain Craven that Isaiah Starbuck would not report for fall term. When one classmate quipped that they could all breathe more easily now that the snitch was laid up, others rebuked him for his lack of feeling. Timothy wondered if they all felt as guilty as he did for not noticing Isaiah's illness.

With the injured man on board and the wind at their backs, Craven hastened the return crossing. In eight days, Boston Harbor came into view, and Timothy and his shipmates crowded the deck for their first glimpse of the United States in more than two months. Timothy's heart felt near to bursting to see his homeport after almost a year. With his second-class furlough a year away, he fought the torturous temptation to jump ship and go home. He longed to see his family, friends, and the home of his happy childhood. But most of all he ached to see Jemima and to comfort her when she learned of Isaiah's tragedy.

The *Preble* sailed into Charlestown Navy Yard, where Captain Craven hired an ambulance to transport Isaiah to the address Timothy had provided. Timothy watched from the deck and winced at each jolt of the invalid's stretcher, although he doubted the patient felt anything. In fact, Isaiah might have been a corpse except for the fever-blush on his pale face. During the voyage back to Annapolis, Hart, Beau, and Wils badgered Timothy with pranks and teasing, but they could not coax him from his depression.

Isaiah ached in every part of his body, but his head and ribs hurt worst of all. Had the pain subsided since its first violent hammering, or had he simply grown used to it? How long had he wandered in and out of consciousness, dreaming first of tormenting demons and then of ministering angels? Weakness permeated him. He couldn't even lift his hands or open his eyes. Was he dying? If so, death was not as dreadful as people thought, for then he could escape this misery.

He knew the ship was still at sea, for he could feel the motion of the waves. But his hammock felt softer, larger, even cleaner, and the stench of his sickness had been replaced by some mild floral scent. Had they put him in the captain's cabin?

For countless hazy days he had felt Dr. Ross bathe him and spoon broth between his benumbed lips, a kindness Isaiah would never forget. Sometimes he thought that Mother ministered to him in the physician's place or that Jemima sat beside him and washed his fevered brow. Pleasant dreams of childhood mingled with memories of Lacy in his arms, waltzing, whaling, sailing, and sighing.

The fever had lessened now, and the ocean had calmed. The fragrance of roses filled the cabin, eliminating every sea scent. A breeze—warm, but not unpleasant, caressed his cheeks, and cool, gentle fingers rested on his hand. A soft sniff, and perhaps a little sob, sounded nearby. He worked to open his eyes, blinking against the dim light of the room. Where was he? Who was this golden-haired angel gazing at him with tears in her lovely dark eyes?

"Lacy." His voice was a soft croak.

She bowed her head on the edge of the bed and whispered, "Thank you, Lord, thank you for your great mercy."

"Forgiveness." Reverend Harris stood on the low podium at the front of Grace Seamen's Chapel, his Bible before him on the lectern. "All of us need to receive it from God for our sins against him. All of us need to bestow it on others who have offended us in some way, whether great or small, whether in truth or in perception."

Isaiah's eyelids drooped, and he struggled to keep them open. Other than mandatory chapel at the academy, he was attending church for the first time in years. Reverend Harris spoke in such soothing tones that one could hardly call his speech a sermon. Lacy nudged him, held her Bible before him, and pointed to the verses as her father read.

"'Let all bitterness, and wrath, and anger, and clamour, and evil speaking, be put away from you, with all malice: And be ye kind one to another, tenderhearted, forgiving one another, even as God for Christ's sake hath forgiven you.'"

The pastor's gaze lingered on the book before him. Then he looked up and scanned the crowded chapel, a kindly smile on his lips. "These words of the apostle Paul to the Ephesians bespeak the very core of how we should live our faith. We are all lost sinners until saved by the grace of our Lord. Think of it, beloved, we believers have been forgiven for every sin we ever committed, every wrong thing we have done, every wrong thought we have given place in our minds. Who are we, then, to deny forgiveness to those we deem our enemies? Let us consider the parable of the unjust steward in Matthew eighteen."

While Lacy turned the pages of her Bible, Isaiah felt a pressure against his other arm. Seven-year-old Sammy leaned against him and gazed up with bright blue eyes just like his father's. Isaiah smiled back, enjoying the hero-worship the lad had heaped on him since the moment Isaiah first sat up in his sickbed. But Isaiah felt a large measure of admiration for the boy as well. Not only had he survived a sickly childhood, but now he flourished as if he needed to make up for lost years.

When Isaiah had been able to consider any matter beyond his own illness, he felt relieved that the boy had not wasted away. The loss of this brother would have broken Lacy's heart and devastated her loving family. But now, after weeks of convalescence, Isaiah found Sammy's energetic companionship indispensable to his own physical restoration. Lacy begged Isaiah not to exert himself and would have spoiled him with rich food and indolent pastimes. But this little scamp dragged him outdoors to play ball or run in the park. Even now, the lad's mischievous grin revealed his understanding that Isaiah would prefer to be active rather than sitting in a lengthy church service. Isaiah gave him a sober frown, but also winked.

"But in his wisdom …" Reverend Harris's words broke into Isaiah's reverie. "… God has ordained this powerful benefit: When we forgive our enemies, when we no longer carry the burden of bitterness against them, we are the ones who are set free. We are the ones who find peace within our hearts."

He concluded his sermon much sooner than Isaiah expected, but no one else seemed surprised. How gratifying to see a preacher who spoke briefly so folks could go home to dinner, their duty to

God completed. After a solemn hymn and a final prayer, the pastor dismissed the congregation, but no one seemed in a hurry to leave. A few even approached the front of the chapel to speak privately with Reverend Harris while the hundred or so other congregants chatted with their fellows. Sammy ran off to find a friend while Lacy looped her arm in Isaiah's and tugged him across the room.

"There is someone you must meet—a good friend of our family."

Something in Lacy's tone warned him, but it was too late to refuse. Beside Mrs. Harris stood a tall, elegant lady with auburn hair. She wore a dark green dress made of expensive-looking fabric, and her bonnet appeared new. Despite her fancy clothes, her pretty face seemed clouded with doubt as she stared straight at him.

"Mrs. Lazarus, this is my good friend, Isaiah Starbuck." Lacy urged his arm forward to take the lady's hand. "Isaiah, this is Mrs. Lazarus."

Isaiah felt a wave of weakness, but he took the offered hand, bowed over it in proper form, and muttered, "Mrs. Lazarus." When he stood back up, he blinked in surprise at the tears sparkling in her beautiful green eyes.

"Isaiah." She breathed out his name in a whisper, and her gaze exuded such kindness and warmth that a blush of shame rose up his neck. He could not hate this woman, no matter whom she had first married, no matter who her son was. Because of her generosity, Jemima's dream of becoming a teacher would one day be realized.

"We were so distraught to hear of your illness." Her expression reflected her words. "But I can see you've had the best of care. Will you be able to return to classes next week for the fall term?"

Isaiah shook his head. "No, ma'am. Like Miss Harris, these Boston physicians think I'm some fragile invalid who needs to be coddled a while longer. I should be back to classes by November."

"I do not think you are an invalid—" Lacy began.

"Isaiah!" Stef Lazarus strode over to the small group and extended his hand. "Good to see you in church, friend."

Isaiah reached out in response, grateful for the young minister's warm but gentle grasp. "Stef, good to see you, too."

"Has anyone seen Jemima?" Stef glanced around the room.

"She's still with the children," said Mrs. Harris. "They enjoy her Bible lessons so much. Isaiah, your sister has a wonderful gift for teaching. When she came up with the idea of taking the little ones out for story time during church, many young mothers greeted the idea with delight." She gave him an encouraging smile and bent her head toward Mrs. Lazarus.

He cleared his throat. "Teaching. Yes. She likes it." Lacy nudged him once more, and he shot her a look of annoyance. She was right, of course. He should say more.

"We're very grateful, Mrs. Lazarus." He hoped that was sufficient.

She gave him a beatific smile. "You're very welcome, Isaiah. We love our Jemima and want what's best for her."

"Thank you, ma'am."

Lacy squeezed his arm and beamed at him.

"Now for dinner," Mrs. Harris said. "Hannah, will you and your family join us? The girls will play nursemaid to the children so we can have a grand party. Do say yes. Stef, you're coming, aren't you?"

While the others chattered their agreement to the plan, Isaiah studied the affable young minister. Here was a fellow he would like for a brother, one well suited to Jemima. In spite of his sickness and injuries, Isaiah decided good fortune had brought him here to give his sister guidance. He must convince her she would make a fine minister's wife, like Lacy's mother.

He glanced at Mrs. Lazarus. Despite a family resemblance, her flawless face bore no trace of her son's arrogance. How could such a refined, elegant lady have married Captain Ahab, that mad old whaler, or given birth to such a pompous dandy? He had heard it said there was no accounting for another person's taste, so his question had no plausible answer. But he would spend these next months doing all he could to ensure Jemima did not make the same mistake as Hannah Lazarus. He would spend time with Stef and commend him to Jemima at every opportunity. With Ahab away for another year, surely she would forget him. He would see to it.

Chapter Nineteen

SO

Spring 1859

S top, Beau, just stop it. I am sick to death of hearing about states' rights." Timothy clenched his fists but stayed seated in his barracks room chair. "How can you be so thick-skulled? The only issue is this: Enslaving another person is wrong—it's nothing but evil—and slavery needs to be abolished, not just in our Southern states but all over the world."

Across the table, Beau shook his head and stared down at his hands. After a few moments, he raised his eyes and looked at Timothy with that irksome, paternal expression of his.

"You've never understood, Jake, maybe never will. I know you read that book *Uncle Tom's Cabin*, and it's got you all in a dither." Beau glanced over at Hart and Wils, who reposed on the room's two beds, as if to enlist their aid in the debate. "But that little lady who wrote it, that Mrs. Stowe, she only saw a few bad apples. She never saw how it is for most of us. Do you think your Northern factory owners treat their workers any better than Simon Legree treated his chattels in that made-up story? Cruelty is cruelty, but you Northerners don't get rid of it by burning down the factory, do you?"

"Burning down the factory—?"

"If you take away our workers, you destroy our Southern economy, and that's the same thing."

"So you admit it. This is how you justify keeping slaves—your economy. Your way of life. What about the lives of your slaves?"

Beau blew out a long breath. "Listen, my friend, each of us has to answer to God for how we handle our responsibility, and my family takes care of all its members ..."

"Family? Balderdash!"

"You think my family is balderdash?" Beau's face lit up with annoyance. "Listen, my boy Cordell is like a brother to me—"

Timothy jumped up, slammed his fist on the table, and glared at his friend. "Can't you hear yourself? Your *boy*—your *slave*, you mean—is like a *brother?*" He leaned nearer, almost nose to nose with Beau. "What if your *brother* decides he wants to go north and—"

Hart and Wils jumped up and moved close to the table. Timothy stood straight and drew in a deep breath. "Don't worry. I'm not going to hit him." He jerked around and ran his hands through his hair. He must calm down. He had almost given away the family's secret enterprise.

A hand clamped on his shoulder, and he turned to see Beau's pained expression. With difficulty, he did not pull away.

"You're my good friend, Jake. I never want to lose your friendship. We've had this conversation too many times. Let's put it to rest."

"Good idea." Hart stepped over and elbowed Timothy good-naturedly. "Let's quit thinking about being from Massachusetts or Louisiana ..." He jerked his head toward Wils. "... Maryland or Vermont. We're all Americans."

Wils bobbed his head. "Isn't that why we're here at the Naval Academy, letting these old fellows put us through such a rough course? We haven't dropped out like some, but we couldn't have made it without each other."

"And when we graduate," Hart said, "we'll all go on to defend the United States—*united* together in the navy. My country, right or wrong, isn't that right?"

"Right," Wils echoed.

Beau appealed to Timothy with a look, then grinned. "Right."

Timothy heaved out a great sigh. "Right."

An awkward silence descended on the room until Wils began to hum a familiar tune. At the end of the first bar, they all joined in:

Come all you gallant middies who are going on furlough:
We'll sing the song of liberty; We're going for to go.

They hung on one another's shoulders and stumbled out into the hallway where other school-weary midshipmen joined the raucous, cheerful, discordant song.

Take your tobacco lively and pass the plug around;
We'll have a jolly time tonight before we're homeward bound.
Our sweethearts waiting for us, with eyes brimful of tears,
Will welcome us back home again from an absence of two years.

The mood spread throughout the barracks, and an impromptu stag ball was staged, with music from one midshipman's fiddle and refreshments from several bottles of forbidden spirits. No one bothered to study that evening except one or two like Starbuck, who closed their doors to the bedlam.

Back in his room later that night, Timothy stared up at the ceiling, unable to sleep. Maybe Beau was right. Not about slavery, of course, but about letting the argument rest. If lawmakers in Congress could not solve this slavery problem for the country, what could two eighteen-year-olds do? He and Beau had argued because they were tired of schooling and needed their upcoming furlough. In two weeks, he would be off to Boston to reunite with Jemima and his family. Come October, he would begin his next-to-last year of study. Where had the time gone?

Timothy's heart felt near to bursting. At last he was back home with his loved ones, seated in Grace Seamen's Chapel with Jemima

on one side and his family on the other. Laz's weathered face wore a
few more wrinkles, and both he and Mother showed a bit more gray
in their hair. Matthew, who had recently turned ten, took pride in
his position as the household's eldest child. Eight-year-old Deborah
was a poised miniature of their mother. As for four-year-old Gracie,
ah, well, surely she would settle down soon. Added to his happiness
was the upcoming sermon, for Uncle Jeremiah had stepped aside this
Sunday to give Stef some preaching experience. Recalling his
cousin's scruffy childhood appearance, Timothy thought Stef had
become a fine-looking minister—not as tall as his father and uncle,
but with their noble, Nordic brow and his mother's dark Portuguese
coloring. In his well-cut black suit, he made an impressive sight.

Across the aisle, Isaiah sat with the Harris family, his eyes forward
and his posture military straight. Timothy had hoped that Jeremiah's
influence and preaching would get through to Isaiah during his
convalescence last fall, but when he came back to the academy, he
still held onto his senseless grudge. Perhaps Stef's message today
would smack Isaiah in the face, and he would finally grow up.
Timothy turned his eyes toward the front and listened expectantly.

As Stef opened his Bible, he announced the passage, 1 Kings
16:28, and pages fluttered throughout the room. Glancing sideways,
Timothy noticed with annoyance that Lacy held her Bible in front
of Isaiah. She deserved better than this obstinate fellow, and
Timothy might just tell her so one of these days. For now, he minded
his own Bible and shared it with Jemima.

"So Omri slept with his fathers, and was buried in Samaria: and
Ahab his son reigned in his stead."

Timothy's head jerked up, he stared at Stef, and his ears seemed to
ring, shutting out all sound for a moment. Why had Stef chosen to
preach on this king of Israel today? After many years of keeping
Father's name a secret, had Mother or Laz, Jeremiah or Aunt Kerry,
told Stef the truth? He knew Jemima had not said anything because

she had promised never to tell a soul. Indeed, she was so thoughtful of his feelings, she never even brought up the subject.

"And Ahab the son of Omri did evil in the sight of the Lord above all that were before him—"

Now Timothy's jaw went slack, and he blinked. A movement to his side caught his attention, and he glanced over as a smirk flashed across Isaiah's face. With heat rising up his neck, Timothy clenched his jaw and turned back to the front. Had Isaiah said something to Stef? But that could not be. Even if Isaiah had blurted out the truth, Stef would never knowingly hurt him.

Timothy sat benumbed, barely hearing the remainder of the verses Stef read. At last he forced himself to pay attention, for Jemima would want to discuss the sermon later. Even now, her sweet smile revealed her innocence. He was being foolish. Stef could preach about whatever he wished and would do a good job of it in the bargain.

"And so we must ask ourselves, for which evil deed, what wicked act, did God curse Ahab that he should suffer such a shameful death and the loss of his eternal soul?"

Wicked. That word had haunted Timothy all his life. Why had Father been named for this evil biblical king? Had his name prophesied his character? Had he been wicked too?

"Was it because he married a foreign princess and followed her in idolatry?"

Well, never mind that. Mother is a saint. She never did a wrong thing in her life.

"Was it because he murdered God's prophets?"

Why did Isaiah now cast that smug look at him? He said my father murdered his. I suppose he thinks his father was some sort of prophet.

"Was it for coveting Naboth's vineyard and murdering him to obtain it?"

My father worked hard. He earned his wealth. He was honest. Laz told me. The only thing he ever killed was whales.

"Was it for his refusal to acknowledge God after lightning burned Elijah's water-soaked sacrifice?"

Lightning! Father's face had borne a scar because he was struck by lightning at sea. Timothy felt a shiver run up his spine.

"Listen to what God said to Ahab in 1 Kings 21:20–21: 'Because thou hast sold thyself to work evil in the sight of the LORD. Behold, I will bring evil upon thee.' Verse 22: 'Thou hast provoked me to anger, and made Israel to sin.'"

Stef gazed around the room, his eyes blazing. "Ahab *made Israel to sin.* He was to be the leader of God's people, and yet he led them astray, bringing on himself and on all the people of Israel great suffering and judgment. Like Lucifer, he exalted himself above God. His great evil, his great wickedness, was that he rejected who God is—our sovereign Creator and Lord. He rejected his God-ordained responsibility to his people."

Stef scanned the room again, and his gaze lingered on Timothy for the briefest instant. "And so, beloved, what of us? Are we like Ahab? Do we fail to acknowledge who God is? Do we exalt ourselves above him? Do we lead others to do the same?"

Timothy lifted his chin and shot a glance toward Isaiah. *My father was a great captain and a great whaler. Mother says every man in Nantucket wanted to sail with him. And I always take care of my responsibilities. No one can ever say I led them astray.*

"No. Never. We are good. We are righteous. We do not partake of wickedness as Ahab did. But does that make us any more righteous than he? Or are we like those of whom the apostle Paul speaks in 2 Timothy 3:5, 'Having a *form* of godliness, but denying the power thereof'? Do we merely go through the motions of goodness?" He paused and then leaned forward over the lectern. "Brethren, we do not earn our salvation through good behavior—"

Timothy expelled a quiet sigh. *Yes, Stef, that's the biblical person to talk about. Timothy, a man who did what God wanted him to do, just like me. Maybe Isaiah will get your message.* He glanced down at Jemima, moved by the tears now sparkling in her eyes. She was worried about her brother, but she need not fear. Unlike the wicked King Ahab of Israel, Timothy would be a good, wise leader. He would watch over Isaiah whether Isaiah liked it or not.

Jemima's heart ached, but she put on her best smile and helped gather the children for their carriage ride to the Harris home for Sunday dinner. When Stef had announced the Scripture verse for his sermon, she feared it would cause Timothy pain, and from his expression earlier, it probably had. Why, oh, why had his father been named after that wicked king? Even Aunt Charity, one of the last of Captain Ahab's generation still alive in Nantucket, had not been able to answer Jemima's question. In fact, Aunt Charity could not even recall the last name of Ahab's father, for she had been a small child when Ahab had been left a year-old orphan. Although descended from the island's earliest English settlers, the captain had never laid claim to Macy, Coffin, Folger, or Starbuck, and none of them had claimed him. What a tragic legacy for Timothy to carry.

Seated beside him on the driver's bench, Jemima glanced back at the others crowded into the large, open landau. Matthew and Deborah could be counted on to behave, but Grace was a handful. Molly, however, seemed to have a way with her. Instead of scolding the little one, Molly took her on her lap and asked her to describe the passing sights, and Grace gave intelligent answers for one so small. Jemima decided she herself would use that clever ploy with difficult pupils one day.

Daisy and Sammy, the two youngest Harris children, squabbled playfully, and Isaiah had eyes only for Lacy. Before they left the chapel, an awkward moment had passed when both Timothy and Isaiah seemed inclined to drive. Then Lacy took charge and told everyone where to sit. Jemima laughed to herself. Lacy might not have been raised in Nantucket, but she was a true Nantucket girl.

Behind the landau, Captain Lazarus drove another carriage for his wife, Reverend and Mrs. Harris, and Stef. Jemima's heart went out to Stef. His place was with the adults, but she knew he would prefer to be with the young people. She smiled and waved to encourage him.

"Good old Stef." Timothy leaned toward her and spoke softly. "It's hard for me to see him as a preacher when I remember the scrapes we got into as boys."

"But don't you think he preached a fine sermon this morning?"

Timothy shrugged. "His discourse was a little awkward, but he'll improve with practice."

"Why, Timothy …" She must not scold. The sermon had indeed bothered him.

"I suppose he visits the Harris home often these days?"

Jemima's face grew warm, and she turned away so her bonnet brim would hide her blush. His crossness did not concern the sermon or his father after all.

"I saw the way he looked at you after the service. I never thought …"

"How true. You never thought. And you don't need to. It isn't Reverend Lazarus's midshipman ball I have attended for two years in a row, braving the cold of winter to come to Annapolis, I might add." She turned to face him, and his dark scowl dismayed her. "Stef is your best friend."

He nodded, but did not respond. Jemima sighed. How difficult it must be for him to come home and discover, without a word being spoken, that his cousin was in love with her. But she never encouraged Stef beyond friendship.

Timothy's large, strong hands gripped the laces, and he drove the horses as if he had never been away. A wave of admiration surged through her. How handsome he was, how capable, and how she loved him for it. Yet this bit of insecurity endeared him to her all the more. *Lord, please show me how I can reassure Timothy that my heart belongs only to him.*

Timothy could not swallow the knot in his throat, for it was not caused by Mrs. Cook's savory roast beef. He couldn't blame Stef for falling in love with Jemima. She was the most beautiful, loving, smart young lady in the whole world. But she was also young— sixteen in a few weeks. Although she seemed to love Timothy now, perhaps she would be swayed by Stef's smooth talking.

A twinge of guilt pricked Timothy. He should not have belittled his cousin's fine preaching. What a childish thing to do. The time had come to do something befitting a man. After dinner, with the younger children upstairs for naps, the adults chatting on the broad, covered front porch, and younger adults playing parlor games, he asked Jemima to give him a tour of the Harrises' new neighborhood. Although Stef had frowned at their departure, Isaiah appeared relieved to see them go.

Despite the June heat, they walked around the block, commenting on architecture, landscape, foliage, and other banalities, as when they first had met. At last they found a small shady park and sat on a stone bench. For some reason, Jemima still held her ivory parasol between them. When he gently moved it aside, she peeked around her bonnet brim, and a coy smile graced her face. Had she guessed his plan?

"You know," she said, "you cannot avoid my brother this entire summer."

Not coyness, after all. "He seemed pleased to see us leave. Or at least me."

"Yes." Jemima sighed. "But he'll see plenty of me. Beside, it's Lacy's company he prefers."

Timothy brushed his already-clean trouser leg, then gazed up at the sky, removed his hat, and ruffled his sweat-dampened hair in the warm breeze. "Nice day. A little warm—"

Jemima giggled. "Nice day, indeed. Why are you so nervous? I know you don't wish to discuss this morning's sermon, for you've already said enough about that."

"Will you marry me?" Timothy could hear his heart pounding, but nothing else. Had he said the words or only thought them?

"What?" Jemima's face grew pale, then pink, and her dark eyes were round.

The lump returned to his throat, and he could not repeat himself. He turned away, wanting to apologize for his clumsiness, but afraid to speak again.

She took his arm and tugged him back to face her. "Of course I'll marry you ... when you graduate from the academy." She gave her head a little shake. "You do mean then, don't you? Not now."

"Yes. Then. Not now."

Her blush had faded to a happy glow, and her smile beamed sunshine into his heart. "So then," he said, "we may now consider ourselves more than sweethearts. We are betrothed."

Her blush returned. "Does that mean you wish to kiss me?" Her expression seemed so sweetly hopeful, he laughed.

"Ah, um, well ..." Yes, indeed, he wished to kiss her, but that might prove dangerous. "I might give you a little peck on the cheek before I go home today."

She laughed, seeming to understand. "Why, Mr. Jacobs, then everyone would know we're betrothed."

"Hmm. Hadn't thought of that." A lie, but not a bad one. "But we don't need to keep it a secret. Mother and Laz have been expecting this for nearly two years. And of course I'll ask Uncle Jeremiah for your hand."

"Uncle Jeremiah? But—" She released a deep sigh and gazed

across the park, her eyes filled with sadness. "Yes. Best to ask Uncle Jeremiah. Isaiah would never say yes, and he knows it would be useless to say no."

Timothy took her hand and pulled it up to his lips. "No one will be surprised, not even Isaiah. If people can't see we're in love, well, they just need to put on their spectacles."

"Just to be sure, let's go tell them." Jemima jumped up from the bench, tugged him to his feet, and looped her arm through his. "Goodness. Who would have thought this hot day would turn out to be so pleasant?" She stopped and faced him. "Oh, my goodness, I just realized something!"

"What is it?" Timothy's heart stood still. She would not change her mind, would she?

"Just a while ago, I asked the Lord for some way to show you that my heart belongs only to you, and look at how he has answered. Oh, Timothy ..." She pulled her bonnet off, stood on tiptoes, and kissed his cheek. "I know I shouldn't do that, but I'm so very, very happy, and I love you so very, very much."

His throat filled with an unexpected lump, and he bent down to put his forehead against hers for one sweet instant. "And I, as well, my darling, my love." He straightened, pulled up her hand for another kiss, then offered his arm. "Miss Starbuck, shall we go tell the world our happy news?"

With a radiant smile, she looped her arm in his again. "Mr. Jacobs, what a grand idea!"

Chapter Twenty

ℰ

October 1859

Isaiah dropped his duffel bag on his bed, pulled out its contents, and began to stow them in proper order in his barracks room. He saw that Sampson was already back, as evidenced by his neatly placed books and gear. He probably had searched for his friends as soon as he returned, not caring if his roommate came back or not. But after a summer in Boston with Lacy's family, Isaiah's heart felt full. What grand times they'd had, despite Ahab's constant presence.

Early in the summer, he had resigned himself to Jemima's engagement to that fool. Still he held out hope that Stef might win her heart through some miracle. He had made sure Molly and Daisy accompanied them all on every outing so Stef would not feel like the odd man. As for Lacy, Isaiah had not dared to ask her to marry him. Such youthful pledges could be made by rich boys and officers, but Isaiah had yet to earn his place. Still, he felt certain he owned her affections, if not her love.

This academy year would be a challenge, but Isaiah faced it without a qualm. He needed to make up for several courses he missed last fall, but by next summer's first-class cruise, he should be caught up with his classmates. His gunnery skills needed some honing, but only Sampson could touch him in his academics. Ahab had fallen behind in Spanish and received several demerits in deportment, dropping to third place. Unlike him, Isaiah never wasted time with foolish games or carousing around Annapolis with friends. If a man didn't keep his nose in the books, how could he expect promotions?

"Say, Starbuck." Sampson burst through their bedroom door, a smile on his face and his arm extended. "Good to see you, fellow. We're trying to scare up a game of baseball. Come join us. What do you say?"

Isaiah stared at his roommate's outstretched hand as if unable to identify what it was. Lacy's voice echoed in his mind. *Oh, do try to be sociable, Isaiah. You must let people know what a fine fellow you are.* Sampson gave him a quizzical look, so he stepped over to accept his handshake.

"I don't know, Samp. Do you play the Massachusetts Game or the New York Game? You know baseball began in Boston, so we Massachusetts folks have the original. If you don't use the overhand pitch, it's a sissy's game."

Samp guffawed. "Don't say that too loudly or Smitty's bound to challenge you, and we'll end up with fisticuffs instead of playing ball."

Isaiah found himself laughing, and it felt good. "Give me a minute. I'll be right down."

"Good man. Hurry up, now. They're choosing sides." Samp gave Isaiah's shoulder a playful slap on his way out and ran down the hall toward the stairs.

Isaiah stared into the mirror above his washstand. What a stupid grin he had on his face. But, like the laughter, it felt good. His roommate had invited him to play ball.

"Old Longwood got the sack?" Hart leaned back against the railing of the dormitory porch and shook his head in disbelief. "Who would have thought such a thing?"

"Now I didn't say he got the sack," said Beau. "I said he's not on the faculty anymore. Maybe he's had more health problems. Wasn't that why he left active duty, Jake?"

Timothy shrugged, not wanting to join the conversation. "That's what I understood. I haven't really spoken with him about personal matters for over a year."

"Well, I'll wager he got the sack," said Wils. "In a town as small as Annapolis, it's hard to hide it when a man's living with his ... with a lady who's not his wife."

"And he's supposed to be an example for us?" Hart said with a snort. "Reprehensible."

"The least he could have done was to keep it a secret." Beau said. "There is such a thing as discretion."

"Say, Jake," said Wils, "aren't you glad you cooled your friendship with him?"

Again, Timothy shrugged, and with his movement, the papers inside his jacket crinkled, a sound only he seemed to notice.

"Say, they're marking out a game of baseball over there." Beau pointed toward the parade ground. "Let's go." He started across the field with Hart and Wils behind him.

"Coming, Jake?" Hart called.

"Maybe in a bit." Timothy watched until his friends became involved in the game, and then pulled out two letters. The first had been in his mailbox when he returned to the academy yesterday and had come from Captain Longwood, asking Timothy to visit him. The second and more troubling letter arrived this morning. In it, Señora Cervantes implored him to visit Longwood but gave no reason. Should he go?

He had tried to keep his nose clean, but things kept coming up that made breaking the rules seem reasonable at the time. He would never regret catching the scalawag who got that Doone girl in trouble. Or hauling Wils in over the wall that time he got drunk and couldn't walk on his own, even though it looked as if Timothy—who had signed the midshipman temperance pledge—had been out carousing too. Or the time he had joined his friends in dumping garbage on the front stoop of an Annapolis merchant who had over-charged a midshipman and refused to return the money. That time he deserved the demerits, but they had been a badge of honor among his fellows.

Now he must decide whether to risk visiting Longwood or to ignore him. Perhaps he could have won his own academy appointment, perhaps not. But Longwood had secured it for him and had vouched for him before Blake. He owed the man a great debt. But fraternizing with a man in disgrace, if indeed Longwood had been dismissed in disgrace, might jeopardize Timothy's future. What would Laz say to all this? While spending the summer at home, he had grown used to consulting with Laz, as in his childhood. But the urgency of Señora Cervantes' letter gave no time for an exchange of letters.

Timothy watched the ball game for a while, surprised and pleased to see Isaiah in the thick of it. Yet he had no wish to join in, even though they did not have to report for duty for a few hours. Without a conscious decision, he stood and walked toward the gated archway at the academy entrance. With each step his confidence grew that he was doing the right thing, the responsible thing. A man should never let a debt go unpaid.

Longwood now resided on Market Street at the city's edge in a white clapboard house, clean and tidy, but far less elegant than his brick mansion in town. Señorita Consuela, shy but serene, admitted Timothy, took his hat, showed him to the parlor, and went to summon her mother. When Anna Cervantes entered, her resemblance to his own mother struck him once again. Her graying auburn hair was swept up in a pretty arrangement and adorned with a tortoiseshell comb, and her gown was a black morning dress, much worn and slightly out of fashion.

"Mr. Jacobs." She extended her hand in a halting manner, as if she doubted he would take it.

He grasped her slender fingers, bowed, and brought her hand to his lips. "Señora."

At his greeting, her shoulders relaxed, and the furrow in her brow softened. "Please be seated. Of course you wonder why we asked you to come."

Timothy sat on the tattered divan. "Yes, ma'am."

The woman glided into a chair across from him. Tears glistened in her eyes, but she gave him a sweet, sad smile. "Please do not believe the rumors concerning our Captain Longwood."

"Rumors?"

She laughed softly and put her finger to her lips. "Shh. Do not pretend. We know what is whispered about us."

Timothy's face burned. Perhaps coming here was a mistake after all.

"The academy did not dismiss Captain Longwood. He resigned his position." She looked down at her hands. "They permitted him that dignity."

He tugged at his collar. This room lacked ventilation.

"I do not know, at least not completely, why my Duncan cares so much for you. But even when we met so long ago in Mexico, he often mentioned an exceptional young boy in Boston." She gazed at him and spoke in a tranquil manner. "Are you his son?"

Timothy coughed, certain he would suffocate. When he could catch his breath, he shook his head with vehemence. "No, ma'am, most certainly not. I knew my father, and I am his spitting image."

She smiled, unmoved by his distress. "*Si*, yes, I believe you. Then it was another reason that perhaps I shall never know."

Timothy scooted forward on the divan, preparing to leave, but Señora Cervantes held up her hand. "Stay. Please. He desires to speak with you."

He swallowed hard and chewed his lip. "Ma'am, I'm not sure—"

She lifted her chin and arched her eyebrows. "Captain Longwood wishes it, and he shall have it." Her imperious tone resonated throughout the room, reminding him of Queen Victoria.

She escorted him to the second floor where, in the front bedroom, Longwood lay in a large, iron-framed bed, his eyes closed.

Timothy drew back. How changed the captain was from just last spring. Very little black remained in his hair, and even in repose, new wrinkles were visible around his eyes. His complexion, so often tanned by his life at sea, was sallow, almost ashen. Timothy turned to leave, but Señora stood in the doorway. When he turned back, Longwood had stirred and now beckoned him to sit by the bed. The sickroom smelled surprisingly fresh. Señora must work hard to keep it so.

"Are you well, my boy?" The strong, authoritative voice had faded to a whispered croak.

"Yes, sir." Timothy took a silent, deep breath to control his distress. "And you ...?"

Longwood chuckled, which brought forth an unpleasant cough. "As you can see, I am *not* well."

"Yes, sir, I can see that." He settled in the chair. "Sir, what can I do for you? Do you need a physician? I can arrange it ..."

Longwood shook his head. "I am not destitute, despite appearances. The physicians have done what they can. They attempt to cheer me with promises of recovery, but the old fevers return and the body disproves their claims."

He closed his eyes, and Timothy wondered if he slept. Of what fevers did he speak? Malaria? Yellow fever? Some other lingering tropical malaise picked up during the war?

Longwood opened his eyes and looked beyond Timothy. "Anna, my dear, would you excuse us?"

A sad sigh and the swish of her skirt gave evidence she obeyed.

After a pause he spoke again. "You wonder why I have summoned you."

"Yes, sir."

"Three matters."

"Yes, sir?"

"First, you misunderstood about Consuela. I could see it from the way you avoided me after I offered her help for your Spanish studies."

Timothy grew warm again. Why must he bring this up?

"I have always known I could depend on you to become a strong, responsible man. I hoped you would forget your young lady back home, fall in love with Consuela—poor, sweet child—and marry her."

Marry her! "Sir, please ..." He tried to stand, but Longwood caught his hand.

"Please hear me out. Young men often fall in and out of love. I can see now you have a constant heart." He breathed out a melancholy moan. "As do I."

You, constant? To whom? Timothy's sigh resounded with exasperation, and Longwood raised his head and arched his brow with sudden energy.

"Is that how you show respect to an officer, boy?" He dropped his head back on the pillow. "Never mind. Perhaps I no longer deserve respect." He fell silent for a few moments. "I hoped that after graduation you would marry Consuela and take care of both her and Anna. As you can see, my care for them has been costly. I have, however, managed to purchase this little house in Anna's name."

Timothy turned and peered out the window at the red- and gold-spangled treetops. What possible response could he give?

"I felt the need to explain so that you would not mistake Consuela's character."

"Yes, sir. I never thought ill of the señorita."

"No. No, you wouldn't." Longwood closed his eyes again.

"You said three matters, sir."

Longwood opened his eyes and frowned. He seemed to struggle to recall his purpose. "Ah, yes." A wry snicker. "A lesson for living, my boy."

"Yes, sir?"

"Never make hasty decisions in affairs of the heart, no matter how desperate things may seem."

"Sir?"

Longwood rolled toward Timothy, a sardonic grin on his lips. "A gentleman never speaks ill of his own wife."

Eyes wide with disbelief, Timothy gulped. He must hasten the end of this interview. "And that third matter, sir?"

A pained expression filled the captain's face, and he rolled back against his pillow. "Please tell your mother ..."

"My mother!" Timothy braced his feet to stand. If Longwood said one disparaging word against Mother, he would leave.

"Tell her I have never forgotten her. Tell her everything in my life went wrong after her rejection. Tell her ..." He grew feverish and grasped Timothy's arm. "... I will love her until the day I die and, God willing, forever beyond that."

Timothy slumped back in his chair as memories filled his mind. The captain, tall and regal in his uniform, taking Timothy and Mother on a tour of his newly commissioned ship, USS *Lanier Wingate*. His kind interest in the boy. His friendly fight with Laz when they dumped each other into Boston Harbor. Longwood going off to war. Then, many years later, Timothy's appointment to the academy—an "atonement," he had whispered to Mother. An atonement for what?

"I wish you happiness, Timothy. You are a son a father could be proud of." Longwood lay back against the pillow. "Will you please send Anna up on your way out?"

Timothy stood slowly. "Yes, sir." He walked to the door, then turned back. "Captain Longwood, sir?"

"Yes, lad?"

"Thank you."

Longwood smiled, gave him a weak salute, then dropped his hand to his chest and closed his eyes.

Timothy found Señora in the parlor. She took his hands and thanked him for coming. "I do not know why he wished to see you, but perhaps now he will have peace."

"Yes, ma'am. I hope so."

She saw him to the door, but before he could leave, she touched his arm. "Would you grant me one last request?" Her lovely face clouded with doubt, as when he first arrived.

"What can I do for you, señora?"

"Please tell me your mother's name."

The pain and fear in her eyes caused Timothy to draw in a breath. Now it all made sense. This beautiful, tragic woman had been a substitute for Mother in Longwood's life, and she suspected it. "Why do you ask?"

"Ah, well, you see, sometimes he calls me Hannah. I thought perhaps … but never mind."

"Um, it's … it's Rose, ma'am."

A girlish blush spread over her face, along with a pleased smile. "Ah. I see. Well, then, good day, Mr. Jacobs. *Vaya con Dios*. May God bless you always."

Three days later word came that Captain Duncan Longwood had died of heart failure. His funeral took place in the academy chapel with every midshipman in attendance. Mrs. Longwood and her sons made a hasty trip from their Richmond plantation to Annapolis, and they all wailed through the entire service.

Chapter Twenty-one

ॐ

December 1859

John Brown got what he deserved." First-class midshipman McGary stood in the mess hall, fists on hips, daring anyone to disagree. "He was a murderer and a thief, and to my way of thinking, it's just too bad a man can be hung only one time."

Timothy trembled with rage, aching to plant a facer on McGary's smug countenance or at least to shout his disagreement. But he had promised Laz he would lie low in these matters to protect their enterprise. Besides, starting a fight would not solve anything, at least not here, where the ever-present slavery debate rumbled below the surface. All the midshipmen, whether from North or South, pledged their first loyalty to the United States, "my country, right or wrong," and their second to the navy "first, last, and always." Their job was to defend the country from outside aggressors, not to solve all its internal problems.

As for that John Brown fellow, Timothy did grieve his death, but the man had been a loose cannon in the abolition movement for years. In early 1857 the fugitive Brown had secretly visited Timothy's neighbors in Louisburg Square and had met with other like-minded men who took the name "the Secret Six." It would have been "the Secret Seven" if Laz had agreed to join them. But despite his own work in delivering slaves to freedom, he told Timothy he would prefer to die rather than to kill. Timothy might doubt such a proclamation from anyone else, but when Laz said it, he knew it to be true. When debates arose among the midshipmen, Timothy sometimes felt like a coward for not telling everyone his opinions, until he remembered Laz's quiet heroism.

Several tables away he could see that Isaiah struggled too. He bit back a laugh, wishing Isaiah would go ahead and clobber McGary for both of them. It would do him some good to earn demerits for striking an upperclassman. Too bad he could not see how many things the two of them agreed on.

Beau, however, dipped his head in agreement with McGary. Little wonder. Brown had slaughtered slave owners and delivered their slaves to freedom in Canada. No doubt Beau was thinking of his own home and family. How Timothy wished he could win him over. But how could he when his friend asserted that slavery was the Negro's natural and normal condition? If only Beau knew Ezra John, he would change his mind.

That's it! Timothy bolted upright, so electrified by his idea he almost knocked over Hart's coffee.

"Watch it, Jake. Did you just get struck by lightning?"

Hart, ever the diplomat, was busy with his dinner, refusing to take sides in the slavery debate. Timothy gently elbowed his friend's ribs. "Sorry."

He might not be able to show Beau what a grand, brilliant fellow Ezra was, but he could show him what his own man Cordell was made of. Living with the free stewards and a few other slaves in rundown academy quarters, the young Negro came to the barracks several times a day to attend Beau. Timothy would find a way to befriend him and maybe to teach him to read. The prospect filled him with excitement. If John Brown had listened to Frederick Douglass and worked to educate the Negro instead of killing slave owners, he might be alive today to continue his holy mission. Despite his disagreement with Brown's methods, however, Timothy knew more than ever he must follow the cause of the martyred abolitionist.

Isaiah ground his teeth and clenched his fists. If McGary didn't shut his face pretty soon, somebody should hit him. What a loudmouthed fool. Ahab sat close by. Why didn't he stand up and at least say something? Isaiah wished for stronger debating skills, but then, these Southerners were beyond reason. John Brown had been right to snatch away those slaves. Too bad his insurrection failed. His courage and his death now stood as an example to others who decried slavery.

Last summer for two weeks of his furlough, he and the Harrises had visited the country home of some staunch abolitionists, Maurice and Antoinette Pendergast, where he learned much about their movement. Further, while Reverend Harris did not attend the more radical rallies where speakers urged violence, he did preach passionately of freeing the Negroes, and he seemed deeply grieved when others could not be persuaded. Yet Isaiah did not embrace his views merely to please Lacy's father. In Nantucket, he had seen whalers of every race prove their mettle, but struggling to prove his own worth had consumed all his energy. Now that he had gained some success, he could consider helping other worthy men who struggled. He had no plan, but one thing was certain. He would not get slapped with demerits for striking a fool like McGary. Better to bide his time and watch. One day he would enter the fray.

Timothy wandered down the hall toward Beau's room. With everyone else in class, he had played sick so he could find Cordell. Like the other stewards in their assigned rooms, the young, light-skinned Negro was cleaning Beau's toilette articles, emptying the chamber pot, brushing his extra shoes and uniforms, and dusting the floor around his bed. When Timothy entered the room, he stopped his work and ducked his head in respect.

"Marse Jake, you missing class? I hope you're not feeling poorly." Now that he had come, Timothy did not know what to say. "Aw, just a little. Mostly I didn't want to recite my Spanish."

Cordell chuckled. "Law, sir, you having trouble with Spanish? I can help you, if you like. I know Marse Jean-André wouldn't mind."

Timothy stared at him. "You speak Spanish?"

"Yes, sir. And French too. Can't live in N'Orleans and not know the languages. It's a port city, you know, and o'course the French folks settled there."

Timothy ran his hands over Beau's books. Not a mite of dust on them. "You're a pretty smart fellow, Cordell. Do you read?"

Cordell blinked his amber eyes and frowned, and his light brown cheeks turned pink. "Oh, not that smart, marse." His cheerful voice now sounded lackadaisical.

Timothy frowned too. He had made Cordell nervous, for laws forbade teaching Negroes to read. How he wished Ezra were here to help him show Cordell what a free black man could become. "Well, you're doing a fine job. You have a good afternoon."

"Why, thank you, Marse Jake. You get better, you hear?"

Back in his own room, Timothy considered the exchange and took heart. It was a beginning, and he would see it through until Cordell understood that he could be free any time he chose.

June 1860

Isaiah tucked Lacy's letter into his duffel bag along with his new brown sweater. Without any direction from him, for these past two years she had chosen colors and patterns different from Jemima's choices for Ahab. Lacy's thoughtfulness and affection continued to amaze him. With her beside him, he knew he could succeed at anything. Just as grand were the kindnesses of Reverend and Mrs. Harris. Despite Mother's Bible instruction, Isaiah had never thought much of religion until he met this family. They made belief in a deity, or at least some sort of faith, seem reasonable, even desirable. If he were superstitious, he would think Mother was watching from above and smiling at his thoughts.

Both Lacy and Jemima had written about his sister's graduation from Boston Normal School. Jemima told him only that it was a lovely event, but Lacy had bragged about Jemima's honors. Though not ranked first in her class, she had proved herself to be so gifted the faculty had invited her to return next fall for extra studies. Because she would turn just seventeen this summer, she had decided to accept their offer and postpone teaching for one more year, a decision Isaiah commended.

Now if only she would receive the attentions of a man of whom he approved, life would be perfect. With that hope, he maintained a correspondence with Stef, another man whose religion and humble bearing impressed him. But his stubborn sister refused to see what a fine minister's wife she would make.

The time had come, however, to put aside thoughts of loved ones. Today Isaiah and his class would embark on their first-class midshipman cruise. This time they would be in charge of teaching the new third-class men what sailing was all about. To his chagrin, one lesson concerned how to avoid sickness in foreign ports, with his own case held up as an example. "Be careful what you eat and what you drink," Craven had ordered, "and whom you fraternize with." He scanned the young men before him, and his look had held many meanings.

But that foolish error paled beside Isaiah's outstanding seamanship and scholarship. His own classmates might still give him wide berth most of the time, but the younger men held him in high esteem. Rank and ability transcended social frivolity.

Isaiah packed his last toilet articles, pulled the ties of his duffel bag, and hoisted it over his shoulder. This year 115 acting midshipmen would sail the *Plymouth*, an old but larger and seaworthy vessel that had replaced the *Preble*. Their voyage would take them once again to Cadiz, Brest, and Madeira, among other ports. This time he would find a better gift for Lacy, for the mantilla he had purchased two years before proved to be out of fashion and it faded when washed. In spite of that, dear Lacy had worn it several times during his convalescence. Surely some divine hand had given him the love of this beautiful girl. He almost felt tempted to raise his eyes and say "Thank you."

September 1860

As the *Plymouth* sailed closer to Annapolis, Timothy hung in the rigging and watched for the old mulberry tree on the academy grounds, for the first man to sight it would win the midshipmen's secret lottery. He had no need for the money, but his love of any sort of competition spurred him on.

The cruise had been a great success. From the third-class men's stormy baptism into seasickness to the layovers in the Azores to the sightseeing in Madeira and Santa Cruz, the voyage had held nothing but adventure. In addition to facing down storms, they had visited foreign dockyards and arsenals and met many fine Spaniards, Italians, and Frenchmen, thus expanding their worldview. Captain Craven commended the first-class men for their leadership, with special mentions to "Sampson, Starbuck, and Jacobs." Craven also gave a commendation to the entire third class, for due to over-crowding at the academy, they had been berthed and taught for the past year on this very ship as it lay anchored in the Severn River. To these men, the ship seemed like home even before the two-month voyage.

Now, as they neared home, Timothy and his classmates laughed to hear the third-class men hone their salty tales of travel and adven-ture to pass on to the incoming fourth-class midshipmen. Thus would they instill in the new men reverence for their superiors as it had been instilled in them only the year before.

"There! I see it!" Flusser pointed across the water toward the great mulberry tree that grew beside old Fort Severn.

All the men cheered, and Timothy lifted his voice with the others. He might not have won this lottery, but a far more important success lay just ahead. In only ten months, he would graduate from the academy and earn his first promotion. Best of all, he would marry Jemima, and a full measure of happiness would then be his.

Chapter Twenty-two

❧

January 1861

Timothy glanced around his group of friends lounging in his barracks room, knowing their bleak expressions mirrored his own. "How many, Beau?"

"Eighteen. Each one signed the petition."

"You think Toucey will actually grant them early graduation?"

"Well, Blake refused to do it," said Wils. "But Toucey sees how things are. I mean, if the Secretary of the Navy will give his approval, you can bet it will mean something."

Timothy looked at Hart and then studied his two Southern friends. "What about you? Are you going to leave?"

Beau shrugged. "I wrote to my father. I guess I'll do whatever he tells me." He stared down at his hands. "I have no doubt Louisiana will follow South Carolina in secession."

Wils bent his head. "I expect Maryland will secede, as well. If we do, I'm bound to my home state."

Timothy thumped his fist on the table. "Come on, fellas. What happened to 'My country, right or wrong'?"

"'Navy first, last, and always'?" Hart added.

Beau and Wils traded a look, and both shrugged. They all sat in silence for several minutes. No one wanted to study or even go out in the cold to play ball.

Beau put his head in his hands. "I can't think of it. I just can't think of ever firing on the Stars and Stripes. Why did that fool

Lincoln have to get elected anyway? He received less than forty percent of the popular votes and not one Southern electoral vote. You'd think our opinions didn't even matter to the rest of the country."

How Timothy burned to tell Beau whose fault it really was—the slave owners. But he had no heart for a fight. Until coming to the academy, he had considered all slave owners as nameless, faceless monsters. But Beau, with his bright, cherubic face, blond hair, and blue eyes, looked like a Botticelli painting, and he possessed a character equally as golden. Loyal, fearless, strong, kind, generous—and completely blind to the evils on which his family fortune was founded.

"You think there'll be war?" said Hart.

"Only if that Lincoln fellow causes it," said Wils. "He just needs to let us go. We'll establish our own country, and pretty soon we'll have a treaty with the United States. Everything will be fine and neighborly. If he's got a lick of sense, he'll just let us go."

Timothy stared at Wils. Did he really believe it was that simple? Lincoln had promised in his campaign to keep the country together. Yet looking at Wils and Beau, he could not think of fighting them. In gunnery practice, they had always imagined real-life enemies and gleefully demolished them. But to stare down the sight of a gun at one of these men.... No, he could never do it.

As if reading his thoughts, Beau gazed at him, his eyes filling with tears. He shook his head and brushed them away. "It shouldn't be this way. It just shouldn't."

Timothy, Hart, and Wils hummed their agreement, unable to say anything more.

The following week, Beau returned to Timothy's room clutching a letter. It could mean only one thing. Timothy held his breath.

"I have to go," Beau choked out. "My father said to come home right away."

Timothy hung on his friend, trying unsuccessfully to hold back his own tears. He skipped class and helped Beau and Cordell pack. Despite their spartan quarters, Beau had managed to accumulate many belongings in his three and a half years at the academy. In his grief, he seemed to have difficulty focusing on which ones to take home.

"No, not in the valise, you fool." Beau snatched a book from Cordell, his tone ringing with anger. "This goes in the trunk."

Timothy stared at his friend as if he were a stranger. Beau had never before treated Cordell this way, at least not in his presence. Was this the way he treated his slaves down in Louisiana?

Cordell merely bowed his head with respect. "Yes, Marse Jean-André." He then hurried to fold Beau's clothes.

Once the job was done, Cordell and other stewards carried the steamer trunk, two valises, and a wooden box downstairs to a waiting carriage. Wils and Hart, along with classmates Sampson and Flusser, joined Timothy to bid Jean-André Beauchamp farewell. They hung on each other and formed a procession on their way out of the barracks, singing discordant friendship songs in an attempt to bolster their spirits.

As they reached the ground floor and headed toward the Main Gate, the commandant, Lieutenant Rodgers, rushed from his quarters, his eyes blazing. "What's the meaning of this rioting? Why aren't you men in class?"

Timothy could not speak, but Sampson said, "No riot, sir. We're only bidding our classmate good-bye."

Rodgers regarded them for a moment, then sighed, and gave them a sympathetic nod. "Ah, yes. Carry on, men."

At the gate Beau shook hands with each of his friends while Cordell stood waiting. Timothy's heart clutched. In the past several months, Cordell had seemed to avoid him, surely from fear of his master. If he did not act now—

"Cordell," he burst out. "Stay here with me."

Cordell's light brown face grew pale. "Sir?"

"What are you talking about, Jake?" Beau looked as confused as his slave.

Timothy ignored him. "Cordell, you don't have to be a slave. I offer you freedom. I can get you safely up north. Just say the word—"

"Jacobs!" Beauchamp stepped over to Timothy and glared at him, fists clenched at his sides and his face red. "What are you doing?"

Timothy trembled with rage, and he could hear their classmates taking sides. "Can you not see it, Beauchamp? It's slavery that's destroying our country, not Lincoln. Set Cordell free. Give him a choice for his own life. You—" he poked his finger in Beauchamp's chest—"*you* can be the first one to do the right thing and end all this before it gets worse."

Cordell moved closer to Beauchamp. "Marse Jake, sir, meaning no disrespect, sir, but you don't understand how it is." For the first time, Cordell stared straight into Timothy's eyes, and his own eyes exuded wisdom and something indiscernible. Not resignation, but something much stronger. Clearly, he knew the choice he was making. "Don't make trouble for Marse André. He's a good man."

At his words, the whole group grew quiet. Beauchamp lifted his chin and glared at Timothy again. "You see. He knows where he belongs, and to whom." Tears filled his eyes and he swiped them away. "I thought you were my friend, Jacobs, and here you try to steal my most valuable property. I thought you were a Christian."

Timothy's eyes burned, as did his heart. "And I thought you were. I guess one of us is wrong."

Beauchamp backed away and glanced around the group. "Goodbye. God be with you." He leveled a grief-filled gaze on Timothy. "All of you."

He climbed into the carriage with Cordell close behind. The Negro did not so much as glance at Timothy, but attended to his master. The carriage driver turned his horses toward the train station, and the small group watched until they were out of sight.

"What's the matter with you, Jake?" Wilson's usually impish face blazed with rage. "What were you trying to do, start a war here and now?"

Hart put his arm around Wilson's shoulders and turned him back toward the barracks. "Never mind, Wils. We can't solve it here."

Sampson and Flusser chorused their agreement in a few words, then they all wandered back through the main gate.

Wilson never spoke to Timothy again, and their shattered friendship typified the feeling of distrust and despondency that fell over the entire academy. Because not every Southerner favored secession and not every Northerner opposed slavery, Timothy, along with officers, professors, and his fellow students, watched silently to see what course the others would take. Timothy noticed that Isaiah wore a perpetual frown and seemed even more detached from his classmates. One weekday, he nearly collided with Isaiah, who was emerging from the chaplain's office, but Isaiah did not seem to notice him.

While Hart and many others avoided all discussion of secession and slavery and attempted to restore the former spirit of unity, some midshipmen wore secession badges, inciting anger in Timothy and others of the antislavery contingent. Throughout March and into April, Hart still voiced hope that the storm of controversy would pass, despite the secession of Mississippi, Louisiana, and other Southern states.

When Maryland failed to secede, Wilson resigned, packed his belongings, and headed south to join the newly formed Confederacy, which offered generous commissions to academy students. Timothy noticed across the parade grounds that his former friend left unattended. Perhaps the men had wearied of tearful farewells.

In early April, Timothy and Hart braved torrential rains to attend an informal hop arranged by the second class aboard the USS *Constitution*, which was anchored at Fort Severn. Dashing across the academy grounds with oilcloth slickers for covering, they reached the school's recently acquired ship just before a great sheet of rain made boarding the vessel impossible. Below deck, the hosts had strung up Chinese lanterns and decorated a table with fresh flowers and punch and cookies made by Mrs. Blake and other faculty wives. Despite the trappings of gaiety, the old ship smelled of mildew and age. Further, due to the weather, only a handful of young ladies from town attended. Timothy did not know whom to ask for a dance, for he did not wish to embarrass a girl whose sympathies might be far different from his own, so he sipped punch and listened to the band play "Hail Columbia" and "Yankee Doodle."

Before the end of the second song, Flusser dashed in, soaking wet. "The Confederate army fired on Fort Sumter, and Major Anderson has surrendered! Now it's war for certain! Lieutenant Rodgers has given orders for everyone to report to the chapel to hear the Articles of War."

For a moment, no sound was heard but the pounding of rain on the deck above. Timothy breathed out a soft sigh, both believing and denying the awful pronouncement. So the game was on. The time had come for every man to choose sides. Timothy stared at Hart. Despite being a peace lover, in these last four years, this capable lad had been transformed from a naïve country rustic into a courageous fighter. Although still ambivalent about slavery, Hart reached out to Timothy. Nodding mutely, the two shook hands. The assembled midshipmen set down punch glasses, bowed to the young ladies, and began a silent trek through the storm.

Timothy and the remaining students continued to perform their duties as they observed the wisdom of their superiors. When Maryland secessionists threatened to seize the *Constitution*,

Superintendent Blake arranged for the ship to sail north to the New York Navy Yard. When Southern officers declared that the academy would become a Southern training school, Blake fortified the academy grounds and welcomed the Seventh New York State Militia Regiment, which transformed the school into a Union fort. When Secretary of the Navy Gideon Welles commanded the immediate transfer to Washington of much-needed naval personnel, Blake sent him all the officers he could spare, along with ten able midshipmen, some of whom were just short of graduation.

On April 22, Timothy watched with dismay as Isaiah Starbuck marched away with the others, regretting his failure to win Isaiah's friendship. In early May, he joined the task of moving the United States Naval Academy from Annapolis to Fort Adams at Newport, Rhode Island. Only a few days after classes resumed in the new location, Welles ordered most of the remaining upperclassmen to active duty. Despite their eagerness to join the action, Timothy and a few others received orders to stay in Newport to supervise the fourth classmen. Once again he shook Hart's hand, this time bidding him farewell and Godspeed as his friend sailed off to war.

May 11, 1861

Isaiah hummed a jolly academy tune as he worked the softening lanolin into his new half-boots. Today he would report to his first ship, USS *Mississippi*, an old side-wheeler steam man-of-war that had served in Japan as Commodore Perry's flagship. The ship's captain, T. O. Selfridge, had received orders to assist the Gulf of Mexico blockade in preventing rebel troop movement in and out of New Orleans.

At last Isaiah would see some action. Although ordered to duty before graduation, he was determined to work hard and earn wartime promotion. Several other men whom he knew from the academy also would join Selfridge's crew, among them Passed

Midshipman George Dewey and Midshipman Jackson Hartley.
Heeding Lacy's admonition, he would try to be sociable with them,
as duty permitted. Surely in wartime, no man would put another in
Coventry, for that man might be needed to save his life one day.

He added black polish to his boots, buffed hard, then held them
up to admire the shine. What a fine gift Jemima had sent him even
before he wrote of his need. How had she known his already-worn
shoes had been finished off when he and the other midshipmen had
been forced to march twenty-two miles from Annapolis before
finding a train that would take them to Washington? That he had
brought only one change of linen and a toothbrush? Yet her package
included linens, a white shirt from Lacy, woolen socks knitted by
them both, the new leather boots, and some cookies. He would not
ask his sister who had provided the money to buy any of it, for each
was a gift from God, no matter who paid the earthly bill.

His heart felt so full, he almost ached. The last letter he had
received from Lacy at the academy had changed his life forever. Who
but his forthright sweetheart could have affected him so deeply? Who
but she would have addressed him with such innocent candor?

> *Beloved, we do not know what this war will bring to us or*
> *take from us. I only know that you are in my prayers, waking*
> *and sleeping. Of course, I always pray that we shall be*
> *reunited before the summer is through. Yet, if our Sovereign*
> *God should choose another path for us, if the war takes more*
> *from us than we would willingly give, I rest my soul in him,*
> *knowing I shall see you in Heaven in God's good time.*
> *Without that assurance, I would not be able to bear it.*
>
> *You cannot know what it meant to me when you recited the*
> *salvation passage from the third chapter of John's Gospel last*
> *January at the ball. Who but a true believer could speak with*
> *such conviction? It was as though an angel spoke.*

Even at her most perceptive moments, his artless Lacy had never discovered his disbelief. Nor had wise Reverend Harris discerned it. But Mother's and Jemima's lifelong prayers and the living love the Harris family showed him cut deep into his skeptic heart and demolished every shield he had used to keep God out. The final thrust came through Lacy's blissful assurance that he would be in heaven if he died. Her ill-founded assertion had troubled him so deeply that he sought out the academy chaplain.

He blushed to think of how he put old George Jones through his paces, for Isaiah did know the Scriptures. But the chaplain blasted away his renewed defenses. "And so, young man, you are willing to admit there might actually be a God? The devils also believe, and they tremble. Yet you do not seem to tremble. Do you not fear falling into the hands of the living God? What man but a fool goes into war without anchoring his soul on the Rock of Ages?" Jones had paused, relenting from his bombast to take on a kinder tone. "If you cannot believe, pray that God will help you in your unbelief. Open your heart to hear that still, small voice. God is true. He will speak. He will answer you."

In his room that night, long after Sampson fell asleep, Isaiah had knelt beside his cot and prayed for the first time since childhood. "God, I am going to war. I will be courageous, for I do not fear dying. In your great mercy ..." He paused. What does a doubting man say to God? "... for Lacy's sake, for Jesus' sake, I place my life and my soul in your hands, to keep or to take away." As he whispered the words, he knew that he meant them, and his heart exploded with inexplicable joy such as he had never known. He pressed his face to his pillow and laughed with abandon. Why had he waited so long?

The following morning, he had written to inform Jemima of where and on whom he had anchored his soul. He had smiled to think of the sweet, happy tears she would shed. Then he wrote to Lacy, but did not contradict her assertion. He merely told her that, beyond all doubt, he would see her again, whether in life or in eternity. Frowning at the look of the words on the page, he added, "Now that we have discussed this matter, let no more be said, for I shall return to you, dear one."

Chapter Twenty-three

ॐ

February 1862

Isaiah stood on the foretop of the USS *Mississippi* and watched for enemy activity on the horizon. For eight months he had seen little else but seagulls, herons, and pelicans as they dove into the Gulf and scooped up writhing fish. How he wished this ship could dive into the river for which it was named and scoop up some rebel territory. Other than the many Union warships in the area, only supply vessels bringing coal and other supplies to the steamships ventured into these waters.

Early on, Isaiah and the other young officers had assumed that their captains would sail up the delta and take New Orleans. But then the Federal steam sloop USS *Richmond* and three smaller vessels entered the river, only to have a rebel ship, the ironclad ram CSS *Manassas* strike the *Richmond* and drive them all back into the Gulf. After that incident, the *Richmond's* Commander Pope apparently swayed Captain Selfridge and the other blockade captains into a more passive stance, for they all seemed disinclined to engage the enemy again. While reports came of the Union army's many battles against the rebels, the navy had few skirmishes. Instead of action, Isaiah and the other equally eager junior officers saw only dreary monotony.

In late February Isaiah's boredom turned to renewed hope when Flag-Officer David G. Farragut sailed into the midst of the fleet with new orders from Washington. From the moment Isaiah saw Farragut, he observed a strong, resolute spirit, like the indomitable whaling captains of Nantucket who set off to conquer the seas and bring back a greasy harvest. Cutting an urbane figure in his dark-blue uniform with its gold braid and bright brass buttons, sixty-year-old Farragut exuded a confidence and decisiveness unlike other, more cautions naval captains of his age. Soon the entire blockade fleet knew he had come to capture New Orleans.

After spies provided news that the rebels had almost completed two new ironclad ships, which he did not wish to engage in battle, Farragut pushed the men to their limits in preparation for the attack before those formidable vessels were battle ready. More than once, Isaiah breathed a prayer of thanks that he had kept physically active beyond the call of duty during the long stretch of military idleness.

Among other changes in the fleet, Farragut replaced Selfridge with Commander Melancthon Smith as captain of the *Mississippi*, and George Dewey advanced as his executive officer. Both promotions encouraged Isaiah, for these were men under whom he was pleased to serve.

Each day Isaiah's respect for Captain Smith grew. The commander had dark, bushy hair and a beard and mustache. His gaze could pinion a disobedient sailor to the deck, and his moral character was faultless. In addition to his temperance, he could give decisive orders without swearing. When the much-pressed sailors used excessive profanity, Smith ordered all the crew aft, where he announced that any officer caught swearing would be suspended and any swearing sailor would be put in double irons. Several times Isaiah forced himself to keep quiet when a shipmate burst out under pressure, thus gaining several friends. Why had he felt it his duty to report small infractions at the academy? Although he did not break rules, he often wanted to. Although he did not curse, many times exhaustion and hard labor forced profane words to his lips, and he restrained them with difficulty.

By April 7, Farragut's fleet consisted of fifty ships that boasted more than two hundred cannon. His force was complete. Intelligence reports indicated that Southern General Lovell and the commanders of two forts protecting New Orleans expected invasion from the north but none by sea. With the advantage of surprise, on April 18 Farragut launched a bombardment of Fort Jackson on the Mississippi River, then led his squadron upriver and blasted his way past Fort St. Philip. On April 24, the startled rebel commanders sabotaged their own heavy guns and surrendered the forts. In a campaign of less than three weeks, Farragut captured New Orleans through his audacity.

Isaiah had killed before, but only whales for oil, sheep for food, and rats as pestilence. He had seen dead men before, but none blown apart by cannon balls. He had been covered in animal blood, but never human blood—the blood of his shipmates and friends. Holding the hand of a broken, dying sailor, a man over fifty whom even young officers called boy, Isaiah wondered why he had been so eager for war. Was he the only man in this violent fray to be haunted by nightmares of men who had died from his cannon fire striking the two forts?

Yet once New Orleans was taken, he knew he had acquitted himself admirably. Captain Smith and Executive Officer Dewey had nothing but praise for him—in fact, had promoted him to the rank of ensign. He in turn recommended to the senior officers that Midshipman Hartley be likewise advanced.

While Farragut sailed his ship up the river, Captain Smith received orders to anchor the *Mississippi* in New Orleans to support the Union army's occupation. Isaiah and his companions, who had so recently been the targets of enemy fire, now found themselves targets of fiery invectives from the city's Creole population. At last the Union army commander, Major General Butler, took a firm hand and demanded at least outward demonstrations of respect for his men and those of the naval fleet. From then on, the crews could occasionally enjoy liberty on dry land.

Not all residents of New Orleans had pledged fidelity to the Southern cause. Several Northern sympathizers, recent transplants to the South before hostilities began, welcomed the officers into their homes. Isaiah now appreciated all the more Mrs. Blake's insistence on those etiquette lessons for academy midshipmen.

One family in particular became a haven for Isaiah during the blazing hot summer of 1862. Charles Randolph, a coffee importer, had a charming wife and two daughters who endeavored to ease the boredom of the midshipmen through teas and socials. Miss Amelia Randolph seemed drawn to Isaiah, and he to her. Unlike young ladies seeking husbands, she had already given her heart to a young soldier fighting with Major General McClellan, which made her friendship safe and innocent.

Pretty Miss Randolph had dark hair, large brown eyes, and medium stature. Only her dimples reminded him of Lacy, for she deferred to Isaiah at every turn. Whether he wished to stroll, sit, have lemonade or tea, read a book, or listen to her sister's music, she preferred the same. Her merry disposition lifted his spirits, and he whiled away many pleasant hours in her home. But he longed for Lacy's spirited candor and her discourses on intellectual matters that seemed beyond Miss Randolph's capabilities. In turn, he could see in her eyes a wistful yearning for a certain young lieutenant far away.

Yet in her genial company and from her childlike references to faith, Isaiah drew strength to soothe his raging guilt over the men he had killed in battle. He had not started this war, but he would do his part to end it.

February 1863

Timothy watched from the quarterdeck as his ship sailed against the flow of the Mississippi River. At last he would have an active hand in this war, even if only to bolster the occupation of New Orleans. He had brought along a package of woolen socks and other articles of clothing for Isaiah, gifts from Lacy and Jemima. Knowing his clever girls, Timothy laughed at their blatant attempt to force Isaiah into friendship with him. For his part, he would do the right thing and try again to win Isaiah over.

Timothy had never felt any rancor toward him, except to be annoyed by his senseless, persistent grudge. Now Timothy carried his own grudge, but its roots were not deep. He only wished he could have taken part in the Battle of New Orleans. Isaiah's wartime promotion did not bother him, but his wartime opportunities provoked a natural, if mild, resentment or, perhaps, just his competitive nature. Timothy knew he could have acquitted himself just as admirably as any man in Rear Admiral Farragut's fleet. Perhaps now he would have a chance to prove it.

The past twenty months had not been without rewards. Superintendent Blake had petitioned Secretary of the Navy Gideon Welles to keep Timothy at the academy after his 1861 graduation to teach history and French. In that honorable position, Timothy's leadership abilities had expanded to include a gift for instruction. He could picture himself in years to come. After the war ended and he had gone on to distinguish himself as a captain or even a rear admiral, he would return to the academy and guide other young men as he had those formerly ragtag lads he had turned into disciplined students.

His plans for the future also included marriage, of course. Against the wishes of their hearts, good sense prevailed when he and Jemima postponed their plans until the war ended. After his graduation, they had considered an immediate union. But then Aunt Kerry established a convalescent home for wounded soldiers and sailors in the Harrises' old house by the mission. Already busy sewing uniforms, knitting socks, and rolling bandages, Jemima joined Lacy and her sisters in ministering to the shattered men. Timothy knew she could have found ways to help the war in Newport, where the academy had moved, but her heart seemed set on staying with loved ones in Boston. After Blake finally granted Timothy's request for active duty, their decision proved the wisest course.

New Orleans came into sight, and the ship docked at its assigned berth. Soon Timothy reported to his first ship, the USS *Mississippi*. Did Isaiah know that he was one of the new additions to the crew? Timothy could not wait to see his face when he found out.

Climbing aboard, he reported to the executive officer, George Dewey. While Timothy saluted and greeted his fellow Annapolis graduate, over Dewey's shoulder he spotted Isaiah, whose face was devoid of expression, though his chin seemed to lift a little. Dewey was cordial, even affable.

"Mr. Starbuck, come see who's to join us. Your old classmate Jacobs."

Timothy forced his smirk into a pleasant smile and stuck out his hand. "Starbuck, good to see you. I envy you men. Everyone at the academy thinks you fellows walk on water for taking New Orleans the way you did."

Isaiah regarded him through narrowed eyes, but stepped forward and briefly shook his hand. "Admiral Farragut deserves the credit."

"Starbuck," said Dewey, "show Jacobs his quarters. Give him the lay of the land so he understands what we're about here."

"Aye, sir." Isaiah picked up Timothy's valise while Timothy gripped his own small sea chest and followed below deck to the large room all the junior officers shared. "There. That's yours." He tossed the valise in front of a locker and turned to leave.

Timothy dropped his chest and touched Isaiah's arm. "I have something for you—a package from our girls."

Isaiah jerked away, but pointed to the floor in front of another locker. "Put it there. I'll get it later." He walked toward the stairs.

Timothy snorted. "Of course. Then I'll write to Lacy and Jemima and tell them how graciously you received their gifts. Say, weren't you supposed to give me the lay of the land?"

Isaiah spun around. "This is a ship. Follow orders. No cursing, no drinking, no card playing." Starting back toward the stairs, he spat out, "I can write my own thank-you."

Timothy blew out a long sigh of exasperation. "Idiot," he murmured.

"Jake!" Jackson Hartley dashed into the cabin, strode quickly over to Timothy, and pulled him into an enthusiastic embrace.

"Hart! I knew I'd find you here." Timothy slapped his friend's back, then held him at arm's length. "Look at you with that ensign braid."

Hart shrugged and patted a similar patch on Timothy's shoulder. "Likewise, my friend. Land sakes, am I glad to see you. How've you been? How's everything at the academy? How's that lovely young lady of yours?"

"Good, good. But look at you, all in one piece. Say, you've been in the thick of it, haven't you?"

Hart bobbed his head, and his eyes sparkled. But then he shrugged. "Aw, it's nothing you couldn't handle. Just you wait and don't worry. You'll get your turn before this is over."

"What's brewing?"

Hart glanced over his shoulder, as if looking for eavesdroppers. "We're going to take Port Hudson so we can shut Vicksburg off from getting supplies by river."

"You mean I'll see some action right away? What luck! When?"

"Pretty soon, I'd say."

Timothy clapped Hart's shoulders and laughed. "Ha! I can hardly wait."

A brief shadow crossed Hart's face, but he shook his head as if to rid himself of some sad thought.

"What is it, Hart? Something troubling you?"

Hart's brow furrowed. He turned away and brushed his sleeve for invisible lint. "The army hung a man last week. A local fellow named Beauchamp."

"Beau? Oh my—" Timothy's heart twisted.

"No, not Beau. I don't know where he is. This was an older fellow. He tried to kill General Butler."

Timothy sighed his relief. "Thanks be it wasn't Beau. Why'd you bring it up?"

Hart bit his lip. "Well, he looked like Beau. Could've been his relation."

"Ah." Again Timothy breathed out his relief, but the painful memory of his good friend-gone-enemy lingered.

Hart shook off his mood and grinned. "Tell me about the academy. Did you whip those boys into shape like Dewey did us? How about Miss Starbuck? How's she?'"

Timothy began his tale as he unpacked his belongings and put them in his locker. As he talked, his heart filled with excitement over Hart's good news. He would get to fight. He even felt a flash of sympathy for Isaiah. After all, in spite of Isaiah's wartime courage and promotion, Timothy held the same rank because he had graduated from the academy and passed his exams. The rank formerly designated by the navy as "passed midshipman" was now called "ensign," and both he and Isaiah held that rank. Surely, it must stick in Isaiah's craw. But Timothy was certain of one thing. He would earn his rank in battle every bit as much as Isaiah had.

Isaiah tried to be thankful for the new shirt, socks, and other clothes from home, despite the way they arrived. He should be pleased, for mail could get lost in these uncertain days unless carried aboard a naval ship bringing reinforcements. When he picked up the brown paper package and untied the string, he attempted to shake off thoughts of the one who had brought it and think only of the loving hands that had sent it. But Ahab's smirk had not escaped Isaiah's notice. Too bad Dewey had not noticed it, for he would have straightened Ahab out in an instant. Now Isaiah must contend with an arrogant novice just before another big campaign. Ahab could be rash at times. Maybe his old friend Hartley would whip him into shape, even though he had been one of Ahab's sycophants at the academy.

Sometimes Isaiah wondered about the way the navy did things, especially when it came to choosing officers. Ahab had taken second place in their class after Sampson. He had passed the qualifying exams and gone on to teach at the academy. But he had done nothing tangible to earn the rank of ensign, nothing to qualify for leadership in battle. Did that fool think he knew about war? He would find out in a hurry once the fleet sailed upriver to take Port Hudson. He had just better not get in Isaiah's way.

Chapter Twenty-four

ᴈ

March 1863

Even more than during their academy days, Isaiah admired Executive Officer Dewey for his strong leadership. He had made the most of the idle times in New Orleans by drilling the gun crews until they developed the strictest of discipline in their procedures. Since most of the men had been under fire, Isaiah felt confident that they would perform as efficiently in battle as they did in drills. Only Ahab concerned him, for he seemed to approach the drills as if playing a game of bandy on the academy parade grounds. But if Dewey failed to notice, Isaiah would not point it out. Let the upcoming battle reveal his ineptitude.

On March 14, with the *Mississippi*'s three-hundred-man crew assembled for instruction, Captain Smith stood on the quarterdeck and stated what most of them already knew.

"Tonight Admiral Farragut will take the *Hartford* upriver first, then the *Monongahela* will follow, then the *Richmond*, each with a gunboat lashed to the port side to help with maneuvering the river's tight bends. The *Mississippi*, because we are most likely to run aground, will be bringing up the rear and steaming alone. We will have to pass Port Hudson, which is on the east side of the river and has bluffs over eighty feet high. There's a dangerous shoal-point on the west bank that we must avoid. If we attract the rebels' attention, as surely we will despite the darkness, they will be shooting down on us, and we will have the disadvantage of firing upward. Every man, keep an eye out and keep quiet. We may slip by undetected, but that's unlikely, despite how broad the river is. We are sure to come under fire, and we will give as good as we get—or better."

Isaiah's stomach fluttered, but whether from excitement or fear, he did not know. At least he kept his face composed, unlike Ahab, whose eagerness shone from his eyes and proud grin. Perhaps that grin would be wiped off his pretty face for good tonight when he saw what war was all about.

That night, as the *Hartford* tried to slip past the first rebel batteries high on the bluffs, the enemy threw up a rocket to announce the incursion. Soon cannon fire rained down from the eastern bluffs on all the ships, and bonfires burst out on the west bank to expose the flotilla.

"They can see our outlines," cried one man. "We're sitting ducks!"

They were, but not for long. The air soon grew thick with smoke from heavy firing on both sides. Isaiah lost sight of the other vessels, but he concentrated on his own cannon crew, ordering them to load, fire, and reload, returning fire at the flashes from the bluffs as the *Mississippi* slowly neared the dangerous shoal point.

"Torpedoes!" one sailor called out.

"They're firing chain-shot at us," yelled another.

Isaiah felt certain their calls were exaggerations, but he could not fault them because chaos reigned in the midst of all the smoke and clamor of battle. Each man could only see to his own responsibilities.

As the *Mississippi* neared the shoal-point, the ship's pilot cried, "Starboard the helm! Full speed ahead!"

"No!"

Isaiah tried to stop the order, for he could see they were not past the shoal-point at all. It lay straight ahead, and the ship's renewed momentum drove it hard aground. The *Mississippi* listed to port with a shudder. The gunners continued to fire while the engineer tried to back off the underwater entrapment, but the ship could not be moved. Heavy enemy shelling struck down more and more men. Certain he would die, Isaiah kept at his post, inspired by the courage of his gun crew, every man of which was full of fight.

From the concentration of cannonading from the bluffs, they understood that the enemy knew they were aground and fatally damaged. Dewey soon announced Captain Smith's order to abandon ship. Still under fire and with only three seaworthy boats available, Dewey directed the evacuation, on one occasion accompanying the boats to ensure the oarsmen would do their duty and return to the inferno to convey survivors to safety. The wounded went first to be taken to one of the other ships. Next the oarsmen delivered uninjured crew members to the river bank. Then the officers left the ship, with Dewey next to last, and finally, Captain Smith, who stepped off his broken vessel like a gentleman leaving a social event.

In the last boat, Isaiah rowed with the other junior officers toward the *Richmond*. From its decks they watched as the fire spread that Dewey had started in the ward room. The ship pulled loose and drifted downstream, a mass of flames lighting the night sky. Isaiah listened to the rebels burst into a great cheering yell and felt just as galled as the other Union survivors. The enemy had beaten them this time, but at least Farragut and the *Hartford* managed to get beyond the port. The shipless crew encouraged each other with vows to return to the point and blow the rebels off their bluff.

"Good man, Jake." Hart slapped Timothy on his shoulder. "You did fine. You never flinched. Your men took courage from you. Good job."

On the deck of the *Richmond*, Timothy shook his head and watched across the water as the *Mississippi* faded and sank into its namesake. "Thank you. You didn't do so bad yourself." He coughed out an ironic laugh. "That was something, wasn't it, losing our ship that way?"

"All the men did their best. No one can expect more. The old man—" He jerked his head in the captain's direction. "He's taking it like a gentleman. We just need to follow suit."

Timothy nodded his agreement and brushed at his torn, dusty uniform. He would need to change. Then he realized his foolishness. "Now doesn't that just beat all?"

"What are you going on about?"

"Our clothes, our things, all of it went down with the ship. All we have is what's on our backs." Jemima's miniature portrait, gone forever!

"Well, of all the—" Hands on hips, Hart stared across the river at the spot where their ship had sunk. "And to think I had some grand rebel souvenirs stashed in my locker to take home to my family. Guess I'll just have to find some other ones along the way."

"Say, that's not bad. At least we're still in one piece." Timothy glanced over at several wounded men who lay on the *Richmond*'s deck, attended by the ship's surgeon and the purser. "I've never seen so much blood. I've never seen—" His voice broke, and he stopped and looked about furtively. A few others seemed as affected as he was by the carnage, but most stood by, stoic, silent, awaiting orders.

Hart reached up and placed a hand on Timothy's shoulder. "I know. It's all right, Jake. May God forbid that we ever get used to this."

Timothy wiped his eyes and cleared his throat. "Yes, I agree." He noticed Isaiah kneeling beside a wounded man from his gun crew. Was he praying? Shame filled Timothy. This is what a leader should do. But looking further, he saw none of his own down. He knew two men had been hit and had died before the ship ran aground. In the thick of battle, their deaths had seemed unreal, yet reality now began to grip his heart. He would write to their families of their courage. But other men lay wounded here and now. He would follow Isaiah's example and encourage them as they sailed back to New Orleans.

 "Let's go, Hart. Let's see what we can do."

July 1863

Isaiah shoved his new toilet articles, books, and extra uniform into his locker, vexed almost to distraction. Dewey must have some perverse sense of humor. Not only had he requested that Isaiah, Hartley, and Ahab be reassigned with him to the *Monongahela*, he also must have assigned them these adjacent lockers. The cockpit, the junior officer quarters on the lower deck of the man-of-war, was crowded enough. Now Isaiah would have to bump into those two obnoxious coconspirators any time he needed to shave or change clothes. Just as he decided he would never escape them, the two proved him right by entering the quarters chattering as if going to a tea party.

"Hello, Starbuck." Ahab's tone intimated a friendship they all knew did not exist. "What do you think? Will we make it past those levees up ahead without taking fire from the rebs? Pretty clever how they can get a little shooting practice on our ships then duck back behind the levees. Too bad our return fire gets buried in the dirt."

A book in hand, Isaiah slammed his locker door, found a seat, and feigned reading. After one battle and losing their first ship, how could this fool still act as if war were a game?

Hartley stepped over to Isaiah. "Say, Starbuck, Jake was just saying how much he appreciates your example with your men—"

"Never mind, Hart," said Ahab. "Let him read."

Ensign England stuck his head down the stairs and blinked in the darkened cabin. "Jacobs, Dewey wants you up top."

"Thank you." Ahab gave Hartley a light slap on the shoulder. "See you later." He bounded up the stairs two at a time.

Hartley slumped down beside Isaiah. "I don't understand you,

Starbuck. You and I got along fine before Jake joined our crew. Now you barely speak to me, and I know it's because of him. Why do you keep holding a grudge against a man who never did anything against you? Since our first day at the academy, you've hated him."

Isaiah snorted his disgust. "He thinks he knows everything. He always has."

"You don't really know the man for all your hatred."

Isaiah slapped his book closed. "You're the one who doesn't know all about him, Hartley. He lived a lie long before you ever met him."

"A lie? What lie?"

"His name is not Jacobs. It's Ahab. His father was a Nantucket whaler just like mine, who murdered my father and all the rest of his crew."

"What? You're crazy."

"There's even a book written about it. One man survived from the crew and wrote the full account." Isaiah waited for Hartley to defend Ahab, but the other man seemed to grasp the significance of what he had said.

"Ah, now it all makes sense."

"Yes. You see it, don't you?"

Hartley seemed not to hear him. "No wonder he felt responsible for you. He was trying to make up for what his father did. And we thought it was just because he cares for Miss Starbuck."

"Felt responsible? You're crazy. He wanted to best me in everything. Still does. He's a spoiled, rich, pretty boy who—"

"Spoiled? You're the one who's crazy, Starbuck. You have no idea how many times Jake has saved you."

"Saved me? What—?"

"Don't tell me you never figured it out. Way back in our plebe year, that girl who blamed you for fathering her child, who do you think got you out of trouble?"

"How do you know about that?"

"Beauchamp's slave Cordell knew all the dirt on everyone. When he told us about your predicament, Jake insisted we get you out of it. He and Beauchamp went over the wall, even received demerits, to drag the right man in. If they hadn't, you'd be married to that woman today and probably getting shot at by General Lee in some Virginia battlefield. Jake swore us all to secrecy, but I think it's time you saw the light. And that's not the only thing."

Isaiah's stomach churned. He did not want to hear more, yet could not leave.

"When you had your accident on our third-class cruise, he went to Craven and asked him to take you up to Boston. Even offered to pay for it. If he hadn't had the idea, you could have died or been crippled forever being transported over land to get back home from Annapolis. You do remember, don't you, Starbuck? You almost died."

Isaiah stood and shoved his book back into his locker. He must defend himself against all this. "I suppose he bragged about it to you?"

"No. Nobody else ever knew about it but me. I eavesdropped. I felt bad about it at the time, but now I know why I did it. So you could find out what a fool you are."

A wave of dizziness swept through Isaiah. Hartley was an honest man. Even being Ahab's friend, he had no reason to make these things up.

"Jake never let us speak ill of you," said Hartley. "When you kept reporting every little boyish prank we did, some fellows wanted to tar and feather you, but Jake stopped them. Almost came to blows! Don't tell me he's not a good man. All this time I wondered why he kept at it, but now I see. He needs a kind word from you, Starbuck. But more than that, he needs your friendship to erase the awful thing his father did to your father and all those other poor whalers."

Isaiah leaned against his locker and put his head in his hands. *Dear God, I've made a mess of it.*

"When we first received orders to leave the academy," Hartley continued, "when we shipped out on the *Mississippi*, I saw you come alive with a whole new outlook. I thought it was because you didn't have Jake around to hate or compete with. Then I saw you read your Bible and pay attention in chapel services instead of wearing that know-it-all face like back at the academy. I thought you had taken on a more Christian view of things. Guess I was wrong."

Isaiah gulped down the bile rising in his throat. How could he have been so blind? Why had he not seen that Ahab took after the mother who had raised him, not the father whom he had barely known? It never occurred to Isaiah that Ahab might want to make up for his father's sins. But then, there was that arrogance … no, maybe not arrogance at all. Maybe just confidence in himself, something Isaiah had to fight for every day of his life.

Lord, forgive me.

"You think about what I've said, Starbuck. Maybe you'll get some sense in that stubborn brain of yours." Hartley walked away, shaking his head.

Isaiah did not know how long he stood leaning against his locker. Surely he should be about his duty. Where was his gun crew? He should prepare them in case those enemy batteries behind the levees opened fire. But his legs, heavy as his heart, refused to move. "What a waste, Lord, what a waste. I've been such a fool," he murmured.

Forgive. The word came unbidden to his mind, but it made no sense. Timothy had done nothing to require forgiveness. Timothy? Yes, Timothy, his first childhood friend, whom Isaiah now longed to embrace in gratitude for all his hidden good deeds. But whom must he forgive? Captain Ahab, of course. Whatever his offense in killing his crew, his offense against God was greater. Ishmael had recorded how the poor fool Ahab had died cursing his only hope of eternal life, while Isaiah knew his own faith-living father now stood in the presence of God.

From the depths of his soul, he cried, "Yes, Lord, I forgive the poor fool. Please forgive me for being a fool, as well."

For the second time in his life, Isaiah's heart seemed to explode with happiness, as joy and overwhelming peace flooded him from without and within. He recalled Reverend Harris's saying that God, in his wisdom, had ordained that one who forgives no longer wears the chains of bitterness. After a lifetime of bitterness, truly Isaiah had now been set free. Yet before he could bask in this marvelous new peace of heart, he must find Timothy and ask for *his* forgiveness.

Timothy stood on the quarterdeck with the executive officer Lieutenant Dewey, Captain Thornton A. Jenkins, Farragut's chief of staff, and Commander Read, commanding officer of the *Monongahela*. As was his custom, Dewey kept one or two junior officers handy to relay orders as well as to show them how the brass operated. Timothy now took his turn for the first time, his heart filled with pride and satisfaction. Only Farragut's presence could make this experience more exciting, for everyone called the admiral a pleasant fellow and not at all officious. But the admiral was aboard the *Hartford* in New Orleans preparing to sail back to the New York Navy Yard in a few days.

How Timothy wished they would engage the enemy today. Recalling how he had loved fencing at the academy, he eyed the rack of cutlasses on the ship's side and permitted himself a few moments of fantasy about fighting off rebels who, like pirates, tried to board the ship. In reality, the rebs liked to play hide-and-seek behind the levees, firing their field guns through small embrasures, then ducking behind the protection of the great piles of dirt that held back the mighty river. This ship was a big target, but one shot could still do some serious damage if it struck a vital place. Timothy felt every nerve in his body ready for action if they received fire.

The *Monongahela* now steamed up river with two other ships, the *New London* and the *Ida*, to convey supplies to the Union troops. Twelve miles below Donelsonville, Timothy got his wish. Rebels began firing at close range.

"Sir," Captain Jenkins said to Commander Read, "I suggest you get out of range. They're going to do us some damage."

"Sir," Read said, "I will not cower before these rebels. It is my duty to make certain the supplies on that transport get through to our soldiers." He turned to Dewey. "Lieutenant, reduce speed and engage those guns."

Dewey stepped over to the speaking tube and shouted the orders down to the engine room. "All ahead one third."

Heart pounding, Timothy watched his superiors take their stance in preparation to engage the rebel battery. As the great ship slowed, the captain and officers conveyed orders. Gun crews quickly took their positions and returned fire, causing the rebels to back off.

Timothy saw Isaiah emerge from below deck. He appeared dazed. At that moment, with renewed energy the rebels rained fire on the ship. Isaiah seemed not to comprehend his danger. Not waiting for orders, Timothy plunged down the steps from the quarterdeck to tackle Isaiah just as a blinding brilliance flashed nearby. The stunning concussion of an exploding shell only a few yards away slammed Timothy into Isaiah, and both of them crashed to the deck. For an instant he saw nothing, heard nothing, felt nothing.

Then screaming! A man, screaming. He, screaming. Pain screaming through every part of his body.

"God help me! Help me!" He tried to rise, but his limbs would not move. He tried to open his eyes, but only one would respond, and what it revealed made no sense. Blood and flesh covered the deck. His blood? His flesh? He screamed again. Then all went black.

Chapter Twenty-five

ﾂﾂ

Isaiah gulped in air to fill his empty lungs. What had knocked the wind from him? His head and back throbbed, but he managed to sit up and shake his head to try to clear it. Sounds invaded his aching ears. Choking smoke and the metallic smell of bloody flesh plagued his nostrils and chest.

"Full speed ahead," cried Dewey from the quarterdeck, and the *Monongahela* lurched forward, picking up speed.

Isaiah blinked his eyes furiously to clear his vision. Before him on the deck lay a shattered, bloody body.

"Timothy!" he screamed, caring nothing for military deportment. "Lord, help us. Mr. Dewey, help us. We need the surgeon *now!* Mr. Jacobs is down. Dear God, please help us."

For one instant, he stared at the executive officer, wondering why he did not respond. But Dewey knelt beside Commander Read, who lay as bloody and torn as Timothy. Behind Dewey, Captain Jenkins sat on the deck. He appeared dazed, and he nursed a badly wounded leg.

Still not fully aware of himself, Isaiah began to grab at Timothy's worst wounds, trying to stanch the flow of blood. His entire right side had been slashed in countless places, but not from a shell. The last enemy volley had shattered a rack of cutlasses stored on the ship's side, exploding their sharpened blades into a hundred deadly shards. His larger body had shielded Isaiah from injury. Once again, Isaiah's guiltless enemy had saved him, and now he clutched at the bleeding wounds to keep Timothy's life from flowing out in dark-red streams.

Ensign England joined in Isaiah's struggle against the tide of blood. Hartley and others appeared and lent hands and prayers. Dr. Kindleberger, the ship's surgeon, arrived and calmly gave orders to his assistant while tying tourniquets to the worst injuries.

"Bring him below."

Isaiah shivered. The surgeon's monotone order seemed to portend impending loss. At his direction, Isaiah gently lifted Timothy's shoulders while Hartley and others gripped him beneath his back and legs. Timothy cried out, but did not seem aware of his surroundings.

In sick bay, they laid Timothy on a table as others brought Commander Read and Captain Jenkins below. The assistant surgeon attended Jenkins, who sat stunned but awake, while Kindleberger gave Read his full attention. Isaiah shot frantic glances between the two unconscious patients. Timothy moaned, shook violently, and gasped for breath, while Read lay quiet, pale, and motionless. How Isaiah wished to cry out that it was no use trying to save the commander. *Let him go. Save Timothy.*

A hand clasped his shoulder, and Isaiah turned to see Hartley, his eyes filled with tears. "Pray, Starbuck. It's all we can do."

Isaiah nodded and brushed his sleeve across his eyes. The two men placed blood-covered hands on each other's shoulders, bowed their heads together, and wept out prayers for their injured friend.

Timothy screamed again, and the surgeon left Read to an assistant's care.

"You two." Kindleberger motioned to Isaiah and Hartley. "Over here. Hold this man down."

Timothy still shook violently, and his left eye opened, seeming not to see. Isaiah observed that many of his lighter wounds had already stopped bleeding, and others merely oozed.

"Thank you, Lord." Isaiah hoped his whispered prayer was not premature. But now he looked at Timothy's bloody face, which had been slashed from forehead to chin across his right cheek. Did the cut go to the bone? Would he lose his sight? Isaiah felt sick, recalling his jealousy—yes, jealousy—over Timothy's handsome visage, the face Jemima loved so dearly. *Lord, please heal it completely, I beg you.*

When the surgeon replaced the bloody bandage on Timothy's right arm, the flesh and muscle opened to show the bone visible but unbroken. Kindleberger checked for fragments of fabric or metal, then quickly bound it again with clean dressings. Isaiah wished he had laid the wound together more carefully. What if it healed in this grotesque shape?

But the worst injury was to Timothy's right leg, where large chunks of flesh and bone had been sliced away below the knee. The surgeon called to his assistant.

"Chloroform. Scalpel. Bonesaw."

"No!" The words escaped Isaiah before he could stop them. "No, you must save his leg. You must." This could not be happening.

"Sailor, if you cannot hold your tongue, I'll get someone here who can. Now shut your mouth and hold him down. Be prepared for him to—"

"No," screamed Timothy. He sat up halfway and gaped with his good eye, first at the bone saw and then at his leg. "No, Doc, don't take my leg. Please don't take my leg."

"Boy, it's almost gone anyway."

"No, you can save it." Timothy shook so hard Isaiah almost lost hold of him. "Look, it's as good as the other. Look, see. Let me move it. It's good. I swear it."

"Lie back, son. You'll be all right soon."

"No!" Timothy jerked around, trying to get off the table. "You don't understand. I can't lose my leg. I can't lose it. Don't you see—?"

Kindleberger poured chloroform on a clean cloth and lowered it over Timothy's mouth and nose. Gasping in the anesthetic, the patient aided the surgeon's purpose and soon fell back unconscious.

"Scalpel." Kindleberger took the instrument from his assistant and cut away muscle and loose tissue, leaving a long flap of skin to one side. He then tied silk thread around the large, bleeding arteries. Next, he picked up the bone saw.

As the jagged blade raked down over the shattered bone with forceful precision, Isaiah plummeted into oblivion.

Deep, searing pain stabbed Timothy in a thousand places, and his parched throat burned. He tried to open his eyes. The right one met resistance, but the left opened to darkness. Pain everywhere … everywhere. He tried to reach up to uncover his eye, but his right arm refused orders. Fear shot through him. His leg! Had they taken his leg? Again his arm would not obey as he tried to reach down. But no, the leg was still there. He could feel it, could even wiggle his toes, though the movement brought more agony. Relief made it bearable. He could stand anything but losing his leg.

Razor sharp pain sliced at his right arm, and he grasped it with his reluctant left hand. Bandaged too, and in a splint. He panted out a deep groan. It would be all right. It would heal. He continued his search. His torso felt uninjured, but his right ribs ached. Minor pain considering the agony in his leg, arm, and head.

He forced his hand to his face. Bandages covered the right side, but the left side seemed unscathed. Touching the stinging spots through the cotton, he felt a jagged ridge from forehead to cheek. It would scar, but how badly? His fingers lingered over his covered eyelid, massaging his eye, which burned but moved. He would not lose his sight.

He could reach both thighs but not his knees. He rolled to his left side, then fell back with a groan, gritting his teeth as pain racked him once more. A deep breath failed to control his shaking, but he clenched his jaw, rolled up on his left elbow, and then tried again to sit up. His head spun, and nausea forced him back down.

Sudden movement at his left side. "Timothy? You awake?" Someone nearby spoke in a sleepy tone.

"Hs'that?" The darkness was playing tricks on him. Isaiah would not be here. Isaiah would not call him Timothy. He blinked his eye and tried to focus on the shadowy form, then blinked again as a match flared up to light a kerosene lantern on the nearby table. Timothy gritted his teeth as hot knives passed through him. "Starbuck." He gulped down a dry swallow. "Why … you here?"

"Waiting for you to wake up." With the dancing light behind him, Isaiah's face looked old and careworn.

"I'm 'wake," he moaned. *No, I'm not. This is not happening.*

"You saved my life."

"Mm. Did? How?"

"Yes," Isaiah breathed out, then folded his arms on the bedside, hid his face, and began to sob. "Forgive me, Timothy," he mumbled into the sheets. "I have been a fool. Please forgive me."

Pain ripped through Timothy again, and he shuddered away a stifled scream.

Isaiah now stood over him, touching him, bracing him. "The surgeon said to give you morphine if you needed it. Will you take it?"

"Yes," Timothy gasped out. "Anything."

Isaiah called to someone, and soon a white-coated surgeon's assistant brought a syringe. With curiously tender care, Isaiah gripped Timothy's hand while the man thrust the hollow needle into his left arm. So great was his other pain that he barely felt the prick. He then lay back and begged the drug to remove his torment.

"Would you like some water?"

Timothy rolled his head to the side to see this wonder. Why was Isaiah behaving so strangely? "Yes."

Isaiah lifted Timothy so the water would not spill. The lantern light made shadows throughout sickbay. Timothy saw the outline of his left leg beneath a clean white sheet. On the right side, only flatness. He blinked and would have shaken his head except for the pain and bandages.

"It's not there." His voice felt thin and weak.

Isaiah coughed out a sob.

"No ..." Timothy whimpered. It was all he could manage before the morphine sent him back into darkness.

Despite Commander Read's death and Captain Jenkins' severe injury, senior officer Dewey ordered the *Monongahela* to continue its voyage up the Mississippi River to deliver their vital cargo. Isaiah and Hartley petitioned Dewey to take turns sitting with Timothy. Perhaps because he understood their history, Dewey granted permission as long as the ship did not come under attack. Once the supplies were delivered to Major General Banks, the ship began the return trip to New Orleans.

Each time Isaiah approached Timothy's bed, he prayed he would not lose control of his emotions. The patient needed for him to be strong. He also prayed for a chance to ask again for Timothy's forgiveness, but Timothy had developed a fever and seemed unaware of all that went on around him. Hartley reported the same condition on his watch. Perhaps the prescribed morphine injections helped to keep Timothy unconscious.

Several nights after the tragedy, Isaiah sat beside the bed and prayed as he had without ceasing since Timothy's surgery. The fever seemed to come and go. At its worst, Isaiah applied cold, damp cloths to Timothy's face and around his wrists. Tonight when he arrived, Hartley said the patient had slept fitfully but had not awakened.

Despite the darkened room, Isaiah determined he would stay awake until morning. Last night, the hum of the *Monongahela*'s engines had lulled him to sleep, and he had dreamed of his childhood. He saw his own father shaking hands with giant, one-legged

Captain Ahab, the father of his dear playfellow. Aping them, Timothy and he had shaken hands too and then giggled at their game. Tiny as they were, they vowed to grow up to be like their fathers. Isaiah's heart ached at the memory of the dream, for he felt certain the scene once had happened.

If only he had been like his father—gentle, good, devoted to God—perhaps Timothy would not be lying here with injuries far worse than Captain Ahab's. Even more than the guilt he felt, he feared how Timothy would respond when he waked up to his awful reality. Would he accept it as some wounded men did, going on to make the best of what God had ordained? Or would he become bitter like his whaling captain father and seek some awful revenge? If so, Isaiah would offer himself as the rightful one to be punished. But Timothy did not take after the isolated, brooding, dark-hearted man in the book. He was cheerful, open, and friendly. Or at least he had been.

Timothy drew in a shivering breath and released it with a long, shuddering sigh. "Hart?"

Isaiah set his hand on Timothy's. "No, not Hartley. Isaiah."

"Mm." Timothy groaned. "What ... whatdyou want?" His words slurred in dry, cracked tones.

Isaiah lit the lantern, poured a glass of water, and lifted Timothy. The patient gulped down the liquid, choking and coughing, desperate to drink. Lying back once more, he seemed to doze, although spasms shook his body from time to time.

Isaiah turned to extinguish the lantern's light, but Timothy groaned again. When Isaiah turned back, Timothy scowled at him.

"Whatdya want? Why're you here?"

Isaiah's heart leapt. Timothy seemed lucid for the first time in days. But in spite of all his prepared speeches, Isaiah could not think of what to say. "I ... I'm keeping watch. Hartley and I are taking turns."

"Mm. Like what you see?"

"What?"

"This's what you want, huh? See an Ahab pay for your father's death? I'm paying, Starbuck. Satisfied?"

"No. No, I never wanted you hurt." Isaiah knew his words were untrue. He felt sickened to realize this was exactly what he had wanted for years.

"Ha! Save your lie for some'ne else." Timothy turned his head away, but jerked back as the bandaged side touched his pillow.

"I was wrong, Timothy. Hartley told me everything you did for me at the academy … that girl, our third-class cruise, everything. I've been a fool. Please forgive me."

"I mus' speak to Hart 'bout that. He swore secrecy."

"But you saved my life. Time after time, you saved me. You—"

"Now we're even. My father killed your father. I saved your life. Now get out."

"You need someone with you."

"Starbuck." Timothy struggled to sit up, and his voice became clear. "I will never need you. Never. Now get out of here before I throw you out."

Isaiah stood and gently pressed the weaker man back on the bed. "Please, Timothy, please let us be reconciled." His tears scalded his eyes and cheeks. "Let us pray together and become brothers."

"Pray! Ha!" Timothy exploded with a string of curses. "To whom shall we pray, Starbuck? The same God who sent our fathers to their watery graves? You think he would hear us?" His dark eye glowed red, and his lips curled in a raging snarl. "Listen, I've done the good thing, the righteous thing all my life just to keep from being like my father whom you hate so much." He slung his left hand across his body and yanked off the covering sheet. "Yet look at my bloody reward," he screamed. "Just like my father!" Trembling violently, he pulled himself up on his elbow, leaned toward Isaiah, and spoke in a savage growl. "Now you tell me why I should pray."

Isaiah shuddered and swallowed away his nausea. Could a Christian man say these things? But what if Timothy was not a Christian? Isaiah slumped down into his chair. Such a thought had never before occurred to him.

"Don't get comfortable." Timothy spat out the words, an awful, pained grimace on his face. "You won't be staying."

Without answering, Isaiah stood again. He must leave, for if he stayed, Timothy might hurt himself or lapse back into a fever. He turned the lamp knob to extinguish its flame, then felt his way along the bed until his eyes grew used to the dark. Behind him, he heard Timothy's ragged breathing and half-sobs, and he longed to console him.

Back in junior officer quarters he lay in his hammock, his heart aching. He feared for Timothy's immortal soul, but his own culpability lay heavy upon him as well. Why had he held on to his blind, foolish, *wicked* bitterness? When did it begin? From whence did it spring? Perhaps as far back as childhood when his bosom playfellow had deserted him in their hour of shared grief. With each passing year, entrenched in poverty, he had fueled his bitterness with the knowledge that Captain Ahab's family did not likewise suffer. Now he knew without any doubt that both Timothy and Mrs. Lazarus would have done anything, everything in their power to prevent that suffering. He also knew that he possessed not a whit of power to redeem his once-and-newly-beloved friend.

Sleep would not come, and so Isaiah rose and found his way out to the ship railing. The *Monongahela* moved down the Mississippi River toward New Orleans, and warm summer air breezed over the vessel's decks. Kneeling in the dark, Isaiah gazed up at the starlit sky and whispered.

"Father in heaven, I do not deserve your forgiveness, yet you give it freely, and I am so humbled and thankful to receive it. Timothy cannot forgive me, but I fear more than that, he cannot forgive you. Preserve his life, I beg you, Father, until he can understand your goodness and grace. Please, for Jesus' sake, don't let him die as his father did. Don't let him die without knowing you."

Chapter Twenty-six

ဢ

August 1863

"Tell us again about Admiral Farragut. Tell us what he said to you." Matthew lay draped over the end of Timothy's bed, and Deborah and Gracie both snuggled under Timothy's left arm.

He forced out a chuckle at his brother's wide-eyed expression, hoping the children would not notice his pain. He had told the story a dozen times, or so it seemed. Once Union troops and ships had taken Vicksburg and Port Hudson, the North controlled the Mississippi River. Farragut, whose flagship the *Hartford* needed repairs, felt free to sail back East to the New York Navy Yard, bringing with him Timothy and other badly wounded sailors and soldiers.

"He's a good old gentleman." Timothy tried to come up with something new to add to the story. "Not at all what you'd think America's first rear admiral would be like. More like a kind old uncle. A very nice fellow. Not stuffy at all. He doesn't have a big staff. Even writes his orders himself, sometimes propping his foot on a railing and writing on his own knee instead of sitting at some big desk. He was always asking us how to spell this or that name of some place or other."

"But what did he say to *you?*" Deborah batted her dark eyelashes at him and gave him a sweet smile. Soon this young lady would be breaking hearts.

"I know. I know." Gracie broke loose from Timothy's arm and bounced up and down on the bed.

He tried not to wince, but the movement jarred his wounds. Eight-year-old Gracie still had not settled down. Why could she not be more like Mother and Deborah? Timothy gritted his teeth to hide his pain. If he could just get rid of them, he could give himself a dose of morphine, but he would not permit them to watch his injections.

"He said—" Gracie spoke as she bounced—"that you're a great hero and that you saved Isaiah's life, and he wrote you a fine letter of commendation." She stopped bouncing and grinned, clearly pleased with herself.

Timothy tried to smile, but the rough motion had brought on a stronger wave of pain, inducing nausea. He closed his eyes and laid his head back against the pillow. A soft, cool hand touched his left cheek.

"Timothy, you're pale," said Deborah. "We should leave you alone and let you rest."

He smiled at her, this sweet, sensitive young replica of their mother. "Thank you, Deebee. That would be nice."

She placed a gentle kiss on his left cheek and carefully slid off the bed.

Gracie bounced to the floor and hopped around the bed toward the door. "Gingersnaps!" She turned and raced back toward the bed. Timothy gritted his teeth and braced himself, expecting her to jump on him, but by some miracle she stopped short.

"Want some milk and gingersnaps, Timbee?" She grinned in a silly, unladylike way.

"No," he snapped, "I don't want milk and gingersnaps!"

She blinked, frowned, and seemed about to cry. Before he could apologize, Deborah took Gracie by the hand and tugged her toward the door.

"But I want some, Gracie. Let's go."

Gracie wrinkled her nose at Timothy, smiled again, and skipped out with her sister.

Matthew moved closer to sit cross-legged by Timothy and stared at him with his serious, Laz-like expression. His face resembled his father's, but his shorter, stocky frame came from Mother's people.

"What do you need, Matt?" Timothy managed a pleasant tone, despite his wish that his brother would leave too. The morphine box lay in the drawer of the bedside table—so near and yet so far. Dr. Kindleberger had provided the syringe and a drug supply, as Union doctors did for all amputees. Yet to take the opiate would seem like a weakness, though he had depended on it since his surgery. How could he have borne this suffering without it?

"I want to join the army."

The statement was so unexpected, Timothy burst out with an explosive laugh, which only increased his pain. "You? Join the army? You're only fourteen."

Matthew did not flinch. "I can still help in the war. Even if they won't let me fight, I can play the bugle. They need men to play the bugle, and I'm very good."

"That's right. They need *men*, not little boys." Timothy spoke dismissively, then closed his eyes and again lay against the pillow. *Go away. Go away!*

"I'm going to join," Matthew continued. "Father won't hear of it but—"

Without thinking, Timothy roused, grabbed Matthew's shirtfront, and pulled him up nose-to-nose. "You aren't going anywhere, you little brat. You think Mother needs that kind of grief? I'm going to tell Laz what you said so he'll keep an eye on you."

"Ouch. Let go. You're hurting me." Matthew's eyes were wide, but he did not struggle.

"Not until you swear you're not going to run away." Timothy began to shake. His strength had not yet returned, but he would not let go of his brother. Why was Matthew not resisting? He could have easily broken Timothy's hold on him.

Matthew's eyes now filled with tears. Timothy could see his

indecision. He summoned energy and shook him, but still his brother did not fight back.

"Swear it!"

Matthew blinked, and tears splashed down his cheeks. "I swear."

Timothy shoved him away with the last of his rapidly dwindling strength, then dropped back on his pillow. "I don't trust you. I'm still going to tell Laz."

Matthew climbed off the bed. "No. I mean it. Please don't tell Father. I won't run away. I promise."

"All right then." Timothy jerked his head toward the door. "Now get out of here."

Halfway to the door, Matthew gazed back at Timothy, his eyes exuding pity. "I'm glad you're safely home, Tim. We missed you. I missed you."

Timothy swore under his breath. *Pity*. That's why Matthew had not fought back. He felt sorry for the wounded cripple. Timothy muttered another curse. How he hated the pity. From the moment he had come home, everyone looked at him as if he were half a man … or less. At least on the voyage aboard the *Hartford*, no one had pitied him. In fact, in his stories about Farragut, Timothy made sure he did not mention the admiral's sound scolding.

The old gentleman showed compassion and respect for the wounded, but he lit into one injured fellow something fierce for feeling sorry for himself, saying no one needed to listen to a gloomy grumbler going on about how much he had lost in the war. Everyone had lost something or someone in the war. "But you cannot make an omelet without breaking eggs." It would be wrong to demoralize the folks back home with complaints over what the Union successes had cost. Victory lay just around the corner. Then he strode over to Timothy's cot. "Boy, I order you to start eating. You arrive home looking scrawny like this and your mother's going to think we don't take care of our boys."

From that moment, Timothy knew better than to let anyone know how he really felt. He would eat. He would put on a smile. He would laugh heartily. His wounds? A trifle. A mere inconvenience. Soon he would have this new arrangement mastered. He would ask Uncle Jonathan to carve a wooden leg and help him figure out how to strap it to his stump. With the help of the new limb and the contents of Dr. Kindleberger's small wooden box, he soon would be up and about again, ready for the future.

Once the *Hartford* had docked at the New York Navy Yard, navy personnel notified families about their wounded. Laz had sailed the *Hannah Rose* down to New York to bring Timothy home. Timothy had watched him carefully, but his stepfather gave no hint of pity or dismay over his injuries. Stoic as always, Laz had gently carried Timothy aboard the ship for the voyage back to Boston and then, as always, let Timothy talk or not talk. Timothy chose not to talk about his injuries. Uncle Jeremiah and Stef had met them at the docks with similar stoicism and respect for his silence.

The females were a different matter. When Mother, Deborah, Aunt Kerry and the girls, Aunt Patience, and Jemima saw his leg missing and his bandaged body and face, all of them wept over him. All except Gracie, and that was the only good thing he could say about the little brat. Despising the tears, he refused all visitors, even Jemima. A stone fortress seemed to enclose his heart. Somehow he must escape this as soon as he was able.

Weakness and pain threatened his resolve, and the morphine dulled his mind. His stump continued to heal, but he could not imagine ever putting his weight on it, even with the morphine powder he dusted on it, as prescribed by Dr. Kindleberger. His arm also healed slowly, for the surgeon had cut it open to try to put the muscles together in a more natural shape. Working to move his unresponsive hand, he wondered if it would ever regain strength.

His face would never be the same. Although the cutlass fragment had not reached the bone, it had cut deep into the flesh. The surgeon had managed to clean and sew the skin together, but the broad scar line would never disappear, and on it an odd strip of white hair blazed through his hairline, eyebrow, and newly grown beard. How could he shave when looking in the mirror sickened him? Without the morphine, how could he bear the still-savage pains that so often cut through him?

Timothy wakened in a darkened room. But what room? Was he still aboard the *Monongahela*? The *Hartford*? The *Hannah Rose*? No, not on shipboard at all, for he could not feel the familiar motion of waves. This unmoving room was home, the place of his childhood happiness now lost forever. As he often did these days, he lay in the dark and wished for one foolish moment that he could reach down and touch his right leg. Sometimes he still felt his foot itch—a maddening sensation.

A knock sounded on the door, but before he answered, Mother opened it and peered in. "Good. You're awake." She walked to the windows and flung open the heavy brown drapes. Daylight flooded the room. "Did you sleep well?"

Timothy put his left arm over his eyes. "I could have slept some more if you hadn't done that. Please close the drapes."

"You've slept enough." Mother sat on the bedside. "Do sit up. You have a guest." She pushed his tousled hair from his face.

"Mother!" He shoved her hand away, but then she tweaked his nose.

"*Mother*," she mocked. "Don't push my hand away. You're a mess, and you have company. Let me—"

"I have told you that I don't want to see anyone."

She studied him, and her tight smile, blinking eyes, and quick sniffs revealed her efforts not to cry. He released an explosive sigh and looked away.

"It's not 'anyone,'" she said. "It's Jemima. You must not refuse her, my darling." She gripped his chin and turned his face back toward her. "She loves you. A few scratches and wounds will not change that."

He tried to turn away again, but she held him fast and stared hard into his eyes. "I know what I am saying, Timothy. You must believe that I know."

Her eyes filled with tears, and her expression became so intense that he grimaced. She was thinking of Father, of course. "Very well, you know. I never suggested you didn't."

She drew back, a haunted look replacing her intensity. Then she gave her head a little shake—one of her most endearing gestures that now annoyed him—and smiled, this time seeming more like herself.

"Your father and I have had a discussion, and we would like to purchase the house next door as a wedding gift for you and Jemima. With slavery ending, we no longer will need the secret doors, but think of the fun my grandchildren will have visiting us without ever going outside in the heat of summer or the cold of winter."

Timothy shrugged his good shoulder. "You and Laz can buy it if you like, but you'll have to save it for Matthew. Once I have my new leg, I won't live in this place."

Mother's smile grew tight again. "Don't you think you should consult with Jemima? These Nantucket girls expect their husbands to listen to their opinions."

"I'm not—" Timothy stopped. Mother was not the one to hear this. He blew out a sigh. "Very well. Send her up."

Mother stood, walked to his washstand, and brought back his comb. "Let me make you presentable first." She raised the comb toward his hairline, but once again he stopped her.

"Let her see me as I am."

That haunted expression darted across Mother's face again, and Timothy's stomach turned. More memories of Father, he supposed.

"Silly boy," she said brightly, the deepening lines in her forehead belying her tone. "Here's your comb and hand mirror. Fix yourself up a bit before she comes in." She set the two items on his bed, wrapped her arms around his chest, and tried to pull him up. "Do help me, darling. This isn't easy."

He pushed his left arm down into the feather mattress and wiggled upward, grunting and panting with pain, until seated against the pillow at the headboard. Mother's eyes revealed her pity, but she continued to smile as she helped him adjust his nightshirt.

"There. Now comb your hair and cheer up. You barely spoke a word to her when you came home. Think of all the catching up you'll have to do."

Humming a tune with brightness that sounded artificial, she sailed out the door.

Timothy drew the mirror up slowly, trying to see only his hair, but the hideous red slash drew him with a dreadful fascination to the right side of his face. How had the blade failed to kill him? How had it failed to take his sight? More than that, how could his family bear to look at him? His face had been bandaged when Jemima had seen him, but now she would see the worst.

If only his bedroom door were on the left side, he could stare straight ahead and she would not see the scar. As it was, his disfigurement would be the first thing her gaze fell on when she entered the room. Would she cry again? Would she pity him?

His wounds began to ache, and he reached for the comfort of the morphine hidden in the bedside table drawer. But a tap on the door stayed his hand. He glanced about in confusion. Wasn't there some way to avoid Jemima, some place he could hide?

"Good afternoon, sleepyhead." Jemima peeked around the door then entered.

She had grown a little taller, though not as tall as Mother. Her pretty yellow walking gown graced her flawless form. Her golden hair was parted in the middle and curled in fashionable ringlets on each side of her head. And her lovely dark eyes—no pity there, only the radiance of love far more womanly than her youthful affection. She glowed like sunshine. Her beauty took his breath away. His eyes were the ones to burn with tears.

"Mother Hannah said you might be a little grumpy." Jemima walked to his bedside and placed a gentle peck on his right cheek. "But I told her I would fix that. I have had plenty of experience cheering up grumpy students at Beacon Hill School on hot summer days." She pulled up a small chair, grasped both sides of her hoop skirt, and eased herself gracefully down. "There. My goodness, I can't wait until these things are out of fashion."

Still wincing from her kiss, Timothy watched her. How unlike her to begin with such superficial topics as weather and fashion, especially when her inner tension revealed itself through her subtle trembling.

"Hello, Jemima."

"Hello, Timothy. My, don't we sound formal? One would never know we're engaged."

There it was—the catch in her voice, the pity he could not bear. The fortress sealed around his heart. She deserved a whole man, one she could respect and depend on—someone like Stef. But with her sense of honor she would never break their engagement. He must set her free, but how?

She stood, took the comb from him and began to work it through his hair. "My, so many tangles, and you do need a haircut." She tapped away his hand when he tried to reclaim the comb. "But I rather like the beard. All the whaling men back home wear beards. Just a little longer, a nice trim, and you'll look very distinguished for our wedding portrait."

"Jemima—"

"I thought a spring wedding would be lovely." Her voice sounded strained. "April or May when all the flowers are blooming." She set the comb on the table and fussed with the books lying there. "Although Christmas would be nice, too. Still, if we wait until spring—"

"Jemima, I cannot marry you."

She stopped arranging the books, but she stared down, and her hands rested on the table. "Don't be silly. Of course you can marry me." She turned and gave him a smile so beautiful that he feared his resolve would shatter. "Do you think I cannot love you now? Did you think I fell in love with your handsome face or strong limbs? Do you really think I am that shallow?

"You are still the handsomest man I have ever seen, and even more so with this magnificent battle scar." She reached over and traced it down the line of his face. "Every time I see it, I will remember how you saved Isaiah's life, despite the terrible way he treated you for all those years, and I will love you all the more for your courage and goodness." Tears sparkled in her eyes, and her brave, radiant smile threatened to breach his defenses.

"He wrote and told me all about it. He said that even before the … the accident, he realized what a fool he'd been." She gave a short, ironic laugh. "My brother—figuring that out after all this time. He said he was on his way to tell you when …" Tears now splashed down her cheeks, and she sighed. "Will you forgive him?"

Timothy clenched his jaw. Just as surely as the surgeon's saw had sliced through his leg, he must sever this bitter, painful cord.

"I met someone else."

"What?" Jemima's face drained of color.

"I met another woman. I'm going to marry her."

She stared at him, looking deep into his eyes. "You're making that up. You're trying to send me away."

"No. When I was a student in Annapolis … her name is Consuela." What lie would convince her? "There was a child." A half-truth.

"No! No, you're lying. I can see it in your eyes. Why would you say such a horrible, ridiculous thing? If it were true, you would have told me before you left."

"Go away, Jemima. Marry Stef and be happy. I … I don't want you." The words sounded so cruel, her face looked so stricken, that Timothy felt as if his heart would explode like the rebel shell that had shattered their future. "Go!" he shouted.

She stared at him for what seemed like an eternity, and her tragic expression again almost penetrated his defenses. Then she bent over him, and her face flushed red. "I will not release you from our engagement. I will not let you go. When you are finished with this foolishness, we will marry and begin our happy life together."

"Foolishness?!"

"Do not, *do not* keep me waiting. But no matter how long I must wait, I will never let you go." She whirled around, and her hoops knocked over the chair as she strode toward the door. She flung it open, turned back again, and spoke with simple dignity. "I will never let you go." Then she was gone.

For as long as he was able, Timothy restrained his emotions until he could no longer hear her footsteps descending the staircase. Then he grabbed a pillow and held it to his face, screaming out in his rage and anguish, "*Jemima!*"

Then he reached for the morphine.

Chapter Twenty-seven

ℰℬ

September 1863

"Easy does it, lad." Jonathan Lazarus put his arm around Timothy's waist and helped him stand ever so slowly.

"Ah! Ow! Ow!" Timothy dropped back down on the side of the bed, grabbed at his wounded leg, and gulped in deep, quivering breaths. "It feels like a hot knife. Like ten hot knives." He reached for the drawer that held his morphine kit, but Uncle Jonathan stopped him.

"Wait a minute." His uncle sat on a chair, removed the wooden leg strapped to Timothy's stump, and inspected it just as he would any other work of his hands. He had carved the device from live oak and designed it to attach five inches below Timothy's knee at the site of the amputation, making certain both legs would be the same length. A cup-shaped portion held the rounded stump, and leather straps extended above the knee to belt it in place while still allowing the living joint to bend naturally. The rest resembled a tapering human calf, with a hinged foot shape at the end that would fit into a shoe or boot.

"The inside of the cup is smooth, and Maria's little cushion should help. Give it another try, boy. It's bound to hurt the first few times, but you'll never walk until you stand."

Timothy closed his eyes, taking more deep breaths.

"Let's try again," Jonathan said. "Ready?"

"Let me get a little help." Timothy reached again for the drawer.

"Let's try it without that first."

"I need some help," shouted Timothy, but Jonathan remained calm.

"The morphine may dull your pain, but it also dulls your mind and saps your energy. Be a man, lad. Bear the pain."

"What do you know about pain?" Timothy snarled, quickly regretting it. He needed his uncle. He could not afford to alienate him. But he must take the morphine.

Jonathan's dark-gray eyes reddened. "What I know or do not know of pain is not in question. You must consider whether you will live a full life or become half a man. At the mission, since the war began, we've seen far too many once-valiant soldiers who easily surrender to their suffering without a fight." He placed his large, strong hand on Timothy's shoulder. "This is not easy, but I will stand by you until you can stand alone."

Timothy felt his eyes burn too. His uncle's words—a long speech for him—touched a place deep in his soul. Would he fight, or would he surrender? He took a glass of water from the table and gulped down half of it, putting the glass back with a thud that sloshed moisture all over his books.

"Ready." He growled. He draped his arm around Jonathan's shoulder, his right hand hanging useless. With his left hand, he grasped Jonathan's arm and slowly pulled himself up onto his left leg. It held strong, for he had been hopping around his room for a few weeks. He began to lean into the wooden appendage, and deep, searing pain once again shot up his right leg. He shifted back to his left so quickly that he would have fallen had Jonathan not held him tight.

"Again," Jonathan said.

"I can't." Timothy despised his own whimpering tone. He reached again for the drawer.

"Wait a minute." Jonathan's patient tone did not change. "Let's try again."

"I need—"

"You can have it after we finish, son. Come now." Jonathan positioned himself to assist. "Again."

Timothy expelled a long, quivering breath, braced himself once more, and moved toward his uncle. Jonathan's stance showed readiness for any mishap. Trembling and shaking, Timothy leaned into the artificial leg, backed off, then leaned into it again. After several minutes, he clung to Jonathan with both hands, gritted his teeth, and lifted his left foot from the floor, only to set it down quickly.

"Ah! That's enough."

"That's my boy." Jonathan's tone was neutral, but his eyes shone with pride.

"Whoo, that was hard." Timothy blinked away tears caused by the pain.

"Let's do it again."

Timothy grimaced, but seeing a glimmer of long-lost Cousin Pal in his uncle's eyes, he tried again. He could do this. He *would* do it.

In the next few months, sixty-year-old Jonathan made the trip across town twice a day to exercise Timothy until they both proclaimed the project a success. Timothy now could walk on his own, although he used a cane when he went up and down the stairs or out for a stroll on the town.

The time had come to complete the rest of his plans—finding a new career. The navy had dismissed him from service, for they needed two-legged men to fight the war. Never mind that many an officer continued to fight with one arm shot away. He would show them. With more practice walking and the clever design of Jonathan's device, he would have no difficulty sailing.

The *Hannah Rose* sat docked at Commercial Wharf, for since the war began, Laz no longer imported cotton from Virginia. But other markets might prove profitable, such as California. The country's westernmost state had many needs, and Timothy was just the man to deliver them around the Horn. At dinner he proposed his idea to Laz.

As usual, Laz listened to Timothy's entire presentation, nodded thoughtfully, and looked to the far end of the table. "Hannah, what is your opinion of this?"

Laz was giving himself more time to think, a clever tactic, but Timothy loathed it when his stepfather used it on him. Of course, Mother would hate the idea.

She wrinkled her forehead and frowned. "Is it safe to sail so far during the war, dear?" As expected, she did not care for his idea. He should have spoken to Laz alone.

"Mother." He worked to keep the irritation from his voice. "The Union has hundreds of ships blockading the entire eastern and Gulf coasts, and California doesn't even know the war is going on. Sailing there is as safe as sailing anywhere."

"Hmm." Laz gave another thoughtful nod. "Let's take a look at the old girl and see if she's up to it. She was all right for that short trip to New York in good weather, but remember she's nearly sixty years old. Going around the Horn can be much more challenging."

"She could be refitted."

"Perhaps. But I'm not certain she can compete with these new steam-powered cargo ships. People out west want their goods as soon as they can get them."

Timothy slumped back in his chair and stared at his plate. He wanted to blame Laz for not supporting his idea, but in truth the ship probably was too old and out-of-date.

"Well, son," Laz said, "we'll take a look at her."

True to his expectations, the *Hannah Rose* required far too many repairs to fit her for long voyages. Nor could money be spent for a new steam-powered ship, for the family fortunes had suffered losses both in the 1857 stock market crisis and now during the war. Although Laz had tried to protect Timothy's inheritance, as he had from the moment he married Mother, he had by Timothy's permission invested some of it in the Union cause. The family would manage, but could not risk investing too much in any one venture.

Robbed of the enterprise by cruel reality, Timothy grew morose, and more so as winter deepened. He cared nothing for war news, for it only provoked his desire to take part. He refused an offer from the Naval Academy, still in Newport, to return to teaching. Why should he put himself in front of rowdy midshipmen to be mocked for his infirmities, as he and his fellows had sometimes mocked the old men who had taught them?

Uncle Jeremiah asked him for help at the mission, saying that many wounded men needed encouragement in their convalescence, and Timothy's recovery would raise their spirits over their own futures. But his wounds had proved difficult enough to cope with. He could not imagine viewing other shattered bodies with any semblance of composure. When Jeremiah mentioned Jemima's good work among the wounded, Timothy changed the subject.

Stef came to call, but Timothy likewise deflected his interest and his attempts to reestablish their boyhood camaraderie. Still, hoping to relive some happy childhood memory, he questioned Aunt Patience about Ezra, only to learn his friend now fought with the Massachusetts Fifty-fourth Colored Regiment somewhere in the South. His friend's remarkable courage did not surprise him. News had filtered north that rebel troops abandoned all rules of warfare and were excessively savage when taking the Negro soldiers captive. Timothy wondered if Beauchamp or Wilson engaged in such atrocities.

He spent endless winter days slouched in a front parlor chair reading all the books Mother had left on his night table, except for one. The book about his father, with its simple brown leather cover and title *Moby Dick*, appeared harmless enough, but the thought of reading it sickened him. What perverse notion caused Mother to torture him this way? He knew all he needed to know about the man, and despite his nearly identical injuries, he would not be like Father. He would do the right thing. No one would suffer because of him.

Since his confrontation with Matthew, his brother no longer gazed at him with wide-eyed admiration, nor did he seek Timothy's company to hear war stories. Deborah seemed to understand his desire to be alone. Only Gracie continued to pester him, even when he ignored her and kept his nose in a book.

"What are you reading?" She leaned against the arm of his wing-back chair one morning and laid her head on his right shoulder.

"Don't." He flinched, but not only because of the pain. Right now, he ached to give himself a morphine injection. But Uncle Jonathan had convinced him it was best to manage without the opiate, and he had permitted his uncle to take away the wooden box. Maybe that had been a mistake, but he would not let his uncle—or anyone else—see him weaken. "That's my bad arm."

She moved back, but just a little. "It's getting better. I can tell by the way you move it." She tapped his upper arm. "See, that doesn't hurt."

He shrugged her hand away. "I said don't. Now go away. I'm reading."

She put her hand on the page and pressed the book down to his lap. "I'm angry with you, Timbee."

"Don't call me Timbee. You're too old to talk like a baby."

"All right, Tim-o-theee. But I'm angry. Aren't you going to ask me why?"

"No."

She snorted. "I'm going to tell you anyway."

"Go away, Grace." Timothy clenched his jaw. This child was intolerable.

"You hurt Jemima and now she won't even come for Sunday dinner anymore."

"Shut your mouth. You don't know what you're talking about." If this brat did not leave, he did not know what he would do.

"I most certainly do know. She always came for Sunday dinner, and now she doesn't. You said something mean to her. I just know it."

"I said shut your mouth." His left hand swung toward Grace, but even before it touched her cheek, the horror of what he was doing slammed into Timothy. He tried to stop, but his palm made contact—hard. She flew backward, bounced off the brocade divan, and fell to the floor.

"Gracie!" he wailed, and heard Mother's scream from the hallway echoing his cry.

Mother ran to Gracie, threw herself down on her knees, and seized the stunned child, who made no sound, just stared at her brother, her eyes round with shock.

In an instant, he saw a different scene: Mother, her cheek flaming red, on the floor, holding another terror-stricken child—he himself—and Papa standing over them in a rage. *Dear God, I am becoming my father after all.*

Weeping as she held Grace, Mother touched the fiery injury, then searched for other wounds. Grace gazed up at her. Tears glistened in her eyes. How had the blow failed to break her slender neck?

Timothy slid out of the chair to his knees and crawled toward them. What had he done? How could he repair the damage? Both Mother and Grace recoiled as he came near and leaned against the divan. He reached out. "Come to me, Gracie. I will not hurt you again. I'm so sorry."

Mother stared at him, her eyes wide with that old, haunted look. Was she too reliving their long-ago ordeal? She pulled Gracie closer. "No. Just go upstairs. Just leave us alone."

Grace, always a crybaby, still had not wept, despite her tear-filled eyes. "No, Mama, let me hug him. He's all broken and can't help it."

She tugged free and crawled into his lap. "I love you, Timothy, but you must not hit anyone again. Promise me you won't."

How could she bear to touch him? How could she trust him after what he had just done? "I will not, little mite," he choked out. "I swear I will not. Please forgive me."

She flung her arms around his neck and hugged so hard it nearly strangled him, but he did not resist. Shaken and sickened, he gently delivered her back to Mother, and then struggled to stand. Mother still stared at him, shaking her head in horror, but he had no words to console her.

He pulled up on the divan, then stood, limped from the room, and dragged himself upstairs to his fourth-floor bedroom. Although this had been his beloved home for over fourteen years, it had now become an alien habitation, a dwelling in which he belonged no more. He grabbed his navy duffel bag from his wardrobe and began to stuff it with shirts, linens, shaving gear, and socks.

Mother entered the room without knocking. "Running away from home?" Her tear-stained face still looked stricken.

He shrugged. "I don't want to hurt anyone else."

"Why Grace?" She removed his shirts from the bag and began to fold them. "Why the littlest one? If you needed to hit someone, why not someone your own size?"

The comment was so unlike Mother that he must defend himself. "She's always been a pest. You and Laz never correct her." This was insane. He had no excuse for striking his sister. "Why can't she be like Deborah? Or like you?" He took a folded shirt and stuffed it back into the bag.

Mother's laugh came short and bitter. "Grace is exactly like me. How my father must have wished I was like Deborah, for he could never keep a governess. I drove them all away."

He glared at her. "I don't believe you."

"I could not be tamed. Once when Papa took me to greet a

whaling ship, I dashed about the docks like a street boy and almost fell into the harbor. Uncle Jeremiah saved my life. He was only a boy of fourteen, and I was eight, just Gracie's age." She stopped folding shirts and stared into his eyes. "When *I* was fourteen, the head-mistress almost dismissed me from boarding school for missing church and going on a lark with my friend Nan."

Timothy shook his head. She was making all this up. He refused to believe it. He could see their friend, Mrs. Nan Pendergast, going on such a lark, but never Mother. Why would she lie to him like this? He took the rest of the shirts and stuffed them back into the bag, brushing against her with his arm. He stepped back, not wanting to touch her for all his uncleanness.

"Where will you go?" She walked to the bedside table, picked up a book, and placed it in his bag.

He shrugged. "Don't know." Why was she not begging him to stay? Of course. She wanted him to leave.

"Why not go out to the farm in Indiana? Cousin Johnny is in the army, the girls are married, and James is in California. Aunt Willa writes that Uncle Solomon is in poor health. I know he would be pleased to have your help."

"Enough. All right. I might do that."

"Will you eat dinner with the family before you go?" Her voice sounded thin and tired. "Father will be home soon."

Timothy felt his heart twist. Laz would kill him for hitting Gracie, and he deserved it. "No."

"Any message for him?"

"No. Yes. I'm sorry."

She patted his shoulder. "I will have Patience fix some food for you to take."

"Thank you, Mother."

As soon as she left, he removed the hated book from his bag and stuffed it under the mattress. He glanced around the room and found nothing else to take, so he tied the leather straps of the duffel bag, lifted it over his shoulder, took his cane, and walked downstairs.

Laz stood in the front parlor with Grace in his arms. The raised bruise on her cheek had already begun to darken.

A few times in his life, Timothy had seen Laz angry, so angry he seemed like a rumbling volcano about to erupt. His eyes smoldered that way now, and Timothy wondered why he did not put Grace down and give him his much-deserved punishment. Just as he appeared about to do so, Grace whimpered and squeezed him about the neck.

"No, Papa. Please hold me."

Laz did as she asked, leaning his head tenderly against hers.

Timothy swallowed a lump in his throat. Was he mistaken, or was Grace protecting him? How much better he would feel if she hated him for what he had done.

"I'm going."

Laz gave him a curt nod, and Timothy could see his jaw clench.

He shifted the bag on his shoulder and walked out the front door. Halfway down the block, Grace caught up with him, thrust a parcel of food into his hands, and dashed away before he could speak.

Chapter Twenty-eight

&

February 1864

An icy wind blew across the Annapolis harbor where Timothy leaned against the cold brick wall of some waterfront business. He stared out across the water, feeling as impervious to the winter chill as the dead fish whose odor permeated these docks. The small city had changed in the past three years since the academy had moved to Rhode Island. The school property had become an army encampment and hospital, and some of the buildings were almost in shambles. Wounded soldiers lay sprawled everywhere. Many had lost limbs, and one poor man had only an arm still attached to his body. Others wore bandages over sightless eyes. Disease and infection were rampant. Among the wounded soldiers, attitudes ranged from raging bitterness to ridiculous optimism. Timothy wondered why he had come. He was not like these men.

Leaving Boston, he had decided to visit his old school. The train ride took him on a journey of happy memories as he recalled his excitement over the coming adventure and the enjoyment of meeting Hart. They had become friends instantly, but then, Hart liked everyone. He and Starbuck probably had become great friends by now.

As his trip continued, he thought of his lie to Jemima and conceived a plan. Poor old Captain Longwood had wanted him to care for Señora Cervantes and Consuela. He would search for them and see if they needed help, for many people had become destitute because of the war. But when he arrived at their house, a new owner greeted him who knew nothing of the former residents.

Without direction, he wandered the town searching for memories but discovered only loneliness. At last as daylight faded, he found himself here at the waterfront pondering a blank, black future. A swish of skirts sounded on his left, but he did not turn.

"Say, pretty boy," a woman said, "are you looking for a place to stay tonight?"

For a moment he did not answer, for Laz had taught him that a street woman might misunderstand a gentleman's courtesy. But why should he not respond? If he turned his face, she would see his scar and leave him alone. He stood tall and turned so she might see whom, or what, she had addressed.

"Ma'am." He doffed his broad-brimmed hat and gave her a shallow bow.

"Ah." Her gaze took in the scar, yet neither in tone nor in expression did the pretty, dark-haired woman show pity. "A hero, I would imagine. Well, you look hungry. Come home with me, and I will feed you."

He studied her for a moment. Her tattered blue dress dipped low on her shoulders, far too low for a winter evening … or decent company. Her perfume was strong but not unpleasant, and it competed with the fishy stench of the place.

"Come." She gripped his forearm and gently tugged, so he picked up his bag and went with her.

She took him to her home on East Street, a narrow house with two stories and a basement. No one else seemed to live there, but he could hear rats within the walls. She hung his Inverness great-coat and dome-crowned hat on the hall tree just inside the front door, then took him to the kitchen and, true to her promise, fed him from a simmering pot on the cast-iron stove. The thick gruel, flavored with tiny bits of ham, smelled inviting and tasted good.

Her coffee rivaled the delicious brew that Patience made. She sat across the table from him and talked about the war, lamenting the losses; President Lincoln, without revealing her opinion of him; and the academy, stating boldly how much she missed the fine young men who had attended it. She had a pleasant way about her and seemed to hold no strong opinions or judgments. On their way here, she had not commented on his strange, limping gait or even looked down at the trouser leg that covered his wooden appendage. While he ate, she did not seem offended at the brevity of his responses.

When he had finished his meal, she took him upstairs.

"This is our best guest room." She seemed almost innocent in her pride in the shabby accommodations: a large iron-framed bed with often-mended quilt and sheets, a scarred bureau, a simple wash-stand, and a mirror. She turned an equally innocent smile on him. "We can share the bed, if you like … for warmth on this cold night."

He drew in a breath as his body flooded with unbidden feelings. This was wrong. He should not be here. But why not? He would never marry Jemima and certainly not anyone else. Why save himself for something that would never happen?

She laughed softly and pushed him to sit on the bed. "Come, my pretty boy, let me take care of you. I have wine, if you like, and we can tell each other stories all through the night."

Her words sounded sweet, like honey. Laz's proverbs echoed in his head, but he dismissed them. Without Jemima, they no longer mattered. Why should he not learn a new way to enjoy himself?

She reached out and began to unbutton his jacket, humming and cooing more compliments, but he could only stiffen and draw back.

"Wait." He took her hands and held them away from himself. "Don't you even want to know my name?"

In the dim candlelight, she appeared surprised. "Why, I suppose, if you want to tell me." She laughed softly. "But if you prefer, you do not have to tell me your real name." She slipped her hand from his and pressed it against his shirt front.

"It's—" He drew in another breath. How could this feel so pleasant and so uncomfortable at the same time? "It's Ahab."

She blinked and sat back. "Ahab? Like in the Bible?"

"Yes."

"That's your true name?"

"Yes."

"Ah, my pretty boy." She reached up and ran her fingers through his beard. "Ahab was a very wicked king, you know. Are you as wicked as he?" The idea seemed to please her.

"I hope not," he blustered, but then a bitter laugh escaped him. "But perhaps so." He stopped her hands again. "What's your name?"

She regarded him for a moment. "Meg. Meg Doone."

"*Meg?*" Timothy jumped up so quickly that he lost his balance and crashed to the floor. A sickening crack sounded at the base of his wooden leg, and he cursed the pain ripping up his stump from the jolt.

"Oh, you poor dear. What made you jump so?" Meg helped him to a sitting position on the floor and sat beside him while they both inspected the damage. The foot had caught under the edge of the bed and snapped off, pulling the hinges with it and leaving the end splintered.

"Now what shall I do?" he muttered. Many years had passed since he had helped Jonathan with woodworking. He would never be able to fix this mess.

"Why, nothing now." She retrieved the broken piece and removed it from the shoe. "It's too late to find a carpenter. But just look at this clever device. I know a lot of men who would like something this grand to replace their lost limbs." Her tone had become practical, almost flippant. She helped him stand and sit back down on the bed. "But we don't need to interrupt our party. This is just a trifle."

"No, Meg, it's not. I have to leave."

A scratch on the door drew their attention. "Mama," a child's voice called.

"Who is that?" Timothy felt his insides twist. He knew exactly who the child was.

Meg hurried to the door, opened it, and knelt by a pretty, dark-haired, blue-eyed little girl. Even in the dim candlelight, Timothy could see that her face bore traces of the scoundrel who had deserted them, the man he and Beauchamp had captured, dragged to Mrs. Doone, and forced to confess.

"What is it, my darling? Mama said you must stay in your room until I wake you in the morning. You must obey."

"But who is that man?" The child's eyes were round with curiosity and perhaps a measure of fear.

Meg glanced over her shoulder. "Just a nice man who is renting our room tonight. You run back to your room now. If you do not stay there, I will lock you in."

With a whimper, the girl hurried away. Meg stood and returned to Timothy's side. "Well, Mr. Ahab, what will it be?" From her businesslike tone, she could be selling him apples. "Shall I take you down to the street, or will you rest here tonight?"

A wave of weakness swept through him. He had no other place to go and certainly could not walk far on the splintered leg without destroying it. "I will stay."

She gave him a short nod. "Shall I keep you company, or will you sleep alone?"

"Alone." The word came out of its own volition, but he felt relieved.

Meg's expression softened once more. Clearly she was pleased at his response. "Very well, Mr. Ahab. I will have breakfast for you in the morning, and then we'll see about finding a carpenter to fix that wooden leg."

The carpenter, a slender old mulatto man, knelt by Timothy's chair and studied Jonathan's design with great interest. "I could sell a hundred of these in a week." His dark eyes snapped with delight at the prospect. "You don't have a patent on it, do you?"

"No. Can you put the broken foot back on?"

The man shook his head. "Don't think so, sir. It's all splintered where it was attached. But maybe I can make you a new one. Will you be here long?"

Timothy glanced over the man's shoulder at Meg. Her eyes revealed hope, but he would not stay in this place. "No. I must leave as soon as possible."

"Well, sir, give it to me, and I'll go file it down and nail on a square piece so's you can walk on it. I'll do my best to keep it the same length. If you like, I'll go over to the blacksmith and have him secure a bronze cap to it to prevent wear."

Timothy gave his assent, and they agreed on a price. Trapped in Meg's parlor as he waited for the man to return, Timothy slouched in a well-worn chair. Meg sat on another chair and tried to draw him out, but her voice sounded like the annoying drone of a mosquito. At last she sighed and stood to leave.

"If you want to read, there's a book over there another fellow left behind. Now if you'll excuse me, I've got to tend my daughter."

He glanced at the side table and picked up the book, but dropped it in revulsion. *Moby Dick.*

March 1864

The ship pitched fore and aft on the ocean's light swells. Timothy held the railing, still not used to his peg leg. With its new shape, he could not hide his injury with clothing and a shoe, so he tucked the trouser leg around his stump and strapped the wooden device over it. In some ways his leg felt better, but now people stared at him more often. One would think they could keep their eyes on their own business. Had they not seen enough wounded men these days? His injury could not be considered unique.

The ship pitched forward into a trough, and to keep from falling to the deck he grasped the nearby lines. Just placing his hand on them stirred his heart. How he longed to go aloft and watch as the ship sailed toward Nantucket. How he longed to cry "Land ho" to the captain, and then trim the sails so the vessel could glide into its berth. But this square peg would never hold on the lines, nor could his right arm compensate to keep him there, despite its increasing strength. Could he not find some way to make himself useful aboard a ship? But now, other more able men clambered aloft to answer the call of bringing this merchant vessel into Nantucket Harbor.

Why had he returned to the island of his birth? What did he expect to see or learn? Yet come he must, as if some invisible hand was leading him. The whaling business had almost completely died out here, and those who still sailed around Cape Horn to the Pacific whaling grounds would not hire a cripple with no whaling experience. His beloved Aunt Abigail had died, as had her sister Tishtega, and with them was buried the last true knowledge of his father. Cousin Daniel, whose eldest son had died at Gettysburg, had moved his family to the mainland. Aunt Charity Coffin, old and feeble, dwelt with the Harris family in Boston, but her mind dwelt far in the past.

Cane and duffel bag in hand, Timothy stood on the wharf, and the ship's crew jostled him as they unloaded their cargo. He hobbled out of the way, walking toward town as best he could with his brass foot slipping on the Main Street cobblestones. The shops and businesses seemed tired, sad, and desolate. Or perhaps he saw in them what he felt in his own heart. Why, why had he come?

He made his way through the winding streets past once-glorious mansions, some now going to ruin. Six years had passed since he last walked this road to the ancient graveyard, but he easily found the way to his father's monument, which towered over all the other gravestones. Empty of all emotion, he traced the letters of the dedication carved into the granite. Yet he thought not of his parent, but of the brave, sweet, beautiful girl who had gently tended this stone with her lovely tapered fingers.

Jemima. He could never go back to her, no matter what. She deserved the best of everything—a man who could support her, love her, and give her all her heart's desires. He could give her only a broken body and a dwindling inheritance.

He leaned against the obelisk and watched as the winter evening drew on. How easy it would be to curl up like a child and sleep here next to all that remained to him of his father, but it would be a sleep of death. Mother would grieve, at least for a while, if he surrendered his life so foolishly. The bitter wind increased, cutting through his Inverness and causing his slouch hat to flap around his ears. He shivered, surely a sign that he did wish to continue living, no matter how desolate his life. Rousing himself, he bid his father one last good-bye, devoid of any emotion. Then he walked back toward town to find an inn.

Along the way, he could not fail to notice that several people stared and pointed at him. What ill manners these Nantucketers had. He would leave tomorrow, never to return.

He located a small, old hotel called the Try Pots and requested a room. The young man at the desk signed him in and directed him upstairs. After stowing his bag, Timothy returned to the first floor and took a table in an alcove off the large dining room. An elderly woman with a well-stained apron bustled to his table and said, "Clam or cod?"

This must be Mrs. Hussey, whom the desk boy had described. "Ma'am?"

"Clam or cod, boy? What kind of chowder?"

A beefsteak would be much more to his liking, but this formidable woman, who wore a necklace of polished fish bones about her long, thin neck, somehow reminded him of Tishtega, and so he said, "Clam."

"Ale or wine?"

"I understand Nantucket water is much to be desired." One drunken binge in his plebe year at the academy had been enough spirits for him.

She eyed him as if he were crazy. As she continued to stare, her face grew pale. But then she shook her head. "Nantucket water." On her way to the kitchen, she almost collided with an old sailor or whaler. Timothy could not tell from his clothes which occupation the old fellow might claim.

The man stumbled away from her and sat down at a round table some twenty-five feet from Timothy. He ordered cod chowder and ale, and while waiting, glanced about at his neighbors. He had a ruddy, wrinkled, seaman's complexion, gray-brown hair, and a muscular build. His faded blue eyes wore a troubled look, and his gaze darted here and there as if on guard against danger. He did not leave any part of the room unchecked.

When at last his searching gaze fell across Timothy's shadowed alcove, he drew back in his chair and cried out, "Captain, my captain, is that you?" He leapt up and raced toward Timothy, whose heart pounded as he pulled up his cane for a weapon and braced to stand for the madman's attack. Could he protect himself with one hand, for the other was useless?

The man stopped short, leaving the table between them. "See here, Captain Ahab, what mean you coming back to haunt me after all these years? Did I not tell your story faithfully? Did I not spread the word of your magnificent death? Is it my fault they do not listen? Why do you stare at me with those wide, dark eyes?

Why do you haunt me? Speak, my captain. Do you not know your Ishmael?"

Timothy struggled to stand, terrified, stricken, remembering. This was the man who had told his father's story in the church all those years ago. This was the survivor of the *Pequod*, the last man to see his father alive. "I am not who you think. I am not your captain." Timothy edged around the table to get away.

"See, you are the man," cried Ishmael, pointing to Timothy's wooden leg. "Resurrected to haunt me, despite my faithfulness. See the leg. See the scar on that noble visage. See God's judgment on that blazing brow. A younger face, but Ahab just the same." He moved closer and blocked Timothy's path. "Why do you haunt me?"

Beyond him, Timothy saw Mrs. Hussey and the other patrons creeping nearer. Would they help him? Or would they too be haunted by his presence? The woman had already recognized the resemblance. Had all these people gone mad? *Can I never escape my father? God, please help me!*

"Very well, Mr. Ishmael." Where were these words coming from? "You are correct. I am Ahab. I came to commend you for a job well done."

The man fell to his knees weeping, but only for a moment. He jumped up. "I have the account. I have it in my bag. You must take it and read. See how faithfully I reported your courage and your madness." He gasped. "No, not madness. Wisdom. I meant wisdom."

Timothy shifted where he stood. "I'm certain you did your best, sir. Don't be troubled. Perhaps there was a measure of madness in me." Yes, perhaps Father had been mad, not evil after all. But which left the worse legacy for him?

Ishmael hurried to his seaman's bag and pulled out the book. Timothy marveled that such a lunatic could write the large tome, and more so that someone would publish it.

"Take it. Read it. I must know what your judgment is."

His lip curled with disgust, Timothy took the book, holding it as if it were a piece of refuse. "Thank you."

"Now, Ishmael," Mrs. Hussey said, "let's have a seat and eat your chowder before it gets cold." She took hold of his hand as one would a child and directed him back to his table, where he fell to eating and seemed to forget the entire incident.

"Fine job there, lad." A man clasped him on the shoulder.

Timothy turned to all the men who had witnessed his ordeal. "Sir?"

"That poor fellow has just about driven us all crazy over the years. You handled yourself very well."

The others murmured their agreement, and Timothy released a long sigh of relief. If the crazy man had attacked, they surely would have helped him.

"I must say he's right about one thing. You're a bit young, but you do have the look of an old whaler who died almost twenty years ago, a man named Ahab," another man said. "O'course, I never sailed with the man, and my memory might have slipped over time."

"Did you lose your leg in the war, boy?" A bent old fellow pressed forward, his eyes rheumy.

Timothy inclined his head. "Yes, sir, I did."

The men murmured their appreciation, and several more reached out to shake his hand or clap him on the back and shoulders.

"It's mighty good to see you alive, boy. I know you're going to miss that leg, but many of our Nantucket lads won't be coming home at all."

"And with whaling dying out," a third man said, "the island seems pretty desolate these days."

"We need young fellows like you to bring in some new ideas. Is that what you came here for?" Hopeful old eyes pierced him clear to his soul.

Timothy began to edge away. "No, sir. I ... I have to leave

tomorrow at first light. Mrs. Hussey, will you please bring my dinner to my room?"

"Of course, my boy. I'm sorry about the old fellow, but he really is harmless."

Timothy disengaged himself from the disappointed ancients and hastened to his room. In the morning, as his ship sailed northwestward toward New Bedford, he dropped Ishmael's book into Nantucket Sound. Mother was right, of course. He should have gone to Indiana in the first place.

Chapter Twenty-nine

❧

May 1865

*L*ieutenant Isaiah Starbuck." Lacy's eyes sparkled as she sat beside him on the divan and gripped his hand. "You look so handsome, and I am so proud of you. Who needs to graduate from some old naval academy? You won your stripes the hard way—in a war."

"You do look very fine, Isaiah." Jemima sat in a nearby chair in the front parlor. Her eyes also glistened, but Isaiah knew her tears were of a different sort.

"It's good to be home." Yes, the Harris house had become a home, a haven of love to two lost orphans, Jemima and him. Isaiah smiled at his sister. "Do you hear from Timothy?"

She took out a handkerchief and dabbed her eyes. "No, but Mother Hannah and I continue to write all the news from here. His Aunt Willa wrote to say he has saved her farm this past year, since his cousin Johnny has been away in the army since '62 and her husband died a year ago. With the war being over, I do hope they will discharge Johnny soon. Then perhaps Timothy will return—" she sniffed back tears "—return home too."

Isaiah nodded his understanding. He looked back at Lacy and almost felt guilty for the happiness her adoring gaze gave him. Last night he had asked Reverend Harris for her hand in marriage and now had permission to make his happiness complete, for he had no doubt she would accept his proposal. He glanced at Jemima, not wishing to dismiss her sorrow but hoping she would grasp the meaning of his wink.

"Oh," Jemima said. "I must go help Daisy. Brother, did you know she is going south to minister to the poor people so terribly devastated by the war?"

"Indeed? How grand. Her given name of Dorcas is appropriate, like Dorcas of the Bible known for her good works."

"Yes." Jemima stood, her sad mood apparently broken. "Now you two have a nice conversation without me." She returned Isaiah's wink, left the room, and slid the pocket doors closed behind her.

Now that the moment had arrived, Isaiah felt his heart in his throat, but Lacy sat there with a delightful smirk on her face.

"Well, Lieutenant Starbuck, what do you have to say for yourself?"

He placed his arm around her shoulders. "When shall we get married?"

"When? Why, sir, how dare you assume—"

He bent close and stopped her words with a gentle kiss. "Marry me. That is an order."

She sighed and then giggled. "Aye, sir. Any day you choose, and sooner rather than later."

"Hmm." He frowned. "Sooner would be grand, but I wonder—"

Lacy grew sober. "About Timothy?"

"How did you know? No, don't answer, my dear one. We always seem to think alike." He rested his head against hers.

"He truly took the part of an older brother for my sisters, brother, and me, Isaiah. As far back as I can remember, he played with us and took us places and never behaved as if we were a bother. I think that loving him as a brother prepared me for loving you. I did not regard young gentlemen as foreign creatures."

Isaiah chuckled. "Foreign creatures? How odd. Such a thing never occurred to me about young ladies, but then, I have a sister." He brushed his hand across her fair cheek. "Ah, Lacy, I owe him so much—you, my academy days, my very life."

Lacy moved from his embrace, took his hands, and pulled them up to her lips. "I long for our marriage, but perhaps our Lord would have you go to him for reconciliation. I cannot think that the young man I've known so well through the years would rebuff you."

"Will you kneel here with me to pray that he won't?"

She leaned forward, kissed his cheek, and blew out a sweet, small sigh. "Would it be all right also to pray that the reconciliation won't take too long?"

Timothy removed his broad-brimmed straw hat, wiped his sleeve across his wet face, and crossed his arms on the hoe handle, basking for a moment in the breeze that dried his sweat-soaked shirt. Hoeing weeds, like all farm work, could be exhausting, but the rewards made it well worth the effort.

He had arrived at the farm early last summer only to learn Uncle Solomon had died after spring planting. Poor Aunt Willa had welcomed Timothy as her knight in shining armor. Her loving gratitude fueled his resolve to learn about farming and save the land for her and his cousin. Last autumn, with hired help, he had harvested his uncle's plantings. This spring, again with hired help, he had plowed and harrowed the fields, planted crops, pitched hay, and mended fences, and in the fall would harvest his own work. His right arm had regained much of its strength. Although the hand still could not manage a pen well, he could grip the necessary farm implements. He still walked with a slow, awkward gait, especially in the reddish brown silt loam of the fields. But his left leg and what remained of his right had grown muscular again, as when he had scampered aloft in the riggings of a ship.

In the field, spring breezes caressed the tender, knee-high stalks of corn, while nearer the farmhouse, sycamore and sugar maple trees rustled their abundant greenery. The sweet fragrance of Aunt Willa's honeysuckle blossoms vied for preeminence with the pungent smells of horses, chickens, and milk cows. How different the redolence of Indiana from the varied city and sea scents of Boston and Annapolis. How pleasant this safe haven from all his grief.

When he first arrived the previous summer, grieving Aunt Willa had welcomed him with maternal kindness and—being a markedly practical woman—a minimum of pity for his wounds. He hoped she found as much comfort in their quiet companionship as he did. Together they looked forward to Johnny's homecoming any day now.

How curious that Indiana's Eighty-first Regiment had not yet discharged its troops. The war had been over since early April. Did they fear that with Lincoln's assassination the South might find some way to rekindle the conflict? Impossible, of course, for news of the shattered rebel armies and fleeing leaders had reached even to this remote area.

Renewed by his short pause, Timothy took his hoe and began again to hack at the weeds. At the beginning, he had cut through several tender cornstalks but with practice had learned how to aim the tool with precision. Today he hoped to reach the ends of several more rows before Aunt Willa rang the dinner bell.

Despite his childhood visit to this place, he had never thought much about farming. Did all city people take their food for granted, as he had, something that just appeared on the table several times a day? Now he could see that farming gave a man soul-deep satisfaction and confidence in his ability to provide for himself and others.

Aunt Willa would cluck her tongue at such a thought, for to her everything was "the Lord this" or "the Lord that." He laughed softly to himself. Maybe he had begun to agree, for surely aboard the *Monongahela*, he had been spared while Captain Read had died. Standing here in this fruitful field he had worked with his own two hands, how glad he was that Dr. Kindleberger had not amputated his right arm along with his leg. And, oh, how good he felt to be alive!

The clang of the dinner bell rang across the fields. Surprised, Timothy created a makeshift sundial with his hoe. Too early for dinner. Aunt Willa must need him. Using the hoe for a cane, he clumped down the row toward the fence, and his pulse quickened.

On the farmhouse porch, a man stood beside his aunt. Johnny! Clambering around the fence, Timothy dropped the hoe and began to run in his terrible, painful, lumbering way. Why did Johnny not rush to meet him? Couldn't the fellow see how it was for him?

But then, just past the barn, he stopped, for now he could identify the man. Starbuck. What did he want? For a moment, Timothy thought to return to the field, but what would Aunt Willa think? And what if someone he loved had died? Perhaps that news had come in the letters piled unread in his bottom bureau drawer. He continued his labored trek to the house.

"Timothy, good to see you." Starbuck wore a plain brown suit and held a black porkpie hat.

Timothy held the railing, placed his foot on the first step, pulled his peg leg up beside it, and repeated the process for the other two steps. Once he had reached the porch, Isaiah stuck out his hand. Aunt Willa appeared surprised at his hesitation. She knew nothing of his past with this man, so Timothy lifted his weaker hand up to touch Isaiah's as briefly as he could.

"Starbuck."

Aunt Willa now smiled. "You two boys sit down here on the porch, and I'll bring you something cool to drink." She walked inside humming.

They sat in two straight-backed porch chairs. Timothy eyed Starbuck's duffel bag, which sported his name in blocked letters, along with "US Navy." Was he still in the service? If so, why had he not worn his uniform? Timothy would not bother to ask.

"You're looking much better than the last time I saw you," Starbuck said. "I'm glad to see that." He looked as if he expected some sort of response, so Timothy would give one.

"What do you want?"

"For us to be reconciled."

Timothy snorted.

Starbuck's military posture deflated, and he let out a sigh. "Lacy asked me to bring you back for our wedding this July. She says it won't be the same without you."

"She'll be all right. She's a strong girl." *She will need to be, married to you.*

"Jemima asked me to tell you—"

"Have she and Stef married yet? That's what you wanted, wasn't it?"

Starbuck coughed out a laugh. "Don't you read your mail, Timothy? Stef and Molly were married last Christmas. They're expecting a child."

Timothy's heart twisted. Jemima—free. He must get rid of the ache this thought caused.

"Speaking of children," he said, "I ran across a friend of yours in Annapolis, a woman named Meg Doone. She has a child but no husband. I suppose the louse deserted her."

Isaiah groaned. "Poor Meg."

"Don't worry. I left her a little money."

"That was decent of you."

They sat in silence for several moments. Where was Aunt Willa? Where was that cool drink?

"Will you go with me?" Starbuck's eyes grew red, and his brow arched with a hopeful expression.

Timothy turned away, pointing. "See that corn field out there? And the one beyond? And that one over to the west? I am responsible for tending those fields until my cousin comes home. In fact, this farm has enough work for six people, and my aunt doesn't need to be dealing with hired men. I doubt I'll be leaving any time soon."

Starbuck brushed his hand across his eyes. "Of course."

Aunt Willa brought a tray of lemonade and announced that dinner would be served in half an hour. After she went back inside the house, the silence on the porch made Timothy's eardrums throb.

"Timothy." Starbuck's voice made him jump. "I was terribly wrong to blame you all those years for what your father did. What a fool I was. I know now that God does not punish us for our fathers' actions. He doesn't even punish us for our own."

Timothy turned in his chair to study him. When had Starbuck become a preacher? Or even a Christian, if indeed he was one? In academy chapel, he had always worn a sneer throughout Chaplain Jones's sermons, coming just short of snorting out his disbelief.

"I suppose you would say," Timothy said, "that he punishes only our good deeds?" He patted his right leg and thumped his peg on the wooden porch.

Pain shot across Starbuck's face, and he turned away for a moment. When he turned back, sorrow had replaced the pain. "We were at war. More than a half million men died. Who knows how many thousands more were injured and maimed, some worse than you."

Timothy sat up and slammed his fist on the porch railing. "Don't *you* tell me to be glad I'm alive. You're sitting here all in one piece."

"But I wouldn't be if you had not saved my life."

Timothy grunted his disdain.

"Are you sorry you did it?"

He drew back. Was he sorry? No. Saving this man had been the right thing to do, and he would do it again. But the idea of admitting it to Starbuck made his insides twist. "As I said back then, now we're even."

Isaiah leaned forward with an intense stare. "There is no 'even' in the eyes of God, Timothy. There is only mercy and grace."

Grace? Grace! Had his little sister recovered from his cruel blow?

Starbuck blew out a sigh. "I understand your reluctance to accept my apology and my offer of friendship, considering how I treated you for so long. But I wonder if it would help you, for your own peace of mind, to read the story of our fathers. They had a few difficulties too." He pulled a brown leather book from his bag and held it out. "Won't you take it?"

Timothy drew back from the volume as if it were one of the copperhead snakes he often killed out in the fields.

Starbuck bit his lip and set it on the railing. "I'll just put it here." He glanced toward the kitchen door. "Now I know you would prefer that I just go my way, but your sweet aunt would have hurt feelings if I didn't stay for dinner. After that, I'll go."

"Good." Timothy stood and walked into the house, not caring that Starbuck followed.

At dinner Aunt Willa quizzed Starbuck about his war experiences and asked for news from back east, not seeming to notice Timothy's silence. After he left and she returned to the kitchen, Timothy knocked the book from the railing into the bushes before returning to the field.

"Mercy me, look what that boy dropped in the bushes." Willa entered the parlor that evening, brushing dust off the hated book. "We'll have to send it to him. You don't suppose he'd mind if we read it first, do you? New books are hard to come by. Here, you start while I clean up the dishes." She placed it on his lap as he sat in late Uncle Solomon's chair.

"Uh, thank you." He set it on the table between their two parlor chairs and started to stand. "Why don't you let me do the dishes? You can start reading it first."

"Nonsense, boy. Sit yourself back down." She gently pushed him into the chair. "You've been out in the sun working all day. You deserve a little enjoyment. Now pick up the book." She picked it up and placed it in his hands. "Now go ahead and start reading. I just think the good Lord wants to reward you for all you're doing for me, holding the farm together until Johnny comes home."

Her words seemed to slam him in the face. So "the good Lord" wanted him to read this book? After all his thwarted encounters with it, her words rang with painful veracity. All right, then. God wanted him to read this book? He would stop running from that heavenly mandate. He *would* read it. But he refused to like it.

Chapter Thirty

℘

From the moment he read the book's first pages, Timothy observed that Ishmael had not been mad when he wrote it some fourteen years earlier. His words formed an intelligent, coherent, and fascinating tale that rang with weighty truths, albeit with many humorous asides to the reader and much extraneous information about whales. Timothy even felt a sort of kinship with the author as he embarked on his youthful whaling adventure, and he recognized the settings of the early scenes in New Bedford and Nantucket. Even the Try Pots and Mrs. Hussey made an appearance.

So lost was he in the story that when he reached the sixteenth chapter, he almost gasped to see his father's name in print. But then he chuckled to read Captain Peleg's description of Ahab, for this forbidding man seemed so unlike the one he and his mother had loved. When he read the description of her, he laughed again, for no one who knew of Mother's courage in hiding slaves could ever call her a "sweet, resigned girl," as Captain Peleg had. A short mention of Timothy himself, although not by name, brought a tender pang.

Aunt Willa clucked her tongue. "Must be mighty interesting, boy. It's almost eleven o'clock. Those chores won't get themselves done tomorrow morning."

With difficulty, Timothy broke away from the story. "Yes, of course, Auntie." He marked his place, set the book aside, and struggled out of his chair to follow her upstairs. He had been vaguely aware that she sat working on a quilt as he read and hoped she had not missed their usual evening conversation too much. Good manners suggested that he read the story aloud to her, but that would be an impossible task.

He lay awake realizing that the book had ensnared him. He must hurry through his work tomorrow and return to it as soon as possible. In the morning, as if the heavens above agreed with his plan, drizzling rain kept him indoors. Aunt Willa forbade him to tend the fields for fear his wooden leg would be ruined.

"You just sit and read," she said. "I'll put a nice summer stew on to simmer and then maybe finish that quilt."

The rain continued for several days, not hard enough to flood out the deeply rooted crops but steadily enough to keep Timothy and Aunt Willa indoors except for hurried trips to the barn to feed and tend the livestock and milk the cow.

With dark fascination, he began to discover his father's offenses. Among his other unruly deeds, Ahab had once spat into a calabash, perhaps breaking some tribal taboo. At the academy, Timothy had been taught to avoid such diplomatic errors. His father seemed to have no such regard, or even regard for anyone. Some had called his evil name prophetic, and perhaps it had been.

Through Ishmael's account, Mr. Starbuck proved to be all that Timothy had expected, perhaps the only sane voice aboard the ship, the *Pequod*, other than the author.

When Timothy read of Ishmael's first view of Ahab, shivers ran down his spine. Clearly, this writer had admired his captain as a supremely superior, almost-godlike man, just as Mother had. From that moment, Timothy's last doubts disappeared concerning the story's truth, yet he could not acquit his father, no matter how desperately he tried.

Even before Ahab revealed his secret purpose, all the men on his ship had feared him, for as captain he held their lives in his hands like a grand and terrible potentate. But because of the account of how he gathered the crew and goaded them to swear their allegiance to his mad quest, Timothy accepted at last what he had feared all his life. No matter what Ahab had done before, this action proved him an unfit captain and a poor leader of men. Rather than direct and guide them to a successful harvest of whale oil—the purpose of their voyage—he had prodded and manipulated his crew around the globe on a quest for personal, deadly vengeance against the whale that had bitten off his leg. Like wicked King Ahab of old, he had led his people astray.

Timothy shuddered and sickened at the description of the tragic incident in which the whale's sickle-shaped lower jaw had reaped away Ahab's leg like a blade of grass. How well he himself knew the blind madness such an injury caused. But then he read of his father's rationale for his vengeful pursuit, and he longed to cry out with Mr. Starbuck over the years long past, "to be enraged with a dumb brute beast is blasphemy." Ahab—for Timothy could no longer think of this man as Papa or even Father—had responded that if the sun should offend him, he would strike it back. Ahab had hated God even before his wounding, and he declared the whale a pasteboard mask behind which God hid to mete out unjust punishment on mankind. If he but struck through the mask by killing the whale, he would strike God himself and repay the insult.

At the end, thrusting his harpoon into Moby Dick and, with the whale, plunging to his death beneath the ocean waves, Ahab had cried out, "From hell's heart I stab at thee; for hate's sake I spit my last breath at thee."

The hideous iron of truth now harpooned Timothy with shattering force. In Ahab's all-consuming pride and arrogance, he had cursed God. Yet, as the waters closed over the battle scene, both man and beast had died.

But God lived.

"Are you ill, boy?" Aunt Willa bent over his chair and patted his damp cheek. "Look at these tears. I don't think this is a book I care to read if it can make a brave young man like you weep. I've had enough of my own sorrow, and so have you. Why should we borrow grief?" She tried to take the book, but he stayed her hand.

"I'm all right, Auntie." He brushed away tears with the back of his hand. "Just a bit tired, I guess."

"Well, then, let's get a good night's sleep. The rain's blown over, and I think we'll have sunshine tomorrow. Then we'll have some catching up to do out in the fields."

Despite his weariness, why had he thought sleep would come this night? Ahab's death haunted him, and somehow he must find relief from his despair. Why had his father not yielded to Starbuck's pleas or to his own heart's longings for his beloved wife and child back home? Why had he felt driven by Fate—a mere pawn in the hands of a cruel God whose only "right worship was defiance"? What had made him the man that he became? More than that, how could Timothy escape following in his footsteps when his own peg leg and identically marred face seemed to suit him for that very path?

Pride and arrogance. Pride and arrogance. The words echoed in his mind.

He rose, lit a bedside candle, took the book in hand, and turned to a place he had marked. In the midst of a lightning storm, Ahab had acknowledged God's "speechless, placeless power; but to the last gasp of my earthquake life will dispute its unconditional, unintegral mastery in me."

Even with this second reading, Timothy recoiled at the words. How monstrous, how self-condemning was Ahab's blasphemous pride. How different from the men Timothy had known all his life: Uncle Jeremiah, a kind, gentle man of utmost humility; Uncle Jonathan, a tireless, quiet, willing servant; courageous Laz, as generous and loving to him as to his own children—each man like a trusty compass that never pointed him in the wrong direction, but only toward God. Who could know such men and still think the God they served was unjust? Yet not one would claim his deeds to be remarkable, for each would say that he merely served Christ.

Pride and arrogance. Again the words rang in his mind. Wealth and respect had been Timothy's birthright. Perhaps he had assumed that God's approval had also been granted to him from birth as well. But had he served Christ?

All his life he had chosen to do the right thing, no matter what the cost. But it had never cost him much of anything until he saved Isaiah's life. Now his anger and bitterness over losing his leg rivaled his father's rage. Yet, foreswearing such blasphemy as Ahab's pathetic tirade against his Creator, whom else could Timothy repay for this outrageous injury? The rebels who shot the shell that shattered the cutlasses? They now suffered enough in the destruction of their homes and way of life. The shell itself? The cutlass fragments? Isaiah, for finally seeking him out to reconcile? Captain Read had died. Captain Jenkins suffered a horrible injury. Of those on the deck, only Isaiah and Dewey remained uninjured. So now, with whom should Timothy get even?

What had Isaiah said? There was no "even," only mercy and grace. Now he began to understand. Mercy that he had lived. Grace that he had regained his strength and now could work like a man again. Yet even that resounded with pride.

But what about all his good works? Was there no good thing in his life to recommend him for divine favor?

Pride and arrogance, as equally damning in a resolute young man as in a poor old Nantucket whale hunter.

Mercy and grace, mercy that he had not died in his prideful arrogance, grace that he still had a chance to humble himself before God.

Timothy set the book on the night table, rolled to the bedside, and glided down to kneel beside the bed. He lifted his eyes upward, but no words would come. All his life he had prayed, or rather, had talked at God. Perhaps now the time had come to listen. At the thought, his heart filled with a strange new peace. As tears slipped down his cheeks, he bowed his head and prayed as Samuel had: "Speak, Lord, for thy servant heareth."

One sunny day in mid-June, Private John W. Jacobs walked into the farmhouse kitchen just as if he had returned from working in the field. Timothy feared for a moment that Aunt Willa would slip from her kitchen chair and fall to the floor. But her indomitable spirit held her together, and she flung herself into her son's arms and wept and laughed at the same time. Both he and Johnny shed their share of joyful tears as well.

An inch or two under six feet, Johnny stood taller than Aunt Willa by a head. He appeared thin and war-weary, his dark red hair needed a trim, his faded army uniform was tattered, but his blue eyes sparkled with hope for the future. Aunt Willa sent him to wash up in the bucket outside the back door while she added a plate to the table. Johnny had not eaten for two days, a condition he hastened to remedy. After two helpings of stew, he seemed to remember his manners.

"My, the land looks good, Tim. You've done wonders considering—" He glanced toward the peg leg but then winced an apology. "Sorry."

Timothy shrugged off the unintended slight. "I didn't do it alone. We hired a few returning soldiers as they passed through. That helped through the worst part. But most of them wanted to work for only a day or two before getting on home."

"I can understand that." Johnny buttered another biscuit and ate it in two bites. "I suppose you feel the same way. You've sure done enough for us to last a lifetime."

Timothy shook his head. "I'm here till you throw me out."

"Well, that's not going to happen." Aunt Willa reached across the table and squeezed his hand.

"Say, Ma, I was just wondering." Johnny poured fresh cream over the warm rhubarb pie she had served him and plunged in his fork. "I don't suppose you ever see any of the Downs family at church these days?"

Aunt Willa's expression grew wily. "Now why would I pay attention to the Downs family? Especially a pretty young lady named Miss Louisa Maria?"

"Miss?" Johnny's face lit up. "Still 'Miss'?"

"Yes, indeed. And she's even more lovely than when you left. Don't you think so, Timothy?"

Johnny's expression fell as he turned to him. "You've met Miss Downs?"

Timothy's heart grew light. With all his wounds and disfigurement, how could his handsome cousin consider him a rival for a young lady's affection? Better still, how many years had it been since he teased and bantered with loved ones?

"Ah, yes, I certainly have met Miss Downs, and she is indeed a lovely young lady. Why, I said to her after church just last Sunday, I said, 'Miss Downs, you certainly are a lovely sight to behold in that lovely blue dress.'"

Johnny's blue eyes smoldered. "Oh, you did, did you? And what did she say?"

"She said, 'Why, thank you, sir. Oh, by the by, have you received any word of your cousin John?'" He gave him a broad grin and a wink.

"Whoo." Johnny smiled and sat back in his chair, his eyes sparkling once more. "Guess I'll have to ride over there sometime."

Aunt Willa beamed her agreement to the plan. In her clear green eyes Timothy caught a surprising glimpse of Mother, and a question stirred in his mind.

"Auntie," he said, "tell me something. When my mother was a young girl and came out here to visit you, what was she like?"

Aunt Willa grew pensive for a moment. "That would have been about 1830, because Solomon and I had just been married about a year." Then she chuckled. "Oh, son, she was a caution. We could hardly keep her out of trouble. If she wasn't climbing in the old barn"—she glanced at Johnny—"the one that burned down in '57 ... she was riding one of the horses down to the creek all by herself and not even asking, and copperheads all over the place down there. One time she climbed on the fence by the pigpen—we had pigs back then—and fell right in head first. What a sight, all that pretty red hair matted with mud, and she sat there with a big grin on her face like she was at a Sunday social. Took me hours to wash and comb all that mud out."

Timothy snickered, then laughed out loud for the first time since his injury. How good it felt, like a healing balm to his aching heart. He could picture Gracie up to her ears in mud, but never his dainty, ladylike, perfect mother.

Aunt Willa paused, blinking. "Oh, my, I don't suppose I should have told you that. She wasn't naughty, dear, she was just lively. Always exploring, asking questions. Always saying whatever came to mind. When she brought you out here in '46 after your father's death, I hardly would have known she was the same person. Of course, she was a grieving widow then. We were so pleased, Solomon and I, when she married that good man, David Lazarus. Her letters are always a joy to read."

Letters. How many letters had Mother and Jemima written *him* over the past year? Perhaps he could bring himself to read them now—or at least this evening after chores were finished.

"Well, Tim." Johnny stood and took his plate to the kitchen cabinet where Aunt Willa's wash pan sat. "If you can manage the fields just for this afternoon, I'd like to clean up and go on over to the Downses' place. There's a certain young lady I'd like to say hello to."

Timothy's heart seemed to leap into his throat. He also wished to say hello—and much more—to a certain young lady, but after his long absence, did she still care for him?

That evening he forced his feeble hand to wrap around a pen and slowly wrote to Jemima the words that overflowed from his heart.

> *My beloved Jemima,*
>
> *After all this time, you must be surprised to hear from me. I have much to tell you. First, I wish to set your heart at ease. I am certain you recall our long ago conversation concerning faith. You will be pleased to know that in accordance with the passage we discussed in John's Gospel, chapter three, I do know our Lord Jesus Christ. We will talk more of this soon.*
>
> *Please, please forgive me for my harsh words to you last year. You never believed my foolishness, for you have always understood me better than I understood myself.*
>
> *Please tell Isaiah and Lacy that I will be home for their wedding after all. And if you still wish to marry me, perhaps you will begin making plans for our own nuptials. I have never stopped loving you, never for a moment, my dear one.*

He sat back with a sense of great satisfaction. If the penmanship was poor, the thoughts should more than make up for it.

His hand ached from the effort, but he must write one more letter. Taking another sheet of paper, he began, "Dear Mother and Laz—" He sat back in his chair once more and studied the unsatisfactory salutation. Why did it trouble him?

Memories flowed through his mind—a tour of Europe, family picnics, fishing excursions, long talks around the dinner table, and dangerous voyages with forbidden cargo, all led by a tall, fair-haired captain whom Mother called her mighty Viking—the one who had stayed at her side and lovingly guided another captain's son to manhood.

A pleasant feeling pulsed in his chest, and he crumpled the page, tossed it aside, and took another sheet.

> *Dear Mother and Father,*
> *With your permission, I would like to return home …*

Epilogue

❧

Spring 1873

"Isaiah!" Timothy's voice boomed throughout the two-storied house. Within seconds, a tow-headed cherub came running into his father's study, where he sat at his wide oak desk.

"Yes, Papa?" Six-year-old Isaiah blinked his round brown eyes and gazed at his father expectantly.

With difficulty, Timothy forced a frown to his face. "Son, what have you done with my leg? I must leave for the academy soon, and you would not have me hop like a rabbit to get there, would you?"

"But, Papa, I didn't take your leg."

Timothy studied Isaiah's sweet face and believed him. "Well, then, what do you suppose happened to it?"

Isaiah bit his lip and stared at the floor.

"Ah, so you won't tattle on your sister, eh?"

Isaiah gazed back up at him. "No, sir. Oh!"

Timothy chuckled. The trick always worked.

"Young lady." Jemima's voice came nearer. "What are we going to do with you?" She entered the study carrying the stolen leg under one arm and gripping their errant daughter with the other hand. Timothy's gaze, however, did not linger on either child or limb. After seven years, his heart still leapt with wonder and happiness whenever his wife appeared in the room.

Jemima pushed their five-year-old daughter, pouting and defiant, in front of Timothy, and he leaned forward with an artificial scowl.

"Hannah Grace, what's the meaning of this? Why did you steal Papa's leg?"

The chubby redhead must have seen his struggle not to laugh, for she giggled and flung her arms around his neck. "Oh, Papa, please stay home and play with us. Mademoiselle Trudeau is so old and Mama is so fat that they are no fun at all."

"But, my little minx, I must go teach my classes at the academy. That is Papa's responsibility. Your responsibility is to learn your lessons from Mademoiselle. Once we have accomplished our work, then we can play."

"Very well." Hannah once more pouted her disapproval. Then she brightened. "And may we have some ice cream and gingersnaps?"

"That is up to your mother." Timothy gazed beyond the children and winked at Jemima.

"Perhaps, if you're good. Now, my darlings, run along to Mademoiselle."

The two children turned to obey, but Timothy set his hand on Isaiah's shoulder. "You're a good lad, my son. Always be loyal to your sister—and to your friends."

Isaiah gave him a broad smile and a snappy salute. "Aye, sir." Then he ran from the room.

Jemima lumbered over to him and would have knelt to attach his leg, but he took her hand and pulled her down on his lap.

"Are you feeling well this morning, my love? You seem a little flushed." He placed his hand on her abdomen, enjoying the busyness of the child within.

She nuzzled as close to him as her large belly would permit. "I feel grand. You know we Nantucket girls can manage anything. Look. I have good news." She pulled an envelope from her apron pocket. "Isaiah wrote us a letter. I did not wish to disturb you while you prepared for class, but I couldn't wait to read it."

"And what's the news? Another promotion?" Timothy felt only a small twinge of longing at the thought.

Jemima seemed to understand. "Yes, he has been made commander, quite an honor for one so young."

"But well-deserved. Before long, he'll have his own ship."

She set the letter aside and took his face in her hands, as she often did, tracing with slender fingers his faded scar—God's mark on him that reminded him every time he looked in the mirror of what he could have become. Over the years she had placed many kisses up and down the jagged seam. "Do you still regret that you are not in the navy, rising in the ranks like my brother?"

Did he regret it? Perhaps in some small way, but not for long. "No, I would not wish to be away from you and the children so much. I know he must miss Lacy and the girls terribly as he sails around the world keeping our country safe."

She nodded her agreement.

"How about you?" He chucked her under the chin. "Do you wish your husband wore a handsome, brass-buttoned, medal-adorned uniform? That he took you to grand balls and introduced you to admirals and presidents?"

She wrinkled her nose and shook her head. "Oh, goodness, no. I would much rather go on family picnics or visit all our loved ones in Boston."

"But what about the uniform?" He no longer yearned for such things, but how he wanted her to be proud of him.

Jemima's eyes grew misty, and she gazed at him with tender understanding. "You look just as you should in this handsome suit, for black is an austere color and masks your playful nature from those unruly, young midshipmen. No, in my opinion, this is a far more commanding 'uniform' for your profession."

"And you are pleased with me for taking this position at the academy? We could have stayed in Boston."

Jemima gave him a radiant smile. "Oh, yes, I am certain our Lord wills for us to be here in Annapolis, for we see every day how much the students admire you and set you for their example of all that is excellent in leadership, character, and—most important—godliness."

She kissed him tenderly on the lips and then rested her forehead against his. "Oh, my beloved, set your mind at ease. I am so very proud of you, my dear Professor Lazarus."

Readers' Guide

બ

For Personal Reflection or
Group Discussion

Readers' Guide

ℰℐ

$\mathcal{T}$imothy Jacobs is "a chip off the old block." Just like his father, Captain Ahab, he is a successful sailor, a competent leader of men, and extremely intelligent. He even bears a remarkable resemblance to his dead father. But he is also full of self-righteous pride and arrogance. He is determined to become a "righteous" man through the work of his own hands—he will not make the same mistakes as his father. But the path he has chosen is one of folly, for Timothy fails to recognize his innate need for God. In so doing, he denies the power and authority of his holy, righteous, and loving Father.

This deception is nothing new—pride is as old as sin itself. The Bible says, "Pride goes before destruction, a haughty spirit before a fall" (Prov. 16:18 NIV). Pride led to the fall of Lucifer, the ruin of Adam and Eve, and the destruction of Captain Ahab. Why is mankind so susceptible to the lie that we can be like God? Why do we try to live life on our own terms, without regard for his ways? Why do we believe we can succeed without him?

The lesson gleaned from the life of Captain Ahab's son is that we are all "sons of perdition," for each one of us must contend with our own sinful nature. Whether we realize it or not, if we do not surrender wholly to God, we walk a path to certain destruction. The good news is that if we have the courage to judge ourselves honestly … to confront the reality of our sin, Jesus is waiting to receive us with open arms. He said, "I tell you the truth, everyone who sins is a slave to sin…. So if the Son sets you free, you will be free indeed"

(John 8:34, 36 NIV). As you consider the following questions, search the depths of your heart. The Truth is waiting to set you free.

1. Hannah is devastated and grieved to learn the nature of Ahab's death. Why is her first impulse to protect Timothy from the truth about his father? What wisdom does David Lazarus offer? How has Hannah's "maternal grasp" affected Timothy's development? Is she really protecting him, or merely hindering his growth? How have you handled similar situations in your own life?

2. Timothy longs to know more about his father and Laz obliges his curiosity with heroic tales of Captain Ahab's exploits. Why is Timothy's identity so inextricably connected with his father, despite barely remembering him? How are we the same—not only in how we identify with our biological parents, but with God the Father?

3. Jemima and Isaiah are unwitting victims of Captain Ahab's treachery. Although they have suffered equally, Jemima finds healing in forgiveness, while Isaiah is consumed with rage and bitterness. Which is the more effective way to cope with grief and loss? How does Jemima's gentle spirit and sweet nature affect those around her? What are the inevitable consequences of Isaiah's determination to see justice served—even if he must bring it about himself?

4. When Isaiah encounters Timothy, he quotes Scripture with a vengeance, "The sins of the fathers shall be visited on their children …" Is there any divine truth in this statement? What evidence exists in our own culture today that children do indeed pay for the sins of their parents? Are there recurring problems or sins in your own family that seem to be repeated from one generation to the next? How can the gospel of Jesus Christ affect these generational curses?

5. Timothy is an accomplished and affable young man, while Isaiah is more reserved and somewhat surly. Despite their differences in personality and background, in what ways are Timothy and Isaiah similar? What do they both feel equally passionate about?

6. What are the consequences for Timothy not knowing the truth about his father? How might his life have been changed—for better or worse—had Hannah told him the truth from the beginning? Would he have been more likely to turn to God early in his life, or would the truth have led him to rebel? How might his relationship with Isaiah have been different? Is there ever a time when such secrets should be kept?

7. At a young age, Timothy decides to "be good," determined that no one—not even God—will ever be able to find fault with him. What prompts this decision? How does his attitude resemble pride? Does Timothy really live a "righteous life"? Is it possible for anyone to live in such a manner that even God can't find fault? (See Rom. 3:10–12, 20–24; Gal. 2:21, Matt. 9:13; John 14:6; Eph. 2:8–9.)

8. At this critical point in America's history, the infamous Dred Scott case helped propel the nation on a course toward civil war. In retrospect, is it surprising that the Supreme Court could make such an unrighteous, ungodly decision? How does this compare to current trends in our nation today? Given the power that the court system wields, what responsibility does each one of us have when judgments are made in contradiction to God's Word? What is the inevitable outcome when a nation turns away from God and his laws and precepts?

9. When he falls in love with Jemima, Timothy attempts to convince her that they are on equal spiritual footing, knowing that

she would not approve of his lack of faith. Does Jemima hear only what she wants to hear? Why is she so easily deceived about the true nature of Timothy's beliefs?

10. Even though Isaiah finally turns to Christ, he still harbors his old grudge against Timothy. Why is forgiveness such an important part of salvation? How does bitterness hinder our ability to live for Christ? What eventually brings Isaiah to a place of true forgiveness and repentance?

11. When Timothy reads *Moby Dick*, he finally comes face to face with the truth of his father's sins. What characteristics does he recognize within himself that he shares with his father? Is Timothy really destined to follow in his father's footsteps, or does he have the ability to choose a different path? What events bring him to the place where he is receptive to truth? Is there a redemptive aspect to the suffering and loss he has experienced? How is this evidence of the work of grace in his life?

Read all of Ahab's Legacy

Ahab's Bride
Book One of Ahab's Legacy
Louise M. Gouge

Before Captain Ahab encountered Moby Dick, he met the woman who would capture his heart—Hannah Oldweiler. This voyage to 19th century Nantucket introduces you to the woman whose spirit and determination matched the man she loved.

1-58919-007-6 • Item # 103292 • 5.5 x 8" • Paperback 336P

Hannah Rose
Book Two of Ahab's Legacy
Louise M. Gouge

In this second book in the Ahab's Legacy Series, the captain has become the victim of his own mad pursuit of the great whale. Hannah, his widow and her son, Timothy, seek to distance themselves from the Ahab name by planning a trip to Europe. During a visit to friends in Boston, Hannah finds she must first search her heart regarding some important life issues, not the least of which is slavery. Hannah's journey reveals the unexpected ways that God fulfills His plans for us beyond our own plans and desires.

1-58919-040-8 • Item # 103817 • 5.5 x 8" Paperback • 320P

Louise M. Gouge is a member of American Christian Romance Writers, Romance Writers of America, Central Florida romance Writers, the Nantucket Historical Association and the Bostonian Society. She is also the author of *Once There Was A Way Back Home* and *The Homecoming*.

Additional copies of *SON OF PERDITION* and other RiverOak titles are available from your local bookseller.

If you have enjoyed this book,
or if it has had an impact on your life,
we would like to hear from you.

Please contact us at:

RIVEROAK BOOKS
Cook Communications Ministries, Dept. 201
4050 Lee Vance View
Colorado Springs, CO 80918

Or visit our Web site: www.cookministries.com

RIVEROAK®
Good News in Fiction